Songbird

a novel of the Tudor Court

Karen Heenan

Published by Authors 4 Authors Publishing
11700 Mukilteo Speedway Ste 201 PM 1044
Mukilteo, WA 98275
www.authors4authorspublishing.com

Library of Congress Control Number: 2019953024

E-book ISBN: 978-1-64477-041-2
Paperback ISBN: 978-1-64477-042-9
Audiobook ISBN: 978-1-64477-043-6

Edited by Rebecca Mikkelson
Copyedited by B. C. Marine

Cover design and illustration ©2019 Coverkeepers. All rights reserved.

Authors 4 Authors Content Rating and copyright are set in Poppins. Titles are set in PlainBlack and UglyQua. Correspondence is set in Almendra. Part decorations are set in TypeMyMusic. Scene breaks are set in Nymphette. All other text is set in Garamond.

Songbird

A NOVEL OF THE TUDOR COURT

KAREN HEENAN

Authors 4 Authors Content Rating

This title has been rated S, appropriate for adults, and contains:

- intense sex
- moderate language
- moderate alcohol use
- abortion
- suicide

Please, keep the following in mind when using our rating system:

1. A content rating is not a measure of quality.

Great stories can be found for every audience. One book with many content warnings and another with none at all may be of equal depth and sophistication. Our ratings can work both ways: to avoid content or to find it.

2. Ratings are merely a tool.

For our young adult (YA) and children's titles, age ratings are generalized suggestions. For parents, our descriptive ratings can help you make informed decisions, but at the end of the day, only you know what kinds of content are appropriate for your individual child. This is why we provide details in addition to the general age rating.

For more information on our rating system, please, visit our Content Guide at:
www.authors4authorspublishing.com/books/ratings

Dedication

For Mario, my good and patient man,
I love you.

Table of Contents

𝔓art 1

The Cuckoo - 1516

Chapter 1

Two days before my tenth birthday, my father sold me to the King of England.

When my mother shook me awake in the gray December dawn, I was told no more than that we were going on a journey. I wondered why my father would choose to travel in such bitter weather, and my questions only grew as we spent the day on one frozen road after another.

The sky was black when we finally arrived at Greenwich, and I was exhausted and near tears. We trudged past the gatehouse through deep drifts of snow. The thin soles of my sister's boots might as well have been paper against the rutted track.

By the time we reached our destination, all I could see through swirling flakes was an endless expanse of brick rising to melt into darkness and more glass windows than I knew existed. A glow issued from the panes on the ground floor, and higher up, slivers of light escaped tight-closed shutters. The warmth of those windows made the outdoors, layered in shadows, seem barren indeed.

A gust of wind slammed into us, and I leaned against my father. It seemed days since Mum had dressed me in my heaviest kirtle and handed us bread and cheese for the journey. I was very hungry.

"None of that," he said, his voice gruff. After a long look at the doors, he reached for my hand. "It will be warmer inside."

Greenwich Palace was only five miles downriver from London, but it was a world away from the mud-choked streets of Southwark and its cramped, squalid houses. I tried to take it all in: lofty beamed ceilings, vivid tapestries, scented rushes underfoot. At home, the rushes were changed yearly and didn't smell sweet when new, and I had never seen a tapestry. I stored it up to tell Madlen, whose jealousy would know no bounds when she learned what she'd missed. I didn't understand why we'd left her home.

"May we stop now?" I was weary of trying to match Da's long stride, but he had me firmly by the hand.

"Hush, child." He hauled me along until we encountered someone. My father loosed his hold on me and bowed to the man, who glittered in the wavering light of the torches mounted along the walls. They spoke briefly, and then my father bobbed again and reclaimed my hand.

I started to ask where we were bound, saw his expression, and sealed my lips; when he looked like that, there was no reaching him. What fretted him, other than the cold and our distance from home? It could not be those things, since he was the one who caused us to make the journey, and surely, he knew it was cold; it was Christmas, after all.

We stopped before another set of doors, tall and wonderfully carved, with golden handles worked in the shape of dragons. There was a guard outside—I supposed he was a guard, though he was dressed as splendidly as the last man, wearing a green-and-white striped velvet tunic that was heavy with embroidery—and he asked what business we had within. I tried to listen to their conversation, but my ears caught the strains of music inside, and I was lost.

"Take yourselves in," he said and swung the door wide. "You'll see him. Whether he will see you, I cannot say."

I still knew not whom we were there to see, and I grew even more stupid on entering the chamber. It was immense, far larger than our house, larger than the inn where I delivered Mum's washing, larger even than the church where I dozed and shivered on Sundays. Many times larger, and like the men in the passage, it seemed to shimmer with a light of its own. There were tapestries on every wall, worked with fantastic figures and beasts for which I had no name. Candlelight gleamed off silver and gold plate.

"Come along," my father said, prodding me.

The chamber was full of people, I noticed then, men and women dressed in colors and fabrics far grander than men in the corridor. I'd fallen into one of Madlen's tales; people like this did not exist. Something in their grandeur frightened me, and I tried to turn away, but Da towed me forward, and the crowd parted.

They were staring, their eyes hard and shiny as the diamonds on their sleeves. I'm certain they wondered, as I did, what we were doing in their midst. They appeared unwilling to come too close, and we continued until my father halted so abruptly that my split soles skidded, and I sat down hard on the floor. Silk rustled as the nearest ladies whisked their skirts away.

Embarrassment was new to me, but it was easy to see we were horribly inferior to these people. It seemed best to remain invisible, so I crouched on the floor, watching my father straighten and take a deep, shaky breath.

A tug on my hand made me scramble up, and I caught Da's annoyed glance. I hoped that by the time we got home, he would forget to tell Mum, and I might avoid a thrashing.

3

My father spoke now, his stumbling words directed upwards. I forced myself to follow his gaze and nearly folded at the knees again.

While my sister told me stories of princes and fair maidens to lull me to sleep, Mum's tales were of another sort. If I misbehaved, she warned, one day, a giant would carry me off and eat me bit by bit until there was nothing left but bones to pick his teeth. I examined my conscience for a crime that merited the extremity of such a punishment.

The giant was immense, and from his bright hair to the tissue-like fabric that made up his costume, he seemed to be fashioned entirely of gold. My eyes fastened on the chain he wore about his shoulders: it was as thick as my wrist.

"What have we here?" The giant's voice was deep, a rumble of summer thunder.

"Your Majesty," my father stammered and launched again into the speech he'd been muttering since daybreak. I thought the giant was unkind to make him repeat it, but perhaps he hadn't understood with all the noise; I'd heard it so often during the journey, the words had no meaning.

I forced myself to look around as my father spoke. If only Madlen could see these gowns! It would take the glory out of her new sleeves, for certes. The thought gave me a mean pleasure, for it was not often her opinion of herself was brought low and rarer still I was the one to do it.

The ladies' garments were no more splendid than those of the gentlemen. Aside from the golden giant, I saw men in radiant blues and greens, rich-figured velvets of crimson and black, and everywhere, more of that dazzling gold cloth. So many gems glittered around me, it was as if the heavens had scattered themselves upon the room.

I noted a young man nearby, dressed all in tawny velvet, with an intricate trimming of pearls and gold thread on his doublet. On his shoulder-length dark hair, he wore a matching cap, which sported a yellow gem big as a bird's egg. His eyes met mine for a moment. Unlike the others, he actually seemed to see me.

I began to feel safe, despite my surroundings. Who, after all, would notice a child in a place like this? My mother's instructions were that children, especially female children, should remain silent. I felt no larger than a moth among all these flickering candles.

"God's teeth, she's filthy!" The giant leaned forward in his chair. Jewels flashed and shimmered when he moved; he was a veritable rainbow.

Thus spoken to, it seemed I must look at him. For all his size and magnificence, his shining pink face appeared kindly. I gave him a tentative smile, thinking of Mum and the rough scrubbing she had given me at dawn. I wasn't clean enough for the giant—perhaps he wouldn't want me after all.

"So she sings," he said, rising and placing broad hands on his hips. Rings sparkled on nearly every finger. "We would hear her."

My father knelt. "He wants you to sing."

Sing? My heart thumped in my chest. I concentrated on a grease spot on my father's gray hose to keep from shaking. "I'm scared," I whispered, then dropped to my knees when he clouted my ear in a perfect imitation of Mum.

My father's hand rested on my shoulder, and his fingers tightened as my silence persisted. It mattered so much to him that I sing, and I could not. I let the music filter into my consciousness again. It showed the depth of my fear that I had ever lost it; it was wonderful, like a river, bewildering me with torrents of sound. My mouth opened and shut, but my throat produced no sound. It was almost as if I had forgotten how.

"Your Grace, may I?" A boy threaded his way through the crowd and offered himself with a bow. "Perhaps she needs a song."

The giant considered this, dropping back into his intricately wrought golden chair. "Then play for her, Tom."

This boy had the giant's favor. He grinned at me through unshorn hair the color of straw and began to lightly pluck the strings of his instrument, bringing forth an age-old tune known to everyone.

"Look at me," he said under the music. "Don't be feared."

With his smile to give me courage, it was easy to mouth the gay lyric and pretend I was singing to him instead of these strange and brilliant people. The minstrels in the gallery ceased their song and took up the air the boy played for me.

I cared not for the scrutiny of the shining courtiers now. I didn't even care if they listened. I sang, and the thing inside me that was my voice washed away my fear and made me all but insensible to the jeweled mob standing hushed around me.

The cuckoo, she's a merry bird; she sings as she flies.
She brings us glad tidings and tells us no lies.
She sucks the white flowers for to keep her voice clear,
And when she sings, "cuckoo," don't the summer draw near.

I will rise up and meet him
As the evening draws nigh.

I will meet him as the evening,
As the evening draws nigh.

My voice spiraled up and out, filling the chamber, stirring the pennons suspended from the gilded ceiling.

Like the flowers in your garden
When their beauty's all gone,
Can't you see what I've come to
By your loving that one?

Oh, the grave she will rot you;
She will turn you to dust.
There's not one man out of twenty
That a young girl can trust.[1]

The song was over. I sought the boy's face. He jerked his head, and I looked up. The giant's expression was stern. I remembered the curtsy my sister taught me and cautiously tried it.

He smiled then, by all appearances, delighted. I looked from him to my father, wondering why Da brought me all this way to sing when I was punished nearly every day for wasting time with music.

"She shows much promise," he said. "We will have her." He waved a hand at one of the men by his side. "Richard, take this fellow out, and give him what he asks." The hand waved again, this time in the boy's direction. "Tom, take the child to Cornysh. He'll know what to do with her."

"Mayhap a bath, Your Grace," Tom said.

There were a few snickers. I glared at him, and the laughter grew louder.

My father patted my head, picking at my snarled hair in a belated effort to make me presentable. "Goodbye, child. I'll give your love to Mum and Madlen."

Until that moment, I hadn't understood that he was leaving without me. I wrenched away from Tom, my mud-covered skirts flying. "No!"

Bending swiftly down, he spoke in my ear. "'Tis for the best. Be a good girl, and do as they ask."

Sobbing, I caught at the hem of his cloak, but Tom peeled my fingers loose. I wiped my tears with one hand and, with the other, fetched him a blow similar to the one bestowed by my father only minutes earlier. He yelped and staggered back. I swung again, but this time, he was wary, catching my wrists in square, brown hands.

The chamber came to life, the courtiers' laughter echoing off the walls. I stood quietly, enduring their mirth, watching my father retreat through the crowd. He did not look back. When the doors closed, my shoulders drooped with despair and fatigue.

"Now, little one," came that jovial voice so far above me. "Tell us your name." His palm stopped just short of touching my hair.

"Bethan," I said, trying hard not to snivel.

He was tremendous on his feet. I found myself at eye level with the padded and pearl-encrusted codpiece that jutted out like a bizarre jeweled egg.

"That was my lady mother's name." Emotion softened his voice, and I forgave the pearls, though I wondered what sort of man decorated his cod.

Mum never said anything about kindly giants. Perhaps she knew nothing about this variety? More likely, I thought, she knew and never told. I held tight to Tom's hand. Kind or terrible, I needed to know what was to become of me.

"Are you really a giant?" My voice, strained from singing after hours in the cold, was barely audible, but I knew he heard me by the flash in his eyes.

His laugh boomed out. With a flick of his hand, he gestured for Tom to raise me up. The boy lifted me under the arms, holding me so we were almost the same height. "I'm not a giant, Elizabeth," he said, and this time, he did touch me, laying one finger lightly on my chin. "I'm your king."

Tom took me on another journey through endless rooms and corridors. "Come along," he said, catching me by the sleeve when I dawdled, stopping to inspect my surroundings.

"I want to see." I had envied my mother's neat stitching, but the work on these hangings was a marvel far beyond her skills. I touched the tapestry, pulling away quickly when I found the hanging chilly as the corridor. "It's wet."

"They've purposes other than beauty," he said, raising an edge and showing me the slick stones behind. "They keep out the damp tolerable well." His matter-of-fact words took some of the loveliness from the tapestry.

"If I don't touch it, I won't know that, will I?"

He grinned, and I found myself smiling in spite of myself. Out of the king's presence, Tom was quite a normal boy, scuffing his feet and whistling as he walked. He was a good bit taller than I, though nearly as thin. I didn't see how he'd had the strength to pick me up.

Abruptly, he said, "You didn't know he brought you here to sell?"

The king's words, spoken so easily, rang in my ears. "Take the fellow out, and give him what he asks."

I had been sold. Tom's words made it real. "No," I said, surprised how calm my voice sounded. I would think about it when I was alone.

There was no sound now but our footsteps and the muffled shriek of the wind outside.

"Will I ever see them again?"

Tom shrugged. "That depends on the king."

"Why?"

"Everything depends on the king."

I digested this. It took my thoughts from my father, no doubt making his way home in the cold. Even if he spent a shilling to travel by river, he wouldn't get there until morning.

I knew the king, of course—I was almost ten and not always stupid—but I hadn't yet fathomed I'd been so close as to be touched by him. Not only touched, but purchased. The man made of gold paid money for me.

That led to another thought. "How much did I cost?"

"A few years back, the king gave twenty pounds for a boy for the Chapel Royal."

Twenty pounds was an incomprehensible amount. "How many shillings is that?"

"Hundreds," he said with some assurance. "I don't know what he paid for you—it might be more or less."

It would be less since I was a girl. But even so, what could be done with such a sum? Perhaps my parents could leave the city, as Mum had always wanted, and properly dower their daughters. Daughter, I amended. Mum only had to worry about Madlen now.

"Is that what I'm to do?" I asked. "Sing in the choir?"

Tom looked down his nose at me. Although he had a palace position, it was clear from his honeyed skin, he spent a good deal of time outdoors. "There are no girls in the choir," he said. "Only men and boys, twelve of each."

8

The stairs grew narrower as we climbed, the torches less frequent. There were no hangings on this floor, and the stones were damp and splotched with green. I looked around, feeling a draft on my face. "Are there ghosts up here?"

"Don't tell me you're feared of ghosts, a girl who doesn't flinch at singing before hundreds of people."

"I was scared until you played your— What is that?" I asked, pointing at the instrument he carried.

"It's a lute." He caressed the smooth wood. "I can play the rebec as well, and I've begun to learn the virginals, but the lute is my true love."

"What's a rebec?" I hadn't heard of virginals, either, but I didn't want to ask too many questions.

He stroked the wood again where it swelled to a curve. "A rebec is somewhat like a bowed lute but shallower through the body and smaller."

"And played with a bow," I guessed.

"Exactly." Tom favored me with another smile. "What can you do?"

"Sing."

"Of course, ninny. We can all do that. Can't you play an instrument?"

I shook my head. Perhaps the king would think Da was trying to cheat him and would send me home. I hoped he would until I thought of Mum.

"Well, that means he truly liked your voice. Did you see the queen?"

"No." I saw no one but the king, Tom, and the young man who hadn't looked away from me.

"She was right beside him."

"Is she beautiful?" I tried to imagine a suitable consort for that golden man.

"She's Spanish," Tom said as if that explained it. His eyes flicked over me. "You look like a gypsy."

"I'm not!" I cried, insulted, though I barely knew the word.

"What are you, then, that your skin and hair are so dark?"

"My mum says I'm Welsh." I was not about to be squashed by this boy for all that he was enviably fair and had a fetching dimple in one cheek.

Tom was silent for the space of a breath or two. "The old king did bring half of Wales with him." With another of his lightning changes, he asked, "What's your name, then?"

"Bethan. Or Bess."

"No. Your other name."

I shrugged, attempting to copy his movement. "My father calls himself Peter."

He stopped walking. "Elizabeth Peters? No." His eyes narrowed. "You must have two names, else they'll laugh at you."

I wanted no more laughter at my expense. "But I don't know—"

"It must be Welsh." He chewed his lower lip. "I've been up since dawn. I can't think." The snap of his fingers echoed in the stairwell. "Llewelyn," Tom said. "Your name is Bess Llewelyn."

Bess Llewelyn. I considered the name, mouthed it silently. It sounded well enough. "I'm sorry I hit you."

"I've been hit before. Never by anyone so little, though."

"I'll be ten soon," I told him. "Three days afore the new year, I'll be ten."

"That's the day after tomorrow. Don't expect a gift."

"Never have," I said, matter-of-fact myself on this issue. I'd never had a gift just for the sake of the giving.

We stopped before an ordinary door with no carving or brass handles. Tom knocked and waited. "This is Master Cornysh," he said in a low voice. "He's the choirmaster."

"Was he not in the big chamber downstairs?" Someone so important should have been there, I thought.

He shook his head, his hair falling into his eyes again. "He'll be busy with plans for tomorrow's revels. Besides, he's had too much wine, and his head aches."

When the door opened, he offered a brief explanation of my presence.

"Again?" The voice was pained. "Why can't he just buy jewels and horses?"

Tom pulled lightly on a lock of my hair. "You'll be fine," he said and vanished down the dim corridor. The last I saw was the flutter of his lute ribbons disappearing around a corner.

William Cornysh was a middle-aged man with a flushed face and warm, worried brown eyes. He told me I was now a member of the King's Music, a group of performers kept for court entertainments. It was a great privilege; the king was very particular about the musicians in his employ.

"King Henry takes a keen interest," Master Cornysh said. "His Majesty is more than competent on the lute and plays other instruments. He sings and writes music as well." He raised a hand to smooth his thinning hair, then dropped it to the writing table, where it met and clasped his other hand. He looked at me earnestly. "In other words, if he were not a king, he would be a more than adequate minstrel. You must bear that in mind when performing. He knows your job as well as you ever shall."

I tried to listen, but my eyes were drooping. Even my wish for a quiet place to cry had faded in my desire for sleep.

Master Cornysh called for a servant. "Take her to the chamber of the girls." To me, he said, "Sleep. I'll listen to you sing tomorrow, and we'll discuss your lessons." He gave me the now-familiar look. "After you've bathed, of course."

I followed the servant, a tall, sturdy girl, who smiled reassuringly. "'Tis a big place, but you'll be getting used to it in no time."

The chamber was dark, and the light of the stinking tallow candle showed little beyond a sagging bed, with several others beyond. All were empty, and the maid explained that the others were either performing or off on their own mischief. "There aren't many girls in the Music, only seven or eight."

"What about the boys?" I asked, sleepy but curious. The servant's chatter was more to my taste than Master Cornysh's seriousness. "I met one tonight. Tom, his name was."

"Aye, Thomas Minstrel, he's a love of a boy."

Minstrel. I wondered how he'd come by such a name—whether music was his family's profession, as some men were called Smith or Chandler, or whether he chose it, as he had chosen my name. I wanted to ask, but even as I formed the thought, I began to yawn.

"You should have a bath, but I'll not carry water at this hour." She spat on her fingers and rubbed at a smudge on my face. "The state you're in, you'd drown anyway." She pulled back the bedclothes and turned to me. "Undress whilst I think. There's the choirboys, about a dozen, and a few more here in the Music. Perhaps sixteen altogether and twice as many men." A cluck of her tongue indicated disapproval of my shift. "You can't sleep in that thing."

Naked and shivering, I sat on the bed while she fetched something clean for me to wear. When she returned, I was capable of no more than putting it over my head and falling back against the pillow.

❧

It was quiet. No street noise, no fishmongers or vegetable sellers bawling outside. I opened my eyes to an unfamiliar room. The covers were rumpled, but my bedfellows had come and gone without disturbing me.

The door opened, and a young woman entered. She was no taller than a twelve-year-old child, though her breasts plumped up from her square neckline in womanly fashion. Her expression was sweet, and I warmed to her immediately. "I've been waiting for you." She held out a soft white hand. "I'm Mistress Keith. Get up now, and follow me."

I sat up and saw the garments folded neatly at the foot of the bed. "Those aren't my things."

Mistress Keith raised her eyebrows. "You have new things, Bess. You have a whole new life."

Chapter 2

My new life hardly seemed real. After having been called lazy all my life, I discovered that I liked rising at first light and practicing for hours. No lesson was too difficult, because it was in preparation for the day when I would again perform for the king.

That first morning, after a scalding bath and a huge breakfast, and wearing my new clothes, I met with Master Cornysh. He asked me to sing for him—anything I wanted. I obliged, watching his face carefully. He then led me next through a series of exercises. After an hour, he announced himself well pleased with my attempts. I sagged with relief. I saw no way in which I would be allowed to leave, other than to displease Master Cornysh or some other powerful man. Though I'd wept in the tub, I'd also decided to make the best of this new situation.

By rights, Master Cornysh said, he should put me with the other minstrel children, since he dealt mostly with the choristers, but for the time being, I would take my lessons with him alone. My voice was untutored, and he wanted the training of it. "The king has heard you once," he said. "Let him not believe his ears when he hears you again."

I took a liking to the overworked, kindly man, and I hungered for what he could teach me. I never knew music could be written down like words, and the transition from sounds in the air to marks on paper was fascinating.

Master Cornysh showed no surprise that I was illiterate, and though he said education was of little importance to a minstrel, especially a girl, every member of the Music must have some formal schooling—how else was I to read lyrics?

I did not get on well with Hubert, a spotty boy of fifteen, who was tasked with teaching me my letters. He spent much of my lesson scribbling music and ignoring me. When I finally complained, he turned surly. "No girl needs to know how to read. What little you know puts you ahead of half the women at court already."

The next day, Mistress Keith appeared in his place. She was patient with the turnings of my mind and answered all my questions about the court just as soon as our lessons were through. Under her tutelage, I learned quickly.

Jenny Keith had been at court for ten years, which made her twenty-three, but her girlish air made her appear far younger. She was wife to

Ralph Keith, one of the adult choristers, a stocky, dark-haired man whose eyes always found her in a crowded chamber. After six years of marriage, they were still childless. She said wistfully that although caring for us was her job, she sometimes pretended we were her own children.

Her affection was genuine, and I returned it with my whole heart. My fancy of being Mistress Keith's daughter kept me going when loneliness clawed my innards. I loved her pretty face, with its clear, pink skin and the smooth dark red hair under her snowy coif. I wondered that she would want a child like me.

As for the other children of the Music, though I met them and learned their names and shared a bed with two of them, I remained isolated by the wall of silence they erected.

I looked often for Tom. At meals, he sat at the long trestle table with a group of other boys, but occasionally, he would glance at me and smile. Though he was a lofty thirteen, I liked him very much. Something in Tom's face reminded me of Da: not his features, which were quite ordinary but for his surprisingly dark blue-gray eyes, but a hint of something in his expression—a watchfulness, as if anticipating a harsh word or a blow. I glimpsed it rarely, and it vanished when he knew himself observed, but its presence endeared him to me. I thought he'd not always led an easy life. Privileged people did not have the look I saw on his face.

This made me think of home, which I did with some guilt. I didn't miss the everlasting cold, the hunger, or the tempers of my mother and sister. I missed my Da and wondered if he missed me. His absence was a hollow place in my new life.

After the first weeks, I began to have trouble sleeping. Mistress Keith offered a cresset for my bedside to keep the terrors away, but I refused; my fears had nothing to do with the dark. When it came, my sleep was peaceful, but I was afraid to close my eyes—afraid I would wake in my Southwark cot and discover that my new life had only been a dream. For weeks I suffered, and then it came to me: perhaps if I kept food at hand, I might feed the demon that plagued me, and sated, it would sleep, and so would I.

This lasted until Mistress Keith discovered bread under my pillow. The thought of disappointing her was worse than leaving, and I began to cry. "I'm sorry," I said when I could speak.

She stroked my head with those light, motherly hands. "You needn't be sorry for being hungry, Bess. You're a growing girl."

I knew she understood my real fear and loved her for her tact. "I won't take food from the table again, Mistress."

"I wouldn't recommend it." She cuddled me, and I sighed happily at the warm roundness of her. "If you go down to the kitchens, you can ask one of the boys for a bit of bread or fruit."

I crept often through the long passage to the kitchens, where one of the under-cooks took pity on my scrawny frame and wrapped apples and bread in a cloth. Occasionally, there would be a sweet tucked in with my store, and those, I left on Mistress Keith's pillow.

The kitchens were as large as the great hall, with smoke-stained walls, scarred wooden tables, and vast hearths. It was always warm there, and my friend Gordon saw to it that I was treated as invisible. He found me a corner near the larders, and I often sat there, watching as fantastical dishes were prepared for the king's pleasure.

The head cook spent his days in a passion of rage, and when he ventured to my end of the kitchens, I scurried under a table and watched his feet, no less terrified of him than his workers were. Despite his temper, he had a deft hand with pastry, and he made spun-sugar subtleties as beautiful as anything I'd ever seen. He carved castles and dragons, and once, a whole tourney, with tiny silk pennons flying over a field of black and white sugar horses.

In a society bound by religious observance, my attendance at church had left me almost untouched. I went to mass because I had to and because of the music. I had no relationship with God beyond a belief in His existence. Before I sat down with a priest, I had little comprehension of heaven or hell, a state of mind which suited me but appalled and upset my elders. I was very close to being a heathen, they assured me, and from their tone, I assumed this was very bad. Father James set to instructing me in the ways of the Lord with as much fervor as Master Cornysh explained the workings of a motet, but with far less success.

With his help, I was soon fluent in biblical lore, though it was difficult to keep the characters straight in my head. I assigned familiar faces to the distant, unknowable saints and got along much better knowing Moses looked like the cook, and Master Cornysh, with us as his menagerie, was Noah. Tom was Adam because he was the first male I met at court. The king, of course, was God, a choice even Father James would not fault. For the Virgin, I applied the features and disposition of one of my fellow musicians.

Agnes Hilliard shared my chamber, and she the only one who was not unkind to me. Accustomed to tight quarters, the space did not seem small, but on my arrival, the others made much of moving their possessions about to make room. Agnes shifted her few things quietly, her expression distant.

In a court where fair hair and complexion were considered a lady's greatest claim to beauty, Agnes was exceptional. Her hair was the color of butter and, when loose, hung in waves to her waist. Her skin was so translucent that a blush caused her to glow. She, more than anything, made me believe in God: I took it as proof of His existence that someone as beautiful as Agnes walked among us.

I watched her in chapel and saw the light of ecstasy in her eyes. I did not wonder why she felt the truth of the mass, and I did not—Agnes, with her saint's face, was assured of heaven, and I, who annoyed my parents so much they sent me away, who could not remember the rosary, was not.

Her pale eyes focused on me now and then, and I would feel privileged by her attention. She spoke rarely and never addressed a word to me. She was almost twelve, and I adored her before she knew I existed.

Sometimes I arrived early for my lesson and heard Agnes at practice, and I discovered I could be critical of one whom I worshipped. Her voice was pleasant but not strong; she sang from her throat, which Master Cornysh told me was a sign of a lazy singer. She had a tolerable hand for the lute, he said, noting my interest, and none of the older girls came close to her on the virginals.

I was always a solitary child, my labors keeping me close to home, but now, with no family, I wanted a friend. Master Cornysh or Mistress Keith was there if I had questions, but they were adults; something in me held back from them. There was Tom, but he was a boy. A friend of my own, a girl, was what I wanted.

In time, Agnes might warm to me, but this seemed impossible while she remained friends with Mary Wynne and Flora Leggett, who, from the first day, chose me as the butt of their jokes. They were within a year or so of my own age and of similar situation. The difference—and it was a vast one—was that they were placed in the king's service by their families, whose willingness to part with them was proof of their importance, as my father's selling me was proof I was unwanted.

Each night, as I lay in bed, conversation flowed over my head. Despite the hollow feeling caused by loneliness, I felt superior to those girls. The only thing that mattered was music. Music was air and food and sunlight. That Mary and Flora gossiped and prattled told me they cared less than I.

Even after the novelty of my purchase wore off, my relationships were still strained. Agnes smiled at me once, and hope rose in my heart, but Mary dragged her off, whispering in her ear. I felt more alone than ever.

The one friend I could swear to was Tom, who warned me not to expect gifts but who had left a velvet rose on my pillow on December 28. He would not confess to the kindness, but the color that stained his cheeks gave him away.

I'd never owned anything so pretty. I wanted to wear it, but my simple bodices weren't grand enough to merit such a treasure, and I was afraid it might be taken by one of the older girls. Mistress Keith gave me a small casket with a lock, and I tucked the rose inside and wore the key on a ribbon.

Possessing a treasure, even a locked-away treasure, gave me confidence. There were still words that cut me to the quick, but when my feelings smarted, I felt for the ribbon at my throat and pretended the rose was there instead.

Envy of that sort—for envy it was, Mistress Keith said with assurance—was something new. In my old life, I was the one who envied others. Jealousy because the king was willing to pay money to possess my voice was something I never considered.

I had never before possessed anything worthy of the envy of others.

Winter passed grudgingly into spring, and the atmosphere began to change. In the summer months, King Henry went on progress, and his musicians accompanied him. This was exciting; I knew but a small corner of London, and now I might have the chance to travel all over England.

If I pleased the king.

All depended on that. I remembered how scared I had been that first night and wondered if I would feel that way again when it was time or if I would sing without my knees knocking beneath my skirts.

This was a predicament I could not take to Master Cornysh, always busy with the choir or helping the revels master, Henry Guildford, plan new fancies for the king's entertainment. Mistress Keith would be sympathetic, but she was feeling the quickening of her first babe, and I had no wish to disturb her springtime miracle with my petty worries.

In the end, I turned to Tom.

I found him in the common practice room, nursing a sore throat and staring moodily at the fire, his beautiful instrument idle in his lap. I sat down beside him, holding my hands out to the flames until my skin prickled. The day was warm, but inside the palace, it was always damp, and I felt it dearly.

"How is the little gypsy?" Tom asked, tweaking a curl from my cap.

I pushed it back, knowing it wouldn't stay. "You sound awful."

"You don't sound too right yourself," he said. "Someone been unkind to you?"

I shrugged. It was his gesture, made my own as I used it in response to so many harsh words.

"That's not the girl who made free with my ear in front of the king." He settled his lute on a cushion and turned toward me. "What's wrong?"

Now that I had his attention, I was scared to tell him I was afraid of performing for the king. I stared into the fire. "I don't like Mary and Flora."

"Have they been plaguing you?"

I ducked my head. "A bit."

He put his arm around my shoulders and let me burrow against him. "They're just girls, Bess." He squeezed me encouragingly. "What do they say?"

I remembered all their taunts and summoned up the worst. "That my parents sold me because they didn't want me." My fingers twitched, remembering. I'd wanted to tear out Mary's red-gold curls when she said it.

"You know that's not true." Unconsciously, he reached for his lute and began to rub one finger along its curve. The pale wood bore the mark of many similar rubbings, and I knew stroking the instrument soothed him.

"I don't know that." I wished someone cared for me the way he cared for his lute. "No one else had to be bought. Families give their children gladly for the king."

"They may not ask for silver, but they expect payment." Touching the strings, he brought forth a few sorrowful notes. "They get gifts, preferments. It's no different from what your father did. He was just more honest about it."

"But it is different." I hopped down from the bench. "The king bought me like I was something in a shop window."

Tom raised an eyebrow. "He has bought other children, I told you, though not for your price."

In spite of my wounded feelings, I was intrigued by this hint of a knowledge I did not possess. I perched beside him again, drawing up my skirts so that the heat reached my legs. "Do you know what he paid for me?"

He nodded and picked out another phrase while I squirmed in my seat. "Thirty pounds," he said, clearly not wanting to tell me. "That's more than what he paid for the last one." His expression darkened. "I hope you keep your value."

"What do you mean?" This was not the conversation I intended. The idea of being worth thirty pounds was impressive, but it would not stop the others from teasing, and I'd somehow made Tom unhappy.

"I meant naught, Bess." He grasped the lute again, this time with a sure knowledge of what he held. "I must practice. The king has asked for me tonight, and I've a new song to learn." He left me sitting by the fire in a worse state of bewilderment than before.

⁓⁓⁓

"Here's a farthing if you'll sing, Bess!" Mary's voice was pitched so I could hear it down the length of the table. I focused on the trencher before me, but she continued, making the others laugh. "Surely, you need a farthing. Mayhap you could send it to your father."

I looked up through a haze of tears. My talk with Tom had not lessened the sting of her barbs, but I would not let her see that she upset me. "At least people would pay to hear me," I said. "If they want to hear a crow scream, that costs nothing." The laughter as I left the table was not all at my expense.

The strain began to show. Despite my desire to learn, I could not concentrate, hearing Mary's mocking voice whenever I did something particularly well. Master Cornysh grew impatient with my blunders.

"God's teeth, child, you knew that yesterday!" He set me to working with the choristers as extra practice, and I was singing the kyrie we'd rehearsed earlier.

I looked down at the rushes. It was a careless mistake.

"I'm trying very hard to make you ready. Don't you want to sing for the king?" His annoyance was obvious, though he suffered from the same cold as Tom, and his voice held only a suggestion of its normal asperity.

19

"Oh, aye!" I was both anticipating and in terror of the occasion. "I'll be better, Master Cornysh. Let me try again."

I closed my eyes and put the girls out of my mind, focusing on the music. Disappointing Master Cornysh was almost as bad as disappointing Mistress Keith. Or the king.

My lingering anger made itself known in my voice, and the depth of feeling I achieved surprised us both. I finished the passage, and Master Cornysh broke into spontaneous applause. "Splendid! Whoever it was vexed you, remember how it felt." He pushed a stool toward me.

It was the signal for a lecture. Now that I'd tied my emotions to the music, I wanted to be left to practice, to see if I could turn my hurts to my advantage. It would serve Mary right if her unkindness made me better. When he finished, I asked, "Master Cornysh, am I good?"

He looked up from his sheets. "Your voice, you mean? Yes, you're very good—the best I've had the pleasure to teach in many years, else I would not waste time with you."

Men like Master Cornysh did not dissemble. I trusted Tom, but he was my friend. Master Cornysh was different. I would be able to bear their taunts more easily, knowing he believed in me.

"Have they abused you?"

"A bit, sir." I hoped his adult sensibilities would put my mind at ease.

"I should have seen it. They persecute you to be reassured they are different—better—because their parents did not take money for them."

I pleated a bit of my gray fustian skirt between my fingers. "Tom told me their families get gifts anyway if King Henry is pleased."

"True. Too often a child is given to curry favor, as it's known by all what value the king sets on music." Master Cornysh rubbed his nose and gave me a penetrating, watery-eyed glance. "So you've had words with young Tom, have you?"

"Yes, sir." I inched closer to the warmth of the charcoal brazier, letting it toast my back.

"And did he make you feel better?"

"He did say I wasn't the first."

"That's true enough." He made a tidy pile of the music we'd reviewed, looking at me from beneath his shaggy brows. "He does not speak of it, Bess, but Tom was bought, just as you were."

Tom's words rang in my ears, and I winced. Why had I not guessed? "Was it long ago?"

"Five or six years, if I recall. The king heard him in a street pageant and bought him outright, just threw his mother a purse." His voice caught, and he cleared his throat with a painful rasp. "The king insisted that Tom be put on the back of a horse and brought along with the procession."

At least I'd said goodbye. I tried to imagine how it must have been for Tom, at seven, to ride away from all he knew, looking back at his mother's face in the crowd. Did he cry? Did she? "The king must have truly liked him."

Master Cornysh blew his nose like a trumpet. His words emerged muffled from the large white kerchief that covered most of his face. "He was very taken with Tom's voice."

I ceased thinking about the cold. "His voice?"

"He sings no more," Master Cornysh said and told me why.

As Prince of Wales, Henry Tudor was allowed only two minstrels; as king, he acquired musicians from all over Europe to make up for his earlier lack. Most especially, he sought out choristers for the Chapel Royal, and it was for this he wanted Tom.

The king was enamored with his perfect soprano and never wearied of listening to him, sending for him at all hours and showing him off to visitors. He was a beautiful child, Master Cornysh said, with engaging manners, and within a year, he'd advanced to first boy of the Chapel Royal. The choir was the envy of all who heard it.

He should have been safe. He should have had years. Boys' voices often didn't change until they were fifteen or sixteen, some even later. Indeed, there were sopranos in the choir who were near old enough to marry, but early in his twelfth year, Tom's voice broke.

He never sang for his king again.

It was a rule that all choristers be proficient in at least one instrument, for general usefulness and also against such a day. Tom already knew the lute, and with the loss of his voice, he applied himself and became a prodigy, no small achievement in a musical court such as this. I knew his love for the instrument and King Henry's evident affection for him, but now, I wondered how often Tom thought of what he had been, rather than what he'd become.

By the time Master Cornysh finished, I was weeping. He tried to comfort me, but when his efforts failed, he summoned Mistress Keith. I took her hand, unable to look up when Master Cornysh patted my head. "All will be well, child," he said and shut the door behind us.

I cried all the way back to the girls' chamber. Eventually, my sobs subsided, and I made out Mistress Keith's words. "What on earth has so distressed you, child?"

I wiped my eyes with my sleeve and gave the reason for my sorrow.

"Oh, Bess, it's common knowledge," she said, one hand on my shoulder and the other resting on the barely visible curve of her pregnancy. "We all felt for Tom at the time, but he's turned his hand elsewhere, and I'm sure he doesn't think of it. There's no cause for such tears."

I couldn't let go of Tom's tragedy. To have just one precious possession, one thing that gave him value in the eyes of the world, and to lose it! Illness wouldn't have affected me so deeply; I was accustomed to the hand of God striking with disease, but what happened to Tom was an innocent, stupid accident, a part of growing up.

I realized the power I held, the sheer luck by which I possessed it, and the work it would take to keep it. After that, I knelt daily at mass and before sleep and prayed to keep my voice, even before I petitioned for the health of my family and the king. I felt no contrition in asking to be spared Tom's fate.

Knowing he had come to court in the same way only strengthened the bond I felt, and the fact that both of us were poor, relying on our talents to keep us in the king's favor, made our kinship even stronger.

I kept quiet for almost a week until Tom looked at me narrowly one day and asked, "Who told you?"

There was no point in dissembling. "Master Cornysh." I looked at him. "He thought to ease me by telling. I'm sorry."

"For what?" His gaze held an unaccustomed challenge, and I realized Mistress Keith was wrong. There was pain in his eyes, and resentment. Tom had found another way, but he mourned what was lost.

"For making you talk about it," I said. "You only tried to help."

"It's not your fault." I did not recognize my quicksilver friend in this sullen-sounding boy.

I bit my lip, tasting blood. "Nor is it yours."

"True." His dimple appeared, and he touched my chin with a rough-tipped finger. "I don't speak of it, though."

It was his right, as I chose not to speak of my family. We would be friends forever; there would be plenty of time.

Chapter 3

I was nearly finished my morning practice when Mistress Keith looked in. "Your father is waiting for you in the great hall." I left the chamber at a near-run, surprised at my own eagerness, and promptly got lost in my new surroundings.

The court had recently moved to Westminster. Five years past, the palace suffered a fire, and repairs were still ongoing. If the royal lodgings were uncomfortable, the servants' quarters were even more so. This, combined with the noise and dirt of London, made an unfavorable comparison to Greenwich, which already felt like home.

I found my way to the hall and, after a moment's anxiety, located my father. He waited by the doors, tall and bony, dressed in the same threadbare clothes he'd worn at Christmas. He looked tired and ill, but when I called out to him, his eyes brightened, and he held out his arms. I went into them joyfully.

"You look well." He looked me up and down. "I can see I made no mistake in bringing you here. Are you happy?"

I nodded, my ears harkening gladly to his liquid Welsh tones. "Most of the time, Da. I've made a few friends."

"That's good." He seemed uncomfortable out in the open, so I led him to an alcove where we could sit. A soft breeze from the doors ruffled my skirts, and I thought, at least he'd had a pleasant day for traveling this time.

"How are Mum and Madlen?"

"Well enough." He explained they had all been taken by a fever early in the year, and it left him easily tired. Admitting weakness shamed him, and he changed the subject. "Your mother hopes you're being a good girl."

"No one has complained." As ever, her only concern was my good behavior.

"She only wants you to do well," he said. He hesitated, then added, "She wasn't always hard, you know. It was Cefin. When we lost him, something broke inside her."

I nodded but disbelieved his words. Madlen had not been mothered with blows and shouts. I knew it was because of my part in Cefin's death, no matter what he said.

Da stroked his chin. "To think I fought for and followed a king I never met, and my child sings before his son. The daughter of Peter Davydd—a servant to the King of England!"

Davydd. Something twisted in the region of my heart. How had I forgotten? Elizabeth Davydd, I said to myself. Bess Davydd. It was someone else's name.

"They don't call me that."

"Don't call you what, Bethan?" I'd almost forgotten his pet name for me as well and felt a pang. How quickly my old life had drifted away!

"Davydd," I said and held my breath.

His hair needed trimming, and there was a line of silver stubble along his jaw. His smile faded. "How do they call you, then?"

"Llewelyn," I told him. "Bess Llewelyn. Tom gave me the name that first night."

The silence between us was terrible. He was a man without sons, and I, who might carry his name into some kind of posterity, had given it up without a backward glance. I braced for whatever blow would follow.

Instead, he laughed. From my earliest days, I'd treasured the sound, but it was edged with bitterness now. "'Tis but right," he said, "as we surrendered you, so should you surrender us. You belong to the king's household now, not us."

His gaze left me then, followed the path of light on the rushes to the open doors. He seemed to forget I was there, and when he spoke, his voice was low. "It's not how I would have wished it, Bess—not for you nor for Madlen or young Cefin."

My eyes burned. I leaned forward and hugged him. His grasp was at first tentative, then convulsive, and I felt his shoulders shake.

"Don't fret, Da. I'm happy." My voice quivered, but I went on. "They treat me well, and I can sing as much as I like. Master Cornysh even suggested I learn an instrument."

I did not tell him I fought the idea, wanting nothing to come between me and my voice; a lute or rebec could be played by anyone with reasonable skill, but few could sing as I did. Also, while it had been prudent for Tom to learn to play, considering what befell him, I feared if I began the lute, I too might lose my voice. It was a superstitious fancy, but I clung to it.

"Learn the harp," my father said. "Our people are great harpers."

I did not want to be a harper, great or otherwise, but I said, "Yes, Da," to please him.

Several men strayed inside while we were speaking, regaling the hall with tales of the day's hunting. No one paid any heed to a shabby man and a child clasping hands on a bench. My father saw them, though, and rose to leave. It was strange to see him so ill at ease when I scarce noticed the bustle.

24

He jammed his cap over his ears. "I but came to see you were well." He kissed my forehead, and I hugged him again. "I'll give your mother and sister your love."

"Of course," I said with as much sincerity as I suspected they gave their own good wishes. "And to you, Da. Especially to you."

His smile was like sunshine, breaking through the weariness on his face. "I'll try to come again, and I'll ask for you properly next time."

I wanted to thank him for coming, for not being angry about my name, for loving me, but I knew it would embarrass him.

"It's a fine name they gave you," he said. "Do you know who Llewelyn was?"

"No." I doubted Tom knew either, for it seemed he'd plucked the name from the air.

"Llewelyn was a great Welsh prince during the time of the English King John of evil memory. His people called him Llewelyn Fahr, Llewelyn the Great." He fastened his coat, smoothing it where it was roughly patched. "A proud name."

Da's visit changed everything for me. I was not so naïve as to think that I'd come to the king solely for my own benefit; no doubt, the money served my family well. But Da chose the way that would give me a life worth living, and I knew he'd done it from love.

After the meal, I went in search of Tom, for there was no one else who would care about my father's visit. He was not to be found within the walls of Westminster. I spied one of the other young minstrels in the practice room and risked a rebuff. "Have you seen Tom?"

Harry seemed taken aback to hear me speak. "The last I saw him, he was in the courtyard." He then surprised us both by adding, in a civil tone, "You might try the stables."

It was a reasonable suggestion, for Tom loved the beasts, and at Greenwich, he spent much of his free time there.

At Westminster, the stables lay a fair distance away, in an effort to keep foul odors from the royal nose. My distinctly non-royal nose also proved sensitive, and I half hoped not to find him within.

The double doors, with their crests bearing the intertwined initials H and K, were flung wide. I stood outside and called his name, venturing in only when I received no response. The stables weren't as large as those at Greenwich, but as I feared, the tickly smell was the same. I sneezed explosively, and several horses shied, bumping against their stalls.

A movement caught my eye. "Tom!"

He glanced toward me, and his face wore the watchful expression I knew well. He nodded but made no move. Full of own my news, I cannoned through the stall door and into his midsection. The air left him in a rush, and he put his arms around me reflexively, then backed away.

"I've been looking for you." This distance was unlike him; he always returned my caresses. "Did you not hear me?"

"Is this goodbye, then?" His voice, above my head, sounded strained.

I drew back and tried to look at him, but his pale hair covered most of his face, and I couldn't see his eyes. "What do you mean?"

Tom's posture became stiffer, and he removed my hands from his waist. "Mary told me your father came for you."

My eyes were itching, and I wiped my face with my sleeve, but the sneeze came anyway. "I cannot stay in here." Grabbing his arm, I pulled him after me, exchanging the dusty, hay-scented stables for the sunlit yard. I took a deep breath and waited for the itching to stop.

"I thought you were happy," he said with an unfamiliar scowl. "When are you going?"

Pulling a kerchief out of my sleeve, I blew my nose and looked at him, my eyes brimming. "What are you talking about?"

Tom took a deep breath. "She said you were leaving."

I almost laughed, but instead, I reached for his hand and was glad when he allowed me to take it. "He only came to see how I fared."

"Oh." His body was still taut, but I felt the relief he would not show. I wondered why boys must be brave and was glad to be a girl, who could show her upsets.

"Did you think I would leave?" When I saw Da, it never entered my mind he would want me back or that I would go. Would it even be allowed?

"Would you not if he asked you?" Leaning against the fence, he'd shed some of the furtive air of the stable and looked more like my Tom. His dark green doublet was dusted with fine gold powder, and I resisted the urge to brush him off before I sneezed again. "He's your father, Bess."

"True." If I left, the hollow in my chest would be from missing the court, instead of my father. "But he brought me here, and he did well by me." I brought his hand to my lips in a gesture I'd seen the court ladies use. It was not a gesture of which Mistress Keith would approve. "I can't think of a better life—or a better friend."

Pleasure lit his eyes and spread until I saw the flicker of his dimple. "I thought he wanted you back," he admitted, raking his fingers through his hair. "I was sore worried."

With an inward smile, I realized that my feelings were not one-sided and that Tom, with his legion of friends, nevertheless felt the same bond. It filled me with happiness. Even after a few months, life without him was unimaginable. Knowing he would miss me gave me as much joy as my father's visit.

May Day was always a great celebration at court. It was also the occasion of my first public performance. As the day neared, Master Cornysh scarce let me out of his sight. I was to be part of a great pageant, but I would sing alone, and I had to be flawless.

He often set me to work with Tom, believing I needed encouragement. I appreciated his fostering of our friendship, for when Tom and I were together, I had the two things most precious to me: music and my dearest companion.

"Bess, pay attention." There was reproach in his voice, but I knew by his expression, he understood. Further into the room, the air was chilly, but near the wide oriel window where we sat, it was warm, unmistakably spring. "Try it again."

My heart was not in the song; repetition had long since taken any meaning from the words. "Play something else, Tom."

"You must practice." He bent over the lute to hide his smile.

"Please." I knelt on the seat and looked out the window, listening as he began the May song. "I can't sing it again."

With a sigh, he abandoned the song for something of his own. This time, I listened eagerly, for he coaxed sounds from a lute as to make my eyes well up and my throat close. His music had a wildness to it, something I could feel but did not have the words to express. He scoffed when I praised him, but my opinion was unshakeable.

"That's much nicer than Master Fayrefax's boring song," I said, trying to shove the heavy casement open. It moved a fraction, then stuck.

"Don't speak foolishness, Bess. I'm but fourteen—I can't compete with the masters." He looked pleased, though, his cheeks shading a healthy russet.

"If you're good enough to play for them, why should you not compete?"

"Because I am good enough to play for them," he said. "I'm a minstrel, not a composer. I make up songs for my own enjoyment and yours. But to compete with them—" Lowering his head, he played a snatch of melody that caught at my heart. "That would not be permitted."

"They should fear the competition," I said, as certain of his talent as I was of my own. The king would be pleased with my performance on May Day, but I wondered how much more favorable would be his response if I sang Tom's song instead. "Your music is so different, so much clearer." I tried to shape my muddled feelings into words, knowing already that I would not succeed. "I see pictures in my mind when I listen to your music. As for Master Fayrefax"—I gestured at the sheets before us—"he does not touch me."

Tom drew me close. Through the glass came faint sounds of birdsong and the voices of the lucky ones who were outdoors on this most glorious of days. If only we could escape the palace, it would be perfect.

It was several minutes before Tom stirred, prodding me upright. "Master Cornysh sent us here for a reason, sweet."

"I know the piece already." I wanted to sit with him in the mellow afternoon light, thinking, for once, of anything but music. "I've sung it a hundred times."

To cheer me, Tom played something else, a lilting refrain that fit the tenor of the day. An insistent yearning hid beneath its gaiety, and I laughed at his ability to exactly express my feelings. I shifted on the cushion and put my head back on his shoulder, stilling his song.

"Are you nervous about the pageant, Bess?" He put the lute aside and reached around me to open the window. It obeyed him instantly, and the room filled with the scent of spring.

"You'll be there, won't you?" Master Cornysh had promised, but I wanted reassurance.

"Of course."

"Then I'll not be scared," I said. "I've sung on May Day, and I've sung for the king. The two together won't be difficult, not with you there." I touched my finger to the ribbon I wore, its only ornament, the small gold key. Perhaps, for May Day, I would wear the rose instead.

"Don't you ever miss them?"

"No." My response was as abrupt as his query. I was lonely but not for my family.

He looked at me closely. "Surely, you must. It was different for me, but you—"

"I don't." This was the closest he'd come to mentioning his life before court. "My father, a bit, since he came to see me, but none other."

"But you had a real family, parents and a sister. It must have been nice to live that way."

From what I gleaned from Mistress Keith, I knew he'd left a mother behind in London, but I did not believe he had siblings. "Just because a family has the right number of people does not make it happy." My family had not had the right number since Cefin's death.

He stroked my hair.

"My mum never wanted me," I said, "and my sister and I did naught but quarrel. If I'd been a help, Mum might have forgiven me, but I was always singing or dreaming, and that just made her angry."

"You were a child," Tom said, staunch in support of my daydreaming. "You couldn't be expected to do an adult's labors."

Poor children were expected to labor like adults, however; Madlen assisted our mother, and the other children I'd known worked beside their parents. I thought of Mum, her temper frayed and her back stooped from bending over the tubs of steaming water. She did fine washing and ironing for the "ladies" of Southwark. Madlen did her share, her nimble fingers taking with ease to the frills and tucks, but I was clumsy, and more often than not, I burned my fingers and scorched the linens.

"I'm certain they love you," Tom said, something in him unable to stomach my bleak description.

"Perhaps," I said. "But you don't belong somewhere if no one misses you when you leave."

"Poor Bess."

I forced a laugh. "And poor Tom." I reached up and brushed his fair hair from his eyes. "A fine pair of orphans we are."

His answering laugh was rueful. "I'll tell Master Cornysh I broke a string. You know that song as well as Fayrefax himself."

The still morning air was shattered by the winding of the horn as the hunt thundered from the stables. The sky was pink-tinged, the grass soaked with dew.

I watched as the horses streamed up the slope of Shooter's Hill, the gaily dressed riders looking like figures from a tapestry. Despite their pace, the attitude was leisurely; everyone knew there would be no real sport. King Henry was at the head of the field, splendid in Lincoln green velvet, a jaunty plume in his cap. He kept a close hand on the reins of his black horse as it twitched and bounded with contagious excitement. I clapped my hands when he stood in the stirrups and let the horse have its head and prance along. After everyone had admired his prowess, the king pulled his mount back to ride alongside the queen's well-mannered gray mare.

The murmur of voices behind me ebbed and flowed like the Thames, but I was all impatience like the king's horse and turned from the window. "Mistress, are we leaving?"

"Does it appear that we're moving, Bess?" came the reply from across the chamber. "Don't fuss. You'll spoil your gown."

Mistress Keith, rounded and glowing like an apple, placed a circlet of leaves and gillyflowers on my head. "You're lovely," she said with a pat of approval. "You look like a young lady in that gown."

I thrilled to her words, for hadn't I thought the same? I didn't often care how I looked, but this gown was beautiful, and I felt more tolerant than usual of the girlish chatter of slippers and sleeves. The heady scent of the wreath made me sneeze, and I did so stiffly, careful not to disturb the ornaments sewn to my willow-green bodice and skirt.

The performers left in a series of carts, traveling along the worn roundabout path. We arrived ahead of the hunting party and were hidden away when we heard the horn. Henry Guildford, dressed as Robin Hood, shouted a challenge to the royal party to join his merry men.

I experienced a moment of disbelief that I should be a part of such a world and felt in my stomach a fluttering much like the wings of the captive birds netted for the occasion. I prayed I would not disgrace myself when the time came.

Soft music filtered through the trees as the king and queen were led to the dais inside the vast silken tent. I stayed hidden behind my tent-flap, dreamily watching the grand spectacle, wishing it was what the king pretended it to be: an innocent hunting-party overtaken by robbers and whisked into the forest.

The outlaws served the party with course after course of sumptuous fare carried apace from the palace kitchens. I lost count of the number of peacocks, cooked and reunited with their feathers, their beaks and claws turned to gold. There were courses of fish and fowl, lark and pheasant, and a special dish of stewed lampreys, the king's favorite. There was much wine and laughter, until I thought the performances forgotten, but at last, Guildford rose and bowed before the king.

"Your Grace, if a poor man may make so bold as to attempt to please his sovereign, I would offer you a little entertainment." He flung his arms wide, and three musicians entered. Harry and Gilbert looked well in their outlaw garb, but I was most proud of Tom, who was tall and fine in green hose and a leather jerkin over a soft white linen shirt.

Their music was gay and light and rang out marvelously in the enclosure. I judged no one need strain to hear and would pitch my own voice accordingly. When the trio began the last of their songs, joined this time by a group of girls in white flower-bedecked dresses, I readied myself for my entrance.

The king shouted his approval, and Gilbert and Harry bowed their way out of the tent, while Guildford took the stage again, his handsome, fleshy face smiling at the success of the entertainment thus far. "I would offer another treat for His Majesty," he said. "A small sprite, found in the wood. Fairies, as Your Grace knows, cannot be tamed, but this one has consented to sing for us."

Someone pushed me forward, and in small, springing steps, I joined Tom before the king and queen, dropping into the low curtsy that was now second nature. Master Fayrefax's tune emerged from lips and lute as perfectly as it had sounded in the composer's mind when he wrote the piece. I knew it without vanity, knew it as well as I knew Tom's songs were better.

There was silence as we performed, and when we finished, King Henry broke into hearty applause. Tom put his hand on my shoulder, and we made our bow together, then retreated to let the next performers come forward. Before we ducked out of the tent, I heard the king say, "Methinks I have heard that sprite before. She sings exceeding well."

I threw my arms around Tom. "He liked it!"

"Of course, he did." Laughing, he pulled me loose and set me down on a felled tree, gently, for fear of my gown. "You've an angel in your throat, Bess, and King Henry is too much a musician not to know it."

I leaned back and looked up at the sky, seeing it only as chinks of bright blue through the thick trees. "I would not sing so well were anyone else to play for me."

"Silly child," he said, kneeling and brushing grass from my skirt. "I can't play for you forever, Bess. They won't allow it. You must learn to stand on your own."

Chapter 4

"Running about like a hoyden, Bess. What do you expect?"

I squirmed at her ministrations; Mistress Edith was kindly but not always gentle. "I'm sorry."

A serving woman looked around the door. Mistress Edith let go of my leg while they had a brief, whispered conversation. After she had gone, I listened while Edith discussed the queen with Mistress Keith and two of the older girls.

"Some women just can't carry a babe to term." She wiped my knee and applied a cooling salve. I inhaled the minty scent.

"And what about the little princess?" Mistress Keith demanded, her cheeks flushed. "Born February last and sound as can be. And the other babe, the New Year's boy—how long ago was that?"

"Five years?" Frances hazarded. "But he died."

"Through no fault of hers." Jenny Keith crossed her arms over her belly. In the past month, she had become stout as a small barrel, but no less lovely.

"He was puny," Mistress Edith said, blunt as always. She put the jar in its proper place on the shelf above her work table. "And she lost a babe before him and one after whilst the king was in France with his war."

Mistress Keith was as angry as ever I'd seen her. "And while the king was in France with his war, Queen Katherine was here, taking care of his other war with Scotland. She wore herself out, poor woman."

"I'm not saying it was her fault, Jenny." Mistress Edith's shoulders heaved with stifled laughter. "God in Heaven, you're sensitive these days. Some women just can't drop a child every year, and she's one of them."

I listened to the talk of midwifery and the state of the queen's womb until Frances noticed me. She was a big girl, buxom and red-cheeked, and she enjoyed pushing the young ones around. Ostensibly, she was there to help Mistress Edith tidy her workroom, but Jenny Keith was doing more effective labor as she didn't stop every few minutes to study her reflection in the surfaces of the bottles and jars. "She's listening, Mistress Edith!" she said. "Little weasel."

"Weasel, yourself," I retorted under my breath. I wasn't exactly afraid of Frances, but she reminded me of my sister.

"Child," Mistress Edith said, "this is not for your ears. Take yourself off and be mindful how you run about. You'll be a young lady one day—try practicing that for a change."

I returned to the girls' chamber, no desire in me for more outdoor games. I hoped for some peace to think about what I'd overheard, but when I entered, Agnes was sitting on the edge of the bed with a piece of needlework. I greeted her guardedly, wondering why she was sewing by the smoky light of a rush dip when the common rooms offered brighter workspace.

"Bess!" She patted the place beside her on the rough brown cover. "Please, don't leave."

Her voice was as pretty as her face, low and musical. I sat on the other side of the bed and waited, but what she said next surprised me. "I heard the king asked for you again last night." There was awe in her blue eyes. "That's three times this week."

"I'm glad my voice pleases the king," I said, choosing my words carefully.

She stuck her needle through the cloth. "You're cautious with me." Her hands, with their long, slender fingers, twisted in her lap. "I'm sorry for any part I had in making you feel unwelcome."

I accepted her apology. "Why do they say such things?"

"Did the king truly pay thirty pounds for you?"

"That is what I have been told." I saw no reason to bring it up again.

"That's what started it," Agnes said. "Most of us were sent here to gain favor for our families. We have talent, of course, or we would have been placed elsewhere in the household, but it was rather a blow to hear that he offered so much for you when he already had all of us."

I began to understand. "But the king has bought other children. Tom—"

"All of them, even Tom, were for the Chapel, and that's different from the Music. I suppose you know about Tom, though—you seem such good friends." Her smooth forehead creased with effort. "It's because the king wanted you so badly."

"Why should one more voice matter?"

It was clear the conversation made her uneasy. "It just did. When you were quiet, they said you put on airs, but you knew you were good; what they said did not bother you."

I took a chance that this proffered friendship was genuine and spoke the truth to Agnes. "It bothered me, especially when Mary said my parents didn't want me."

Agnes was working on her embroidery again, her needle pricking the cloth neatly. "Do you not see? That is what we all believe."

I mulled her words while she stitched. Agnes, I forgave utterly, but I wasn't so sure about the others. "I've heard you," I said. "Your voice is very good."

"Not like yours." Her needle flashed with a confidence I would never possess. "Have you always been able to sing like that?"

I shrugged. "Before I came here, my mother beat me for it. Master Cornysh has taught me so much, and Tom has as well."

"He's nice, isn't he?" Agnes held her work out at arm's length and began to pick at a loose stitch in the border. "And a great favorite of the king."

I was about to ask, with some jealousy, if she liked Tom, when the door opened and saved our burgeoning friendship. It was Mistress Keith, loose tendrils of dark red hair clinging to her face. She pressed one hand against the swell of her front-laced bodice. "Bess, there you are! You've been summoned, child."

"Is it Master Cornysh?" I asked, sliding off the bed. I ran a hand over my head. Though my hair was smoothed away under a linen cap, it was still an unruly tangle hanging down my back. I twisted it up into a knot and let Mistress Keith tidy it away.

"The queen has asked for you," Jenny Keith said, moving her bulk around me. "The poor dear lady needs cheering, no doubt. No maudlin songs."

A summons from the queen! When I pictured the royal couple, I saw only the golden giant who'd so impressed me that first night. I'd seen Queen Katherine just a few times since May Day, and my memories of her were eclipsed by those of the king.

The other minstrels were waiting in the corridor outside the queen's apartments. To my disappointment, Tom was not among them, but Gilbert, the other lutenist from the forest, was there, and he winked at me. Harry arrived at my heels, and he, too, smiled.

We were admitted to the anteroom. It was a small, luxurious chamber. A fire crackled behind a painted screen, casting a glow on the Bible-themed tapestry nearby. I tried to take it all in, but we were quickly led to the privy chamber.

The queen's ladies-in-waiting were dressed in gowns of stiff dark cloth and unfamiliar cut, and I remembered that the queen was Spanish, and her ladies, for the most part, dressed in the fashion of Spain. Other women were seated in the inner chamber, working at embroidery frames or talking quietly. Their gowns were brighter, and by their pink cheeks and lighter hair, I surmised, not all the queen's ladies were from her own country.

Queen Katherine was almost invisible behind rich velvet curtains worked with her pomegranate device. I made my curtsy toward the bed before looking at the nearest lady, a stern olive-skinned woman. "What shall we play, my lady?"

She informed me of the queen's wishes in precise, accented English. I moved to the virginals, where Harry sat, cracking his knuckles. To my left, Gilbert fussed with his instrument. I realized they were nervous, and it surprised me, for they had been with the Music for some years.

We played for an hour or more, King Henry's love ballads and other merry songs. There was no comment from the bed, just a constant flow of muted conversation that grated on my nerves. I wondered if they heard us at all.

The lady with the forbidding expression crooked a finger at me. I ended the passage, curtsied, and approached, wondering if my resentment of their chatter showed on my face. Was I to be reprimanded after being honored with such an invitation?

"Her Majesty wishes to see you." She marched me to the bed, one hand hovering over my shoulder. "Your Majesty."

"Gracias, Maria." The voice was faint through the hangings, and even after they were drawn aside, the woman in the bed seemed but a shadow.

Seeing the queen up close for the first time, I felt a stab of pity. She looked as ill as any common woman might after such travail, though no common woman would have such a multitude of pillows, nor a dozen women to wait upon her. Though tired and drawn, her features were pleasant and every bit as regal as King Henry's. Her hands, on the lavish bed cover, were bare of rings.

"You sing very well," she said. Her accent was not strong, but it was there, a barrier to fluency. "Our husband, the king, praises you."

"Thank you, Your Grace. You honor me."

"You have how many years?" One of the cushions slipped from behind her shoulder. It was caught and replaced immediately by a young maid, who curtsied and backed away, leaving us to our conversation.

"Ten," I answered. "Your Grace."

"So young." She drooped, and I was shouldered aside by her women. Pillows were plumped; the long dull red-brown hair, loosely arranged on her shoulders; a golden cup of watered wine was brought. I stayed where I was, uncertain if the queen was finished with me, until a hand closed on my shoulder. "The queen's physician is coming."

We had missed our dinner, and I followed Harry and Gilbert to the kitchens, wondering why I felt none of the exhilaration that flooded me when I sang for the king.

The sweating sickness returned to England that summer. Unlike most diseases, it did not target the weak, the elderly or the young, though, in the case of my family, it had taken my five-year-old brother. The sweat most often struck those in their prime, and it was devastating.

King Henry had a horror of illness. Greenwich reeked of vinegar, and everyone wore their own particular charm. The palace soon grew empty as courtiers scattered, ordered away by the king for their safety and his own.

We were told to keep a cheerful visage, as the sweat preyed on fear. I tried not to worry about my family in London, but I could not keep from fretting about my precious second family at court. When it was discovered I had survived the disease and was therefore "safe," I was ordered to accompany the royal party when it left Greenwich.

"I don't want to go," I said, watching Mistress Keith's awkward movements as she packed my things. Her confinement was very near.

"It's an honor, child."

"It's not an honor," I said. "It's because I can't make them sick."

Her smile said I was being foolish. "All will be well. I would like you here for the birth, but you will be my baby's dear sister, whether you are here or not."

We were gone an endless month. Finally, after learning that no new sickness had been reported in a fortnight, the king decided it was time for us to go home.

I looked forward to our return, knowing I would be able to report nightly requests for music and that I had acquitted myself ably to the accompaniment of sandy-haired, short-sighted Gilbert. The queen and Princess Mary played together while we performed, the baby as fair a copy of her father as could be imagined. Queen Katherine lost years from her looks as she laughed with her child.

Thoughts of the small princess turned my mind to Mistress Keith, and when we reached the road to the palace, I jumped out of the cart, running across the lawns and spinning into the hall well ahead of the procession.

When I reached the top floor, it was deserted. For a moment, I was afraid, but common sense overtook me. Mistress Edith would have moved them to a quieter place. I set out in search of Mistress Keith.

"Bess!"

Turning, I saw Agnes nearly fall up the stairs. She held out her arms. "We were waiting in the courtyard—how did you get past us?"

Returning her embrace, I said, "I came across the fields, I couldn't wait. The king isn't here yet."

"We were waiting for you," she repeated, holding me so hard I could feel her stays. "Tom wanted to speak to you before you came inside."

"I can talk to him later," I said, pulling free. "Where is Mistress Keith?"

Her eyes were as red as her cheeks. "Bess, darling—"

I knew before she said anything further. The silence on the servants' floor was not just absence; it was the stillness of grief.

"She had the babe a week ago, but a fever took her." Her chin trembled with the effort not to cry. "They buried her two days past."

Her voice was tinny through the sudden ringing in my ears. "The baby?"

"A girl. Ralph has taken her to his family in Surrey." I could feel Agnes's cold hands on mine, yet I was the cold one, shivering as if it were January.

If Mistress Keith had to die, why was the child allowed to live? Did God not know she was the more loved? "Rather the baby had died." I realized I spoke my thought aloud only when Agnes looked shocked.

"Mistress Keith wanted that babe more than anything," she said. "She would not have changed places."

I knew that, knew as well that I would never have my friend's assurance that Mistress Keith was in a better place. What better place than with those who loved her, with the baby she had longed for? With her husband?

My own feelings paled at the thought of his loss. Early on, I had been jealous of Ralph Keith, but I soon realized that he worshipped her as much as I did.

"And Mistress Keith?" I began, wanting to know if she had asked for me.

The grip on my hands intensified. "Do you not hear me, Bess? We buried her on Thursday."

"She said she'd be here, that she would be waiting." I looked at her bed with its smooth coverlet. "I was to be godmother, did you know?"

"You've had a long journey. Why don't you rest?" Agnes steered me toward the girls' chamber. "Sleep a bit, darling. You can speak to Tom later."

She left me alone. I was supposed to weep now, as she was weeping outside the door. I stared at the ceiling and tried to make the tears come, but nothing got past the awful cold I felt inside. I fell asleep waiting to hear Jenny Keith's merry voice at the door.

I awoke to silence and the knowledge that I was alone again. Every muscle in my body ached, but I found I could stand, so I washed my face and bundled my hair back in a thick braid. Perhaps some fresh air would clear my thoughts.

I didn't want to see anyone. Tom and Gilbert were in the hall, and I ducked through the doors to the garden, hoping they hadn't seen me, and broke into a run.

When Tom caught up to me, we were almost out of sight of the palace. I gasped for breath, and an insistent pain sang in my head.

"Should you be out of bed?"

"There's no one left to say I cannot," I said with a flippancy I didn't feel.

My flight had taken us into territory familiar only as a view from the upper windows. The studied formality of the gardens blurred, and I caught the damp green scent of the forest. I turned away, letting Tom follow if he would.

"You know she's dead, don't you?" he asked. "Agnes said—"

"Oh, Agnes!" I was angry without knowing why. "She doesn't know everything."

"She's been worried about you. You shouldn't be unkind."

"I am unkind." I wanted to hug him but held back because of his rebuke. "Good things don't happen to me."

Seizing my hands, Tom pulled me down onto the fading grass. "Is that what's troubling you? You came here, and that was good, wasn't it? You found me and Agne, and Mistress Keith."

It didn't do any good to love people. They would only leave me, like Cefin left my parents. They were never the same after his death, and I hadn't understood. I understood now. "She's gone."

"Aye, she is but not because she didn't love you." When I still would not raise my head, he tugged sharply on my braid. I looked up then, my eyes watering. "Good, you felt that. None of it is your fault, you know."

What I felt about Jenny Keith was not just sorrow, as he assumed, but a dreadful anger. Having him tell me I was blameless made it worse. If it wasn't my fault, it could happen again. Nothing I did would prevent the people I loved from leaving. It was my first real adult thought, and it filled me with a blind, unreasoning panic.

I jumped to my feet before he could reach me. How far could I get before the river stopped me, I wondered, and what then? I did not want to go back to the Music; my life there suddenly seemed meaningless.

"Bess, stop!"

The green river flowed swiftly from the autumn rain. I dropped to my knees on the bank and let my sorrow rise up to meet the water, feeling nothing but emptiness. Tom found me and gathered me in his arms, soothing me with his rough minstrel's hands until my sobs quieted to hiccups and whimpers.

"You can't stop loving people just because they might leave you," he said in the soft voice he used with fractious horses. "What sort of life would that be?"

"It wouldn't hurt so."

He kissed the top of my head. "You wouldn't be alive either."

"But she left—" I began, and Tom cut me short, sensing the direction of my thoughts.

"You can't be angry with poor Jenny."

"Mistress Edith says I'll feel better if I don't think about her."

He groaned. "She may know all there is about poultices and potions, but she knows little of the heart sometimes. Why should you not mourn? I do."

The ache in my chest was still there, and the tumult in my head, if anything, was worse, but I felt better for knowing I was allowed to weep.

There were still things I needed to know. "About Mistress Keith," I said. I took a deep breath. "The birthing—no one will tell me anything..."

Tom dropped back on the grassy bank, letting me lean against him. "Mistress Edith did the midwifery, of course, but some of the girls were there. Agnes was there. Can you not ask them?"

I snorted. "Mistress Edith says I'm too young, and Agnes is too accepting of God's will. You're the only one who would tell me."

"I know little of such business," he objected. "Anyway, it's not fitting."

Stubbornly, I said, "I must know."

He looked away. "I can refuse you nothing; you know that." I waited while he collected his thoughts. It was some time, and I thought he'd changed his mind, but then he cleared his throat and began, haltingly, to tell the tale.

"They said it was a difficult birth, that she was too narrow to bring the baby forth." Tom's face was scarlet. He kept on, knowing every word helped me as much as it mortified him. "I came up once, to fetch something, and I heard her—Mistress Keith—screaming. I went back downstairs. I ran back downstairs." His hands knotted against his thighs. "The babe was born near midnight. By morning, she was feverish. Edith scarce had time to call the priest."

"She suffered, then," I said, having hoped at least for a painless, unknowing exit for my dear one.

"In truth, I think she suffered more with the birth," Tom said with a male's healthy respect for that which he cannot comprehend. "Her dying was quick, and she said her farewell to Ralph and held little Elizabeth."

My eyes filled with quick, hot tears. "No one told me."

"That she named the babe for you? She said you were to be godmother, but Ralph took her away before your return."

Somewhere, a motherless child would grow up bearing my name. It was almost enough.

Chapter 5

Jenny Keith's death brought me closer to Tom and Agnes. They were as bereft as I, and we worked hard throughout the autumn to make ourselves into a small family. As the festive season approached, the loss of my adopted mother was a dull, constant ache, but it was bearable because of them.

This year, the court lodged at Southampton, London and its environs being deemed too risky. I had wanted Westminster, with the hope of seeing my father, but Mistress Edith predicted we would not return to London until the first thaw.

Concerns of family were supplanted soon enough. Master Cornysh planned a variety of performances, and we were occupied with rehearsals. The making and alteration of costumes filled any empty hours. When she saw my love of splendid fabrics, Agnes took it upon herself to turn me into a competent seamstress. It allowed us to spend more time together. I would never have her skill, but I could be trusted with straight seams and attaching trimmings.

As it turned out, Agnes and I had much in common. It wasn't until late November, when we were being carried along to Southampton with the rest of the king's baggage, that I learned her background. She would not name her parents, but her mother had been one of the queen's English maids of honor during her brief marriage to the king's brother. Her father, she knew not at all, only that he had seduced her mother, got her with child, and fled to France.

Agnes was a child of shame. Her surname, Hilliard, came from the well-to-do merchant in whose home she had been fostered and who delivered her into the king's service when she was eleven.

"I don't remember her well," Agnes said, her voice muted by the blankets and shawls that swaddled us both. "She was very fair and slender, with a sweet voice. I've never seen her since."

"Could you not find her?" I asked, squirming to sit on my mittened hands. "Someone would know." Court gossip reached back for decades; I heard women recalling with malicious glee events that had happened in the days of the old king.

"I don't want to." Agnes set her delicate jaw and stared out at the snowy road. "She gave me up."

I tried to hug her, and she stiffened. "Perhaps her people forced her." A poor woman could make do somehow, even on the streets, but a gentlewoman cast out with a baby would have no chance.

"Can we not speak of it?" Being raised without comfort, Agnes was unable to accept it, even from me.

As soon as there was a spare moment upon reaching Southampton, she disappeared to the chapel. Her piety made me ashamed of my own scattershot beliefs. While I fidgeted through mass, listening to the music, my lips moving silently with the choristers' voices, she dissolved into prayer. I waited through her confession and her penance and offered my silence when she emerged. She took my hand. "I pray to be stronger," she said, "but I have such wicked thoughts."

I couldn't imagine a wicked thought taking root in her head. "You're so good," I said. "You're almost a saint, how can you say that?"

Agnes laughed aloud, one of the few times she expressed herself without restraint. "If I were a saint, Bess, I would not have to pray to be forgiven for hating the woman who gave me life."

She was subdued, and I hesitated to ask what else bothered her. When we reached our chamber, she sat down on the bed, her hands folded in her lap. I wasn't certain if she prayed or simply needed peace, so I sat beside her in silence.

"I don't have many friends," she said. She wrapped a strand of loose hair around her finger, coiling and uncoiling it. "I don't like people knowing...about me."

Her thin shoulders were tense. I placed my hand against her back and could almost feel the tension vibrating through her. "I do not talk about my life before here either."

"Except with Tom," she said with a curious half smile. "You talk to him."

"He comes from the same place."

She turned away, and I realized she was crying. I thought of Agnes as having everything: beauty, talent, a disposition that made people love her. It surprised me she could be so unsure of my feelings. "Agnes, I am your dear friend," I said, leaning against her. I wondered why she couldn't take comfort in our made-up family. "From the moment I came here, I wanted you as a friend."

Her cold hand covered mine. "I have always wanted a sister."

The uncertainty in her tone brought tears to my eyes. I blinked them back and pressed her hand. "You have one," I told her. "For always."

Our parts in the Christmas masques were limited by our years, but I was filled with nervous excitement before each performance. I had no fear of singing in public, but my talents did not lie in the dance, and I was always scared I would trip over my feet and disgrace myself.

Our most complex routine, which gave me agonies in the learning and terrors as we dressed, was performed on Christmas Eve. We were clad in angel robes of thick ivory satin with silver tinsel wings fixed to our backs and ingenious gilt halos wired to our heads. Our hair hung free, making me wish again to be fair, flanked as I was by Flora, Agnes, and Mary. Behind us were four boys borrowed from the Choir, and together, clasping hands, we danced and sang for the court a special song written by Master Fayrefax in celebration of the season.

I tried mightily with the dancing. My enthusiasm might have been taken for skill by some, but I caught Master Cornysh's glance and wilted. Much of my winter, I knew, would be taken up with dancing lessons.

The king praised us, overlooking my thumping feet. He was grand as a masque all on his own, ablaze with jewels worked on cloth-of-gold. Great pearls glowed on his sleeves, and rubies and diamonds glittered on his doublet. The queen was lavishly dressed as well but in stiff dark brocade, her only ornaments a heavy gold collar and the jeweled cross she always wore. Her hair hung down her back, nearly concealed by the long velvet lappets of her gabled headdress.

I was now able to put names on many familiar faces in the boisterous crowd around the king: fair, florid Charles Brandon, the king's dearest friend and husband to his sister Mary; Nick Carew, whose sharp wit made the king laugh like a boy; dashing Francis Bryan, with his dark roving eyes. All young, handsome men, the king's favorites.

There was another face I knew well, though I had no name for him—the young man in tawny velvet from my first night at court. He wore the same shade this evening, a warm hue that brought out the healthy color in his cheeks and accentuated his unusual eyes. His clean-shaven face was sharply chiseled from his high-bridged nose to his finely drawn mouth. It was a startling, vital face, a touch of arrogance saving him from an almost feminine beauty.

After our bow to the king and queen, we withdrew to a corner, and I asked Agnes if she knew him. She made me point him out, and I wondered, how did she not see him? I noticed him on entering a room in the same way I always saw Tom.

"That is Nicholas Hawkins. He is one of the king's especial favorites." She knew little else to tell me, other than that he was twenty-one or thereabouts, unmarried, and possessed of both a mistress and a large estate in the North, with the expectation of more when his ailing father died.

Agnes knew better than to question my interest, for I was likely to turn about and plague her for her concern about Tom's well-being. She did not like to be teased, especially about Tom.

I was glad of her tact. I couldn't say why I watched Nick Hawkins or admired his feline grace as he danced every measure. On each partner, he fixed an unwavering attention. I recognized a sort of possession in that dark glance, and young as I was, wanted someone to look at me that way.

With the passing of the year, I felt a great contentment, as if a cord pulled tight was finally released. The court was my world now; I needed only remember my old life to think of Westminster, of Greenwich, or even of Southampton, as a blessing. I had friends; I was happy.

I thought I would not change anything about my life in the Music, not for all the king's treasures, and I meant it. But ours was a transient lifestyle, and changes—as well as arrivals and departures—happened whether we liked them or not.

Spring brought a new chorister to our midst. Comings and goings among musicians were not infrequent, and with regard to the choir, they went almost unnoticed because of their relative seclusion, but special circumstances surrounded this boy.

Robin Lewis was dropped into our midst by Cardinal Wolsey to placate the king, who had decided the cardinal's choir was superior to his own. It may well have been true; Wolsey so assiduously gathered to himself those things which charmed his master that he occasionally overstepped and outshone the one whom he intended but to please.

Whatever his intent, the king's refusal to be surpassed led to a competition between the choirs. This threw Master Cornysh into a frenzy of preparation. Until then, it was enough to be allowed to practice with the choir, to let my voice climb with theirs, and to learn music different from that which I normally performed. The idea of a competition spurred me; I wanted to pit my talent against others, and I was sorry I could not participate.

The day arrived. Wolsey, followed by his choristers, came into the Chapel. It was a bad sign that, in addition to the standard twelve men, he had fifteen boys, three more than the king. Despite their superior numbers, they looked as nervous as the choristers of the Chapel Royal. Hidden behind the stalls, the members of the Music waited for the king.

The choirs were placed side by side and compelled to perform the same music, one after the other, while King Henry sat as judge. Wolsey stood to his left, his fleshy face anxious.

On any other day, I would be lost in the music, but the stakes were too high. I stood with the others and awaited the result. When King Henry stood at last and pronounced, as at a criminal sentencing, that Wolsey's choir was indeed superior, I saw fear on many faces.

The cardinal's face glowed red as his sable-trimmed taffeta robes. "Think you so, Your Grace?" he asked, wringing his hands. Covered as they were with costly rings, the gesture did not convey the intended effect. "I would not have it so." His expression flickered between panic and his familiar preening aspect. "Choose, Your Grace—I beg you to choose which of my choristers would suitably ornament the Chapel Royal and remedy this imbalance."

The idea clearly pleased the king, who would have suggested it if it had it not been offered, and the business of choosing began. Back and forth the king paced, pointing a finger at one or another, requesting bits of song or a scale to be sung. King Henry paused in thought, his narrowed eyes roving the ranks of men and boys. They quivered visibly under his gaze.

"The men are safe," Tom's quiet voice said in my ear. "He'll take a boy, for the soprano." From anyone but Tom, the words might have been cynical, but I knew that the spectacle caused him pain. Together, we listened to the king's musical interrogation and breathed a sigh of relief when his pacing ceased.

The royal finger pointed one last time. "We should have that one, Thomas. He is a choir of angels unto himself."

Cardinal Wolsey looked stricken, and the king's choice made an effort to appear pleased but succeeded only in looking petulant.

Robin Lewis was ugly. I thought it then, as I watched him evade the king's gaze, and I thought it after, when he was installed at Greenwich. It was not his lank red hair, bobbed just below his ears, his numerous freckles, or his gangly limbs, but in combination, the result was unpleasant. He needed no physical defect to stand out: his personality alone was all angles and corners, jarring with everyone. If he had not possessed the voice of an angel, we would have treated him like a leper.

His coming should have caused no more than a ripple in the Music. What could an eleven-year-old boy do to disturb his elders and his peers? Robin, it turned out, disturbed by existing, and each time he opened his mouth and brought forth that divine voice, it was an insult to those who labored and practiced but could not equal his gift.

Within a week, he was disliked by every man, woman, and child among us. I recalled my own rough treatment and watched the newcomer for signs of distress, but jeers and taunts rolled off him like rainwater. We learned to dread Robin's casually dropped pronouncements, which were always more brutal than the remarks occasioning his rejoinder. I disliked him, but I envied his unchildlike aplomb.

Mary, who had begun to think of herself as too mature to torment her juniors, made a special effort to be pleasant and offered one day to accompany him on the virginals. He turned and said, loud enough for all to hear, "A pleasing figure and face are, alas, no guarantee of talent—or of a realization of its lack."

There was some laughter, in part because Mary was still not well-loved, but for the most part, it was an utterance born of shock. Mary turned white with rage, and I thought for a moment she would strike him, but instead, she slammed her hands down on the keys, bringing forth a discordant jangle of sound.

~~~~~

The blow, when it fell, was not unexpected, and once in motion, it was difficult to stop. I was in the gardens with Agnes when a page arrived, red-faced and breathless, having run all the stairs in the palace in search of me. "Master Cornysh wants you now!"

It was the first clear day after a week of rain, and the air was redolent with flowers. The sun on my face was almost enough to make me forget the bleak winter months I hated. I was loath to give up my walk, but Master Cornysh was not to be disobeyed nor to be obeyed slowly.

Perhaps it was a new part, I thought as I climbed the stairs behind the laboring boy. Or a new song. Maybe he'd decided at last to use Tom's music and wanted me to sing it.

My head was full of these happy thoughts when I skipped into Master Cornysh's chamber. Then I saw his solemn expression, and my mood fell away, leaving me with fear in my belly.

"Sit down." I dropped onto a stool, wrapping my feet around the legs. "I would ask you a few questions about Robin Lewis."

My nose wrinkled, fear subsiding. It was only a lecture, after all, about treating Robin with more civility. Since I was far from the worst offender, he would have to give the lecture to more than me.

"I've just had the young choristers in here, and they refuse to tell me the truth. You've never given me any trouble before this, Bess, so I would have you tell me."

His eyes, sunk beneath those bushy brows, fixed me with a painful scrutiny. "What would you have me say, sir?" I asked, for it seemed he expected me to know of what he spoke.

"Where he is, of course!" Cornysh exploded. "The boys have had enough, and they've hidden him away somewhere."

I almost smiled, but it would have been fatal. "I don't know where, sir. Why did you ask me?"

The narrow window across the chamber was wedged open with a book. Cornysh sighed and crossed to stand before it. When he spoke, he sounded defeated. "Because the choir is to sing mass in a quarter hour, and they will not produce the boy under any threat. When I asked them who was to sing his part, to conceal this trickery from the king, they suggested you."

Of course, Master Cornysh would try to keep Robin's disappearance from the king. Not only would he be angered at this treatment of his prize—the king did not know or care what an odious little monster his jealousy brought us—but without doubt, he would place all the blame at the feet of the choirmaster.

"In truth, sir, I know nothing of what they've done with him."

His lips curled in spite of himself. "I'm certain he deserved it, the little toad, but that makes my position no easier." He gave the outdoors one last glance and turned his attention to me. "Unless I can get the wretches to produce Robin in short order, there will be a noticeable gap in the choir. The king will surely miss his voice."

"Surely," I agreed, imagining the scene to follow.

"And while I can give out that he has a sore throat or some other ill, it would be too like the king to send a messenger, or worse yet, come personally to see how the boy fared. Then all would be revealed."

47

"Yes, sir."

His expression indicated he was dealing with a particularly dense child. "The choir loft is not visible from the king's pew. I would have you take Robin's place—if you know the mass, that is?"

I replied in perfect honesty that the singing was the only part to which I paid any attention. We did not often mention my participation in the choir's rehearsals, and indeed, these occasions had ceased on Robin's arrival.

Master Cornysh's laugh was grudging. "Go, then, and put on robes. Unless they turn him loose, you'll be the first girl to ever sing in the Chapel Royal."

The others were already dressed when I arrived. Seeing me, they whooped with delight. The men did not appear displeased by Robin's absence, only smiling at me while the boys robed me and gave me instructions amid waves of giggles. One boy tucked my braid down my back before straightening the stiff ruff around my neck.

"Such a joke on him," William said, snickering. He was no more than seven, but he already had a healthy dislike for Robin.

Another snorted. "He'll be worse than ever for this, but we'll bear it easier."

The door opened, and Master Cornysh looked in. "Boys, see what was found locked in a cupboard downstairs." He pushed the door wider, and we beheld Robin, his face dusty and red-splotched. He shouldered past Master Cornysh and pulled on the nearest robe, his face emerging from the neck more disagreeable than ever when he found it did not fit properly.

"Where is my robe?" he asked. "And how were you planning to explain my absence?"

"Bess was to sing in your place," someone volunteered. "It is she who's wearing your robe."

I flushed with embarrassment. Robin had not singled me out thus far, and I dreaded it. His eyes flicked over me. "As if a girl could replace me."

Cornysh shook his head. "We'll talk about this later. Come along now; you're already late."

The choirmaster was scarcely out the door when Robin turned to face the other choristers. "I'll see that you pay for this, you misbegotten sons-of-whores. I will see to it."

They fell back, stunned, and so it was that only Robin was on time for mass, with the rest of the choir scampering behind like mice, twittering at his guttersnipe language.

"You've not given him much of a chance," Agnes remarked when I told her of the scene. "Perhaps he just misses his friends in the cardinal's household."

I hooted. "Do you think he had any? No one here likes him. I can't believe he was so different there."

Agnes turned the ring on her left forefinger. "I do not like to think that of anyone."

"You didn't hear him. He didn't learn words like that in the cardinal's choir." It was not Robin's low beginnings I faulted, but the boy himself.

She continued to plead his case. To make her leave me in peace, as much as to prove myself right, I contrived to meet him in the practice room. The chamber was deserted; the others were either performing throughout the palace or off at their own devices. It was the perfect opportunity to discover the real Robin, if indeed there was one.

A westward-facing window had been pushed open, and the evening sun turned to fire the hair of the slight boy who stood motionless at the sill. Something in his bearing suggested loneliness, but I was too young and awkward to treat the idea any way but clumsily.

"Master Cornysh seems well pleased with you," I said into the silence.

He turned, startled by my intrusion. "Of course he is." His speaking voice was quiet, smug, with no hint of the silvered beauty held in check.

"Do you miss the cardinal's choir?" His response to my opening comment was annoying, but for Agnes's sake, I would give him a chance. "Your friends there?"

He looked suspicious. "I had no friends there. Nor do I need any here."

The slender thread of my patience snapped. "You've your voice to keep you company; is that it? What will happen when it breaks? Then you'll have nothing and no one to care." My venom surprised me. I disliked him, to be sure, but did I wish that on him? I took another look at Robin's smirk and decided I wished him all that and more.

"Perhaps it won't last forever," Robin acknowledged, "but whilst it does, I shall outshine you all. None of you can sing as I can."

"Am I not as good?" I wanted to provoke him. More than Master Cornysh remarked on the similarities in our voices. Even Tom, my highest authority below the king, said as much.

49

"Good enough," he said, "for a girl. You could have never replaced me in the choir. The fakery would have been known immediately."

"Master Cornysh believed me capable. Do you know more than the choirmaster?"

Robin's eyebrows raised. "Cornysh is a man, not a god."

"A competition, then." The challenge tumbled from my lips before I could stop myself.

"No," he said, folding his arms. "You're a girl."

Skirting a group of stools littered with abandoned music, I joined him at the window. "Then what have you to fear? A chorister of the Chapel Royal against a mere girl?" He was growing angry at my goading, and I pushed him further. "I challenge you."

"There is no music," he objected, pushing a freckled hand through the greasy fringe on his forehead.

I affected superiority. "You need music? I can call someone to play for us—and watch your defeat."

"I shan't lose."

"You shan't win," I retorted. "No one likes you now. They'll hate you for certes if you win." I heard myself and wondered where the words came from. I disliked Robin, but I had come to attempt to make friends. How had things gone so wrong?

As I was about to withdraw my challenge, he drew a deep breath. "All right, little girl. I accept."

"Little!" This, from a boy my own age, was too much.

"Match this!" he cried, catching me off guard. His voice came forth, sliding up and down a series of scales. So perfect and shining was the sound that I almost feared to follow, but follow I did, note for note, scale for scale, frolicking from those rudimentary exercises to bits of hymns, snatches of Cornysh's lovely Magnificat, popular songs in both French and English. Robin's voice led the way, and I pursued him, sounding perhaps a bit more workmanlike than his clear purity of tone, but as close a match as ever he would find.

There came a moment when I realized I could beat him, and with that knowledge, I lost all consciousness of singing. I chose the measure then, and it was his turn to follow me, first through the Chapel's own kyrie, as a lesson, and then on to Tom's songs, which I could sing in my sleep and better than anyone else.

Our voices slipped through the open window into the soft evening. I felt as if I were slipping through the window as well, so far was I from my solid body in the practice room. I sang to the bright evening sky, to the sharp sickle moon, to the green treetops on distant Shooter's Hill. I sang a hymn to summer and youth and joy, and in that moment, I surpassed him.

Beside me, Robin faltered. I stopped, knowing my point made but too well. The pain in his eyes was something that would not soon fade. I no longer disliked him then, but pitied his self-made isolation. His world, of which he and his voice were the sole, contented occupants, had been shaken.

If I did not make a friend of him now, he might never forgive me. I discovered, strangely enough, that I didn't want his enmity. Putting my impulse up to Agnes's influence, I held out my hand. "It was a good fight, Robin. I declare a draw. What say you?"

Robin knew little of sportsmanship or good manners, and his injured pride would not allow lessons in either. He slapped my hand away and ran from the room.

Because of that open window, our musical battle had drifted across the gardens, catching the attention of courtiers and servants alike. My elders were mostly silent, but the choristers, the same ones who had locked Robin in the cupboard, were gleeful at his defeat. Several of the softer-hearted members of the Music tried to use the occasion to befriend him, to no avail. Even gentle Agnes was rebuffed and driven to tears. Perhaps my attempt had been misunderstood; I would not feel kindly after being defeated by someone I considered my inferior, but Agnes was different—to look upon her was to know her goodness. Even Robin should have seen that.

The sole reproach came from Tom. "You can't have forgotten what it was like."

We made our way along the dark passage to the kitchens, our performances over for the night. I was still dressed in my costume and moved cautiously for fear of soiling my embroidered skirts on the blackened walls. "No." I skipped to avoid a rat crossing the passage.

"So you, of anyone, should understand."

"I didn't go there with the thought of challenging him." The damp walls absorbed my words, leaving me with but an inadequate murmur for an echo. "I meant to be kind, but at every turn, he threw it back at me." I hung my head, my tone growing sheepish. "I lost my temper."

Tom ruffled my hair, his solemn expression relaxing. "You are too much governed by that temper of yours."

That, he did not have to tell me—I had been told by others with more authority than Tom—and yet it seemed impossible to control. I thought and I spoke, and more often than not, I regretted my hasty words. "He made me angry."

Tom caught my dangling sleeve. "What if Cornysh made you angry, Bess, or the king? Would you lash out then and find yourself on the streets? Or would you govern yourself?"

"You make it sound easy," I grumbled as we reached the kitchens. The searing heat met us at the door. Tom hastily took off his green doublet and flung it over his shoulder. Gordon waved, and we waited just inside, safely away from the cook and the naked kitchen urchins, while he piled a plate for us.

"It's not like straining soup through a cloth," I protested, as we ducked outdoors to eat in the dark garden. The cool air felt like a blessing. "I don't have anything in my head to catch what should not be said. It all just comes out."

"It doesn't make a pretty soup, does it?" he teased, spreading his doublet on the grass. "You'll learn to sit on your feelings, Bess. In a place like this, if you do not pause to choose your words, your temper could lead you to worse trouble than a sulky chorister."

Chapter 6

The years were numbered not by my birthday but the anniversary of my arrival, as they were so nearly the same, and coming to court had been nothing if not a rebirth. The passing of the third of these occasions marked my thirteenth year.

Agnes was an inspiration during this difficult period. At fifteen, she still possessed the fragile beauty of a child, but she was tall and willowy and, to my eyes, lovelier than ever. I envied the grace which made her always know the right thing to say and wondered if I would ever achieve it.

Despite my good intentions, I was still prone to tactlessness and impatience, and though I often studied my reflection, hope springing anew each time, the glass showed no hint I was going to turn into a graceful young lady anytime soon. The only improvement of which I was certain was in my voice, for I still practiced daily and took lessons with Master Cornysh as often as he had time. I worked hard at my dancing and was included in far more performances. Against my will and somewhat haltingly, I also learned the lute. I had no desire to be as proficient as Tom, but the lessons saved me from having to find someone to accompany me when I practiced.

Tom was flourishing. Listening to us practice, his elders were at last convinced of the merit of his compositions, and soon, throughout the court came to be heard melodies familiar to me as my own thoughts. It gave me pleasure to hear him praised, and I enjoyed our performances together all the more. Though Tom laughed at my boldness, I believed our talents meshed perfectly and was jealous if someone else dared sing his songs.

There was much furtive romance among the minstrels, and I envied the happy glow of the girl newly fallen in love. I was too young for such matters, but I admired several young men for their fine clothes and pretty manners, and this contented me well enough. I thought it a shame Tom and I had been thrown together so often, for though I cherished our friendship, it eliminated him, along with the other boys of the Music, from my romantic daydreams.

It was difficult not to think along romantic lines. King Henry was steeped in the legends of King Arthur and his knights, and we heard stories of chivalry and courtly love from the time we understood speech. Many of our plays were based on those tales, and the fact that the king condoned such fancies made our dreams less reckless, even though we all knew the only men suitable were those of our own situation.

Such dreary certainties did not stop the girls from aspiring to more impressive lovers. Several of us sat together on a rainy afternoon, stitching costumes and talking in desultory fashion about the young men of the court. The first we knew of Mistress Edith was her astonished snort as she faced us, hands on hips, her lips pursed with disapproval.

"Have you nothing better to do than spin fancies?" she demanded, striding among us and picking at the work spread on our laps.

Several voices protested, but Agnes's low tone undercut them all. "Mistress Edith, they're just dreaming."

"You cannot work and dream at the same time." She snorted again.

Mary threw back her curls and held out the murrey satin doublet she had been mending as she related her fancy for Charles Brandon. "There's nothing wrong with this!"

"Not if the wearer minds being naked before an audience. Look at these stitches, you silly wench. I'm surprised you haven't broidered some man's name there, the seam's that crooked." She turned quickly. "And don't laugh, Bess. You're no better, giggling like there's not more important things to be thinking of."

For a few minutes, nothing was heard but the sound of rain against the windows. We knew well enough there were concerns afoot more serious than our romantic dreams. The king had changed in the past months, sitting in conference with his ministers and meeting with advisors and ambassadors, when once, he'd played tennis or hawked the day away. He did not give up the pursuits which gave him pleasure, but he spent far less time at them.

With the death of the Holy Roman emperor, England was drawn deeper into the changing scene on the Continent. Calls for music were less frequent, and when King Henry was cheerful, it was an uncomfortable, forced merriment. Excuses were made for his behavior, but the one that explained it best was one I recognized in myself: the king was growing up.

He was a man of many talents: singing, dancing, languages; he possessed a keen intellect and could lead an army as easily as he led a dance. But despite his responsibilities, the king was notoriously light of mind regarding the duties of kingship and was easily distracted by his roistering companions.

The request came officially from the Privy Council, but its effects were ascribed to Wolsey, and eventually, the dismissal of a half dozen of the king's favorites in Maytime, 1519, became known as the "cardinal's purge."

The tennis courts and the tiltyard lay idle in the sunshine, and the king's interminable games of mumchance and primero finally found an end, the cards untouched in their enameled boxes. We thought the whole matter pointless. A bad-tempered monarch has little need for music, except to soothe his melancholy, and our lives were made dull by the change.

During this time, the king developed a quirk that likened to drive us mad. He would not be in one place for too long; he decreed after several weeks, a palace "lost its sweetness." That made us smile, for the king, with his velvet-padded closestool, never ventured into areas which were less than sweet; anyone with a nose knew when it was time to move on, for the stench of the common jakes spread through the palace like a mist.

Much of the household was already gone, and that which remained was a welter of confusion. Everywhere were wagons and carts, loaded with the furniture and provisions essential to the court's comfortable existence.

I made certain my possessions were stowed before I made my escape. It was a warm day, too warm to be about such efforts, and I sought shade trees along the riverbank. Sinking down, I rested my chin on my knees and stared out at the water, trying to block out the sounds drifting from the courtyard. It was a rare opportunity for solitude. Stretching out on the grass, I closed my eyes and knew no more until I heard footsteps.

Raising my head, I saw Robin, moving at a good pace. I had no desire to leave the river—judging by the sounds, there was still time before the carts left, and I didn't want to be put to work among the sweaty throng in the yard. A shower of pebbles warned me as he started down the hill. He would have stepped on me but for my agility in rolling aside.

It pleased me to see he was dismayed by my presence.

He nodded. "Bess."

After our contest, he tried to ignore me completely, but it was difficult since I again practiced with the choir. Our dislike had evolved into a stringent civility.

"Robin." I straightened my skirts. His opinion of me was low enough; he needed no reason to call me hoyden as I sat with my legs bare to the knees. "Isn't the Chapel ready to move?"

"No. The cardinal must go with the king, and there is no one to supervise." The cardinal was a clerk at heart and reveled in the petty details of organizing and moving the royal household. I imagined the chaos which reigned in his absence.

"I am in hiding," I confided. It seemed silly to be so stiff with him, and I decided to try again to make things right.

"From Master Cornysh?" Robin looked suspicious, but he lowered himself to the ground nearby.

I shook my head. "Mistress Edith." It was a dreadful job, loading the contents of her workroom, all those bottles and jars, into coffers for the journey. "I would only drop something—I always do. Agnes is not nearly so clumsy."

"Agnes is a kind girl."

"You made her cry," I pointed out.

Robin flushed to the roots of his rusty hair. "I regret that. She was the only one who was kind."

I saw an opening, but was it a chasm to be bridged or an abyss into which I would tumble? I gathered my courage and said, "I know you'll not believe me, but I came with good intentions that day. You made me angry, and when I'm angered, I do stupid things."

I hadn't intended to mention the horrid competition. He undoubtedly disliked having his memory refreshed.

Robin looked at me for a moment, his eyes narrowed. He seemed to be fighting the same battle within himself. He turned his head away. "You were as a nightingale is to a sparrow," he said. "You won fairly."

Surprised, I protested, sorry to have opened the wound again. "You're the one touched by heaven. Hasn't the king said as much?"

Robin laughed. It was a nice sound for such a sullen boy. "And he calls you his songbird."

I reached my hand across the abyss. "Can we not forget it, Robin, and make friends?"

There was a long pause, and then he clasped my hand briefly and pulled me to my feet. "They'll be searching for us."

I followed him back to the palace without further conversation. One need not have friends, but I disliked having enemies. When I climbed into the cart beside Agnes, I carried my good mood with me, and we sang duets all the way to Eltham.

England and France were ancient enemies, but Cardinal Wolsey, with his usual energy, was trying to bring about a miracle. His attempts filled the court with representatives of the French king, and as a king must entertain his visitors, music once again filled the court.

Strangers passed through Greenwich for weeks on end, and we performed for them all. The French were gallant and gay, dancing as much as the English. Though the older girls spent much time flirting, I was not ready to forsake music for romance. Neither was Agnes, which disappointed the Frenchmen. They made eyes at her while she played or sang, but they might as well have ogled a statue.

Late one evening, after we had finished performing, one of the strangers approached. Something in his bearing told me he was English, for all that he was with the French party. He caught my attention early in the evening, for though he danced with many ladies, he stared often at Agnes, with an expression different from the hungry interest of his companions.

He removed his feathered cap with a movement quite graceful for such a large man. When he spoke, his words were addressed to Agnes. "I beg pardon for my boldness," he said, and something in his face said he did not often beg. "I wonder, miss, if you are related to Margaret Stanton? Of Dorsetshire?"

Agnes's face was a lovely mask. "No," she said, her voice pitched below the sounds of the court at play. "I do not know that name."

The hope in his eyes faded, but he recovered quickly. "You look so like her—the same eyes and hair." He pushed his fingers through his own close-cropped brown hair, a boyish gesture for a man in his mid-thirties. "She wasn't much older than you the last time I saw her."

"What happened to her?" I asked since Agnes appeared to have turned to stone. She stood slightly in front of me, her hands behind her back, gaze glued to the floor.

The gentleman smiled crookedly. "I lost her. I joined my uncle's household in France for a few months, and when I returned, she was gone. Her parents said she grew tired of waiting for me and joined a convent." He clasped his hands together, and I saw that he wore only one ring, a thick gold band. "Ah, well—I'm sorry to have bothered you, but I had to ask. It's been so long since I had word of Mags."

As he crossed the chamber to rejoin his companions, Agnes turned and sat down again at the virginals. Her back was very straight.

"Poor man," I said, watching him still. "Shall we find Flora and get some food?"

She shook her head and pushed the cover back from the keys. Her hands were shaking.

"Who was he, I wonder?"

"He was my father," she said and began to pick out a song, note by painful note. The remaining minstrels heard her and raggedly took up the tune. "Did you not realize? He took me for my mother's child."

I saw by the set of her shoulders, she was trying not to cry, and I did the only thing I could: I sang and kept attention from her as she played for a hundred people—and her father—with tears streaming down her face.

⌒‿⌒‿⌒

The next morning, she was gone before I rose. When she joined me at the noon meal, she no longer looked like the girl who'd spent the night sobbing into her pillow.

"What's happened?" I asked, laying a hand on her sleeve. "Are you all right?"

She smiled faintly. "Better, at least. I stayed to pray after mass this morning. One of the priests asked if he could be of help." Spots of pink stained her cheeks. "I do not know why, Bess, but I told him...everything."

"Did it help?" I asked, trying not to feel jealous that Agnes opened her heart to a priest, instead of to her best friend.

I leaned to one side as the dishes were set between us, and reached for several slices of meat before Harry and Gilbert, seated across from us, could grab more than their share.

"It did," she said, seeing I expected an answer. She looked into my face and laughed softly. "Don't look like that, Bess! I know what you're thinking."

I ducked my head.

"He was able to help because he does not know me. We talked about my mother and how angry I was that she gave me up and about my father." She twisted the narrow ring on her finger, and I remembered her hands had been hidden in the folds of her skirt. Was she afraid he would recognize it, remember it on the hand of his lost Mags?

"He seemed very nice," I said.

Agnes nodded. "I cannot but feel sad that I did not know him—or her."

"Can you not know him now?" I reached for the leather bottle of ale as it made its way down the table. "He is still here. I saw a member of his party just an hour ago."

She pushed a chunk of boiled beef around with her spoon. "Let him think her gone and love her. I would not want him to hate her as I have."

I wiped my own spoon with a piece of bread and reluctantly passed my plate toward the voider. "Do you still hate her?"

Agnes handed along her plate, its contents almost untouched. "We prayed over that. She was young and scared. I cannot be a Christian and hate her for being a frightened child."

Her expression was tranquil. Speaking to the priest had done her good. Still, I felt sorry there were now three unhappy people. Her mother perhaps was beyond reach, but her father was not, and while his feelings might be changed by the knowledge that his lover had given up their child, he would have a daughter to console him, and Agnes would have one parent. I thought to say as much, but something in her eyes prevented me from speaking.

I took her arm as we left the hall. "I am glad you have found some peace." A thought occurred to me. "It was not Father James, was it?"

She smiled, looking almost like the girl she had been a few days before. "I would not burden him after all you put him through. No, it was one of the Spanish priests."

The French party stayed several more weeks. Through diligent questioning, I learned Agnes's father was named Alexander Crawford. He lived in France, managing the estates of an elderly relative. Little else could be gleaned; he was pleasant; he was distant; he was discreet. From time to time, I saw him watching Agnes, but he never spoke to her again.

Nor did she mention him, though I knew she prayed daily in the chapel. I wondered the priest did not counsel her to speak, to take the burden from Crawford's shoulders. Perhaps there was some knowledge of the human heart that I did not yet understand.

The sky above us was a perfect pale blue. Tom and I were together and happy because we had the day to venture into London to visit our families.

I knew not how Tom felt, but despite lingering regrets for the royal menagerie, I was excited. It was two years since I had seen them, and that visit had been fleeting, as the king passed through on his way to Westminster.

We walked at no great pace along the road. I felt we were embarking on an adventure, and when I turned to Tom to share this thought, I found him smiling as if he already knew.

By noon, we were in Southwark, the poorest section of the city, hard in the shadow of London Bridge. The streets were clotted with filth, torn up by wheels, smelling rankly of garbage and the contents of chamber pots flung from upper windows. The first breath brought tears, and I forced down the bread and cheese I'd had for breakfast.

The tiny, shabby house where we lodged was even more rundown, and when I knocked at the door, I found it occupied by strangers. I asked where my family had gone, fearful of accident or disease, but the woman, holding the door open only a fraction, said they'd moved some time back, she knew not where.

After inquiring at several other houses, I finally found them. At the news that my parents had been in Aldgate for six months, Tom's expression turned somber. "I'd hoped to leave you with them, Bess, while I visited my mother." He shifted from foot to foot, his boots making sucking noises in the mud. "Why don't I take you there, then visit my mother and return for you later?"

"Is your mother near to here?" I didn't see why he should spend the day crisscrossing London to accommodate me.

"Yes," he said, "but I didn't want you to see her."

At first, I thought he was ashamed of me and took a breath to protest I had become quite presentable, when his meaning, as well as his embarrassment, became clear. Hot blood suffused my cheeks, and I looked down. There was not a child raised in Southwark without an understanding of sexual matters by the age of six. It is a coarse age, and in such a place, too much is said and done in the open.

"I'd like to meet her, Tom." I linked my hand with his. "She can't be worse than my mother."

As we left Southwark to find my family, I marveled at the hour we spent there. I hadn't expected to find Tom's mother living in the very stews, an aging, painted harlot who couldn't find a civil word to speak to her son. After abusing him for neglect, she berated him for spending money on a meal at a tavern. I cringed at her harshness and wanted to clasp his hand again, but I feared her tongue.

"'Tis not extravagance," Tom said. "Where would you have us go?"

She propped her elbows on the scarred wood table, showing the worn spots on her faded marigold sleeves. She gave off a sharp, unpleasant scent, something rank and floral, with a musky undertone. "You always come to the house before."

Looking between us, Tom said, "You think I'd bring her there?"

"I don't know why you brought her at all." Petulance gave way to an ingratiating smile, showing blackened teeth. "Do you have any money, Tommy, or have you spent it all on this feast?"

He slapped her wheedling hand away and drained his ale in one swallow, but before we left, I saw him hand her a small purse.

I spared him a glance now, found him pensive. "How long since you've seen her?"

"Almost a year," he said. "I don't know why I go back. She earns a decent living still; I've no responsibility for her. But she...she wasn't always like that. Sometimes it was like having a dozen mothers, with all the women in the house, and other times, it was like having none at all."

Tom never spoke of his mother, and I wondered if he would object to my next question. "You never knew your father?"

"I might know him now," he said with an odd smile. "My mother always said he was a nobleman." His gaze, more gray than blue, was impenetrable. "She never would tell me his name."

"Does it matter?" I loved my father, but being his child meant little enough to me. With a pang, I thought of Agnes, with a family she would never know, and decided perhaps it did.

"Not for any practical purpose, but I should like to know who I am," he said, his expression earnest, "other than Thomas Minstrel."

I ransacked my brain but recalled no one at court who bore any resemblance to my dear Tom, yet he certainly did not favor the haggard woman we just left.

His expression tore at my heart. I was learning that men felt pain as deeply as women, and I hated Tom's mother for hurting him. I was ever one to pick and probe at my troubles until they disappeared from lack of substance, but he was not that way; talking would do little good, and I thought spending time with my family was no remedy for melancholy either. Taking his hand again, I said, "We need not see my people." He looked down, understanding my motives as if I were made of glass. "We'll see them."

"They're not all that nice, Tom. We could go to the menagerie instead."

"We haven't been set loose to go there." He smiled to prove I had cheered him, but I did not believe it for a moment. Was it this easy for him to read my thoughts? "And they haven't seen you for a long time. They'll be pleased."

"Not likely. The last time I saw them, my sister fussed because my dress was finer than hers."

Tom drew me to him in a quick, affectionate hug that did much to make us both feel better.

We found my parents at last in a tall, narrow house in Aldgate, smaller even than the place they left behind but with no outward signs of disrepair. It was, Da said proudly as we followed him up the stairs, only two streets from the inn where he worked.

He led us into a chamber that seemed small due to the number of things that were crammed into it. In the myriad of coffers, stools, and tables, I saw almost nothing I remembered. Despite the new furnishings, the rushes were sticky underfoot and did not smell clean.

My mother's appearance was surprising: prosperity took years off her age. She no longer smelled of harsh soap, and her hands were smooth with balm. She was attentive to Tom, and I compared her to his mother and was pleased with Mum's efforts.

Madlen also showed a great interest in Tom, and I smiled at her wasted coquetry. She was seventeen, and her looks, though similar to mine, were neater and more agreeable. Her black hair was restrained under a clean linen cap, and her figure was likewise restrained by stays so tight that her breasts plumped above her square neckline like risen dough. I saw her note with a frown that my dark skirts, though plain, were of better cloth.

My parents insisted we share a meal with them and, not wanting to admit we'd already eaten, we agreed. It was a way for them to show how their lot had improved, and I was surprised at the quality of the meal my mother brought forth: it was comparable to the plain, savory food at court when there were no banqueting leftovers.

Afterward, Tom and my father stayed around the table to talk, and we cleared up. My mother and I had nothing to say to each other, and Madlen ignored me, her dark eyes on Tom. I warmed with pride that she would think him worthy, for although he had grown tall and manly in the past year, as well as being the kindest boy alive, I could not judge him by his face after knowing him for so long.

My parents asked questions about the king and court, and we tried to satisfy their curiosity. Da gathered much gossip at the inn, and the breadth of his knowledge was surprising.

"Be it true that he has taken another mistress?" my mother asked with a scornful face. "Wasn't Mistress Blount enough?"

This was very recent news indeed. "Mary Boleyn is her name."

"A pretty woman," Tom added, and I looked sharply at him. Mary Boleyn was small and blonde, with soft, complaisant gray eyes.

"We'll be leaving any day now," I said into the silence that followed his comment. "To meet with the King of France."

Cardinal Wolsey's efforts had not been in vain. He had managed to arrange a face-to-face meeting between King Henry and his French counterpart. Even before it was announced, I had known the Music would accompany him, for how could he hope to properly impress the French without us?

"We've heard about that," Madlen said, looking envious. "I'd love to see France. Tell us about it, Tom."

"The entire court is upside down with preparations," he said and told her of some of our plans. "We were fortunate to get away today."

He did not exaggerate. I was glad to escape the flurry of packing and the fitting of new garments. Even the most menial servants were to have fresh livery for the occasion.

Soon, it was time for my father to go to work. When he rose, I took Tom's hand, and we followed. I felt no reluctance at leaving. It was good to see them and know their lives were better without me, as mine was better without them. Madlen would be married soon, my mother informed me, her eyes glittering—the son of Forsyth, the wool merchant, had asked for her hand. This was the culmination of my mother's dreams, and it would not have been possible for Madlen to be dowered if I had remained at home.

They embraced me in turn, my father most warmly, wishing me luck in France and in life, my mother with some distraction, for as we left, a boy arrived with a note to announce a visit from Madlen's intended. My sister embraced me last, with little grace.

"You must come see me once I am married," she said, smiling at Tom over my head. "We shall have a lovely home."

"I'm certain you will," he said and put his hand on my shoulder. "We must go, Bess."

The expression on her face remained with me on the walk back to Westminster. It looked like envy, but what did I have that Madlen could want?

SONGBIRD

Part II

Great Matters - 1520

Chapter 7

The morning sun caught the gold-painted sails of the king's flagship, the *Henry Grace-a-Dieu*, making them shimmer like butterfly wings. My stomach lurched, and I turned my gaze to Calais, that one small part of France that still belonged to England. Beyond the harbor swarming with small boats and our fleet of twenty-seven ships, the streets were draped in the king's colors, and the waterfront was packed with people.

"A bit different from his last visit," said a voice over my shoulder, reminding me that this French expedition was unpopular with many people. The war with France was but seven years past, and many courtiers complained they should not have to bankrupt themselves to impress a hereditary enemy, that the king would never make the visit but for the cardinal's scheming.

Despite the queen's nephew being the new emperor, the far-sighted cardinal saw the future in France, and this meeting was his way of leading England toward that future. Every detail was planned to foster an impression of peace, down to the very location of the camp where we would live, set up on the border of the Pale of Calais, a scant twelve miles into the French countryside. We would camp at Guisnes; the French would be in Ardres, a mile or so distant.

Precisely in the middle, the two kings would meet.

Some of the court would stay in Calais, where lodgings had been arranged; others would be at the camp, which accommodated every rank of courtier and servant in a combination of tents, pavilions, and wooden houses. The king must have music, so space was reserved for the choristers and minstrels.

After almost four years at court, I was accustomed to grandeur, but the splendor of Cardinal Wolsey's temporary city was something entirely new. The whole of the arrangements were entrusted to him, and once again, he did that which he did best, pleased his master and stunned even the most jaded courtiers into silence.

King Henry sat his white Spanish stallion at the head of the company, with Queen Katherine beside him. Behind the royal couple, the rest of the court, numbering well over five thousand, stared out over the Field of Cloth of Gold in amazement.

Three thousand pastel-tinted pavilions dotted the field, and standards of every color fluttered in the breeze. The tent city was arranged to form a circle, with five broad streets running from its center, where stood a fountain carved to represent the pagan god Bacchus. Someone murmured that it spouted claret and hippocras as well as water and ale.

In the distance stood the old castle of Guisnes, which would lodge the highest-ranking members of the court, with the exception of the four inhabitants of the temporary palace at the center: the king and queen, Cardinal Wolsey, and Mary Brandon, the king's sister and former Queen of France.

The palace was the culmination of Wolsey's artistry, tied to the skills of half the artisans of England. It stood two stories tall on a brick foundation, a graceful, timbered building with diamond-paned windows. The roof was ornamented with fanciful beasts, and a small six-sided cupola offered a gilt angel to the heavens.

The French camp was said to be equally grand, but I did not think anything could surpass our English city, which resembled nothing so much as one of the spun-sugar subtleties from the royal kitchens, a mirage fit to decorate a table, not something to be lived in for three weeks.

Behind me, the other girls twittered like birds, their excitement more voluble than my own. My gaze shifted from the city of tents to the king and queen, visible for a moment through a break in the crowd.

I wondered about Queen Katherine, riding so near her husband; they seemed close, and yet I knew, as did everyone, that he no longer shared her bed. I knew, as well, that Mary Boleyn rode in the procession with her new, hastily procured husband. A wife in the king's most personal service was a valuable asset, and it was assumed that the man who wed Mary Boleyn was either extremely stupid or smarter than he appeared.

My thoughts, though sympathetic, did not linger long on the queen, for the procession shifted again, and I caught a happy glimpse of Nick Hawkins, who was one of the courtiers banished at Wolsey's request. Until his disappearance to his northern estates, I had not realized how often I looked for him in a crowd.

After an endless year, the courtiers had begun to return. Their behavior was circumspect, drawing no undue attention to themselves. I wondered about Nick and learned that he was sent the same summons as his fellows, but he was occupied on his estate due to his father's death. Several weeks later, he made his appearance, and when I saw him, I misbelieved my eyes—first, that he was really there, and more handsome than ever, and second, that he would canter so brashly into the king's presence. I trembled as he swung down from his horse and made his obeisance to King Henry as if he'd been gone a week.

The two courts mingled carefully. Their enmity was centuries old and would not be reversed by a few weeks' choreographed chivalry. I knew our gentlemen were enjoined from fighting. From their careful behavior, I imagined the French had been given similar instructions.

I was eager to see King Francis, who had been touted by ambassadors as our king's equal in every respect. Certainly he was tall and athletic, a fair match in height and muscle, but he was dark and of swarthy complexion, and I thought King Henry, even with his new and unflattering red-gold beard, the more attractive.

I saw little of the revelry beyond that glimpse of the two kings. When my presence among the minstrels was discovered, I was scolded and sent back to my quarters. Agnes was outside when I returned, and she smiled at my dejection and took my arm. "Let's look at the camp. Will that cheer you?"

We met almost no one on our walk through the tent city. The palace drew us like a magnet, its insubstantial beauty shimmering, the statues on the corners caught by the rising moon.

"It doesn't feel real, does it?" Agnes asked. "Not just the palace—all of it."

"The seasickness was real enough," I reminded her. She had been beside me several times at the rail. "Have you seen inside?"

"No."

I hadn't either, but I said, "I heard they brought all the carpets from Greenwich and Richmond, and—"

"I'd like to see the chapel."

I was not surprised. My own prayers were earnest enough, but Agnes had grown more devout over the years. Her fervor reminded me of Queen Katherine, who spent more hours in prayer than at any other pastime. It was even said she wore the rough habit of her favored religious order under her finery.

The chapel was easily found, and it was resplendent as all of Wolsey's creations, with chalices and candlesticks borrowed from Westminster and altar cloths of pearl-encrusted gold fabric. Agnes went immediately to the altar rail, while I explored the rest of the chapel. I saw where the choristers would stand on the morrow, viewed by the king and queen in their elaborate oratories, and paid a visit to a set of statues of the apostles, made of gold and only slightly smaller than myself. I was bored, but Agnes showed no signs of fatigue, her eyes closed, skirts rolled to make a pad for her knees.

"Agnes," I whispered. "I'm going back. Are you coming?"

"I'll be along soon." Her head bowed again; I was dismissed.

As I swung open the door, I walked into the black-clad figure of a priest. Flustered, we exchanged apologies, and I escaped into the night.

Each day dawned clear and warm, and the nobility of both courts spent much time at the lists. The tourney field was specially constructed for use by a great many participants, and at all hours of the day was heard the crash of lances, the thunder of horses, and the cheers of the crowds. During the evenings, talk centered on the day's events, and I feasted avidly on these scraps, since no space in the stands had been allotted for servants.

The closest I came to the field was the tournament tree outside. Cunningly engineered, it bore the arms of all those who took part, in addition to the hawthorn and raspberry devices of the kings. Each time I passed the tree, I sought one shield in particular. Just once, I would like to see him ride.

My curiosity got the better of me before long, and I persuaded Agnes to come with me on a day when Nick's name was shouted for the tourney. It was a brilliant, sunny morning, and by the time we reached the field, my shift clung to my back, and curls had sprung loose from my cap.

We found a place in the shadow of the stands, and from this secluded spot, I caught my first glimpse of the courts at play. Their feelings were well disguised, but there was still bitter intent when two knights, French and English, launched themselves toward one another with lances held high.

I pressed as far forward as possible while still remaining concealed. When I turned to speak to Agnes, I saw that she had gone. I thought to follow her, but then Nick Hawkins, dazzling in silver armor, entered the lists to cheers from both sides. I stood on tiptoe to get a better look and watched as he unhorsed three French knights in rapid succession. Hooves pounded dangerously close to my hiding place, and I found myself near-dizzy from the spectacle. When he was flung from his mount by a lucky blow, I held back a shriek, my hands clapped over my mouth. He rose slowly, clumsy in his armor, and relief flooded through me.

On the stands above me, I heard two men speaking as he left the field. "Great favorite of the ladies on both sides," one said. "You'll note he wears no favor."

"Given too many," said the other. "I heard him tell one lady he would wear her favor under his armor, near his heart. I suppose he couldn't decide which to display, and therefore, which tent to eliminate from his nightly visitations."

There was a shout of laughter from the first speaker. "More likely he could show none of their favors in public."

A burst of cheering drowned part of the response. I strained to hear, and my cheeks flamed at the words I caught. "...more fitting he should tie it round his lance!"

Soon after came our best day in France, perhaps the best of all my days at court. At loose ends because the king was being entertained by the French, a group of minstrels left camp to explore the countryside. "So that," Gilbert explained, "when they change their minds, we'll not be loitering where they can find us." We started down the road between Guisnes and Calais, admiring the scenery. Harry said it reminded him uncommonly of Richmond.

We'd attended a village fete there the past summer, and the memory was dear to us. The king had had his favorite sport that day, dressing up and passing unnoticed among the common people, and we'd joined the other musicians and played and sang until nightfall.

"Remember the fellow who first recognized the king?" asked Harry, skipping along, though the sun blazed down on his uncovered black head.

Tom and Gilbert hooted with laughter, Tom recovering first and striking up a tune on his lute. "Remember the face of the maid he was dancing with?"

Harry bowed before me, offering his hand. "Might I have the honor of this dance, my lady?"

I curtsied, my new hedge-green skirts sweeping the dusty ground. "Your Majesty." I let him lead me off the road. Tom kept up the music, and soon, we were joined by Agnes, Gilbert, and Flora. Others of the Music stood by and watched, and two late arrivals produced another lute and a recorder, making a lively accompaniment to Tom's playing.

The songs were old tunes, known by everyone present in one form or another, and soon, the singing began. It became rather unearthly-sounding with the arrival of a half-dozen choristers. I marked their participation with surprise: they rarely mingled.

I no longer practiced with them, but I danced happily with my old conspirators. One broke free of the ring to ask Agnes to dance, and I saw her shake her head. "I'm fine," she said before I could ask. "Just too warm. I think I'll go back."

Looking wistfully over my shoulder at the lively round, I said, "I'll come with you."

"I might sit in the chapel for a while." She smiled at me. "You won't enjoy it."

I felt guilty, but watching as she walked back toward Guisnes, she looked not the least bit lonely.

Someone tugged at my hand, and I turned away, dancing until my legs were sore, and still dancing, the day and the music and the unaccustomed freedom going to my head. I heard one lute cease its play and opened my eyes to find Tom before me.

"Dance with me, Bess?" he asked and swung me into the circle. He was flushed and smiling, infected with the same gaiety that caught us all. I didn't realize there was such a difference between a real smile and the pleasing expression he presented to the world, but this was a different person.

Suddenly, I noted unfamiliar livery, and a shout went up. "Frenchmen!" For a moment, all hung in the balance, but Mary and Flora swept two of them into the dance, and the others followed without a word being spoken in any language. One man remained on the side and sang for us. I had just enough French to comprehend his lyric, which brought a blush to my face.

LaValle sang several songs, and then I was picked up and carried unceremoniously to the musicians. "We can't be outsung," Harry told me. "Pretend it's the King of France."

"Rather the King of England," Tom said and began to play. The song he chose had a peculiar relevance to the day; though I never liked it before, it now seemed meet, and I sang it willingly.

All is hazard that we have,
There is nothing binding;

SONGBIRD

Days of pleasure are like streams
Through fair meadows gliding.[2]

When at last I stopped for breath, someone else took up a tune. I sat on the grass, my mind drifting. A blissful, floating happiness pervaded my very bones and made me feel light as air. I wished the king, queen, and cardinal back in England, if I could but stay in this field and feel like this forever.

My reverie was interrupted by an unfamiliar voice singing a very familiar song. The singer, I saw with amazement, was Tom, the song the very one he had played for me that long-ago Christmas night.

Oh, it's night—after night, love,
I do lie on my bed
With a feathery pillow all under my head.
Neither waking nor sleeping,
No rest can I find
From the thought of that young girl;
She still troubles my mind.

I will rise up and meet her
As the evening draws nigh.
I will meet her as the evening,
As the evening draws nigh.

I reached up and clasped his hand, too moved to speak. His voice was fine, a sound tenor, a man's voice.

And if you love another,
Your mind for to ease
Oh why can't you love the old one
Till the young's learned to please?[1]

When the song was ended, he loosed my hand to resume playing. I tried to regain his attention, but he played until the gathering began to break up. When he stopped, I was by his side. Flora waited at the edge of the field, but I pretended not to see her, and she soon left with the others.

"Why did you sing?"

He shrugged. His eyes were very blue. "I believe it was the day. All at once, I wanted to sing that song for you."

"I thought you couldn't sing."

"For a long time, I thought so too," he said. "I wanted to die when I could no longer sing in the choir. I swore never to use my voice again, and eventually, I convinced myself I couldn't."

"And yet you stayed at court," I said. Choristers who grew too old for service had two choices: to stay on and sing a man's part, making themselves useful in the meantime by playing an instrument, or, if they showed an aptitude with their books, to be sent off to university. Remembering his help with my lessons after Jenny Keith's death, I wondered why Tom hadn't taken advantage of that option.

"Would you go if you could stay? Most choristers who go to university end up taking orders. I don't fancy myself a churchman," he said. "Do you?"

I shook my head. "There are enough priests."

We caught up to the others and made our way back to the camp as a group, walking slowly through the lilac dusk. Tom escorted us to our tent and lingered after the other girls went inside. "I've never seen you like this."

"I'm happy," I said, though it seemed a tame word for what I felt. "Thank you for 'The Cuckoo,' Tom."

He smiled and touched my hair and surprised us both by leaning down and kissing me on the mouth.

I drifted through the evening, the day's activities coloring my mood, the effect of Tom's kiss warming me still further. It was my first, and though the caress came from one I thought of as a brother, it was nevertheless a milestone.

Always in my thoughts was the one to whom I wished that honor belonged. Dreaming of Nick Hawkins made me feel like every girl I'd ever laughed at for aiming too high. In an atmosphere of deliberate romance, denying my infatuation was impossible, especially when he was so often under my gaze.

It struck me the king must feel thusly, seated beside Queen Katherine and knowing that Mary Boleyn Carey was near.

She was not among the court that evening. I heard from one of the girls that her younger sister was among the French queen's ladies, and they were having a reunion. I imagined another Mary, and my stomach churned. Was I to be surrounded all my life by pastel-pretty blondes who made me look like a gypsy?

I knew myself to be plainer than the fair-haired women favored by the court, but I'd begun to make more of an effort. My dark hair would never straight, but it hung to my waist, and with strict brushing, it no longer looked like the coat of a wild beast. I kept my linen caps as snowy as Mistress Keith's, even if I could not keep them on straight.

The problem of clothes was less easily remedied. We were supplied with everything we needed, but my heart hungered for color and brilliance beyond my sturdy, well-made gowns. I knew better than to wish for cloth-of-gold or silver tissue, but I grew bored with brown and green and gray and thought them nearly as bad as the rat's color I wore as a child.

This new preoccupation distressed me. In the past, clothing was something with which to cover my body. I scoffed at Mary and Flora's chatter of gowns and slippers—what, after all, were garments when one had a voice? But now, my love of music, while not subsiding, made room for me to understand and to wish for a few luxuries of my own.

A gown of wine-red velvet, I decided, with full long sleeves like the French ladies wore. Under-sleeves of the finest cambric, with lace at the wrists. A pearl-encrusted headdress, but not the old gabled kind favored by the queen. I preferred the newer French hood, which showed more hair in the front. I imagined myself in this finery, and when the picture was firmly established, I added Nick Hawkins, noticing me, threading his way through a crowd of many fair women until he reached me. Then he knelt, declaring his love in the humblest tones imaginable.

It was so ludicrous, I had to laugh. Nick would never prostrate himself at anyone's feet; even his bow to the king seemed slightly mocking. I put that down to their closeness, though it was daring even to pretend to mock the king. Despite his arrogance, Nick was popular, and mine was not the only heart that beat faster when he swaggered into view. I believed the tourney-field gossip of his abundant favors and but wished one of them had been mine.

As the visit wore on, competition became more heated. One morning, King Francis appeared in King Henry's chamber and insisted on playing the role of gentleman, choosing his clothes and helping him dress. On another occasion, there was an impromptu wrestling match, which ended with King

Henry flat on his back and two flustered queens trying to preserve the peace.

While the brotherhood between Henry and Francis was at times forced, the affection between their queens seemed genuine. A few of us were called to sing for them one afternoon when it was too hot to watch the men at the lists. We made our way through the English palace, marveling at the painted walls and statuary in every corner. Its transitory loveliness outshone even Greenwich, I thought, feeling disloyal.

"All this magnificence for three weeks." Gilbert shook his head.

"What will happen when it's over?" Agnes asked. She was studying a complicated heraldic painting of fantastic beasts and Tudor roses that ran the length of the wall.

"It gets broken up, and bits will be sent back to England—what of it can travel, anyway. The rest will get left, I suppose," Tom said, steering us along to the queen's chamber.

There were a dozen women seated there, some Queen Katherine's, others belonging to Queen Claude. They talked quietly and seemed at first not to notice us.

Queen Katherine smiled. "Come, children!" She leaned toward the French queen. "The little dark one, the king calls her his songbird."

The king's songbird. Those words reached further than the French queen's ears, and I was teased unmercifully for the remainder of our stay. Secretly, I was proud, though my pleasure was tempered at being called the "little dark one."

The day before our departure, mass was held in a grand outdoor chapel. Cardinal Wolsey officiated, an unusual occurrence, and both choirs sang. Master Cornysh rehearsed the choristers for days, keeping them away from the fountain. A marvel of timing, the English choir sang alternately with the French, each with the other's organist. I was proud for Master Cornysh and envious that I could not sing with them.

After the music ended, Wolsey continued with mass, but a commotion from behind the makeshift chapel intruded, causing him to stumble over his words. He glanced to one side, and several of his men slipped out.

A tremendous bang shook the structure, sending candlesticks rolling into the aisles. Ladies shrieked, and the sharp reek of gunpowder filled the air. There was another bang, and a dragon burst from behind the chapel wall, flying directly overhead with a whiff of sulfur. Its flaming tail had only just cleared the roof when there was a rattle of cannon fire, and all the women screamed again.

Cardinal Wolsey did not move. He fixed a baleful eye on his congregation and said, "A mere firework, Majesties, to have been set off tonight. There is no cause for alarm."

Somewhere in the crowd, there was a bark of laughter, and I surmised it had not gone off accidentally.

Smoke seared my nose and throat, and I wiped my streaming eyes with my sleeve. Beside me, Agnes trembled. "Did you not hear him?" I asked. "There's nothing wrong."

"I don't feel well." A blue vein throbbed at her temple. "Will you walk back to the tent with me?"

Tom caught at my hand as we tried to make an unobtrusive exit, and I leaned down to explain Agnes was unwell. "Too much prayer," he said.

I wondered at his words, for hadn't I felt the same? Piety, rather than giving her strength, seemed to weaken Agnes.

Settling her on the bed, I made her lie back while I smoothed her hair and fanned her. "What is it, Agnes? Is it your stomach? Your head?"

"I just need to be out of the heat for a while," she said.

I was not eager to return to mass. "Shall I keep you company?"

She shook her head. "I'll be fine. Please go back."

The chapel was the last place I wanted to be; I suspected I'd already witnessed the best the Church could offer this day.

Perhaps the heat was the cause of her malaise. Though I walked slowly, I nonetheless felt a trickle of sweat down my back and veered off the path when I reached the fountain. I filled a cup with sweet wine. The sugary liquid flowed down my throat, refreshing me immediately. I replaced the cup and turned reluctantly toward the chapel.

"Mistress!"

I looked about, and the call came again from a nearby tent. I approached, and a hand ventured out, holding a linen fine kerchief. "What chance, mistress, of a fellow getting a wetted cloth?"

The voice was cultured, a nobleman. I curtsied and took the cloth to the fountain, dipping it in the water and wringing it well before returning it to the waiting hand.

"Thank you."

"Is there anything else, sir?"

The tent flaps parted, and Nick Hawkins emerged, wiping his face. "No, little mistress. I thank you for your help."

It was the first time he'd addressed me, and I should have been dumbstruck, but instead, I could only grin at him.

"What is it?"

"Your shirt, sir," I pressed my lips together to keep from laughing. "It has quite a large smudge on the front."

"What?" He wiped at his chest with the black-smeared cloth, making it worse. "Damn."

"It looks to be a powder burn."

"The child has eyes," he said with a sharp look at me.

"And so do kings and cardinals." I curtsied once more. "Mass will be over soon. I must return."

Nick Hawkins bowed elegantly. "And I must change my shirt. Thank you again, mistress—"

"Elizabeth," I supplied. "Elizabeth Llewelyn."

He touched his cap. "You're a pretty girl, Elizabeth, and a canny one."

Chapter 8

That the king had a scholarly side was nothing new, but there had been little reason to dwell upon it before this. In the somber first months of the year, as the palace filled with learned men called to confer with him, we dwelt upon it aplenty. It was rumored that his new work was a tract to refute the German monk, Luther, whose heretical ideas went against those of king, pope, and all civilized Europe. In lodgings reserved for ambassadors and nobles were found clerics and scholars of all kinds, staid, colorless men with no interest in entertainment. Cardinal Wolsey was ever-present, and sober Thomas More was seen entering the king's privy chambers while his gentlemen lingered outside.

Most surprising was the apparent retirement of the royal mistress. Mary Carey was at court but on the arm of her somewhat surprised husband. The queen appeared less worried now that her husband paid his extramarital attentions to the Church.

When the book was completed and copies taken by messenger to the pope, a semblance of gaiety returned to the court. It was a shadow of the old feeling, for soon after our return from France, there were rumblings from nobles dissatisfied with this new view of England's age-old enemy. This dissent was capped by the speedy accusation, trial, and execution of the Duke of Buckingham.

Buckingham was rich, with valuable manors and land, and he ranked high in the succession. His enmity with Cardinal Wolsey was well known, and when he publicly criticized the new pro-French policy, the king's notice fell upon him. He was taken to the Tower and, soon after, made the brief journey to Tower Green to meet the headsman and exercise the sacrament of confession and penance that the king defended.

Executions were public events, but I didn't know many who witnessed this one. The death of a criminal was one thing, but Buckingham was a duke and, until recently, a friend of the king. It had been years since a peer died on the block, and not a few were squeamish about it. Robin Lewis, who did attend, told us Buckingham's speech was short and bitter, and it took three hard strokes of the ax to end him.

I learned a few unwelcome lessons during that crisp autumn. One nearly destroyed my friendship with Agnes. Another shook my relationship with Tom to its very foundations.

My friend was, as ever, devoted to her religion, but as the year wore on, I began to fear a far different devotion held her in thrall. Tom's enigmatic warning, which I had shrugged off as unbecoming to Agnes, appeared to be true. Whether it was so at the time I never dared ask. I knew only that my friend was infatuated with Fra Domenico, the Spanish priest who was her confessor, and that her infatuation was making her ill.

Agnes was still beautiful, but her face was thin to gauntness, and her visionary eyes were fever-bright. Her gowns sagged, and in dressing together one morning, I saw with shock the changes love had wrought. The smooth skin was the same, but her breasts were almost non-existent, and below, her ribs showed through taut flesh.

I went to Mistress Edith. Having the same fears, she had already questioned Agnes. She was fine; she felt perfectly well; she had no headaches or pains or ailments. She was a brittle vessel with a thin, hot flame inside.

My suspicions grew slowly, because I would not believe the evidence before my eyes. She was thin because she ate too little, because she danced too much. Her eyes burned bright because she was growing up and suffered the same strange yearnings I did. She spent too much time at prayer because she was pious, not to mask any private purpose.

I kept myself in ignorance as long as possible, but one afternoon, I ventured to the Chapel of Observant Friars in search of her. At first, I did not see them, only the shadow of two heads together, nearly touching. I dropped a prayer book, and the shadow resolved itself into two silhouettes with guilty speed.

Agnes was the color of a midsummer rose, and even the priest seemed flustered. I kept my own counsel while she chattered on about the loveliness of the day. I understood the heart knew no logic, but a priest! It was not just ridiculous, it was sinful. How could Agnes love a priest?

She brought his name into conversation now, as if he were a secret too good to be kept, and I learned more about him. He belonged to the Spanish ambassador's suite and was a favorite of the queen because he came from Aragon as she had. My friend extolled his goodness and piety.

Somehow, I had to make her see reason, but I had no words to accomplish this task. Tom might help, but I would not betray Agnes's trust.

I brought up the subject casually. "I saw Fra Domenico talking to one of the cardinal's men. His English is very good." She brightened, though I only parroted her words.

"He's only been here a few years, but I do think he speaks exceedingly well."

Diffidently, I said, "You like him, don't you?"

"I do." Her voice lowered, allowing me access to the secrets of her heart. "And I think he cares for me."

God in Heaven! I wanted her to scold me for thinking her capable of something so against the tenets of her faith. I wanted her to laugh at my fancies, to embrace me and say she would never risk herself in such a way. I wanted her to say my fears were groundless, that I was making something from nothing.

Agnes did none of these things.

"I don't understand," I said in the face of her silence. "How did it happen?"

One did not fall in love with priests; priests were not even men; they were God's representatives on earth. Agnes's faith was too strong to defy this. She never looked at any man that way, save Tom. "He is like the others, only finer," she'd said once. I'd been jealous, then, that she looked at him.

"Without my knowing," she said. Her cheeks were flushed, but her gaze was steady. "You remember, I spoke to him about my parents. It felt good to speak to someone." Her expression clouded. "At some point, I began to think of him as a friend. I imagine it's how you feel about Tom."

"I don't feel that way about Tom." Even as I spoke, I wondered why I always devalued our friendship.

She sighed, impatient with me. "I didn't say you were in love with him, but you cannot deny he is your friend. He would do anything for you; you know that."

How had we gone from discussing Fra Domenico to Tom? "Of course he's my friend," I said. "But we were talking about you."

Agnes folded her arms. "And now we are not."

Her rebuff made me realize the seriousness of the situation, for Agnes was never rude. How had she come to see Fra Domenico as a man, as Domenic, instead of the dour Spanish priest everyone else saw? I granted he was handsome, but physical beauty would not make Agnes betray her principles. There had to be something more.

"Do you want him to love you?" I asked. I understood her desire for affection, for who would not wish for love in such surroundings? "He is a good man, you say. A fine priest. Do you want him to dishonor himself by loving you?"

"Our love is chaste." Her tone was calm, but I watched the glow fade from her face as she stared down at her beautiful hands. "There is no dishonor."

"Is he chaste in his heart?" I asked. I was too upset to choose my words with the care she deserved. "Are you?"

She did not speak, and rashly, I ventured to fill the silence. "It seems a pity to spoil what you most admire about him, just for love."

"Just for love," Agnes repeated, and it was no longer the sweet voice of my dearest friend. "You have never loved, else you would know there is nothing 'just' about it." She rose from her seat, gathering her skirts. "Wait, dear Bess. You will see."

Nick Hawkins took less notice of me than the king, who at least knew my name and paid me compliments. While I daydreamed about smoke-stained young men with pretty speeches on their lips, he did not acknowledge my existence. If there were minstrels in the chamber, he might glance our way, but he was always caught up in dancing or gaming. Even when his gaze rested on me, I did not flatter myself that I was seen. It suited me thus, for I could watch him to my heart's content and yet escape detection.

The king still courted the French, and on one evening, our presence was required at a banquet in honor of the French ambassador. To my delight, I found Nick seated just above the salt, in plain view from my spot in the gallery. I sang mechanically and watched his every move.

He spoke with great animation to a lady across the table. She was unknown to me, but he treated her with great familiarity, and jealousy flooded my heart as he smiled in her direction. I remembered the ribald tiltyard conversation and wondered about this new lady. What did he find so fascinating in such a plain, sharp face?

I paid little notice to King Henry or the Frenchmen, but my eyes occasionally strayed to the queen. Her sad face and dark clothing were out of place in the colorful gathering. I sympathized with her; I always had. It was common knowledge that King Henry was disgusted by her inability to bear him a living son.

The little princess, six years old now, was soon to be shunted off to the Welsh border with an establishment of her own. She clung to her mother and openly adored the king. He made much of her accomplishments, but it was obvious that he wished her a boy. It would not be easy, growing up under such a yoke.

There was a shout of laughter from the table, which had nothing to do with diplomacy. I saw Nick and another courtier trying to stifle their hilarity. The dark-haired woman smiled behind her hand, looking all eyes without her wide mouth to balance her face.

I was so intent, I missed my cue and felt Tom's fingers prod me sharply between my shoulder blades. "Stop mooning, Bess! Hawkins cares not how you sing, but Cornysh does."

I whirled to look at him, horrified. He knew! Somehow, Tom knew my secret, knew it and shamed me by speaking it aloud.

Those below took no notice of the break in the music, but Master Cornysh would know. He always did. I decided to plead illness and let myself be put to bed for a day.

When we were dismissed, I escaped up the narrow stairs to the girls' chamber. Though as a rule, I was all arms and legs and skirts that caught on everything, now, I was glad to be thin and quick, so Tom, a full-grown young man, could not catch me.

I closed the door and sat down on the bed, drawing my knees up to my chin. He saw through to my most hidden thoughts. Was he the only one? What if the others—even Nick himself—knew and laughed at me? I would have laughed in other circumstances. A little nobody of a minstrel infatuated with a man who could have any woman he wanted. It was the stuff of farce, and the king's dramatists could turn it into a comedy that would have the court roaring with mirth.

The loss of my secret was worse than any ridicule I might have to endure; I knew Nick was not mine and never would be, but my love for him was the secret I hugged to my breast each night, and Tom had taken it from me.

Flora crept in later and asked why I was in bed with my clothes on. I told her of my sore throat, and she flew off to ask Mistress Edith to prepare a remedy. Moments later, she was back. "You're to go to her and be dosed properly."

I turned over and pulled the covers to my chin. "I don't want to get up. I'm sick."

She pulled back the bedclothes with a snap. "You're not the king's songbird up here. Get out of bed."

Such firmness from Flora surprised me into standing, and by way of apology, she straightened my clothes and peered hard at my face. "You're all hair and eyes when you're sick, Bess; it's quite alarming."

Mistress Edith, rumpled and obviously roused from her pallet, made me drink a cup of foul brown liquid. She assured me it would cure whatever ailed me. I was doubtful. Remembering the older girls' chatter, I wanted to ask for a love posset. When I handed back the empty cup, she patted my shoulder and told me to go back to bed. "Sleep the night through. If you still feel unwell in the morning, I'll give you another dose."

I did not want a miracle cure, but I also did not want another dose of Edith's medicine; I simply wanted something to keep me abed so I did not have to face Tom while my mortification remained.

On such a day, however, I would not be so fortunate. The corridor was quiet and dark, lit only by the occasional torch, but as I stole back to my chamber, a hand shot out from an open doorway.

"Let go!" I dug my fingernails into Tom's wrist.

"Not until we've talked." From somewhere, he'd filched a tallow candle, and he lit it from the torch before marching me into the stairwell to the attics. "Promise you won't run."

"There is nothing to talk about," I said, wondering why it was true. We rarely spoke these days. Ever since France, a distance had grown up between us. He was eighteen, one of the men, while I was fourteen and still a child. If I had been born into a wealthy family, negotiations might have been underway for my marriage. Many girls, even poor ones, were married by fourteen. But servants, especially royal servants, fell into a different category. We would stay young until we were suddenly old.

"There is much," he said, fixing the candle in a gap in the stones, where it cast a flickering light over his face. "What I said—"

"Was none of your concern. I would appreciate you not mentioning it again."

A draft from above caused the candle to smoke, and he shaded it with his hand. "You can't ask that. I'm but trying to look out for you."

"I can take care of myself." My voice echoed against the stones.

"Shouting at me won't do your throat any good."

"There's nothing wrong with my throat," I said, rubbing my hands together against the chill. "I just wanted to be away from you."

Tom looked stricken, but the uneven light did not let me see his eyes. "I cannot say I'm happy to hear that," he said, "but if you strain your throat shouting at me now, Edith will think her medicine has done no good, and Heaven knows what she'll pour into you tomorrow."

He sat down on the steps. His hand, warm through my sleeve, suggested I do the same. "I know you can take care of yourself, Bess, better than most lasses your age, but there are some things a girl can't—" Tom stopped, clearly embarrassed. "I don't want you to make a spectacle of yourself over him."

It was bad enough he knew; I would sooner die than anyone else know. The thought of Nick finding out was enough to make me want to leave court.

"I've seen you watching him before. It worries me, to see you hurting over someone like that."

My resentment flared at this slight to my darling, whom I endowed with all the knightly, chivalrous qualities gathered from my favorite tales, the same qualities I refused to attribute to Tom. "What do you mean, someone like that?"

He sighed, his patience wearing thin. "Bess, look at who he is. And who you are." He turned further from the light, so I had to squint to see him properly. "I'm not saying he'd never notice you, but what would come of it if he did?"

His imaginings went so much further than my own. I was shocked into silence. The thought of Nick showing any real interest in me was ridiculous, and I laughed in Tom's face. "Do you think he'd ever look at me? With all the women at court?" I could not hide my laughter. "He seemed well contented tonight."

"Anne Boleyn."

Later, I would mark that as the first time I heard her name. "Mary Boleyn's sister?" I asked. It was difficult to believe they were related, one so dark, the other so fair. "She's not what I would have expected."

"No. she appears plain until you look at her. Then she's quite pretty, and you wonder how you did not see it straight off." Tapping my nose with his forefinger, he added, "Rather like you, which is why I worry."

"Well, don't," I said, more sharply than necessary. I saw blood on his wrist and felt bad about hurting him. "If he's got Anne Boleyn to look at, he doesn't need me. Tom, do you honestly think I'd be such a fool?"

"No, but—"

"A cat can look at a king. Is there anything wrong in that?"

"Nicholas Hawkins will not love you back, and you deserve better."

I rose from the step. When he failed to restrain me, I edged one foot cautiously down. "I thank you for your wisdom." I blew out the candle. "I'm sure I'll see the error of my ways before heartbreak puts me in my tomb."

Why, since hearing Anne Boleyn's name, did I feel this curious connection, as if our paths were destined to cross? The question was on my mind that winter, as she was often in my sight. Of those times, she was frequently with Nick Hawkins.

Strangely enough, she was not his mistress. Nor did she appear to be involved with the other man to whom her name was linked, the yellow-haired poet Thomas Wyatt. Anne Boleyn laughed and danced and flirted with both men, and a score of others besides, but she never passed the bounds of propriety. I found this surprising, in light of her sister and Mistress Anne's own upbringing at the licentious French court.

It was safe to malign the French because King Henry had switched his allegiance again. There was talk of a visit, even of the emperor marrying the little Princess Mary. Because of these hopes, a party of ambassadors from Brussels was feted with great expense, prefatory, we were told, to the arrival of the emperor himself.

Lent was fast approaching, and the prospect of an end to merrymaking added an edge to the proceedings, which took place at Westminster and the cardinal's palace at York Place. The embassy, along with the king, sat through indoor tourneys, feasts, masques, and music of all sorts. Through it all, the king's energy was boundless. The ambassadors looked impatient and somewhat tired.

Shrove Tuesday was capped by a riotous disguising devised by Master Cornysh, which was christened the Battle of Chateau Vert. It celebrated jointly the themes of unrequited love and King Henry's long-standing affection for his wife, which was much more on view during this visit. It also gave me occasion for a closer study of Anne Boleyn. She was one of the eight maids of honor chosen to portray the qualities of womanly perfection, playing Perseverance to her sister's Kindness.

All the pleasing qualities were assigned to ladies, who might take offense at being labeled Disdain, Jealousy or Scorn. Master Cornysh told the girls of the Music that our role was to protect the Virtues and defend the castle from the qualities of the ideal, chivalrous male—led, of course, by the king.

The castle was a creaking, wooden affair used many times before, covered all over with bits of shining green tin. Three towers held the Virtues, and at the base of these towers, the Vices were to stand ready with weapons of rosewater and sweetmeats.

The ladies joined us for only two rehearsals and chattered throughout as Master Cornysh tried in vain to set down their parts. Mary Carey, temporarily returned to the king's good graces, tried to hush them, but Anne Boleyn and their brother's fiancée, in particular, laughed at every word Cornysh uttered and refused to heed his scolding.

"Such a shrew, that Jane Parker," Flora said. "She has that sharp line between her brows. She'll not give George Boleyn an easy life!"

"She's cast as Constancy," Agnes remarked. Recovering from a chill, she was with us only as a spectator. "Do you not think the parts well cast?"

Mary laughed. "The king's sister as Beauty is apt, but Jane must be constant, for who else would have her?"

"What of the Boleyn sisters?" I asked, hoping for gossip. If Mary Carey was condemned as promiscuous for bedding the king, her sister was garnering a worse reputation while remaining virtuous.

"Mary Boleyn is kind, 'tis true, but Anne is just forward," Flora said, looking to our Mary for approval. "Yet Mary is the one in the king's bed."

Mary Boleyn Carey had nothing to show for her relationship with King Henry but a lackluster husband and some fairly insignificant property. And, of course, a baby, a girl-child, who was shown none of the favor lavished on Bess Blount's boy. There were even shameful rumors that her child had been sired by her husband.

Despite the inconsistency of our rehearsals, the masque went off well. The king led the attack, dressed as Ardent Desire, and demanded surrender of the castle in ringing tones.

"Nay, sir!" I called, Disdain having been given the first opportunity for refusal. "We shall never surrender."

For a moment, the king, in his scarlet satin doublet, looked like a child refused a treat. Then he threw his short cloak over his shoulder and called to the others, "We shall take them, my fellows! We shall take them!"

A volley of fruits and sweetmeats showered over us, and the maids of honor began to squeal in unison. We returned a bombardment of dates and splatters of rosewater, but shortly, we were overcome, and the castle walls were breached.

In his siege, Ardent Desire managed to capture both Kindness and

Perseverance, but Anne regained the safety of the castle and began to cheer on her protectors in a shrill voice.

"Doesn't she want to be rescued?" I heard Flora ask as she flung an orange at Charles Brandon carrying off his white-gowned wife. The fruit bounced harmlessly off his broad shoulder, and Flora herself had to duck as the king's sister laughingly aimed a handful of sweets at her.

I dodged the missiles easily, my costume as yet unmarked, returning each with a quick throw that was a legacy of my first summer at court. Each gentleman came due, except for two. I was afraid to pelt the king with dates, no matter my instructions, and I had no desire to stain Nick's deep blue costume.

"Go on, Disdain—hit them!" Anne Boleyn cried, alone in the highest tower. Above her head was a banner showing a slender hand clutching a broken heart.

Moments later, I was flung aside as she was abducted by Pleasure. Nick's boot caught the hem of my gown and nearly tumbled me from the rock-strewn float. I knew not what he said to her, but Mistress Anne flung back her head and laughed in his face.

The imperial ambassadors seemed confused by our English vigor, but they enjoyed the dancing afterward. I did not dance but sat in a corner with Agnes while the musicians played, my mind divided between worry for her and the puzzle of Anne Boleyn.

I still did not see why Tom thought her attractive, other than the wealth of black hair which was, to me, her only claim to beauty. Jealousy did not cloud my thinking, for I found my opinion shared by a majority of the women at court, most of whom made snide comments about her popularity.

But popular she was, and if the men were not to be discounted, pretty as well. Pretty, even with her pale, almost sallow skin, her too-wide mouth, and her large eyes, unusual and discomfiting to look upon. Her manners, when she exercised them, were French, and she conducted herself apparently by whim, laughing inappropriately and favoring many gentlemen with her slantwise smile.

Nick's attachment to her worried me at first, but Anne Boleyn favored no one man over the rest, and while I deemed Nick the handsomest of all courtiers, if and when she made a choice, there were better catches in terms of title and fortune.

In time, I saw that she had chosen, and well. Henry Percy was heir to the Earl of Northumberland. In his early twenties, he was pale and studious-looking, with weak gray eyes that focused on Anne with fascination as she conquered the males of the court with the ease of a seasoned coquette. When she finally noticed the quiet young man from the North, he was already in love.

She seemed to see the man inside the boy and treated him with surprising gentleness. There would be no mocking laughter or coy smiles for Harry Percy; her dark eyes were solemn and depthless, her small shapely hands grasping his sleeve. It was plain to see she cared for him, made even more obvious by her lightning change from heartless flirt to demure young lady.

I watched them, as I watched everyone, observing the little tricks employed to gain a moment alone, the glances like warm embers. I did not envy them—how could I? That was the life of the Lady Anne, not the life of Bess Llewelyn.

Chapter 9

When I was free of an evening, I often escaped to walk in the gardens. I liked the peaceful time of day, and even more, I liked to watch the courting couples, flitting from the path like moths. It seemed to me that magic was possible within those precious minutes between light and darkness, and more than anything, I wanted to experience that magic.

Those were my thoughts as I wandered through the rose garden, only to have a hand clapped over my mouth and be dragged, struggling, into the bushes. I was folded into a crushing embrace, and a mouth covered mine, hot and urgent.

The kiss sent a shock through me, even as I panicked at the suddenness of the assault. I shoved hard at the man's chest. My struggle must have told, because the mouth tore free and said, "Oh, God in Heaven, miss! I am sorry!" Harry Percy's face flamed to the roots of his hair. He released me so abruptly that I stumbled.

Harry Percy had been seen with no one but Anne Boleyn for weeks. I imagined her nearby, waiting impatiently for her lover. He got his breathing under control and continued his apologies. "I meant no offense, miss. It was an honest mistake."

I curtsied low to the flustered young man, wanting to escape before the lady found us. "I take no offense, sir." Raising my skirts, I fled back to the safety of the crowded hall.

Later, when I saw Percy and Anne Boleyn, I searched their faces for clues. He still seemed flushed and nervous, but she looked relaxed, a bit bemused. For the rest of the evening, they watched each other's movements, and once, when he passed in a dance, I saw her reach out and touch his sleeve.

By the end of the night, I decided to forget the matter. Other than having been in the wrong place at the wrong time, it had nothing to do with me.

Over the next days, I busied myself with learning a new piece for the queen, while my mind, unable to let go, reworked the encounter until I was sick of it. Whenever I thought the matter had been put to rest, I remembered Percy's horrified face or the feeling of his fingers buried in my hair, and the cycle would begin anew.

To be taken for Anne Boleyn was a surprise. All we had in common, to my mind, was a mass of black hair. Certainly, we were unlike in looks, and Anne's gowns were as extravagant as mine were plain. Mayhap Percy had been overwhelmed by impatience and had not looked before he leaped from the bushes.

My reaction confused me. Percy did not appeal in the least; if he hadn't been a Percy, I would have called him a milksop. But he was rich and powerful, someday to be Lord of the North, which meant he was no milksop for all his unassuming looks. Still, he had not the brash, swaggering sensuality of Nick Hawkins, or even Tom's ill-disguised gentleness. If it were possible to feel thus with a man one considered unattractive, what would that caress feel like from a man like Nick? Why did my first kiss have to come from Harry Percy?

My second, I amended, thinking of Tom, though I was not certain that brief touching of lips constituted a kiss now that the term had been redefined. Besides, that was the kiss of a friend, with nothing of passion in it.

If Percy did not appeal, why did his kiss set my heart to pounding? Why did it awaken vague, itching desires that had nothing to do with him? My heart was set on one man. Could my body be led astray so easily?

For the first time, I felt some compassion for the king and his marital foibles. I still disapproved, but I also disapproved of my own reaction.

I wondered if this was how Agnes felt about Domenic. Their friendship—for I refused to think of it any other way—continued, but Agnes no longer spoke of him. My candor had lost me my confidante.

Once, I could have taken my questions to Tom, but after our conversation in the stairwell, we spoke on only the most circumspect of subjects. Telling him I'd been kissed by Harry Percy would bring a lecture I didn't wish to hear; Tom would start on walking alone in the gardens, and by some circuitous route, he would end with Nick Hawkins.

It was a sign of my desperation that I appealed to the Church. I attended mass daily and confession often enough to keep worry at bay, but I was skeptical about its assistance in matters of the heart; relying on the Church had done Agnes no good. I revealed my confusion to a priest, told him that since the incident, I was plagued with feelings I didn't understand.

He told me sternly that I was a weak and immodest creature and gave me sufficient penance to keep me on my knees long enough to make desire disappear. Praying for strength and guidance did not suit me. If I prayed, it was for answers.

Instead of a solution, I was given another worry. Several days later, I received a summons from Anne Boleyn. Rumor made much of her temper; I wondered how much of it had been spent on Percy and how much reserved for me.

A Boleyn servant escorted me to their apartments. He glanced at me repeatedly and with such a curious expression that, finally, I asked if I had grown a second head. He said no and seemed content to leave the matter until I asked if he knew why I'd been summoned.

"I've no idea, miss. The Lady Anne told me to find the girl singer with the black hair."

It was no simple request for music. My last hope turned to dust. It was Harry Percy's weak eyes that mistook me for her, and as for walking in the gardens, there was no rule to say servants must stay indoors. All coincidence, none of it my doing, and yet sure to be my fault.

What could she do to me? The Boleyns were a powerful family, even before Mary's liaison with the king. Anne was proving more dangerous than her sister, aligning herself with the influential Percy family and making other useful friends. As a royal servant, I didn't think she could harm me for such a trivial offense, but she had the power to make my life unpleasant.

I was announced at the door, and it was with a faint heart that I waited, too uneasy to do more than scan the chamber. No one acknowledged my presence, and I began to relax. I was alone.

Then I heard a step, and the lady emerged from behind a carved ebony screen. She crossed the room, silent but for the rustling of her pansy-colored skirts, and stood before me. After a moment, she laughed sharply and put her hands on her hips. "Well, at least now I may be assured Harry isn't totally blind!" She walked in a circle around me. "That doesn't mean I've forgiven him."

Forgiven him! My knees nearly gave way at her words, uttered in a tone that was almost good-humored. She sounded as if she had taken Percy to task for the incident and called for me out of curiosity.

Her black eyes were close to mine. "Were you frightened?"

"Yes, my lady." I wiped my palms surreptitiously on my skirt.

"If you'd thrown yourself at him, I'd not be so easy, but I'll not blame you for a chance cuddle." Seating herself on a three-legged chair near the window, she folded her hands in her lap. "Did he catch you unawares?"

"Quite." I remembered my abrupt descent into the shrubbery and felt my cheeks grow hot.

"Men are fools," she said with a sigh. "We had an assignation. He was far too early." Anne clapped her hands, startling in the quiet chamber, and the same servant appeared, carrying a tray. He offered his mistress a chased gold cup, then held one out to me.

The wine was excellent. It was evidence of the Boleyn wealth, I supposed, that their private stock should be superior to that in the king's own cellars.

Anne watched me drink. "I do not know what to do with him."

I put my cup down with care, knowing it cost more than I had. It was only half empty, but already, there was a pleasant buzzing in my head. "I'm afraid I don't know enough about men to offer an opinion, my lady."

"Good Lord, I shall have to tell Harry he's insulted you!" She turned the cup in her hands, watching as it caught the light. "How old are you?"

"Fourteen, my lady."

"At fourteen, I was at the French court." Her eyes were far away. "Not everyone has had that education, I must remember. But surely, you do live at court?"

I shook my head. "We're kept apart. I suppose some of the girls have...transgressed, but I've always been at my music."

"It's another world." She sounded surprised. Turning away, she walked the length of the room. At close range, I was better able to judge the likeness between us. She was perhaps a hand taller, and being over twenty, her figure more mature, though no more rounded than my own. Her hair was worn loose under her hood, hanging almost to her waist, and she moved with a quick, impatient grace.

Her defects, avidly discussed by her detractors, were not visible. She wore a choker of large pearls, and her sleeves hung over her hands in a fashion she herself set. I thought it admirable that a girl with no real claim to beauty and two visible flaws was able to convince the notoriously choosy males of the court that she was beautiful.

"Your name is Elizabeth, is it not?" She was rummaging in a small chest, and her voice was muffled.

"Yes, my lady. Bess, if you prefer."

"Do you prefer it?" The lid closed with a snap, and she looked up at me.

"Yes."

"Then Bess it shall be. Bess, I apologize for my suitor's clumsiness and for any offense given. Take this for your troubles."

She offered me a small purse, exposing her hand with its superfluous nub of flesh on the little finger. The superstitious reckoned it a sixth finger; I had seen larger calluses on musicians' hands. "I couldn't."

"You must have something for your pains." Her expression brooked no argument. "I shall get repayment from Harry. And besides," she added, "I may have need of a favor someday."

"You need not offer me money, my lady. I would grant any favor you asked, if the means were in my power." I surprised myself with my hasty offer.

She smiled then, and I understood why men found her beautiful; it transfigured her utterly. "Favors should not always come from the heart. It would be better to say you were paid. They would understand that."

"What would you wish of me?"

Her brow creased. "I may need to conduct a bit of a masquerade."

"What?" I was too shocked to remember my manners.

"My father's men have prevented us from meeting on several occasions. It may be necessary to outwit them." For a moment, her eyes lost their brightness. "What say you?"

"Would they not know the difference?"

"Harry couldn't tell us apart for a moment, and he professes to love me more than life. With luck, this would be from a distance."

"I will do it if I can," I promised, wondering why I wanted to help her. "My time is not my own. I can't always get away."

"Of course. You are, after all," she said, with a mocking arch to her brow, "in the service of the king." She tucked the money into my hand and gave me that smile again. "I will be considerate of when I call."

After receiving the Lady Anne's gift, I went alone to London to visit a cloth merchant who dealt with court servants. It was an unimaginable pleasure to go into the shop, knowing that my purchase would be of my own choosing. I inspected one bolt after another, running my hands greedily over the fabrics until the merchant lost patience. With a sigh, I pointed to the bolt I'd selected at first sight, a pleasing Bristol red cloth that was smooth to the touch without being above my station. As soon as my purchase was wrapped, I returned to court.

I did not venture into Aldgate.

My sister was married now, initiated into the rites of womanhood about which I was so intensely curious. Viewing her happiness firsthand would make me feel too keenly my own wants. Madlen would also ask after Tom, and I did not wish to discuss him.

During the sultry weeks that followed, there was nothing to do but practice, watch Anne Boleyn, and stitch at my new gown at every opportunity. It was made in her fashion, and I began to wear a neck ribbon, trimmed with Tom's faded rose, in imitation of her pearl collar. At a distance, it would heighten the resemblance between us, and if the habit was established, it would not seem a purposeful deception later.

I practiced her smooth, gliding walk, watching my reflection in the gallery windows as I tangled in my skirts time and again. Her nervous movements were easier, and the swift toss of her hair was my own gesture already.

It did not matter that she was a Boleyn, a humble branch on the ancient and mighty Howard tree; it did not matter her great-grandfather had been a merchant and Lord Mayor of London. She could have been born as simply as myself and it would not have detracted from the essential Anne-ness of her that I, as well as many others, found fascinating.

No mention was made in the Music of my new airs and graces until, one afternoon at Richmond, Tom made bold to ask, "When did you decide to become Anne Boleyn?"

I sighed. A hint of a breeze rustled the canopy of deep green leaves above our heads, showing patches of a perfect pale blue sky. I did not want to quarrel over something as silly as the wearing of a ribbon, but his words, and the glance accompanying them, nettled me. Though I was loath to gossip, I did not want him to think badly of me. Tom was the soul of discretion: her secrets, as well as mine, were safe with him.

"To please the Lady Anne?" he said, incredulous. "Why?"

I squirmed, but there was no avoiding a response. "Because she was kind and asked my help."

"Jesu, Bess, they are all kind within their means. Have you lost your senses?"

"I'm not a fool!" I turned my back on him and stalked a few paces across the grass. I had as a defense my wine-red skirts, worn this day for the first time. I swished them around me, hoping I looked elegant against the backdrop of the Thames.

Worn with my new gown was a set of red-laced canvas stays, a proper adult corset with bones and a carved wooden busk in front. It changed my silhouette completely, giving me a fashionably flat front while pushing what breasts I possessed right up under my chin. I might not be a lady, but I was shaped like one.

Tom's voice trailed after me, and it sang not in praise of my gown, but in derision of my folly. "Only a fool gets involved in their intrigues. If the king is angered, you've risked everything, and for what?" He folded himself neatly on a rise overlooking the river, his green garments blending with the grass. "Do you believe she or Percy would help you if the king's wrath came upon your head? Do you believe they would think of you at all?" There was an edge to his laughter.

"That won't happen," I said, rejecting his argument. I did not want it to happen.

He raised himself on one elbow. "Who is trying to keep them apart?"

"The cardinal and the Lady Anne's father."

"We already know the Boleyn influence," he said. "And in whose interest does the cardinal act in all things?"

In the interest of the king.

A chill ran down my back. "She asks nothing wrong."

"Perhaps not, but you're the king's creature, not the Lady Anne's."

Voices interrupted our quarrel. A barge was coming in, mooring at the stairs nearby with a great splashing and shouting. Tom heaved himself up, and we retreated to a grove of trees overhanging the river, watching as Charles Brandon landed with a large party.

"Why are you so determined to do this?"

Brandon's entourage made its way up the path, and I left the sheltering trees for the sunlight. "Because nothing ever happens to me."

"Sweet God, Bess!" he exploded, losing his temper. "Nothing ever happens to you? You're a child out of the bowels of Southwark, and look at the life you have." His outflung arm encompassed the palace and all its surroundings. "The only future you had there was in the stews."

I thought of the vile place where his mother plied her trade and shivered again. My stays felt too tight. "I'm not pretty enough for that."

"Yes, you are, especially in your new gown. And besides"—he frowned at me for distracting him—"beauty isn't a requirement, as well you know." He considered me carefully, head cocked. "Perhaps not. You talk too much to be a successful whore.

"But look at yourself. You're clothed, housed, fed. You've traveled and performed for kings. What more could you want?" His eyes blazed, exasperated with my mulishness.

SONGBIRD

"It isn't enough." How could I explain it? I knew there was more to life, and I wanted it. "I love to sing, I love my music, but it's something I do for them. I'm a little nobody who performs when called upon. The king could have a trained monkey do as much."

We were at the water stairs again, our circuit of the lawns complete. Tom leaned against the rail and stared out at the river. "I'm not saying this to hurt you, but we are trained monkeys, and we're lucky. Nobles and courtiers come and go, but unless we do something dreadful, we're safe." He patted my shoulder tentatively, so different from the old Tom, who never hesitated to touch me.

"I didn't know you were so tame." I was distressed at the change in him, and it was easier to be angry. "Don't you have any sense of adventure?"

"Within reason." He withdrew his hand.

I wanted him to comprehend something I barely understood myself. "My entire life has been at the behest of others. I've traveled, and I've sung for kings and queens, but I've done those things because they wanted it of me. I've never done something for the joy of it." I appealed to him. "Don't you ever get tired, just watching everything?"

Something flickered over his face, quickly concealed. "Don't trifle with your life, Bess. You have people who care about you."

Why could I not let it go and make peace? "Not my family—I haven't seen them since France, and you can't tell me I'm worse off for that."

"I don't mean them." Tom let his irritation show. "I'm speaking of Agnes and Mistress Edith. Cornysh. Me. Your friends. You don't need people like Anne Boleyn to make you real."

I looked at him uncertainly. "We haven't been such great friends of late."

The breeze took his light hair and blew it into his eyes. "I know. I'm sorry." He took my arm across the path, and his grip was firm. "I will try not to judge, Bess, if you'll not be so quick to accuse me of judging."

"Don't you ever feel that you're missing something?" I persisted, too moved by his apology to acknowledge it. "You've been here longer. Don't you ever feel it?"

"No," he said, and it appeared to be the truth. Tom was incapable of deceit, even for my benefit. "I leave the intrigue to those who are born to it."

He sounded so superior! I said peevishly, "You should have gone to university, instead of staying here. You're obviously too good for us."

Tom stepped back, and his face showed such sadness that something inside me shattered. He touched my cheek with roughened fingertips. "Why do you fight me so?" he asked, turning my face up so he could look into my eyes.

My heart and soul laid bare, I stared back, unable to tell him of the emotions churning inside me. There was a strength in his touch I could ill resist, a sense that everything could yet be all right if I held on to him.

I put my arms around his waist and leaned my head on his chest. I had grown since the last time we stood this way; the top of my head now fitted under his chin. His heartbeat was quick beneath my cheek, but it steadied when he put his arms around me.

﹏﹏

My comfort was short-lived. I was sitting with Agnes, doing needlework and chatting about everything except Tom and her priest, when the summons came.

Lady Anne was pacing her chamber when I arrived, so angry she seemed to glow. Her wrath was not directed at me, for when I entered, she broke into a merry smile and sent the boy for wine. She exclaimed over my new gown and noted my neck ribbon with a playful, long-nailed finger. "You have thought of everything."

She appeared distracted, wandering to the open shutters, knotting her kerchief in her hands. Her visible anxiety was uncharacteristic; despite her nervous movements, Lady Anne hid her emotions, and I felt privileged that she trusted me enough not to play-act in front of me.

Ceasing her pacing, she sank down on the window seat. Spots of color burned on her sallow cheekbones, but she folded her hands calmly and looked at me. "As you've guessed," she said, "the time has come for our little masque. There seems no other choice."

She waved me to a chair while she explained. "You have heard my father and the cardinal have planned a marriage for me, yes? Not to Harry Percy, but to James Butler. I care not that he's the Earl of Ormond or that the marriage will settle some family squabble—he's an Irish peasant, and I will not have him!" She fussed with her skirt, pleating the rich fabric with her fingers. "I've tried to conceal my feelings for Harry, but we've been found out. The cardinal has someone watching us."

I thought of Tom and wondered why I was involving myself in a situation fraught with such risk. If the Irish match was favored by Wolsey, it had at least the tacit approval of the king.

"You don't agree," she said, and her plucked brows arched. "Go ahead, Bess, say what's on your mind."

I was unable to keep back the words. "Do you really expect to fight them?"

Her laughter filled the room. "I know the limits of my power. I just want time to say my farewells. My father will drag me back to Hever tomorrow and immure me like a nun until I give in."

I was relieved she did not intend something mad like running away or confronting the cardinal. It made my mind easier about my part.

"If you'd rather," she said, "I can find another way—"

"No, my lady." I would go through with it, despite Tom's misgivings and my own. I had promised, and I suspected what her life would be like at Hever. Let her have her farewell.

Anne conferred with her maid. After a moment, the girl returned with an armload of cloth in a color similar to my new gown. Anne continued to talk to me while she was stripped and redressed.

"I shan't ask much of you," she said, taking off her headdress and tossing it aside. She peered into the polished steel mirror while the maid brushed her hair. "Great God, we are alike without all my fuss and bother."

I joined her and found, for the first time, that I agreed. My features, accustomed to subservience, were less animated, and her mouth was wider, but our dark eyes and coloring were similar enough. I smiled tentatively and the resemblance sharpened. Anne laughed and took my hand.

"Do you know," she said, "I really believe this will work."

The thick fingers of the cardinal's henchman dug into my upper arm as I allowed myself to be dragged toward the cardinal's lodgings. What, after all, was there to say?

The charade went well enough in the beginning. I made my way from the palace by a route different from the Lady Anne's, meeting a servant in Percy livery who passed me a note to misdirect followers and turned me from the direction where the real meeting would take place.

I wandered along the path, taking my time and stopping often to look at the view, aware at last of a presence behind me. I prayed I would be able to keep the cardinal's man at bay while Anne spoke to Percy. Finally, I paused, choosing a secluded bench in the rose garden, and opened the note, as if to read again the words of my beloved. The shrubbery parted with a rustle, followed by curses when my face was seen for the first time.

To have it end so abruptly, to be shut in a closet in the cardinal's quarters with the door locked, brought my position home to me. The room was sparsely furnished but still imposing with its oak-paneled walls and massive fireplace. Despite the warmth of the day, I regretted the clean-swept hearth as I waited, shivering.

"Tell them I made you do it," Anne had said blithely, confident no explanation would be necessary.

A commotion erupted on the other side of the door. I heard Anne's shrill voice and Percy's lower tones. Their voices were joined by the unmistakable deep rumble of the cardinal. I trembled on my hard seat. Two more doors slammed shut before a key rattled in my own.

When I opened my eyes, a scarlet figure filled the doorway. I scrambled to my feet and made a terrified obeisance.

"What have you to say?" he asked, his voice ringing in the bare chamber. "I suppose you, like young Percy, were bewitched into doing things the king's fool would not consider."

"She asked a favor, Your Grace." I began to feel a faint hope that his fury was not directed at me.

The cardinal's expression softened, but he still lectured me for some time before stopping to say, "Go back to the music rooms, and stay there. I know who you are."

He preceded me out of the chamber. I hung back when I saw who waited outside; the Earl of Northumberland had come to deal with his heir. The Earl nodded heavily to the cardinal, and they entered the door to my left. I did not envy Harry Percy for having to brave such a pair; in his place, I would sooner face the king.

～～～

"Do you want to leave court, Bess?"

"No, sir." I realized the depth of my disgrace by the disappointment in Master Cornysh's eyes. "No, I do not."

"You've made the cardinal notice you, and not for your voice." He did not look well, and our interview seemed to cause him pain. "It would be better if you left."

"Master Cornysh, please, no!" I pictured myself marooned like a ship in the uncaring harbor of Aldgate. If the court cast me out, I would rather to go Southwark to make my living than return to my family. "I'll never meddle again, I promise."

His smile was strained. "We wouldn't abandon you to the streets. It won't be difficult to find a household in need of a minstrel—a household which rarely comes to court." He looked down at his hands. "You've always been a special case. By rights, I should have no say over your future. You've put me in an embarrassing spot."

"Hasn't the cardinal more important things to worry about?" I never thought my unique position might cause difficulty for Master Cornysh. There would be no question of my fate in the hands of the Master of Minstrels; he was a fair enough man, but I was no favorite.

"Anne Boleyn will be at Hever, and young Percy's being taken north by his father," Cornysh said. "The cardinal is free of them both. But you—"

I held my breath, even as the tears streamed down my face. The end was coming, the end of my life at court. Tom, Agnes—Nick! I sobbed aloud.

"The cardinal did say you'd done him a service. Someone innocent of wrongdoing isn't likely to employ a double so she can meet her lover." Cornysh patted my hand. "Let us hope that his gratitude outlasts his anger."

Chapter 10

Too many people knew of my involvement with Anne Boleyn, and I did my best, in the weeks that followed, to disappear into the Music. If any attention came my way, it would be as the king's songbird, not as the girl who meddled in the affairs of her betters.

I was so preoccupied that I failed to see the changes in Agnes. She had withdrawn from me ever since my clumsy handling of her confession, but I knew the relationship continued, that her feelings had gone beyond respect: it was Domenic the man she loved, not Domenic the cleric. When I first noticed her unhappiness, I assumed she felt remorse over the attachment and tried to comfort her. To my surprise, she was not repentant, only despairing.

"Why is he being sent away?" Seeing that Agnes was close to tears, I attempted to distract her with questions, hoping his recall had nothing to do with their liaison. My own mistake came close enough to touching us all; if their relationship were discovered, there would be no avoiding unwelcome attention. My behavior would be brought up, and the morals of the entire Music could be called into question.

"The Spanish Ambassador is sending him back with an envoy; he was given no reason. Bess, what shall I do without him?"

Her tears came in earnest then, with such racking sobs that I feared for her health. When Tom opened the music room door, I held up my hand behind her back, and he retreated. I murmured consoling words to the girl whom I feared nothing would console.

At last, her weeping subsided, and she leaned against me, worn out. Her voice was softer now, almost inaudible. "I'm sorry, Bess, I shouldn't have brought this to you. I know you disapprove."

I hugged her to me. She felt like a skeleton wrapped in cloth. "Agnes, I worried you would be hurt, nothing more." I closed my eyes, hearing Tom say those same words. "I love you—you must come to me when you're unhappy. I feel a fool not seeing it before now."

"Don't be silly," she said, trying to master herself. She allowed me to rub her back. "Domenic has known for weeks, but he didn't want to upset me."

Voices outside warned we would soon be interrupted. I took her arm and led her away. Tom shielded us from view until we rounded the corner.

When we were safely in the girls' chamber, she continued. "He can't disobey the order, and he won't give up the Church. He's not like Cardinal Wolsey."

Wolsey held more offices than allowed by church law, and his son, a mere schoolboy, had recently been given church office.

"Agnes, you're not—"

"I wish I were," she said, with a depth of feeling that shook me. "I wouldn't care, if he stayed. I could live with the shame if it meant being with him."

"Oh, Agnes."

Her expression turned inward, and she seemed not to hear me. "I never thought to feel this way about any man. I never wanted to. It's all I wished for, Bess, his love, and I had it. I still do, but to be loved by a priest in Spain is not the same as being in the arms of a man in England." Her face was white, and her eyes burned feverishly.

"Dearest, don't upset yourself. Why don't you sit here while I get a sleeping draught from Mistress Edith?"

"It's all well for you to say not to upset myself," she flung at me, dropping down on the bed as directed. "Your man will never leave you."

"You've made yourself ill. Let me get Edith."

"I'm not ill. I'm angry. You're like her, that Anne Boleyn. Half the court heard him crying, saying he'd love her forever."

I had avoided thinking about Anne and Percy. I hadn't witnessed Percy's leave-taking, but the story had been widely repeated. Sentiment was against Anne for leading him astray from the match his father had arranged, and worse, for causing him to unman himself by crying out for her.

"How can you say that?" I sat next to Agnes, hurt and confused. "You've captured the heart of a man who is supposed to be immune to women."

Her cheeks grew flushed, and she pressed her lips together. "I speak of Tom, of course. The poor man loves you, and you waste yourself intriguing with someone like her." She grasped my hands with her cold fingers. "I'm not truly angry, just envious. Tom is the match we all pray for, and you throw his love in his face."

⁓⌣⌣⌐

The Spanish envoy's departure was postponed until January, and Agnes glowed like a torch through the holidays. Her place in the bed beside me was often empty until dawn, but I asked no questions. It was enough to see her happy again, though the end, when it came, would only be worse for the delay.

Domenic's ship sailed four days after Epiphany. They said their farewells in the chapel, and he delivered Agnes to me at the door. He appeared as gutted by the separation as she did, but I watched his figure retreat amid flapping black robes and was glad he was gone.

Bringing Agnes from the gloomy state into which she sunk seemed impossible; for several weeks, I lived with a wraith who neither slept nor spoke and barely took food. She spent hours in the chapel, emerging with tear-stained cheeks and trembling hands. When she wasn't at prayer, she helped Mistress Edith, which I took as a good sign. The older woman cosseted her and taught her simple remedies. Agnes smelled pleasantly of herbs, and if her eyes were red, she blamed the irritating effects of Edith's concoctions.

Despite the example before me, I believed in a different sort of love and wondered why she was so afflicted. To my mind, love was not like this—it was something to rejoice in, to cherish, not something over which one suffered and starved.

It was obvious she did not appreciate my attempts to cheer her, no matter how well-meant.

"You're glad he's gone," she said one morning when mass was over. "You never liked him."

"I didn't know him as you did," I said, knowing if I agreed, it would provoke a storm. "If he had to leave, I only wish it had been sooner, before you were hurt." I tried to take her hand, but she slapped my fingers away.

Her eyes were bright in her otherwise colorless face. "You've never felt pain like this, Bess. You have everything you could want, and you ignore it and reach higher."

"Agnes—"

"No!" Her skirts were bunched in her hands as she pulled away from me, revealing a flash of knitted stocking. "You make a mockery of us all. We're lucky to get one chance for happiness. You're so greedy!" Tears began to run down her cheeks. "Do you think if Nick Hawkins sees you—beds you, even—he'll remember in a month?"

The depth of her bitterness pained me. I could not love on command; I knew Tom cared for me, but I could no sooner forget Nick than Agnes could stop loving Domenic.

The silence was absolute. I raised my eyes and met Tom's gaze. "Will you do it?"

"Why do you think it will work?" he asked, and I knew he would not refuse. "And why ask me? Why not one of the others?"

I took his hands. "It will work, Tom. It has to." I had no doubts about the soundness of my plan, worked out over the past few sleepless nights. "Agnes needs someone to break the priest's spell."

Tom's smile was rueful. "I am hardly a figure of romance, sweet."

"Perhaps you're not cut from the same cloth as her precious Domenic," I said, "may he rot in Spain for what he's done, but Agnes thinks highly of you. You are the match they all dream of," I quoted. "I'm not asking for a plight-troth, just a bit of kindness. Share supper with her, or ask her to walk with you. Make her smile."

His misgivings were plain, but he gave in and left me alone to consider the consequences of my request. Asking Tom to pay court to my heartsick friend was simple enough—he wasn't likely to fall in love with her—but I wondered if Agnes was capable of appreciating his efforts. I vacillated between fear she would send him away or, worse yet, transfer her affections to him. He would be too kindhearted to shrug them off, knowing my own heart was elsewhere.

I cataloged the emotions this thought bestirred and found a few ugly strands of jealousy. Though I did not love him, I didn't want to see Tom with anyone else.

In early March, we were granted a spell of warm weather. The restless king, hoping the false spring would hold, ordered his courtiers to pack for a short journey. My attendance was required on this occasion. After my troubles of the previous year, I was glad of the favor, but once again, I would have to leave my friends behind.

The weather was kind and the progress enjoyable, taking us for two endless weeks through Surrey and Essex. The court was merry, and I was merry too while there were eyes upon me, but I was glad when matters of state called the king back to Greenwich.

The pleasant rose-brick river palace was my favorite of all the royal residences, being both the first I knew of court and the scene of some of my happiest days.

I encountered Tom in the courtyard as I swung down from the cart which had carried me for the last eight hours. He waved a greeting but kept moving. He seemed unchanged. I breathed a sigh of relief. If he was in love with Agnes, I would have seen it on his face.

Before I reached the girls' chamber, Mistress Edith laid hold of me and began to steer me down the corridor. "Thank the Lord you're back, Bess. There's a performance planned for tomorrow night, and Mary's lost her voice, the wicked girl. William is distracted waiting for you."

"But I want to see Agnes."

"Agnes will wait," she said, shoving me toward the music rooms. "Master Cornysh and the king's entertainment, they cannot. Go on with you. I'll tell her you've returned."

It did not matter it was a castoff of the unlucky Mary; the thrill of new music never diminished. My enthusiasm was overshadowed by worry, and I turned back to face Mistress Edith. "How is she?"

She turned round, hands on her broad hips. "No better and no worse. Now go!"

It was near midnight before we were released. I was travel-tired and hungry, and now exhausted as well. I chose my bed over a late meal simply because I could not bear the thought of walking all the way to the kitchens. Some of the beds were already occupied, but the place beside me was empty when I crawled in. I felt my limbs relax on the straw-filled mattress and tried to stay awake until Agnes joined me. After a while, I heard footsteps, and the missing girls began to filter in, talking and laughing quietly. I heard the soft swish as they tossed their clothing over chairs, the creaking of their beds, a few whispers before they slept.

My eyes grew heavy. I couldn't imagine what was keeping her. I had just drifted off when I felt the bed sink beneath her slight weight. I sat up, half awake. "Agnes."

"Shh, Bess."

"I tried to stay up." I rubbed my hands over my face. Her back was to me, and all I could see was her curtain of hair shining in the faint light from the door.

"You shouldn't have," she murmured, sounding more like herself than she had in months. "You must be exhausted."

I reached across and squeezed her arm. "I missed you."

Her soft laugh made me smile. "Don't fuss. Go back to sleep."

I struggled; my eyes were stubbornly trying to close again. "But I want to talk—"

Her cool hands pressed me down and pulled the coverlet up to my chin, and I wrinkled my nose at the sharp, unfamiliar scent on her fingers. "There will be time tomorrow."

⁓⌣⌣⌐

Sunlight was streaming in the narrow windows when I heard a sound at the foot of my bed and opened my eyes.

"Tom!" I sat up, remembered I wore only my shift, and yanked the covers up to my shoulders. "I'm sorry I didn't see you last night. Master Cornysh kept us."

"Have you seen Agnes?" His gaze left my bare shoulders to travel the room.

I shook my head. "Not since last night. I waited up, but she came in very late and said we'd talk this morning."

He plucked at the ties of his shirt. "It's after nine already. No one has seen her, not at table nor in the practice rooms."

I sat up again, knowing he would turn away, and swung my legs over the side of the bed. "What happened while I was gone? No one said anything."

"I wanted to." He risked a glance over his shoulder, caught me struggling into my gown. "Sorry."

I disregarded my stays as something I could not manage alone. "Don't be silly. Here, lace me up." I felt him fumble at my back and realized it was not a kindness, asking him to help me dress. "What did you want to tell me last night? Where is Agnes?"

Finishing my lacing, he took my brush from the table and pulled it through my hair several times before arranging the heavy mass down my back. His hands lingered a moment longer than necessary. "She's been very low," he said. "I'm afraid where she might be."

It had been pleasant, having him brush my hair. I braided it quickly and tucked it beneath my cap. "Tom?"

"She knew I was doing it for you." Tom passed a hand over his eyes. "She said she only stayed here because she had nowhere else to go."

His words, combined with my own suspicions, hit me like a thunderclap. "Have you searched the grounds?"

"I haven't alerted Master Cornysh yet, but I've had the others—Harry and Gilbert and some of the choristers, even Robin—looking these past two hours. Flora's gone through all the places she can reach: the chapel, the practice rooms, the attics. Nothing."

"That doesn't leave much."

His eyes, gray today with hardly a trace of blue, met mine. "Except the river."

The thought of Agnes, alone, offering herself to the river, made me catch my breath. I reached for Tom as my legs lost their strength, and he caught me deftly.

Had it come to that? I cursed Domenic again, but just as quickly, I turned on myself. I should have done something to keep her from this dark place. She was my friend, and I failed her. I saw her pain and offered no comfort, had instead asked Tom to salve her wounds for me. Why did it matter that I didn't approve of Domenic?

"Tom, what if she's done it?" I drew the coverlet around my shoulders at the thought. Something tumbled from the rough cloth onto the floor, and we both reached for it. My hand closed on it first, a small bit of linen wrapped around something. I unfolded it and stared at the contents.

A narrow gold band, thin as wire, seen daily on Agnes's slender hand. It lay gleaming in my palm, needing no note to explain its presence.

"A bequest," he said, and there was a catch in his voice.

"She said it came with her when she was brought here. It belonged to her mother." I rose, my legs steadier now, though fear spread through me like a fever, and went to the next bed, where Flora and Mary slept. I turned their pillows and found small packets under each. I showed Tom my findings, and together, we checked the other beds.

We found two more gifts. The small store, spread out on the bed, seemed not enough to define a life. The ring for me; some ribbons, green and pink, for Mary and Flora; an illuminated page from a prayer book; a small velvet cushion with her sewing needles stuck in it.

My mind turned to the small casket beneath my side of the bed, and I wondered if its contents would seem as pitiful. They were my treasures, but to other eyes, they would be no more than an accumulation of rubbish.

"Tom, we have to find her." I swept her things under my pillow. "She must be here somewhere!"

Feigning calm, he put his hands on my arms. "We will find her, Bess. I promise you."

"I'm coming with you," I said, struggling against him.

He drew me to his chest and pressed a kiss on the top of my head. "I'm sorry, but you're in no condition to search; you're worn out." He went to the door and called for Mistress Edith.

I watched, aghast. Not search for Agnes? I had to—I could not let my friend face whatever was ahead without me. Something could still be salvaged of this, if we found her.

"She needs me," I said. I needed her. "I'll rest later."

"No." Sitting beside me, he slid one arm around my waist. "It's for the best, sweet, truly. Do you think I'll be able to concentrate on finding Agnes if I'm in knots of worry about you? You haven't eaten, you've barely slept, and now you've had a nasty shock." He hugged me to him. "You're only so strong, no matter what you think."

"He's right," came Mistress Edith's rough voice. "Not that I give much credence to a fellow who's not had permission to enter the girls' chamber." She swatted Tom good-naturedly. "Out with you, and find that poor girl. I'll take care of this one—I've a mess in my workroom that needs tidying. Bess will be a great help."

He kissed my cheek. "I'll send word as soon as we find her."

His footsteps receded. "You're encouraging him!" I raged at Edith. "He doesn't own me."

"He'd like to," she said bluntly. "Come to my rooms when you've eaten. And don't let me find you've gone outside."

I took Agnes's things from their hiding place, passing them through my fingers like beads, praying for her safety.

All at once, I was sickened by my own shameful part in it. My tears came in floods so that when Mistress Edith returned, she comforted me but could not understand my words as I choked, "Damn him to hell. Damn Domenic for what he's done to her!" She patted me and wiped my eyes, clucking like a hen, and waited while I put the ring and the other bits away.

"You're not doing her any good by crying," she said. "I told Tom true when I said I needed your help. A shelf collapsed in my workroom last night, and it will take all morning to put the place to rights."

On a normal day, Mistress Edith's narrow closet was a comforting place. It smelled of trapped sunlight and herbs, an almost visible scent. She pushed open the heavy door, and I winced at the disheartening sight. Mistress Edith stared at the jumble with dismay equal to my own. "I've already checked the shelf," she said, picking her way across the floor, her skirts kilted up around her knees. "I can't imagine what happened."

The table where she mixed her remedies was at the end of the space, and above it were shelves holding bottles of concoctions and jars of dried ingredients. Usually, there were four shelves, but the second-lowest had slipped from its bracket, sending everything crashing down on the table. The floor was littered with broken vessels, dried herbs, and powders, and a viscous brown fluid dripped from the table edge to the matted rushes. The smell made my eyes water.

"And Tom worried that walking the grounds would be too much for me." I tried to make Mistress Edith smile, knowing how upset she must be by the destruction of her workroom.

"Tom is worried what they will find, and he wants you far from it," she said.

I pushed her words aside. Tom would find Agnes. "Can all this be replaced?" I gestured at the rubble at our feet.

"Most. Some must wait until spring or summer, when I can collect new plants. Some will have to be bought. The bottles and jars will be the hardest. You become accustomed to using certain things." She picked up a large shard and put it down again. "If you like," she said, "you can help me remake the remedies."

"Agnes is your assistant."

Mistress Edith was disconcerted. "I do mean if she no longer wishes to help. She's become very clumsy. She broke my best mixing beaker just two days past."

I began gathering up pieces of crockery. Edith's voice went on, but I blocked it out, trying to imagine where Agnes had gone. Tom said she was despondent, and so she was, but she would never cast away her religion so entirely as to take her own life.

The process of clearing up took us well past noon. When we were finished and what was salvageable, put in new containers, Mistress Edith showed no pleasure at completing the task.

"Did we miss something?" I asked.

"Nay." She climbed up on a stool and began to move jars on the top shelf, then the one below. "Bess, did you discard a dark brown bottle?"

"Glass?"

"Yes. Tall and narrow it was, with a stopper like that one." Indicating a bottle, she held it up to the light and peered inside. "Have you seen it?"

"No. What was in it?"

"A preparation of mine," Mistress Edith said and sat down hard on the stool, color draining from her ruddy cheeks.

"Edith, shall I call for someone?"

"Pennyroyal," she said under her breath, and then her face crumpled, and she began to weep. "Oh, sweet God in Heaven."

I dropped to my knees by her side. "Edith, what's wrong? What about pennyroyal?" I knew the herb by name but not its properties or why

Mistress Edith was so disturbed by its loss. "We must have discarded it, and I didn't notice."

"We did not." Her expression was stricken. She rose, moving without her usual briskness. "Go on now. Search for your friend if you like."

"Is this about Agnes?" I asked, clasping her hand with both of mine. "Tell me!"

"She is not in the river." That was all Edith would say, but after she locked the door, I heard her muffled sobs.

The search was called off at nightfall. Tom told me, weariness in every line of his body, there was no sign Agnes had gone to the river. By then, everyone knew she was missing, and many curious glances rested on us as we ate together. Neither of us felt the need to speak.

During the meal, I couldn't let go of Mistress Edith's words. Why did the loss of the brown bottle upset her? The herb whose name she uttered with such horror was somehow tied to my friend's disappearance. Suddenly, I connected the scent of Agnes's hands with the tumbled herber. It was logical, but I shied from suspecting her of such destruction.

I excused myself, climbing over the bench. Up the endless stairs, I ran and reached Edith's chamber, short of breath and shaking. It took no time to find the leather-bound book where she recorded her potions. The volume was so old that the paper crumbled at my touch. It must have been given to her, for the first part was written in a tidy, masculine hand, and the accompanying drawings were like none of hers. I ran my finger up and down pages, searching for one word.

I found it several times, in harmless preparations, but then I saw what Agnes found, at the bottom of a page. The ink was faded, but I could still make out the words, the properties of the herb and its various uses. "Useful in powdered form for congestion and cough." The book listed other herbs to add for these remedies, but my eyes were caught by the postscript at the bottom, in a different hand. "Not to be taken when with child, as it will cause bleeding—"

The page was torn there, but I did not need to see more. This was what caused Mistress Edith's tears. A woman with a bastard child had little or no chance of respectable survival, as Agnes knew too well.

There was a soft tread on the doorsill, and I looked up, not surprised to see Mistress Edith framed there. Her face showed she understood my invasion of her chamber.

"Her helping me was a sham." Her voice still held traces of tears. "She knew all the time and waited to find a way."

"Helping you seemed to make her feel better. Mayhap she stumbled on the knowledge and could not resist."

Her heavy shoulders rounded in defeat. "She need only have asked," she said. "I would have done it for her. I've done it before. I know the right amounts."

"The right amounts?" I grasped the words. "Edith, could Agnes—"

"It kills near as many mothers as babes," she said. "Herbs are easy to misuse. I've been tearing myself apart trying to remember how much was in that bottle, and I can't. I can't remember."

Chapter 11

From across the chamber, I heard the roar of the king's displeasure, and moments later, Wolsey scuttled past, moving as quickly as his bulk and his voluminous robes would allow. I saw the queen lean over and speak to her husband, then raise her skirts and withdraw with her ladies.

Despite his magnificent green velvet doublet studded with pearls, the king looked like a small, sulky boy. His eyes narrowed as they scanned the room, looking for distraction. His gaze paused on me, and I froze, but his lips thinned, and he called for his fool.

I had been out of favor since the night of Agnes's disappearance, when I failed to perform, owing to my rattled nerves and the weakness Tom accurately predicted. My part was ably sung by Flora, but the king voiced his displeasure at the substitution. Not so long ago, the thought of his disapproval would have brought me to my knees. I still feared the king, as all sane folk did, but some of the awe had worn away. The giant was petulant as well as majestic, and it made him a bit less than a god. I was sorry to have attracted notice by not performing, but his attention would be elsewhere soon enough.

I neglected my music as I worried over Agnes. At first, I thought perhaps she'd booked passage to Spain, to join Domenic, but that was unlikely as she'd left everything of value behind. My fear was that she'd dosed herself with Mistress Edith's concoction and made herself ill or worse.

"You're too hard on yourself," Tom said as he attempted to revive my lute lessons. "Agnes made a choice."

I wanted to tell him she made that choice because she had no other, but I kept quiet, her secret heavy on my heart. Tom knew more than the others but not the whole tale. Mistress Edith and I agreed no one need know of the baby; if Agnes returned, she should not have to face the shame. "I should have tried harder, instead of shifting the responsibility to you."

"Do you think I don't feel a failure as well? Every day, I think of something I should have said or done."

I lowered my eyes, knowing he might see something he wouldn't understand. "There was nothing you could do."

"Then why are you guilty?" His tone made me wonder if he suspected. "If one friend could not save her, another could do no more."

"How did I not know how to help her?" I bit my lip, tears burning my eyes. "How did I not see what she needed?"

He wound a loose strand of my hair through his fingers. "We give what we can, Bess. No one was happy about the priest, knowing what heartbreak it would mean eventually." Tom had suspected the truth long before I had.

"But that was her concern, not mine. She needed to feel my love, and she did not." I tilted my head toward him as he continued to play with my hair. "I failed her."

The curl dropped to my shoulder as Tom drew away. "Agnes failed herself," he said. "She loved where she should not have loved. All the friends in the world couldn't make her believe it was right."

I scarcely noticed what was going on around me, so wrapped was I in my personal troubles. It was a good time for idleness—the king hunted, hawked and rode out almost every day. As well, Master Cornysh had been gone since July, searching for new choristers. In August, we heard the king had granted him a manor in Kent as reward for his services. He returned to formally accept the grant and gather his family for the journey.

Later in the month, we received word that Master Cornysh was taken ill soon after their arrival. As the sweat was not abroad that summer, we thought no more of it until one morning, scarcely a week on, when Mistress Edith lurched into the practice room, her hand at her breast.

"What is it?" Harry ceased his playing at the sight of her face.

"William," she said through her tears. "He's dead."

It took a moment for us to realize she meant Master Cornysh.

I put out my hand, knowing that Tom would take it. "How?"

"His heart," she choked and put her hands over her face. "He died at Hylden."

We were stunned. Almost as shocking as the news was the sight of Mistress Edith leaning against the doorframe, her face streaming tears, the message crumpled in her hand. Tom handed me his instrument and held out his arms. Edith collapsed against him, sobbing like a girl.

After he led her away, the rest of us were left to take in our loss. The youngest of the choristers began to cry. They had never known a master other than Cornysh and thought of him as a father. Even the men looked distressed, passing their hands over their eyes before comforting the little ones.

Harry and Gilbert gathered around Flora, who was crying noisily into her skirts. I sat in the window, wanting no comfort. While I no longer practiced with the choir, I still worked with Master Cornysh, and it was due to his care that I had reached such a level in the Music. He was my protector as well, and I cared deeply for him.

The others drifted away, and when Tom came searching for me, I was curled in the window seat, trying to pluck out a tune on his lute. "It won't play for me," I said as his hand fell on my shoulder.

"It wouldn't. It's tuned for me." He pulled me from the seat, carefully relieving me of his darling. "Can you make a sleeping draught for Edith? Do you know how?"

"Yes," I said. I hadn't spent much time in the workroom, though I knew she wanted me there. "I know that much."

Tom unlocked the door with Mistress Edith's heavy key. He watched while I found the bottle of poppy syrup on the shelf. I poured a small amount in a cup and added water. "This will make her sleep." At his skeptical glance, I said, "It's very strong. She always waters it."

"I hope so," he said, taking the cup and sniffing the contents. "She's sore upset over Master Cornysh."

"Of course." It would not be amiss to hand out poppy syrup to half the Music. "We'll all miss him."

"Yes," he said, "but she loved him."

By the next day, Mistress Edith had regained her composure, and I almost disbelieved Tom's words. "What of Mistress Cornysh?" I asked, thinking of pleasant Jane, who had several times made us welcome in their London home.

"What of her?" Tom's brows rose. "I don't believe anything ever passed between Edith and Cornysh, only that the love was there."

I wondered whether loving Edith meant Master Cornysh had not loved his wife or if there had been space in his heart for both. It was another lesson for me: that love came in guises I would never expect.

I felt my life in the Music slipping away: first Jenny Keith, then Agnes, and now Master Cornysh. Almost all those who had welcomed me were gone.

~~~

After snatching a few minutes in the September sun, my spirits were higher than they'd been in months. The courtyard was full of men and horses, the beasts prancing impatiently in the sunshine, their coats gleaming like satin. Light caught on the polished bits of their harnesses and glittered, bright and lovely. Late for practice, I sped across the empty hall, only to collide with someone who hurried in the opposite direction.

"Oh, I am sorry!" a male voice said. I wanted to disappear into the rushes; I knew that voice. "Let me help you up." Masculine hands fitted themselves under my arms and set me on my feet. "It's Bess, isn't it?" He looked at me, his head cocked to one side. "The king's little songbird."

"His Majesty has called me that, yes." My voice was barely audible. This was his first notice of me since those careless words three years ago in France, and in my plain gown of ash-gray, I was a drab sparrow blinded by his brilliant plumage.

Nick smiled. "I remember when first you came here."

He had removed his hand, but I still felt the imprint of his fingers on my skin. "Seven years ago, sir."

"Seven years," he repeated. "Good God, you've seen a lot."

"Not so very much," I said. "I was a child." That was an untruth—children often see more than their elders—but I had no better words with his eyes upon me. At that moment, all I could think of was seven years of cherished daydreams. Better to seem an ignorant servant than to say something ridiculous.

"You are not a child now," Nick said. His smile was gone; his lips were a straight line, with faint creases on either side.

"No, sir."

"How old are you?"

Where was this heading? I prayed he would notice me someday and carry me off to be a fine lady, but that was a childish fancy. "Sixteen."

The noisy approach of the Duke of Suffolk rescued me from my bewilderment. The king's companion clattered through the hall with several retainers and a dozen hounds swirling around his feet. "Hawkins! The hunt begins—are you with us or no?"

Suffolk, like the king, was growing older and fleshy but in a different manner. The king would always be regal, despite his widening girth; Charles Brandon's indulgences made him look coarse. I recalled the tales of his beauty, a man magnificent enough to be mistaken for the king, bold enough to steal Mary Tudor's heart and whisk her from the throne of France, brave enough to risk the king's wrath.

"I'll be along directly." Nick turned back to me. "We have spoken before, have we not?"

"It was in France, sir," I supplied. He shook his head, and despite my fluster, I added, "I fetched a wet cloth for you. You had gotten your shirt dirty." I held my breath, damning my hasty tongue. At last, he looked at me full on. There was laughter in the wine-dark depths of his eyes, and something else.

"I remember you now, Mistress Songbird. You helped me out of a bad spot. I recall I said that you were pretty."

I remembered every word, every nuance of our brief conversation, but how strange he did as well.

"You still are."

Tom would tell me, with his wry grin, that what pleased a princess and a minstrel girl were two different things entirely, but as I watched them ride away, Nick's slim dark figure so near his two massive golden-haired elders, I wondered if Mary Tudor ever regretted her choice.

The court was a whirl of activity in the next months, the intensity building toward its customary pitch at Christmastide. Everything was just slightly off, and it seemed the new master tried twice as hard to achieve what Master Cornysh would have done with ease.

Somehow, I always found time to worry about Agnes. I began to spend more time with the other girls of the Music, who were always merry and, if they did not cheer me, at least distracted me from my thoughts. Through them, I made a new acquaintance, as different from Agnes as a girl could be.

Full-bodied and rough-tongued, Gwen Morgan was the youngest daughter of a once-prominent Border family. Given the choice of convent or court when her lack of dowry failed to attract a husband, she chose the court. She wore her ambition like a scent, and while I found her entertaining and outrageous, I had the sense to keep my distance.

"They think I'll never find a husband because Father lost all we had." It was our first meeting, and she seemed intent on shocking the assembled girls. "As if I'll spend the rest of my days here plying a needle."

Maids of honor were supposed to be isolated with the rest of the queen's women, but there was not a door made that would keep Gwen in—or out. She was a tremendous source of gossip, chattering endlessly about the affairs between Queen Katherine's ladies and the gentlemen of the court. Gwen found the queen boring. She said Her Majesty held little interest for the king these days, in or out of the marital bed. The queen's chambers rarely shook with his step; when they did meet, it was over dinner in their private rooms. Afterward, they played cards. It was more a friendship now than a marriage, she confided, for the king never touched his wife.

I always remembered the first time I truly saw the queen, a pale, exhausted woman recovering from the travails of failed motherhood. She'd touched my heart that day by speaking to me, despite her own pain, and Gwen's news filled me with sadness.

"What sort of wife is that for a king?" she asked.

Whatever his feelings for Queen Katherine, Henry had no new mistress in his sights; he dallied yet with Mary Carey, but her star was sinking, and everyone knew it.

Between Gwen's conversation and my own curiosity, I became more aware of the ebb and flow of sensuality in the court. It repelled me, but at the same time, I was drawn to the spectacle because of one who stood in the midst of it all.

My awareness of Nick Hawkins had heightened since our baffling conversation in the hall. Several times, I found him watching me. His gaze made me uncomfortable, yet I was filled with a prickling wonder that he looked at me at all. A cat may look at a king, but it upsets the natural order of things when the king looks at the cat.

In December, I lost another friend to the world outside. I never thought to call Robin Lewis a friend, but he had become one, in his odd fashion, and I would miss him.

Robin still kept to himself, preferring solitude because it gave him time to read. His love of books stood him in good stead now that his usefulness to the king had come to an end. His voice changed at seventeen, sufficiently late that the choirmaster had hopes of keeping his boyish soprano forever, and now he was leaving us.

The week before Christmas, he made his farewells to the choir and the Music and drew me aside.

"How can you be glad to leave?" Our relationship had remained faintly antagonistic, and I could not help but challenge him on what I saw as his rejection of my chosen life.

"Bess!" Robin shook me gently. "There's a whole other world out there. I want to see it." He was flushed, his eyes bright with anticipation. When had he ever looked so happy?

"If you wish to see the world, why not just sign on a ship? Why Oxford?"

"Why not?" He waved one of his ever-present volumes at me, and I wondered in passing how he managed to afford them. "It's my due for all these years of labor."

To me, performing was its own reward, but not everyone thought as I did. I understood Robin's attitude, but to be joyful at leaving was beyond me.

"How long will you be there?"

"Several years." Even his red hair seemed to be crackling with exuberance. "Until I learn enough to make a life for myself. Then I can see all the world I want without having to sign on a ship."

I heard the sound of wheels outside. "Will you come back to court?"

"Of course, I'll visit." He wrung my hand earnestly. "You've been a true friend to me, and I'll not forget." His homely face drew so near that I could have counted the freckles dotting his light skin. I thought he was going to kiss me goodbye, but instead, he pressed his cheek to mine and held me tight for a moment. He mastered whatever sadness he felt by the time he broke the embrace. "I shall miss you most of all," he said, sounding surprised. "Funny, after our beginning."

"Yes." I wished he would stop talking. I was losing another friend, and I didn't want to think about it yet.

"You'd win the competition easily enough now; I sound like an angry goose." He laughed, not at all bothered by the loss of his glorious voice. I thought fleetingly of Tom.

They hailed him then, and he jerked around. "I must go!" He took my stiffened shoulders as sorrow for him alone and embraced me again. The spine of his book cut into my ribs. "I will come back, my friend," he said softly. "Who can say, if I succeed at university, there may be a position for me here better than chorister!"

I put my tears away then and faced him with a smile. "Do well, then, Robin, and come back."

～～～

The king decided to winter at Westminster. As the weather was yet mild, the removal was accomplished by river, but we had not been there a week when bitter cold set in. All around rose the fascinating clamor and smells of the city, but the weather kept us all—king, courtiers and servants alike—crowded indoors. It seemed there was never time nor place to be alone, and I found myself wanting to spend time with Tom. He was restful, even when we disagreed. He felt the same inclination, and we arranged to meet on a January afternoon when we were both free.

The stables made me sneeze much less in the winter, and they offered a haven of peace with little chance of interruption.

Tom leaned against the wall, his arms folded over his green doublet. His hair was in need of cutting and lay over one eye, the same color as the straw in the horse boxes. His expression was far from bright as we spoke. "Bess, I'm not scolding, but—"

"Yes, you are." I had run across Nick that morning, and my body vibrated like a fresh-plucked lute string at the memory of the encounter, his few words, the watchfulness in his eyes.

The air was frigid. At one time, we would have huddled close. Now, I stood apart and felt the lack. "I seem to recall a promise not to meddle. Did I dream that?"

He smiled faintly. "I did promise."

"Well?" I drew my cloak around me, needing to do something with my hands; I was not as comfortable taking the lead over Tom as I wanted him to believe.

"I don't like Gwen Morgan."

"Since when do you criticize the queen's ladies?" I asked, my voice tart. I didn't like Gwen much myself, but it wasn't Tom's place to tell me who to befriend.

"If she's so high, she should act it," he countered. "A friendship with her might do you more harm than that silly affair with Anne Boleyn." Unkindness did not come naturally to him; his words were slow and deliberate. "She's not like Agnes, Bess. She may be highborn, but she's common."

"Don't you think I can see that?" I asked. "I wouldn't want her to be like Agnes—even Agnes proved no good at it in the end." I thought of the terrible knowledge that Mistress Edith and I shared. The truth came, despite my efforts to keep it down. "I couldn't bear to have someone as dear to me as her, because it would break my heart to lose her."

I was mortified; I'd not intended to tell my private fears.

"You need not fear her influence," I said at last. "I know what she is. I can speak with her, Tom, without wanting to be like her."

Through the open doors, I saw the snow begin to drift down, and I drew further into my cloak, dreading the thought of the long, cold days ahead. "Agnes was a piece of me, like you are. I didn't realize what a large piece she was until she became so unhappy. Then it felt like I was being torn apart, and when she left..."

I felt his hands, hesitant, on my shoulders. "I know, Bess. I know."

I turned on him. "How can you know?"

For a moment, Tom's fingers were tight on my shoulders; then he let me go, sliding his hands lightly down my arms. "There's this lass, you see, and she owns quite a large piece of my heart." He brushed his hair from his face. "And sometimes, it seems she cares naught for how she tramples on it."

Chapter 12

The rift between king and queen was now public. As her troubles grew, Queen Katherine spent the hours formerly shared with her husband in prayer or discussion with her priests. She saw few people: her confessor, a handful of ladies, the princess. The queen still liked music, and Mary would play for her on the virginals, her small fingers sure and skillful. We minstrels stayed well back and let the princess shine for her mother.

The likeness between them was deeper than mere physical resemblance. The princess was slight and pale, with red-gold hair, her father's child, but the set of her face, the imperial stiffness of her narrow shoulders, all bespoke her mother's influence. She and the queen spoke Spanish or Latin together; it was obvious that Katherine was raising a tiny model of herself: proud and pious, destined to be a great European princess.

As the queen grew melancholy, the king became gay. During the day, he hunted with Charles Brandon or Francis Bryan, or closeted himself with his ministers; his nights were full of entertainments. His penchant for masques and play-acting taxed the revels master to the limits of his endurance, and at almost any hour, there was a line of carts outside the palace, going to and from the storage houses in the city where scenery, props, and costumes were kept.

It was a fascinating, exhausting period; players and musicians kept at the same rigorous pace as the workmen who erected the fanciful scenery required for the revels—hours of labor, to be followed the next day with the removal and installation of new and more fantastic sets. Each day, there was a new piece or a new dance to learn, and rehearsals would last until we dropped with weariness and hunger. I enjoyed the challenge but resented the inroads the king's entertainment made on my limited personal time.

For weeks, Nick was nothing more than a face in the crowd. I was not deluded that his eyes lingered on me alone; I'd watched him for years, heard the stories and saw for myself his attractiveness to women—and their attractions for him. It hardly seemed fair that, when at last I came due for my limited share of his attention, I should be so occupied as to never see him.

After long days spent in the practice rooms, there were occasional rewards. If we were not cast in the evening's performance, we were permitted ride into the city to spend time as we pleased while the carters exchanged their loads of scenery for whatever new fancies the set-builders had conceived.

I could not withstand the lure of the city, despite my desire to see Nick. He was not likely to cross my path, for if the day dawned clear, he would ride out with the others, and if it rained, he would be at dice or cards with the king. Flora and several of the others hatched a plan, and it took little convincing for me to join in.

The morning sun shone like a promise, with a bright and cloudless sky arching over the road to London.

To my surprise, Tom was waiting in the courtyard with a satchel. He did not notice us until I planted myself in front of him and asked after his plans.

"I'm going into London for the day."

"So are we." I gestured around at my fellow-travelers, all of us dressed in our best. Mine was the wine-red gown of the Anne Boleyn days, as it would be long years before I might afford another. Jenny Keith had taught me to store bags of dried herbs in my clothes to lessen the staleness of frequent wearing. Agnes had sprinkled her body linen with lavender water. I could not yet bear the smell of lavender.

"We're going to see the menagerie at the Tower." None of us had ever been there; it seemed a perfect pleasure-jaunt, and we had discussed the plan for days.

Tom smiled. "You'll enjoy it."

"Come with us," Flora invited. I poked her, and she said, "If you like."

He shook his head. "I'm visiting my mother. She's not been well."

I had not forgotten that shrewish woman. She'd hurt Tom; I did not understand why he would go to see her and said as much.

"She's my mother, Bess. I see her once or twice a year." He frowned. "She isn't young; her looks have faded. Too much paint."

It was frightening, what could happen to a beautiful woman. The compounds of lead used to whiten the complexion could tint it yellow or green, and carmine caused the lips to blister and crack. Tom's mother no more resembled a pretty woman than did one of the revels master's grotesques, and I pitied her. But to spend this glorious day in the confines of Southwark? I would not, and as well, I had no plans to go to Aldgate.

What Tom and I once discussed, I had taken to heart. I was no more the child of my parents than he was the child of that aging whore. We were children of the court, and we made our own family. Thinking of my parents only brought memories of cold and hunger, of dirt and the verminous streets where I'd spent my childhood. Except for my father, I attached to them no happy thoughts at all. I had been the daughter of Peter Davydd, but I was now Bess Llewelyn. We were not the same girl.

The girls traded rumors as we bumped along. Flora had seen the king fondling a new maid of honor in the corridor. No new favorite had come along; even Mary Carey was returned to the arms of her dull husband. We speculated on this too, and across from me, Tom's disapproval was clear. I didn't care. How often did I get a chance to be an ordinary girl? He could visit his mother; I was going to enjoy myself.

I set my chin and determined to be rude if he scolded, but his words were kind, saying that I must be certain to see the lions.

"We will," I said. "And we'll see you this evening."

The bells sounded six as we arrived at the meeting place, having seen the menagerie, eaten meat pies bought at a shop, and wandered the walks by the Thames, watching the great ships unloading their cargo. Tom wasn't there. The cart waited a quarter hour before leaving. "He'll have to walk," the driver said, "it's my hide if this lot's late."

My imagination set itself to listing all the horrible things that might befall a young man alone in London, footpads and cutthroats and ruthless prostitutes with daggers in their bodices. We would not reach the palace in time for vespers, so I said a prayer for his safety as we rumbled along.

The next morning, he was still missing, but at midday, I saw him seated at a far table. I slid onto the bench beside him. "We missed you last night."

"I couldn't get away," he said and took a deep swallow of ale. "Did you enjoy the beasts?"

I cast my mind back to the strangeness of it all, the fierceness of the cats at their meat, the oddly human calling of the birds, the roaring that had filled our ears as we left.

"The whole day was lovely." I touched his arm. "How is your mother?"

He jerked away as if my fingers burned. "Not well," he said. "Did you like the lions?"

"Yes," I said, though I had not. Despite their terrifying roars, they made me sad, stalking about in cages, swinging their golden heads. It seemed to me that no animal should be locked up to be stared at, but when I'd said so, the other girls laughed. "Are you all right? You look dreadful."

"I'm tired, that's all. I was up most of the night." He pushed the plate away, having eaten almost nothing. "I'll be better when I've slept."

He did not improve. Our trip to London was almost a week past, but Tom still looked tired and ill, and Harry complained he kept them awake with his tossing and turning.

My natural impulse was to ask him what happened in London and be done with it. I realized the folly of such directness and devised a more subtle plan and asked him to meet me at the water stairs at vespers.

Greenwich is a river palace, but it never seemed more so than on a warm evening, with the dark waiting behind the gold and purple twilight. The river plashed quietly, brimming with sunset colors. I ran across the wide lawns to the stairs, where he was waiting. Several barges were tied there, and I motioned that we should walk; I did not want to be interrupted by the cardinal's entourage should he decide to journey upriver to view the progress on his new palace.

"To what do I owe this honor?" Tom asked after we walked for several minutes, the soft lapping of the Thames the only sound.

I took a deep breath. Voicing my concern would not be easy, and for a moment, I struggled. "I'm worried about you," I said. "You've not been the same since London—everyone's noticed. What can I do?"

Tom laughed. "This is not a role I've ever imagined you playing." He turned away but not before I caught his expression.

"You've spent years trying to sort out my problems. Don't make a joke of it when I try to do the same for you."

"I've told you, my mother is ill. Is that not enough?" His tone was harsh, but he accompanied the words with a light touch that said my concern was appreciated.

I took his hand, sank down on the grass. He followed more slowly, reluctant to continue the conversation. The setting sun caught his light hair and set it ablaze, and I smiled to see it. "Of course, you're worried over your mother, but I don't believe that's all." He gazed out at the river, and I shook his shoulder lightly. "Don't you think the burden would be less if you shared it?"

124

He avoided my gaze. "If you were anyone else."

The idea of Tom having secrets was incomprehensible. What was so bad he could not tell me? "It's Agnes, isn't it?" It could only be Agnes.

"You're a witch, I swear." He sighed. "How did you know?"

Tom was the perfect servant. He'd performed on the night of Agnes's disappearance, when I could not lift my head for grief, but other than a slight pallor, his sorrow was invisible. A stranger looking at Tom would think he had no inner life at all. "You're protecting me."

"Someone has to." He rose to his knees, brushing at his clothes. "It's getting late."

"Vespers aren't yet over," I protested. "And what of the hour? I'm not performing; are you? You weren't practicing this afternoon."

He shook his head.

Though the ground was growing damp, I sat back down and patted the grass beside me. "Did you see her? How is she?"

A cloud passed over his face as he debated with himself. I waited patiently. Tom would not refuse me where Agnes was concerned, no matter how much he wanted to protect me.

"She's changed," he said at last. "Changed but...but still Agnes. I could still see her."

"Where did you—" I stopped when I realized there was only one place he might have seen her. "Oh, God above, Tom, not there."

He took my hand. "I spent the day with my mother. She's bedridden now and likely to stay that way if she's not lucky enough to die."

I made a sound of sympathy. The pox was a death sentence and often a slow, painful one.

"The women care for her, but my money was welcome. On my way back from the apothecary, I saw a girl. She disappeared into a house before I was certain.

"I'd already missed the cart, and once my mother slept, I'd intended to start back, walk all night to get away from there, but I couldn't stop wondering. I went to the house to prove myself wrong."

"What happened?" Though I had convinced him to speak, I was terrified of what he would say.

"They said there was no one named Agnes, but when I described her, they sent me upstairs." His grip on my fingers tightened. "I needn't tell you what such places are like. I was so glad Agnes wasn't there, I didn't care about giving my money to some stranger just to prove it. When she pulled back the curtain..."

"Oh, Tom." I leaned against his shoulder. The idea of Agnes in a place like that sickened me, but I would think of that later, when I was alone. It was more important now to purge Tom of this horror.

He seemed unable to go on. I stroked his hand, waiting for him to gather his thoughts. "She wasn't Agnes, not at first. She asked for sixpence. I said I just wanted to talk, but she said that cost too."

The dusk did not hide the ruddy color in his cheeks; it embarrassed him to speak of such things to me. "Bess, she was always so lovely." His voice threatened to crack. "She reminded me of my mother."

Pale, pretty Agnes painted like a whore. Behaving like one, with Tom. It was unimaginable. "How did she come to be there? Did she tell you?"

He dropped his forehead to his bent knees, his voice emerging muffled. "It took some persuasion to let me stay. She made me sit on the far side of the pallet. When I told her how upset you were, she softened a bit."

Tears brimmed in my eyes.

"She went to London, hoping to make enough money to sail to Spain, but she soon realized she'd never get there. When that happened, she stopped caring."

"She can't be happy!" Despite his words, I could not see my friend in such a place.

He looked at me as if I were mad. "Of course she's not happy. She just doesn't care whether she lives or dies." Tom turned away again. "We talked until dawn. It cost every farthing I had to keep the room for the night, but I couldn't bear any of the men I'd seen downstairs coming to her next."

Agnes could never survive that life. Raised without love, she'd nonetheless been gently bred; she knew nothing but solid walls and warm clothing and the comforts of the court. Thinking of her there, alone, violated and miserable, made me ill. My head ached, and I knelt at the bank to splash water on my face. It ran off my chin, spattering my bodice. "I would be better off there," I said.

Tom joined me at the edge. "You're stronger than she is."

"We have to do something."

"She doesn't want our help, Bess," he said, his voice tight. "She doesn't want to see me—or you—ever again. She made that clear." He cupped my wet face in his hands. His eyes were bright with unshed tears. "It would only hurt you if you tried to see her."

"She's my friend." The depth of his distress stopped my tears. "Nothing will change that."

"Let's go in." He began to walk swiftly toward the palace, and I followed.

"You haven't told me everything, have you?" I grabbed at the sleeve of his coarse linen shirt.

He turned then, and his face was stark and white. "I've told you enough. She is alive. Be content with that."

I would have, except I suspected the worst demon of all still lurked within his brain. "Tell me the rest." I wrapped my arm through his and leaned against him in a way I knew he found hard to resist. "You needn't protect me."

"Someone must." He tried to disengage my fingers.

"No, someone mustn't." I clung all the harder. "Tell me."

"Damn it, Bess!" He peeled my fingers loose and shoved me away.

"Tom!"

"Can you not leave it alone?" In all the years we had been friends, he'd never raised his voice to me. "Must you know everything?" He paused but spoke again before I had the chance to assure him I did. "Your dear Agnes has changed, Bess." The sun left his face, and I could barely see the glitter of self-hatred in his eyes.

"Of course she's changed." Such an ordeal would not leave her untouched.

"Before dawn, when we'd talked the night through, there came a time when there were no words left." He faced the river, leaving me with his silhouette against the dark water. "She asked me to stay."

"To stay," I repeated. His meaning was clear.

"So as not to waste my money," he said. "That was how she phrased it." His hunched shoulders told me everything I needed to know. I put my hand on his arm. The tension in his body was extraordinary; he flinched when I touched him.

Tom turned to me, his voice soft and full of loathing. "God help me, Bess, but I did."

~~~

The night was endless. I left my bed when the others, at last, fell quiet, climbing the narrow stairs to the attics. There, among crates of unused finery, I burrowed, free at last to indulge my sorrow.

How I hated Domenic! He'd used Agnes and no doubt forgotten her before he reached Spain. I cried for what she must have felt when she

127

realized she was alone, cut off from her friends, her lover's child torn from her by craft or by birth, surrounded by the uncaring city.

It cost sixpence to possess Agnes's fragile body, her even more fragile soul. What had it cost Tom?

Strangely, or perhaps not, I didn't hate him for staying with her. Worse was the thought I was least prepared to confront. Agnes was—or had been—modest, but we'd shared a chamber and a bed for years. I saw her naked almost every day, and it was the image of her smooth white body twined with Tom's which caused a pain so sharp that I doubled over, muffling my sobs in my skirts. He'd been mine for so long that the idea of him loving anyone else, even Agnes, tore at me.

I hated that I was jealous. I didn't want Tom, not like that. He was the one who loved me, who betrayed me, and himself, by bedding Agnes. Yet if he was the betrayer, why did I feel in the wrong? Tom was not mine; I had no rights over him. What would happen when he did fall in love? He was twenty, a man grown. It would happen. Could I wish him well, without this knotting in my innards?

Was misplaced jealousy my only fault? Was there something more to be laid at my feet than not being the friend Agnes needed? If I hadn't asked Tom to play the admirer, would he have stayed? Would she have asked?

The notion that I could have provoked their actions was appalling.

Faint sounds from below told me the earliest servants were up. It was almost dawn, and sooner or later, someone would come looking for me.

Later in the morning, I made my way to the yard, determined to find Agnes myself. I remembered where Tom's mother lodged, knew the apothecary's shop he'd mentioned. If I explored every route between those two points, I would find her, if I had to ask at every brothel in Southwark.

I heard shouting at the gates and began to run. As I called to the driver, Tom's tall figure came around the side of the wagon. I stopped, unsure how to greet him. His approach was tentative, as if he feared I would run from him again. Instead, I threw my arms around his waist, sobbing as though I had not cried all that long night.

Tom rubbed my back and waited until I stopped for breath. "You're going to her anyway."

"Of course." I turned toward the palace, realizing my absence would be unexplained. "I should leave word—"

"I already told Edith we were going into the city."

He'd known all along what I would do. His night could have been no better than mine, yet his first thought was to clear the way for me.

We stayed silent all the way into London. Though our shoulders brushed as the cart rattled and jounced on the rough road, shunting us from side to side, the barrier between us could not be breached.

The cart stopped at the boundary of Southwark, and we got out. I remembered another such trip, the two of us eager and full of joy. It was not long ago, but I felt much older.

"Are you all right?" His eyes showed blue shadows beneath. I wondered how much sleep he'd lost lately, and how much last night, because of me.

"I'm no worse than you are," I said, and it brought forth the faintest of smiles.

Several streets later, we turned down a narrow, dirty passage. My nose wrinkled with disgust at the odor, and seeing, Tom offered me his handkerchief. I thought of Wolsey and his gilded pomander and shook my head. I would bear the stench. Let the cardinal ride with a clove-studded orange to his nose.

"This is it." A tall, narrow house, its three stories overhanging the street, terrible only in its ordinariness. Tom put me behind him and knocked at the door. It was opened by a blowsy, painted woman wearing a loose blue wrapper. Her hair was a bright, artificial gold, dark roots showing close to her scalp, and she had no eyebrows, just two black arches drawn above her eyes. She looked at Tom, a businesswoman's smile lighting her whitened face. Although he did not wear his court clothes into Southwark, some of their authority clung to him; she saw a young man with money to spend.

"Afternoon, sir." Her eyes lit on me, and her expression grew puzzled. "What can I do for you two?"

Brothels had been part of my growing up, but I'd never been inside one; they had been pointed out by my parents as places to avoid because they stole girl children. I stayed at Tom's shoulder.

"We're looking for Agnes."

"There's no one by that name," she said. Her look became sly. "But I have several lovely girls..."

Tom shook his head. "She is here. You sent me up to her only a week ago. Fair, blue eyes, about twenty."

The woman wavered. "I remember you." Her expression softened. "A week ago, as you said." She folded her arms under her breasts, which were barely covered by the slippery fabric. "Mags ain't here."

"Where is she?" Her use of Agnes's mother's name chilled me.

129

"Gone." Her shoulders lifted in a shrug that caused her wrapper to gape. "Left the morning after she saw this one. I don't know where she went, but I have my suspicions."

"Where?" we asked in unison.

She jerked her chin. "Yon river is my guess. I'm surprised it took that long."

Chapter 13

Agnes was gone, this time for good. Though the Church said her soul was forfeit, I lit candles for her in the chapel and hoped her merciful God heard my prayers. God might not forgive her, but I did. I wondered if she'd lost her faith in God, as well as in her friends. She'd found herself alone and unable to bear the unbearable. I understood why she'd chosen the river over the visit she anticipated, but I mourned her desperately.

There was one question that had to be asked. "Was there a child?" I heard Tom's sharp intake of breath.

"No," the madam said, still fussing with her wrapper. "I thought there might have been, once—she was so tender with the girls who got that way, helped them out after."

Edith's preparation had worked. I did not know whether to be happy or sad. I took Tom's hand. "Let's go home."

We spoke little on the way back to court, but the silence was different this time.

"You knew there was a babe," he said at one point.

"Edith and I both knew."

"You should have told me."

I leaned my head against his shoulder. "Someone has to protect you."

Tom let out a deep breath. "Is that what I do to you?"

"Yes." I squeezed his fingers to let him know it was all right.

We did not speak of Agnes's other choice. We never would.

The next weeks were almost unendurable. I resented men—all men—as the agents of Agnes's undoing, and possibly my own. When I came across Gwen wrapped in a heated embrace, I didn't speak to her for days, seeing the marks of passion on her throat as a betrayal.

She thought me absurd. "Men are God's greatest creation," she said.

"I'm glad you think so," I said, tightening a balky peg on my lute. My playing was still flawed; I did not need assistance from the instrument to sound bad. "I don't see it."

"Bah! You would if you let your Tom close enough."

It was a sore point. Though we had spent the ride from the city wrapped in misery and each other's arms, we had avoided each other since. I believed it was mutual; there was nothing to say that did not hurt. "I don't think of him that way."

Gwen rolled her brown eyes. "What is he, your lapdog? Have you looked at him?"

Tom had grown up, his shoulders manly beneath his doublet, his legs long and well-muscled. I noticed but did not like that she had.

"You're fortunate that he's a musician, and I aim higher." She played with the points of her sleeves. "You don't see what sort of lover he'd be if you let him."

Her preoccupation with men was grating, never more so than when I wanted to ignore their existence. "Tom is handsome," I agreed. "I never said he wasn't. But that doesn't mean I must take him to my bed."

Gwen pushed herself off the bench and stretched. There was something rankly sexual in the movement, and I remembered how much I disliked her. "Someone should, just to let the poor man know what a hot female body feels like beneath him."

The color drained from my face. Her words were, more or less, an explanation of what Agnes had done, stated plain enough for even me to understand. She knew Tom would tell me, hoped I would be jealous enough to value him, to react to his perceived unfaithfulness by loving him. Yet I had not, though I knew more than ever, this was what he wanted.

That Gwen, of all people, could reveal this was unsettling. Keeping my eyes shut tight, I tried to imagine Agnes's thoughts as she asked Tom to stay, but Gwen's voice intruded. I looked at her, seeing her afresh: the bright, knowing gaze, the ripe body.

I felt jealousy at the thought of Agnes with him, but hearing Gwen threaten to do the same was different. The thought of her in Tom's bed was not to be borne; if need be, I would remove her bodily.

"You've got ice in your veins," she said, capping a sentence I hadn't heard. "How old are you, with no love affairs?"

"I'm not like you. I'm a servant."

"Servants have to come from somewhere," she said, tossing her head. "They don't just appear when the king snaps his fingers. How many girls in the Music haven't had a lover?"

I thought. Frances was married and gone; Peg was engaged; Flora had fallen in love briefly last year; Mary was currently starry-eyed. Then there was Agnes. I concluded that, of the girls over fifteen, I was likely the only virgin. "I don't know. I don't spend my days thinking about it."

"Most women do. Not in front of the queen, you understand—it would upset her, especially these days." Referring to the queen's neglect was unkind, but Gwen felt the sting of the king's disfavor, for Queen Katherine's rare public appearances resulted in her ladies being kept close. "You may be a servant, but you put a higher price on your virtue than a princess."

The arrival of Mary and two others distracted her, and I breathed a sigh of relief. Quarreling with Gwen would do no good, and if she felt vengeful, she would set herself at Tom. She would not succeed, but I couldn't watch her attempts without wanting to snatch her bald.

I greeted my rescuers warmly, though Mary was still no friend, and the other two were almost unknown. Red-haired Cecily Clare was part of the king's sister's household; she and Mary had recently become friendly. The third girl, Joan Irwin, was only just come to court.

"We were discussing men," Gwen informed them with a bland smile. "Mary, surely you have something to say on the subject?"

"Anyone in particular?" Mary asked.

Gwen shrugged. "Name one."

Cecily laughed at that. Her two front teeth were crooked, but it did no harm to her looks. "Who would you choose if you had the choosing?"

"Cess!" Mary squealed. She looked over her shoulder before she answered. "Anyone, you mean?"

"Yes, who?"

Joan was listening, but she looked anxious. "This is nonsense," I said, hoping to spare both of us the embarrassment.

"Bess thinks men are nonsense. I don't, so I'll go first." Gwen clasped her hands together, smiling broadly. "Francis Bryan."

"Why? He's so dark," Mary objected.

"I like dark men."

She flushed. "Bryan is a libertine."

"But what a dancer," Gwen said as if that explained everything. "I've had that pleasure, though it's the only pleasure he's seen fit to give me. Grace in one act often means grace in all. And I think he looks positively wicked!"

I tried to get into the spirit of their game, fearing I would draw more attention to myself by remaining silent. The hall was almost empty; at least there were no witnesses to the conversation. I tried not to think how I would feel if Tom overheard such silliness.

"What about you, Cecily?" Mary asked, leaning against the window ledge. Her blue eyes were hard.

Cecily giggled, admitting she admired Edward Neville, so tall and fair and successful with women. She stared at her slippers while saying this and then turned abruptly on the new girl. "Joan, that leaves you, because we all know Mary is so smitten with her Jack, she would never look at another man." All dissolved into laughter at this, save Joan and me.

"I don't know anyone very well yet," she said, her voice soft. She looked embarrassed to the point of tears.

"You don't need to know a man to find him attractive," Gwen said. "Sometimes, it's better not to. Are you playing, Bess, or will you run away?"

I was surprised at the hostility I felt. "I admire the king."

"You always did give yourself airs," Mary said.

"I just see no point in dreaming about men who don't notice our existence." I suppressed the urge to bring my lute down on her head.

Gwen plucked at my sleeve. "You've never dreamed?" she asked. "I suppose Nick Hawkins means nothing?"

Taking a deep breath, I prayed for a calm I did not feel. "So I'm mortal after all," I said, trying for a light tone. "You've found me out. I've looked at Nicholas Hawkins."

"You're no better than we are," Mary said.

I let them taunt me, my relief at their dropping the subject so great, I would have allowed them to say almost anything. Let them think I stared at Nick as Gwen watched Francis Bryan, with a lust in her loins that had nothing to do with her heart.

Several days later, Joan sought me out. Curious, I had already made inquiries of Mistress Edith, who knew everything. Joan had an uncle in the royal household who'd found her a place as a fine seamstress. She spent much time with the queen's ladies but was not one of them. I hoped Gwen's coarseness had not bruised her ears.

"I wanted to thank you."

I was struggling to learn a new piece Tom had given me and was glad of the interruption. "Why?"

She smiled uncertainly. Her skin was freckled all over, even her chest, framed by the square neck of her plain, ash-colored gown. "You took their attention from me," she explained. "They're always at me like that."

"It embarrasses me too. Not everyone is like them."

Joan glanced at a nearby chair, asking my permission before sitting. She had a bit of embroidery in her hands that she worked on as we spoke. "You have a young man, don't you? Not the one they were teasing you about. A musician."

"That's Tom," I said. "We're friends. Everyone makes too much of it, Gwen especially."

"I thought you and she were friends."

"Not really." I looked down at the music I had been working on. It was unlike Tom's usual work and required difficult fingering. "Joan, I'll be flayed if I don't know this by tonight." She bolted from her seat, and I had to call after her, "Are you eating with anyone later?"

"No." Her fingers twisted the embroidery.

I remembered the loneliness of the newcomer. "Then we can sit together."

Our friendship was forged with all simplicity. I was able to be myself with Joan, whose contemplative nature reminded me of Agnes without making me sad. We exchanged confidences over the autumn days. Joan pined for a boy she'd been handfasted to in Yorkshire. Aside from embarrassment, that was why she hadn't joined in Gwen's game; her heart belonged to William, and like me, she could not make light of her feelings.

Christmas came, and with it, my ninth anniversary at court. The holiday was full of masques and disguisings, and the revels master kept us busy day and night.

December 28 was the grandest night of all. We performed many different tableaux and dances for the court, followed by the king leading the queen out. Although their marriage had cooled, they were united during this holiday season. I watched them dance and wondered how the king could be unfaithful to a woman who loved him deeply. She moved with deliberation, unaccustomed after all these years to the leaping English dances. Her eyes never left his face.

She retired soon after, but some of her ladies stayed on. I saw Gwen in a new primrose-colored gown. It made her look sallow, even with spots of rouge on both cheeks. She had publicly proclaimed Nick her new favorite, and her pursuit of him was clear. I disliked her all the more, but at least it would keep her from throwing herself at Tom.

I danced with Harry, then Gilbert. Tom and I eyed each other from across the hall, but he made no move, and I did not encourage him.

The players struck up a lively tune. I begged Gilbert to let me catch my breath. He led me to one side and took Flora by the hand, leaving me to watch the dancers.

I found Nick easily, standing with Neville and Bryan, a goblet in his hand. They were deep in conversation as I approached, and when I stumbled into Nick, it took him by surprise. He caught the cup before its contents showered over my gown and offered me his hand.

"Happy Christmas, Bess," he said, smiling broadly.

"Happy Christmas, sir," I returned, rearranging my skirts. "I'm very sorry about that."

"My fault entirely," he said, handing his cup to Neville. "A lovely young lady shouldn't be left without a partner. May I have the honor?"

"Yes, sir." Dazedly, I let him lead me out. I'd hoped for but a few words. I did not look at him, fearing my face would show too much.

"You're very quiet," he admonished, taking me through the intricate steps. His hand was warm on mine.

"I don't know what to say." It was the truth.

"You've been dancing all evening, and you've not run short of conversation 'ere now."

He had noticed me dancing. I blushed and missed a step. I hoped he was drunk enough not to notice.

"My fault," he said again. "Tell me, Bess, why do you look so pretty tonight?"

I turned smoothly in the figure and faced him. My nervousness made me bold. "Might I suggest you've had a lot to drink, sir?"

He shouted with laughter, drawing attention to us. I saw Gwen's face and shivered with delight. "You still look deucedly pretty."

"Thank you." The music ended, and I said without planning to, "Today is my birthday."

His dark eyes focused on me. "That's why you look different, then." Putting one hand on my shoulder, he raised my chin with the other. "May I kiss you for your birthday?"

136

Gwen was watching. Tom was watching. The king and the entire court might be watching, and I wouldn't care. "Yes, sir," I said.

Nick's mouth was warm, exerting a friendly pressure. After a moment, my lips parted. He tasted of hippocras. A warmth started deep in my belly and spread through my body. I knew nothing but the sensation of his mouth on mine; the music, the crowd, all ceased to exist. When he released me, I swayed.

He set me upright. "I'm not alone in indulging, I see." Raising my hand, he brushed his lips over it. "Happy birthday, Bess."

It was not wine that weakened my legs, but desire, flooding my veins, making me want to sway toward him, just to feel his hands again. But he moved off into the melee in search of his friends, and I was alone.

Nothing could improve the evening further, so I decided to retire. My body hummed as I made my way toward the stairs. Almost there, I walked into a wall. The wall wore a soft fustian doublet of Tudor green, brushed to feel like velvet. I looked up into Tom's face and just as quickly looked away.

"Can you walk?"

"Of course I can. I'm fine."

"You don't look it."

"I've just been told I look pretty."

Tom scowled. "Everyone saw, Bess."

"I don't care. It's Christmas. Everyone gets kissed at Christmas." I waved a hand toward the kissing ball in the arched doorway. Mary Carey was there with a man who was not her husband.

"Are you leaving?"

"I'm tired."

He took my arm. "I'll walk you up. There are a lot of men the worse for drink by now."

I ignored the implication that Nick had kissed me because he was drunk.

"Nine years ago, you took me on this same walk," I said. "How little has changed." I ran a hand over a tapestry as we passed, the dampness no longer a surprise.

"A lot has changed."

"I don't look like a gypsy anymore," I said and tugged at his arm to make him look at me. "But you still act superior."

"Nine years," he said with wonder. "Where shall we be in another nine years?"

That stopped me in my tracks. "I shall be old," I said. "Twenty-eight. And you shall be—"

"Older," he finished.

We reached the door to the girls' chamber. I paused, wanting to escape yet drawn by his wistful expression.

"Might we talk a moment, Bess?"

I looked inside. "No one's here yet. You'll be fine so long as Mistress Edith doesn't catch you."

Tom sat at the foot of the bed. I took a while to settle myself, mourning the days when words did not have the power to hurt. This was the first real conversation we'd had since London—since Agnes—and the air was heavy with things we could not say.

He spoke first. "I'm sorry for the pain I've caused you this year." He looked down at the shabby brown coverlet. "It was weak of me to tell you."

"You didn't cause any pain I didn't ask for." I covered his hand with mine. "Not knowing, I would have always imagined I might have been able to help her."

I rested my head against his chest and sighed as he pulled me close. We sat together in silence, but it was a comfortable silence now. His thoughts were still with Agnes; that was as clear to me as if they were my own.

"I'll never mention her again, Bess, if you'll but answer one question."

He had removed his sheltering arm. "What is it?" I asked, expecting him to ask about the baby.

"Can you forgive me?"

His voice, so uncertain, tore at my heart. "I was never angry with you," I said. "I was angry with myself."

"I thought you hated me."

I curled my fingers into his hair. "I can't hate you," I said. It would be like hating the air I breathed, but it would be ridiculous to say that. "I was afraid to speak, because I understood so well why you did it."

"That's quite a gift, understanding on that scale."

I leaned back against him. "You do it often enough, even when you don't approve of what I've done."

"True." There was a hint of a smile in his voice, and I relaxed, happy that things were right between us at last.

"How could she ask you?" I wondered aloud and cursed my stupidity as he tensed. "Don't answer. I'm sorry."

"She did it for you," he said, and the smile was gone from his voice. "Because she said I should know love, and you would never give it to me."

It was so much like what Gwen said that I froze. "Did she hate me so much?" My voice shook.

"No, sweet." Tom stroked my hair. "She knew you."

Agnes had taunted me for making light of Tom's feelings, but to bed him, knowing he would be unable to keep it from me offered no other explanation.

"I can hear you fretting."

Passing my hands over my face, I said, "Your heart is kinder than mine if you can find any meaning there besides hatred."

"She didn't hate you, Bess."

I tried to believe him. Perhaps someday, I would understand her intention, but I would not dwell on Agnes now. It was still Christmas, and it was my birthday. The court's merriment went on below, but the corridor outside was quiet. I felt the same peace fill my heart as I sat, circled by Tom's arms.

"Nine years," Tom said, his lips near my ear. "Has it been so long?"

I looked up into his face and saw what I was not meant to see. The tenderness in his eyes was unmistakable. To acknowledge it was dangerous; he could so easily be hurt by my response. "It doesn't seem that long, does it?" I said, hoping to set him reminiscing.

The arms around my shoulders were protective, comforting, and now, something more. He moved one hand slowly to the small of my back. With the other, he tipped my chin so our eyes met. His gaze prickled through me like lightning.

"Would it be rash to ask for my own Christmas kiss?" His hand was firm on my waist.

I murmured that there was no kissing ball.

"We can either go in search of one," Tom said, "or we can pretend."

It was a jealous whim brought on by my display with Nick. To refuse would cause hard feelings, and now that our silence was broken, I would not deliberately bring it upon us again. There was no harm in a kiss. We had, after all, kissed before, in France.

Tom leaned forward, and his lips brushed mine, tentative, almost diffident. His fingers sketched a line along my cheek, twining into my hair. He drew back for a moment, as if to speak, then changed his mind, and took my mouth again, not so carefully this time.

The touch of his lips brought back the sensation of Nick's kiss, yet they were totally different. This was Tom, I reminded myself as I felt the same warmth surge through me. This was Tom, not Nick.

I pressed my palm against his shoulder, meaning to push him away, but instead of releasing me, he pulled me tight against him. His mouth never left mine.

There were no barriers between us now. I felt his passion flow into me, dizzying. Exhilarating.

My arms wound around his neck. The muscles in his arms and shoulders were taut beneath the cloth, and an image, so plainly erotic as to make me blush, skittered through my mind. I caught myself before I moaned aloud.

Tom lowered me onto the bed. He stopped kissing me at last, but only to seek the skin below the silk neck-ribbon I still wore. When his hand cupped my breast through my gown, I made a small whimper of protest. Taking it as encouragement, he kissed me again.

"Tom, we can't!" I wrenched myself free. My heart was pounding.

"Why not?" His breathing was as ragged as my own.

"It's not right." It was ludicrous to say his caresses frightened me. I would have let Nick fondle me thus, and more, without objection.

Straightening his doublet, Tom eyed me coldly. "You'll not be kissed by many men if you wish for someone else in the midst."

"I don't want to be kissed by many men." I smoothed the covers, tidying the evidence of my near surrender.

"Just by one." He closed in on himself, becoming the smooth, self-contained servant the court saw every day. "I don't appreciate being used as his substitute."

I heard the sharp edge to his voice. I'd hurt him again. "I thought it was but a Christmas kiss. I didn't know…"

"You knew," he said. "I've made it plain enough." Opening the door, he looked back over his shoulder. "I hope he makes you happy. I'm sick of waiting my turn."

❧

Why hadn't I explained myself? Why had I let him believe I thought of Nick? It was far from the truth and part of the problem: when Tom kissed me, I hadn't thought of Nick at all.

I'd always considered Tom the perfect brother, but the man who left me was no brother. I still saw him in the torchlight: eyes, hair, skin, all golden. Could I ignore that because I was in love with Nick? I knew Tom as I knew myself: I knew his thoughts and feelings, especially his feelings for me. Their intensity was a shock, but I should not have been overwhelmed. Nick's kiss had clouded my brain.

Hours later, with Flora snoring beside me, I pondered the strange thing that had happened. I felt stripped, my privacy violated by the oneness we experienced, and the strength of both his desire and my response frightened me. It was like looking into a mirror and seeing his reflection there.

I had to tell him the truth. He could not be allowed to believe I had been repulsed, or that I'd thought of Nick. I'd caused him enough pain not to let such misconceptions continue.

He was not at the morning meal. Joan teased me about my eagerness to catch sight of a certain gentleman, and I did not contradict her. She had only witnessed half the evening's events, and I was not ready to speak of Tom.

The day was festive, but I was out of sorts. Time and again, I looked for him, but he was not among the musicians in the hall nor in any smaller chamber, nor was he in the practice rooms. I braved the cold and searched the stables, but there was no sign of him.

When darkness fell, I thought of Mistress Edith. Scarcely a day went by without Tom visiting her.

"Aye, I saw him at dawn." Despite the fact that she had been up for over twelve hours, the white kerchief that covered her hair was crisp, and her apron was unspotted. "He's gone off with the cardinal's party. They'll be back after the New Year."

"Why?" I had noted the absence of scarlet velvet but assumed the cardinal was closeted away, not gone and Tom with him.

"He didn't explain." Mistress Edith turned away and fussed with some dried leaves on her worktable. Their sharp scent filled the chamber. "He left something for you," she added in a queer tone. "It's on the shelf there."

I inspected the note. The seal was unbroken, but it showed signs of being bent. "Was it interesting?" I asked.

She shrugged. "He was upset, and you were the cause, by the look of it." Mistress Edith leaned against the table. "There are two things Tom won't discuss—his mother and you."

Guilt heavy upon my brow, I slunk off to read his note. There were people everywhere, and I ended my journey on the dark back stairs, my candle guttering in the draft from the river.

I hesitated to crack the seal. It was so important that we talk about this; how could a note manage to say what was in either of our hearts?

141

SONGBIRD

Bess,

My apologies for last night. You know my feelings. I now know yours. Regard my actions as those of a man who had taken too much wine.

Tom

Chapter 14

Spring always made King Henry restless. He gathered his favorites and rode out to hunt, or decided on a visit and appeared unannounced on a noble doorstep; whether the family considered themselves fortunate or unfortunate depended on their situation, as the king's visits were liable to cost a small fortune. I heard secondhand that Hever Castle was a frequent destination.

I knew little of the place, other than its location, some thirty miles from London. The Lady Anne had been exiled there for almost four years, her father's plan for an Irish marriage never having come to fruition.

Gossip speculated of a reunion with Mary Carey, who was absent from court, but in July, it was sister Anne who returned to court in a blaze of finery, with the king doting on her every word.

I watched as she shifted easily back into court life. She moved—and dressed—as if she knew every eye was upon her. Her gowns were always stylish, but now, the fabrics were richer, and a heavy jeweled collar hid the mark on her throat. Long, flowing sleeves concealed her hands, and the lace at her wrists was of the finest weave.

She looked much the same, but her eyes now held a watchful aspect. Exile had added to her allure in many ways, aged her beyond her years in others.

It was several weeks before we met face to face, though I saw her watching me when I performed. I was not eager to speak to her; Anne Boleyn marked a passage in my life at court of which I was none too proud. Nonetheless, I was curious.

～～～～

The king and his gentlemen were shooting at targets, and most of the court clustered around the butts. I had wandered away from practice, drawn by the sounds of shouting and applause from over the hill, and saw her walking toward the palace, trailed by a few of her women.

She stopped short, looking hard at me. "It's you," she said, and I wondered how I'd forgotten her voice, hypnotic as those black eyes. "You're still here."

"It is good to see you back, Lady Anne." I sketched a curtsy.

Anne smiled at me, her old smile. "I feel damnably foolish, but I cannot remember your name."

"Bess. Bess Llewelyn." Why did her forgetfulness prick at me? There would be much on her mind: a climbing brother, a sister rumored to be pregnant, her own unquestionable involvement with the king. But her downfall, and my part in it, had not been forgotten. I tried to cover my hurt.

She laughed. "Of course. Forgive me. I tried to forget as much as possible."

Had she forgotten poor Harry Percy? I wondered. Percy had married the woman of his father's choosing but refused to share a house with her. He looked ever more gaunt and drawn at each of his infrequent appearances. By all accounts, he never forgot Anne.

"I'm pleased you're still at court," she continued, her tone cautious but friendly. "I did worry once I'd gotten over my own upset. There was nothing I could have done, packed away at Hever. I'm glad no harm came to you."

"There was no great demand for my voice for several months," I said, "but they did not send me away."

"It was thoughtless of me. I never believed we would be found out or such a fuss made." Her bottomless eyes turned stormy. "Four years! Thank God for Tom Wyatt, else I would have gone mad from boredom."

Kent was pretty country, and Thomas Wyatt, an attractive young man with a tongue full of pretty speeches. I knew many who would not object to four years of such punishment. "But you're back at court now, my lady." I heard a shout, turned. A crowd approached, the king glittering at its head. "His Majesty comes."

The petulance drained from her face. She looked in his direction, and her scattered graces drew themselves around her. The Anne who lifted her skirts to fly to the king's side was not the Anne of a moment before, and I marveled at her abrupt transformation.

"I am back, Bess," she said, her eyes on him. "And this time, I intend to stay."

"Nan!" King Henry bellowed, and she ran toward him, tucking her arm through his. In matters of the heart, the king was transparent as a babe, and his adoration was writ plain. Lady Anne's expression rivaled his, but I fancied I saw something else behind the façade of esteem, a momentary flash of her old disdain, quickly hidden.

Why come ye not to court?—
To which court?
To the king's court,
Or to Hampton Court?

Nay, to the king's court:
The king's court
Should have the excellence;
But Hampton Court
Hath the preeminence.[3]

The poet Skelton was moved by his dislike of Wolsey to pen those lines, avidly repeated by the cardinal's detractors. His feasts and functions had long rivaled, and on occasion surpassed, the king's, and now, not content with York Place, he had built a palace of his own on the Thames.

Hampton Court was perhaps the greatest of all the cardinal's works. Built in the new Italian fashion, his new residence was fit for a king, and in 1525, Wolsey presented the sprawling red-brick palace and its pleasure gardens, tennis courts, and hunting parks to his clearly expectant master.

Immense as it was, the king, with his love of building, found ways to enlarge and improve Hampton. A tiltyard was added and the tennis courts improved. Extra men were assigned to the herb garden to care for the medicinal plants that fascinated him, and work was begun on a great hall that would take years to complete.

The cardinal, reluctant to pull up stakes, lived there and entertained for the king and ran the place and its five hundred servants with admirable style. The king had a new house that suited him, and the court, one more place to pack up and journey to at a moment's notice.

Greenwich was still my favorite, I decided as I wandered the gardens at Hampton Court in the afternoon sun. It was my first real home, and Hampton, for all its thousand-roomed splendor, could not touch its place in my heart. I did love the gardens: the roses were in full and glorious bloom, their nodding pink and white and red heads large as my hand, the epitome of the gardeners' art.

I heard footsteps behind me, several men by the sound of it, and ducked behind a hedge to let them pass. They did, moving at a leisurely pace, and I peeped from behind the screen of hawthorn. I recognized two as Wolsey's secretaries, and the third, bringing up the rear, was none other than Robin Lewis.

I was shocked at the sight of my old friend, walking so casually in the king's gardens while I hid in the shrubbery. As I stepped clear of my hiding place, I wondered what business brought him back. The Music had last heard from him two years prior, in a letter where he mentioned an appointment and an upcoming trip across the Channel. Since we'd heard nothing more, I envisioned Robin in France or Flanders or even Italy—the boundary of my imagination—but never in England.

My walk brought me out at the far end of the palace, where the servants hurried in and out of doors, their arms full of provisions or laundry or the trappings of the cardinal's mules. Here were the bakehouses and the wafery, the laundry, the scullery, and the great kitchens where the cooks reigned. I ducked through an open door and skimmed through the kitchens.

Chambers opened one off another, and soon, I came to the area set aside for the minstrels. I burst in, surprising Harry and Tom, who were huddled in a corner, arguing quietly over a new piece of music spread in front of them. Tom had begun composing for instruments other than the lute, but his true talent seemed to lie in the poetry of his lyrics. Harry would sometimes assist him with the arrangement of the music, but no one ever touched his words.

"Bess," they said in unison. Their heads, dark and fair, lowered again over the music. It consumed all their attention, and I soon turned to my own work, though I would have listened to their song all day. Indeed, they seemed prepared to play it that long, or until they resolved their dispute. Even when they ceased, the song still sang in my head, a slow, plaintive ballad of love that would suit the king's present state of mind.

> *My heart she hath, and ever shall,*
> *Till by death parted we be;*
> *Happen what will hap, fall what shall,*
> *Shall no man know her name for me.*[4]

When Joan was able, she joined us, her fingers always busy with some bit of needlework. I saw her expression when Tom's love songs were performed; I did not need to be told that her thoughts turned to her William, still in Yorkshire, still in her heart.

"His songs are lovely," she said, her brown eyes damp.

"But they're so sad," I said. "Always pining for his lady who loves another. I wish he would write something gay."

Joan stabbed her needle through the cloth to keep it and looked up at me. "Perhaps when his lady confesses her love, he will write gay songs. I believe Tom writes what he feels and cannot pen a happy song if happiness is not there for him to draw upon."

"Nonsense," I said too sharply. "Tom's as happy as any of us."

Joan smiled wistfully. "William once watched me as Tom watches you; I simply learned to see it."

Agnes had called me blind where Tom was concerned. It disconcerted me to hear the same words from Joan. "Not you, too," I pleaded. "Can't we be friends without everyone thinking we're lovers?"

"I know you're not lovers; that much is obvious." Joan clapped as Tom and Harry took their bows. "Tom will settle for your friendship, but he wants more."

I had never told Joan what happened at Christmas. She wouldn't understand my violent reaction, and I doubted my capacity to explain. In truth, I tried not to think on that night and the feelings left unresolved.

A commotion at the far end of the chamber made us look up, and I saw a knot of people at the door. It was with mixed feelings that I saw Robin for the second time that day.

No one would yet call him handsome, but the arrangement of his features had become more pleasing with age. He was still thin and clad in a plain, fashionably cut doublet; his angularity was even more noticeable. Former chorister perhaps, but he looked every inch the educated young man paying a visit to his past comrades.

"Bess!" he called, hailing me from across the chamber.

I'd hoped for a few seconds to compose myself, but it was not to be.

"Come here, let me see you."

I rose from my seat and went to greet him. He ignored my outstretched hands and embraced me before everyone, planting a smacking kiss on my cheek and declaring loudly how I'd grown.

"Well, I should hope so!" I said. "You've grown a bit yourself, or else you've found a better tailor."

He laughed. I looked around at the smiling faces and recalled his unpopularity. Now, it was as if he'd never left us. I remembered myself and introduced my friend.

"Joan Irwin, may I present Robin Lewis, a former member of the Chapel Royal who has gone on to greater things." I stood back as she curtsied prettily and gave him her hand. "Robin was one of our most beloved choristers."

My words meant nothing to her, but I looked at Robin and saw he took my meaning. The mask of the young gentleman extended only so far; the choirboy was still there. He chatted politely with Joan, but I felt him watching me even as I crossed back to my seat.

"Give him a song, Bess," someone called.

"Come, Bess, do!" This from Flora, who again favored me over Gwen and Mary because of a recent instance of Gwen's flirting with a young man she admired.

The color rose in my face. Now, Robin was watching me as voices joined in from all over the room.

Tom stepped forward. "What shall it be, Bess? They'll plague you until you give in."

"Play what you will."

The opening chords were familiar—an old song written by the king, a safe song, not about love, but a young man's paean to youth and its lack of care and responsibility.

> *Youth must have some dalliance*
> *Of good or ill some pastance;*
> *Company methinks then best*
> *All thought and fancies to digest.*
>
> *For idleness*
> *Is chief mistress*
> *Of vices all;*
> *Then who can say*
> *But mirth and play*
> *Is best of all?[5]*

It was a short song, and I finished and stepped out of the center. "Who is next? Robin, would you give us a song?"

He shook his head. "I regret I cannot."

The rest seemed content to let him go, but I pressed him. "Did Oxford educate the music from your blood?"

"Yes." He turned away, spoke quietly to Tom, then made his farewells. Taking my hand, he said, "I'm certain we'll see each other again, Bess. The court is often at Hampton these days, I understand."

"It is. Will you be here?"

"I'm part of the cardinal's household."

"Choirmaster?"

"Undersecretary." Robin raised my hand to his lips. "Your voice is as pure as ever, Bess. Even in Venice, I never heard your match." He bowed stiffly and left us.

"He seems very nice," Joan said. "Why did he look so queer when you mentioned his popularity?"

"Because he wasn't," Flora said, arranging her skirts to sit among us. "None of us liked him."

"He sounded just like Bess," Harry told her. "They had a competition once. She won."

"She would win again," Tom said, interposing soberly. "He told me he was taken ill when he was in Padua. For a while, the physicians were afraid he would be unable to speak at all."

I felt a prickle of shame. All that glory, stifled! To have been possessed of such a voice and once again to lose it: Tom's nightmare revisited, except Tom could still sing, though not as he had nor as he wished.

But secretary to a cardinal was no small thing. I considered Robin's journey, orphan to chorister, student to secretary, and it seemed appropriate that he should be a companion to one who had gone from a butcher's shambles in Suffolk to a red hat from Rome.

The court remained at Hampton for several more days. Before we left, I spoke with Robin again. We met by chance early in the morning, and he asked me if I had free time that day.

"We're readying to return to Greenwich tomorrow, but I've not much to do." I had planned to spend some time with Joan, but I was intrigued by this new Robin.

"Good. Meet me in the gardens at midday." He touched his feathered flat cap, anxious to be off on the cardinal's business.

I caught his sleeve. "Where in the gardens?"

"Along the wall, where you were hiding the other day."

By noon, I had encountered Nick in the king's outer chamber and been the beneficiary of a smile and a greeting. Robin was late, and I waited among the flowers with equanimity, still buzzing with pleasure.

After greeting him, I apologized for insisting he sing. "Tom told me later of your illness, but I feel a fool for not noticing the difference even in your speaking voice. It never occurred to me—"

"If anyone else had done it, I would have opened my mouth and bleated like a damned sheep, but you did not deserve that."

"Can we walk?" The sun was high, but there was little warmth in it. "I am sorry about your voice."

"Music is for dreamers," he said. "The cardinal deals in realities, and so must I." He pulled a red rose from the wall, plucked absently at its fading petals. "It's a comfort, if you can believe it. To be more than a voice. It's different for you. You love it so, and you don't have a man's options. Losing my voice is seeing that door closed, finally. It's a constant reminder to do my best in the cardinal's service."

"Do you like it, being a part of his household again? It must be very different than when you were a boy."

"It is and not just because of the change in my position, but the cardinal himself. He's grown larger, more important." His words described Wolsey's person as well as his household. Robin's inordinate luck secured him a patron only slightly lower than the king and more feared.

"You've done well."

"As have you. Do not forget, I've heard you sing these two days past. You have improved beyond all hope. Your voice is as clear as when we were children."

"Tom says so too." I don't know what made me bring his name into the conversation, but once said, I waited for Robin's reaction, certain he'd heard the practice room gossip.

"Born with one soul between you," he said. "He doesn't sing, and you probably still can't play the lute."

Robin's words were chilling; I soon found an excuse to leave him and spent the rest of the day with Joan, mindlessly plying a needle.

Nick remained in the fore of my thoughts, despite my confused feelings for Tom, or perhaps because of them. I did not question my obsession; I knew only that his eyes made me warm all over, and his touch made me quiver. He was a simple fact of my life, like Tom or Joan or Mistress Edith.

He was there, watching, as I performed for the court. The queen was conspicuously absent, Anne Boleyn just as conspicuously present. My song was new, fresh that day from Tom's fevered pen, and we had been warned by the revels master not to sing it because of its references to a bewitching black-haired lady and her besotted lover. Tom was obstinate, insisting that we perform the song. I supposed he wanted his disapproval of Anne out in the open, though cloaked in music. It was a mockery of the lover more than the beloved, and the king could find much in the lyric to anger him if he but listened—as the rest of the court listened and held its breath.

I saw muted glee on nearby faces and sensed behind their manners and poses, they would have liked to laugh and shout aloud as we all had when Tom first read out the words. I prayed Anne Boleyn did not see the ripple of amusement at the reference to "darkest beauty, hardest heart." She had many supporters at court who sensed the direction of the wind, but few real friends.

Stubbornly, I still liked her, and yet I sang Tom's song because it was good and it was true and because he wanted it sung. It didn't stop me from being concerned.

The silence was tangible and immense when we finished. The last note was clumsy; Tom was scared too. From beneath my lashes, I sought the king's face, fearing his frown, dreading his wrath.

He rose to his feet slowly, his gold robes glittering. A finger pointed at me, and I quaked in my slippers. "That lass," he pronounced in a leisurely tone, "has the very angels in her throat. I have always said so."

My knees went weak. I felt Tom's hand in the small of my back, steadying. I curtsied deeply to the king, to the court, and made my exit with their applause still ringing in my ears.

"Did you hear them?" I asked Tom, jubilant. "Did you hear?"

His face was white. "It was madness, Bess; he might have thrown us in the Tower."

"But he did not." My smile stretched wider.

He shook his head and turned away.

Instead of following, I ducked through an open door. I was so full of joy at that moment, I couldn't bear to be inside. The lawn and the gardens, the nearby river, all beckoned.

In daylight, the trees would be heavy and golden, but now they were naught, but dark shapes in the moonlit night. Into this colorless world, I ran headlong, filling my lungs with crisp autumn air, feeling the damp grass against my ankles. I hurtled across the lawn, away from the river, where other solitary wanderers would naturally gravitate, spinning myself in circles until I was dizzy, then collapsing on the grass.

It felt so good to be alive and in the king's favor! I laughed aloud.

"May I congratulate you on a song well sung?"

The voice came from the tree line behind me. Scrambling to my feet, I looked around. "Where are you?"

"Where the barbs of your tongue cannot touch me." There was a rustle, and Nick appeared on the path, grand even in the dark. "You are fortunate His Majesty is indeed bewitched."

I dropped a curtsy. Grasping my shoulders, he raised me up and did not let go immediately. Nick twisted a lock of my hair around his finger, touching my neck. "I followed you," he said.

My face flushed, and I was glad it was too dark for him to see me. "Why would you do that, sir?" Dearest, sweetest God, I thought I knew why.

"Must you call me sir, Bess?" he questioned. "Must you always curtsy?"

I raised my eyes. "I am, after all, a servant," I said with some spirit. "What would you have me say or do?"

"I would have you call me Nick," he said softly and led me from the path. "And I would have you kiss me."

I stood still, my astonishment so great, I could manage nothing else, and waited. He took my hands gently, kissed each palm, and placed them against his chest. One of his hands went around my waist. The other was in my hair, then on my throat. His fingers were cool, confident.

"Say it, Bess," he coaxed, sliding those assured fingers around the square neck of my bodice where my breasts were pushed up by my stays. I was certain he could hear my heart. He pushed my gown to one side, pressed his lips to the hollow of my shoulder.

"How can I say anything if you do that?" I tugged my dress back.

He retreated, confounded. "May I assume it is to your liking?" The words were muffled; he had moved behind me. His breath was hot on my neck. It made me weak, and I would die rather than have him stop, but I would not make this easy.

"Aye, I like it fine," I said. "It's just difficult to carry on a conversation, and you seem to desire that. Sir."

Nick groaned, and for a moment, his grip was uncomfortably hard. "I don't desire that, Bess, not at all. Let me tell you what I desire." He drew me close again, one hand cupping my face as he whispered words that made me yearn to give in without a fight.

But he seemed to want the fight. He set out to convince me with a shower of small caresses that set me to trembling all over. Each time he heard my breath catch, he moved to another spot, until it seemed that my whole body was afire with him.

I was overwhelmed by my feelings and his obvious skill. Many times I'd heard women talk about passion, but they never mentioned such burning. He'd not even undressed me, and I felt quenched, fulfilled. What more could there be than this?

Abruptly, he stopped touching me, and it was like a death. "Wait," he said. Leading me by the hand through the maze of shrubs and flowers, we arrived at the silence of the tiltyard, the open space lit only by the moon. "A secluded bower for my lady," he said, throwing off his short cloak and smoothing it on the grass. "May I offer you a seat?"

I lowered myself onto the cloak, trying not to crush the velvet. "How different it is at night."

"You've seen the tourneys, then?" he asked, kneeling on the edge so there was some distance between us.

"When I am able," I said. "I've seen you ride many times, sir."

He took my hand and kissed each fingertip, honoring my palm with a caress that scorched my flesh. His mouth trailed along my wrist. "I've been told I'm a skillful rider."

Nick's lips found my shoulder again, bared it, made a blazing trail to my breast. He fumbled with my laces, never turning his face from his task. I allowed him to lower me full length to the ground. "That's encouraging to hear," I gasped out, "for I've only but watched."

He caught my meaning. "Never a participant?" he murmured, raising me up and parting my bodice so I was bare to the waist. His hands, warm in the cool October air, cupped my breasts.

"No." The word was short, clipped. He had taken my nipple between his fingers and was rubbing it in a way that made my belly fill with warm desire. "Nick."

Dragging my skirts off, he folded them with care and tossed them away from us. He eased my shift over my head and regarded my body in the moonlight. "You'll soon learn the parry and the thrust," he said. His hands ran lightly over my quivering belly, parted my thighs with assurance. "And you'll feel the sting of the lance but once."

⌒〜〜⌒

It was to Joan that I went the next morning, fresh from sleep, my mind full of Nick, the scent of his skin still on my fingers. Dear, level-headed friend, she was not shocked; knowing the ways of the court and the heart, and she embraced me when I told her.

"Do be careful, Bess," she said at last. "I know you love him, but guard your heart well."

"I'll be fine," I said. Nick's ardor made me confident, and I decided I would enjoy this interlude while it lasted and not think beyond our next meeting. "I know his place and mine. My hopes never rose this high. I will not ask for what he cannot give."

"Good." She squeezed me and kissed my cheek. "I must go, dearest. Remember, you have a practice this morning. Do not spend the day in dreaming."

After love, Nick had raised me from the ground and helped me to dress. His hands were sure then, and he laced me quickly. I wondered how many women he had assisted in this manner. I was glad of the dark, for my face reddened again, not at the memory of our passion, but at his matter-of-fact intimacy as he straightened my gown and attempted to tidy my hair. I caught his hands.

"There's no use of that," I said. "It doesn't tame easily."

He touched my cheek with a finger, ran it lightly to my chin. "Neither do you, but it was well worth the effort."

I felt a twinge at his lighthearted words. "I'm not a slut, you know."

He wrapped his cloak around my shoulders. "I know what you are, Bess. I don't take such a gift lightly."

I ducked my head. "I was afraid you would think...because of the way I gave in..." Being close to him made me alarmingly aware of his scent, the texture of his skin beneath his fine clothes. I would not be able to think clearly until I was away from him.

"You gave in gracefully," Nick said, "when you consider I nearly dragged you off the path. I've wanted you ever since that damned drunken Christmas kiss."

Chapter 15

Now the queen was banished, and the Lady Anne all but ruled in her place. The court was gay, the king happy. Some, loyal to the queen, disparaged his happiness, but I did not. My mind was always full of Nick, his latest word, a chance meeting in a corridor, a discreet touching of hands on the dance floor. How could I fault the king for feelings I understood?

Nick's lodgings were in a busy area, so he arranged a small chamber where we could be together. I lived for our infrequent encounters, as much to talk with him as for the fevered straining of our bodies.

We spoke as equals, which surprised me. It took time to learn to speak freely, and still I told him little of my life before court, knowing he would not comprehend. I spoke of myself and my friends, of my love of music, and listened as he told me of his childhood home, his upbringing at another great house, his travels to France and Italy. He spoke often of the king; he held him in great affection and favored the Lady Anne.

"He'll never have sons by the queen," he said with certainty. "She's far too old, and all her children were born dead, except the New Year's boy."

I sat up, pulled the coverlet over myself. "And the Princess Mary." The girl, now ten, was nearly forgotten in the furor of her father's pursuit of a male heir.

Nick shrugged. "A girl child." Winding my hair around his fist, he drew my face toward him. "Girl children have their places," he murmured, pushing aside the covers, "but the throne is not one of them."

"Why not?" I grasped his questing hand. "She seems a likely child."

"More Spanish than English," he grunted and pinned my wrists with his hands. He dropped kisses on my neck and shoulders, drawing his tongue around the curve of my breast. I arched toward him—surrender. He loosed my hands then, and I plunged them into his hair, bringing his mouth to mine.

The candle guttered when we were at last sated, and we continued our conversation as though passion hadn't intervened and left us shaking and breathless.

I lay in his arms, marveling I was so comfortable with a man who I'd scarcely spoken to a month before. He was completely at ease. How often had he used this little chamber before, and with whom? It did not seem to matter. "He'll have strong sons by Anne Boleyn," I said, continuing our earlier conversation. The curling dark hair beneath my cheek was soft and left me with a desire to run my fingers through it again.

"Are you so certain of the divorce?" He brought me closer. "Even Wolsey has doubts."

"Cardinal Wolsey doubts only Anne Boleyn," I said, and Nick's chest heaved with laughter. "He's never forgiven her for Henry Percy."

"You know of that?" He sounded surprised.

"Aye." Telling him of my small part in the Lady Anne's tragedy brought it back with such clarity that I ached for the young woman who blithely accepted the caresses of her king. I thought of being cuddled and caressed by a man I did not love, after knowing this pleasure with Nick, and I shivered.

Nick felt the spasm, leaned over to find the blanket we had kicked aside. "Cold?"

I shook my head. "Uneasy, of a sudden. I should go back to my chamber. It won't do to be missed."

Once again, he helped me to dress, easier since I'd come from my bed and needed only my shift and wrapper and my hair bundled into a braid. He opened the door and kissed me farewell before I crept away, the stone floor cold on my bare feet. I crawled into bed minutes later and slept, with no portent of the trouble to follow.

Something was amiss at breakfast. I sat down, and there were a few snickers, but I was too tired to interpret their meaning and ate my meal quickly before escaping to the practice rooms.

A few of the male minstrels were there, and when I entered, they fell silent, the small chirps and squeaks of their tuning the only sounds in the room. Their eyes were bright, and in the gaze of two of the eldest, I saw a new appreciation. They were looking at me as if I were female and not just one of them.

My face burned as the truth dawned. Somehow, they knew, all of them, about Nick.

"You're staring," I said, scarlet to the roots of my hair.

"Because you look so pretty today, Bess," Ned remarked, putting aside his rebec and favoring me with a sweeping bow.

"Nonsense." I crossed the room and searched out my new piece of music. I had plucked the first few notes when a new thought slammed into my brain with the force of a knight on the tilting ground.

If they knew, then Tom knew.

The lute fell from my hands. I heard the brittle cracking of the wood from what seemed a great distance.

Did I think he would never find out, never see us together or, as was his way, simply sense it? I don't know what I thought, but I was frantic about his reaction. Was he hurt or angry—and who had told him?

He knew, and I knew that he knew. I should speak first and clear the air, but the more I thought about it, the more tangled my feelings became, and the more I dreaded seeing him. I skipped practice; I was late for meals; I steered clear of the hall, the courtyard, and especially the stables, anywhere he would take refuge. I grew more and more ill at ease.

No one confessed to spreading the rumor of my liaison; no one had to. When I calmed down, I knew well enough who had done it. Seen in the hall, Gwen looked smug as a cream-fed cat. My first reaction was to claw her eyes out, but reason intervened. She expected that; instead, I would somehow wear a brave face and ruin her enjoyment.

To make matters worse, Mistress Edith woke me early one morning. I had only been in my own bed for an hour, my distress over Tom no bar to spending the night in Nick's bed. I did not want to get up. She was adamant.

She yanked my laces until she forced the breath out of me and then dragged me down the hall to her workroom. "Mistress Edith, what is the matter?"

"Are you so in love that you've forgotten Agnes?"

My cheeks flamed.

"Well?"

"I haven't forgotten." I had given thought to the matter but hadn't wanted to ask Mistress Edith how to prevent a child. Until I became like Agnes, I realized, and hung my head.

She slammed her hands on the table. "Then why have you not come to me, you foolish girl? I can fix things after, as well you know, but it would be easier if you never got with child to begin with." She started taking jars from the shelves. "It's not foolproof, of course—the only foolproof method is leaving him in his breeches—but it's better than taking your chances. And if you miss a course, you come see me."

"Yes, Mistress." I stared at the floor. She doted on Tom and on me, except when I caused him upset. If he had not confided in her, he had at least let his hurt be seen.

When I saw Tom later that morning, it was by chance, and all the preparation in the world would not have helped me.

"You sounded well last night." His voice echoed in the empty practice room.

"You were there? I did not see you." His absence had given me more time to marshal my wits.

"I was." He sorted through some music on the rack beside me, humming softly.

His presence disturbed me. I moved to the window seat, nursed the lute on my lap. Whether it was the tuning or my emotions, not one true note came from the instrument.

Ignoring my efforts, Tom said, "Gil is working on a song, did you know? He wants you to sing it when he's through."

I made another discordant sound and cringed at my own clumsiness. "Am I the only voice in the Music?"

He made no response, and I looked up to find him watching me. When I saw his expression, I knew what he felt: a loneliness beyond words. He spoke, and without listening, I knew he told me of Gilbert's song, how it was suited to my voice. I heard only what was unsaid.

There was a dull ache behind my eyes. He knew and said nothing. I suppose he thought I was beyond hearing reproaches, but at that moment, the pain I felt erased every bit of pleasure Nick had given me. I stared out the window, holding fast to the lute.

"No wonder it sounds like a scalded cat," he said. "Look at how you're holding it. No weight taken by your left hand, Bess. Like this." After a moment, I felt one of his hands cover mine. I looked down. Square, brown, and capable, the fingers callused—that rough hand, unlike Nick's softer one, was capable of comforting me.

Autumn passed into winter. Soon, Christmas was upon us. It was difficult to remember the rush of rehearsals in the actual glory of the holidays. It was the gayest Christmas I knew, filled with gifts and love.

I employed my rusty sewing skills and, with Joan's help, made a gift for Tom, who shouted with laughter when he opened the package containing his own pilfered flax-blue doublet, carefully worked with roses and leaves in gold, red, and green. The embroidery was somewhat rough, but he exclaimed over it as though done by one of the king's needlewomen. Joan's present was not handmade, because I could never match her skill, but

I spent a morning in the London shops, painstakingly choosing French embroidery silks, knowing she would do wonders with them.

The choosing of a gift for Nick troubled me. There was no opportunity to take something from his wardrobe, and in any event, his clothing needed no embellishment. It was important that his gift be worthy. It puzzled me until, on my day in London, I saw a length of golden brown velvet in the same shop where I'd once bought the cloth for my own gown. It was beyond my meager funds, and the shopkeeper ceased haggling and crossed his arms, waiting for me to decide. I stroked the velvet. Under my fingers, it felt like Nick's flesh, and I grew warm in my clothes.

The shopkeeper grabbed my hand. "I'll take that to make up the difference," he said, plucking at the gold ring I wore.

"No."

He folded the velvet and put it back on the shelf. "We've cheaper goods."

I looked at his goods, and they were just that: cheap. It would embarrass me to give Nick any of it. I looked from the cheap cloth, which was not the right color, to the expensive cloth I wanted. My fists clenched, and I felt the ring cut into my skin. It had not left my finger since the day I'd found it under my pillow. Rashly, I tugged it off, hearing the tiny regretful clink as it dropped onto the counter.

"Take it. I'll have the velvet." I watched as the ring disappeared into the shopkeeper's sleeve, and my lover's gift was wrapped. I tried to tell myself Agnes would understand, but I felt a pang as her keepsake disappeared in exchange for a bit of cloth.

I worked his crest in gold thread, with love, but with no more skill than with Tom's roses. I hoped Nick would not notice my faulty stitches, and my reservations disappeared when he viewed the cloth and hugged me to him. "It's lovely, Bess," he said, kissing me soundly on the mouth. "I'll have it made up at once."

"I thought to attempt it, but..." Having arrived ahead of me, Nick lounged on the bed wearing nothing but linen shirt and dark hose. I ran my fingertips along the line of his shoulder, slipping my hand inside the neck of his shirt.

Making a sound of pleasure at my caress, he sat me on his lap and proceeded to nibble at my neck. "You've done enough. You're a singer, not a seamstress. You needn't have bought anything at all, love, you could have sung for me."

"I sing all the time. You must be sick of the sound of my voice."

"Never," he said, reaching up under my hair and beginning to fumble with my laces. "Especially when you sing airs by that fair-haired lutenist."

"Tom." Even saying his name in Nick's presence felt wrong, and I stiffened as he pushed the gown off my shoulders.

"I have something for you, Bess, lest you think I've forgotten." He reached across me into his doublet, a stunning black and gold affair, pearl-trimmed, and handed me a packet no larger than the palm of my hand.

I opened it eagerly and steadied myself against his shoulder when the cloth wrapping fell away and revealed a ring. Not Agnes's ring, as my contrite imagination first assumed, but a narrow gold band, set with a red stone.

"Put it on," Nick urged, taking my hand and doing it for me. It slipped easily onto the first finger of my left hand and I stared at it. "It's a ruby," he said. "For your birthday."

"It's beautiful!" I threw my arms around his neck. Through my heavy skirts, I felt the stir of his response and the answering surge of longing in myself. "We can't." I tried to quiet my breathing. "The festivities are still going on; we'll be missed." Casting a glance at the barred door, I let him kiss me, his mouth making heat flow to my loins.

His hand was inside my bodice when I gently pushed him back. In a moment, I was on the bed, and he was kneeling between my legs. "It doesn't have to take the whole night," he said, pushing my skirts up around my waist.

Combing the tangles out of my hair with my fingers, I watched as he gathered his clothes. He dressed with painstaking care, smoothing the luxurious fabrics and making sure all his lacings were perfect. His face was smooth now. "I told you," he said, carefully pulling his shirt through the slashes in his doublet. "No one will have missed us."

At the first opportunity, I showed his gift to Joan, and she glowed with happiness for me. I wished, not for the first time, that someone would take her mind from faraway William.

"It does mean he loves you," she said, turning the ring so the stone caught the light and gleamed like a drop of blood. "No man gives such a ring who is not in love."

I folded my hands, holding it to my breast. I hoped she was right.

Joan was as restrained as Agnes in her displays of affection, but she embraced me then. "You are lucky, Bess," she said. "Nick must love you, and Tom..." Her voice trailed away, and I thought of Tom's face when he gave me his gift, a small roll of cream-colored lace, delicate as cobwebs.

It was not an impressive gift when compared with gold and jewels, but I knew his offering cost him more than the ring had cost Nick. I would save it until I had a garment worthy of it. Nick's gift was a gesture but not an expensive one. He ornamented himself like a peacock, and I was certain his New Year's gifts to the king, queen, and Anne Boleyn would be lavish.

In February, Nick received a summons from his steward and traveled to his estate in the North. Between his duties and the harsh weather, it would be a journey of some weeks, and I envisioned the time without him as desolate as the Yorkshire moors he would cross.

He mentioned the visit casually, as if I would not mind his absence. I knew not to press my feelings upon him and kissed him lightly, saying I would miss him. I hoped my desolation did not show on my face.

Nick stretched, muscles flickering beneath the dark pelt on his chest. I sat back on my heels and admired him. He liked to be looked at; he knew he cut a fine figure and was as comfortable in his skin as he was in his outrageous court garb. The candle cast harsh shadows, making his expression seem forbidding. Had I imposed too much by saying I would miss him? Fearing some unconscious offense, I made bold to ask what bothered him.

To my relief, it was but a grasping neighbor, having been caught once again changing the boundaries on his property. "He will be brought to law at the next assizes for laying hands on what is mine," Nick said. "He will learn."

He reached for me, a slow smile breaking across his face. "Come here, Bess. It will be like a Lenten fast without you."

The days without him were long, but I filled them with music, practicing for hours and resuming my long-abandoned lessons on the virginals. I detested playing them as much as ever, but I kept up this time for lack of anything better to do.

My nights were not as easily filled. I remained in my own bed, aching with loneliness. Jealousy prickled like a hair shirt. Surely, there were women at Hawkmoor, and just as surely, they would fall in love with him, or at least into his bed. He had told me he was neither saint nor celibate, and I took his remark as a warning I should not expect fidelity when he left my side. I smiled and bit my cheek until it bled, agreeing that such a man could not be expected to forego women, but inwardly, I seethed.

She would be everything I was not: fair, petite, wealthy, a graceful dancer. Most painful, she would be skilled in the arts of the bedchamber. I was accommodating, acquiesced to his every whim and suggestion, but a novice would not know the tricks of her elders. I was tormented by visions of Nick with a flaxen-haired girl with large breasts, round hips, and an accomplished mouth. These dreams left me shaking.

I performed several times for Anne Boleyn and her ladies. The women murmured among themselves, but Anne, as much a lover of music as the king, scolded them into silence. She was skilled on the lute, and once, I accompanied her while she played for them, but she played in open court only at the king's request.

Confined by the weather, there was nothing better to do than gossip about the divorce. King Henry, confident, wore a perpetual smile that contrasted with Cardinal Wolsey's anxious creases, and Lady Anne hovered somewhere in between, quiet for days, then breaking out with her unnerving laugh. She seemed to have shed her past like a castoff gown, content with her glittering present and hints of an even more spectacular future.

The king intruded frequently on our musicales, sitting at Anne's feet with his head in her lap, one hand, often as not, trying to slide beneath her skirt. Watching him fondle her made me think again of Nick and his bold hands. Anne pushed him away, but he was stubborn, and once she cried out, "Hal!" when I was in the middle of a song, causing the king to storm out.

Rumor was rampant, but I did not believe they were yet lovers. The prize was sighted but still outside the hunter's reach. I applauded Lady Anne's restraint even as I wondered what would make her surrender—the king already showered her with jewels, lodged her in splendid new apartments, gave her brother and her friends positions at court.

Without Nick, the cold months were endless. I spent time with Joan when I could, but otherwise, when not practicing or performing, I sought out the rare quiet parts of Greenwich.

One of my favorite hiding places was a small, curtained alcove off the chapel. It was rarely used, and unless the chapel was occupied, no one saw my comings and goings. Tom discovered me one day when he came to fetch some music stored there. I was so lost in thought that I started at his abrupt appearance.

He held up a hand to silence me and put his head through the curtain. "I don't see it here. I'll look further and bring it up if I can find it." The curtain swung closed, and he leaned against the wall. "Daydreaming?"

I hung my head.

"I'm sure he'll be back soon."

It was the first time he had referred to my relationship. "Yes, soon."

He bit his lip. "He might come back and pick up with someone else." Tom poked at a box brimming with yellowed sheets; no doubt his missing music was there. "Even Gwen."

"You're being cruel." My voice shook.

"Perhaps, but, sweet, there is a need! Someone must make you see him as he is before you ruin yourself for his sake."

A clatter in the next room announced the arrival of the choristers. We were trapped now unless one of us made an exit, and I did not want our presence made public. My liaison with Nick was now an accepted fact. I did not want my name linked again with Tom's.

"It's none of your concern." I spoke quietly beneath the noise outside.

"I know you love him," he said, his voice soft as mine. "It galls me to think of it. I'll even grant he has feelings for you. But what of it?"

I retreated to the corner, Tom's words finding the sliver of doubt that lurked within me. I lived with my love for Nick day by day; I knew it would not be forever, but that made me cherish each moment.

"Jesu, Bess!" Tom burst out, no longer caring about the choristers. "Do you think he goes moonstruck each time he thinks of you?"

I wrapped my dignity around me like a cloak. "I couldn't hope for that," I said. "But I am content. Why must you ruin it?"

He clasped my cold fingers in his and drew me, unresisting, to my feet. "I would sooner give up my hands than wish you unhappiness. While you smile and think of being in his arms, I think of the day when he'll no longer be there. Forgive me if I can't see him in the same light."

I raised his hand and kissed it. "I know it won't last forever. One day, he'll tire of me, or the king will find him a wife. Then it will be done, and I'll go on." I felt a queer vibration in his body as I spoke. "I'm not Agnes. I'll not want to die if he leaves me."

The mention of her name cast a pall, but when I made a move to leave, Tom nodded at the curtain and kept me close. I rested my cheek on his doublet. Beneath the green fustian, I could hear his heartbeat, or mine.

Once, his criticism of Nick would have hurt, but now, my pride was not so great. I accepted that his words were prompted by devotion. I loved Nick with all my heart, but I cherished Tom.

Minutes passed. Eventually, the choristers left, and we were alone. The tension drained from him, and when his hold on me relaxed, I spoke. "You do worry too much." It was a mild reproach, to remind him his rights over me were imaginary.

"I care too much," he said, lowering me on the nearest seat before ducking through the curtain into the empty chapel.

April arrived warm, with a downpour of rain. Everyone grew snappish at being kept indoors. The king roared because he was unable to hunt or ride, because he was bored with his courtiers, because he lost at card games. He was bored with everything, except Anne. I wondered how she made it through the rain with her virtue intact, so mad was his pursuit.

It was hard to keep up a cheerful front with my head filled with worries and loneliness, the court with fractious courtiers and damp, moldy smells. We moved palaces because of the wet, and I worried Nick would not find us; then I worried his horse would stumble, and he would drown in the mud covering southern England.

I lay in bed, hearing the rain and the low growl of thunder in the distance, wishing for summer and sunlight and Nick. Flora slept, lulled by the same sounds that stuck my eyelids open to gaze into the dark.

Muffled footsteps sounded, and the door opened. I leaned up on my elbows and caught a glimpse of a face lit only by a taper sheltered in a cupped hand. A glimpse was enough to bring me scrambling from my bed to fling myself into Nick's arms.

He was cold and soaked through. I caught myself before I cried out. I kissed his wet face and pantomimed how glad I was to see him. In response, he turned into the corridor. I reached for my cloak and ran after him. He put his arm around me, and I snuggled against his body, no longer minding his sodden clothes. He would be warm and dry soon enough.

As we reached the stairs, we were met by the glow of a torch. I shrank back against the wall, but I saw Tom's face as he passed, and he saw mine.

Seeing Tom put no damper on our loving, but when it was over and I lay still in Nick's arms, my mind turned to Tom.

"Seeing him distressed you," Nick said, shifting to look at me. "Why?"

"He shouldn't have seen," I murmured. "No one should have, Tom least of all."

His servants must have been warned of his return, for there was a bottle of wine beside the bed. Nick reached over and poured us each a cup, his face showing displeasure. "Why should no one see us? 'Tis not as though it's the Great Matter."

"There's no need to bruit it about far and wide either." Too late, I heard the shrewish note in my voice and softened it with a smile as I took the cup. "I'm still new to this, Nick."

"Poor Bess." He stroked my bare shoulder, which bore a red welt from his mouth. "It's not so bad."

My reputation as a shy virgin reestablished, I crept back into the circle of his arms. "Let's not talk about him now," I whispered, my lips seeking a favored spot on his throat. "I've missed you sorely."

Nick stopped me. He twined his fingers in my hair and raised my head so that our eyes were level. "I missed you, Bess, more than I expected, but your mind isn't with me. If I wanted no more than a willing body, I would have stopped at a brothel on my way back." He pushed me away and sat up, pulling his shirt over his head. "I don't like the way he looks at you."

He was jealous! My heart leaped at the thought, but I hurried to reassure him. "Tom looks out for me. He's the nearest I have to a brother."

"His thoughts of you are as brotherly as mine," he said and tossed me my shift. "Get along before someone else misses you." His tone made a mockery of all my caution.

My shift was torn along the seam, and I put it on with difficulty, then found my cloak, draped over a chair. "I choose to regard him as my brother."

Draining the cup, he filled it again and took another swallow before responding. "Your reaction is out of proportion to being seen by a brother." He twisted the word, made it ugly.

My fists clenched at my sides. "I was ashamed," I said, very low. "Ashamed to be caught creeping about at night by someone for whom I care a great deal." I saw the impact of my words.

"Creep back in darkness, then." He turned his back and began to dress. "Perhaps no one else will see you."

I don't know what I expected, but it was not what happened next: I ceased to exist. His attentions were lavished on every woman who came into view, making me shake with anger and longing, but I could have paraded in front of him in my shift, and he would not have paid me any mind.

How stupid I was! Of course he would take offense, especially after admitting that he'd missed me. I had humiliated him.

Mistress Edith tried to ease my troubles with a tonic. "You look like a stick, Bess. Do you think you'll do anyone any good if you starve to death?"

I sat down on a stool in her small, cluttered workroom. "I'm not doing anyone any good at all," I said. I played with a jar, turning it mindlessly on the tabletop, until she slapped my hands away.

"Least of all yourself!" she said. "You'll make yourself ill if you keep on this way." She stopped, turned to face me. "You're not with child, are you?"

"No." I imagined the consequences of such a predicament. "My course has just begun."

She sighed loudly. "Well, that's a blessing." Her hands dropped to my shoulders, and she shook me. "Gather yourself together. Pretend you don't care—ofttimes it works, and you forget how much you do."

"I can't forget." I thought of Nick's face as he dismissed me. "And pretend I don't care about which of them?"

"Both of them. I don't know." She shook me again and turned to her work. "Spend time with your friends. Being alone does a body no good at all." Mistress Edith began to sort through the dried herbs that littered the table, her fingers moving surely, discarding what was of no use.

Joan would be sympathetic, I thought, having suffered her own loss. I needed someone's shoulder; Mistress Edith, no matter how she wanted to help, was too brusque for my raw sensibilities. More than her harsh exterior, her affection for Tom kept me from sharing my heartache. The suspicion always lurked that she blamed me for Tom's unhappiness, and it did not help matters since I already blamed myself.

Chapter 16

With the May came a new set of troubles and a new lutenist. With his glossy curls and long black lashes, Giovanni di Rossi was the most beautiful young man I'd ever seen, yet he was completely unappealing. His manners were as pretty as his person, but I disliked him for his patron.

Nick claimed to have found him in the retinue of an obscure Italian nobleman, but I had my doubts. Before his departure in 1525, Dionysio Memmo, the king's organist, had plumbed the city's small Venetian colony for talent, and while they sent a lutenist, the boy soon died, and no replacement was sought. If someone such as this young musician existed in London, Memmo would have found him.

It seemed obvious that Giovanni, or Gianni as he soon came to be known, was more than a mere musician. Something in his attitude was too refined; his clothes, while not of the latest fashion, were of a cut and cloth beyond the pocket of the average minstrel; though not prosperous at present, he had been and was still far from being the itinerant Italian musician he claimed to be. Worse yet, he was talented. On his first evening, he played simple Italian airs that brought tears to the eyes of many. A more practiced performance made the throat close with wonder.

He seemed genuinely pleased with his reception, smiling sweetly through loose black ringlets, making a most charming picture. A ripple ran through the women in the crowd; his reception was also unlike that of most other musicians. He would not sleep in his own bed unless he wanted to.

The king was taken with him, as he had been with Memmo, who had been tempted away from St. Mark's in Venice. The king demanded Gianni perform every night, making petulant requests for songs he'd not had time to learn. Gianni learned quickly, as suited his interests, and within a few weeks, he was able to gratify a majority of the royal requests.

I refrained from calling attention to myself, for fear that I would be asked to sing with him, a request I could hardly refuse, though I loathed the idea of joining my voice to his music.

If I stayed in the background, Tom made himself invisible. He was in the hall for the Italian's first performance, wearing a diffident expression, even as the rest of the Music held its breath. After the first song, he turned away, but not before I saw the shock on his face.

I tried to offer comfort, running after him as he threaded his way through the crowded chamber. "You are the better musician," I said, catching hold of his wrist. His bleak expression chilled me. "And you have the king's love; do not forget. Don't let him take that from you."

He shrugged loose. "Perhaps I don't want it."

In truth, Gianni was perfection on the lute, better even than Tom. His instrument was an extension of his body; he seemed never to think when he played but only to hear the music in his head to have it flow from his fingers. His intensity reminded me of myself, new at court and in love with the power of my voice.

Gianni's voice was no more than passable, but his accent added interest to his light countertenor. That was another point in his favor, as Tom still did not sing and needed a voice to accompany him. Gianni did not make songs, I thought. All he could do was play and sing.

It was enough.

Hating Gianni on Tom's behalf made me feel better for a while, but I realized his talent, and even his taking of Tom's position, was not his fault. The fault lay with the man who'd introduced him to the king, the man I still loved and would never trust again.

Even if I made Nick see reason, the king would never give up this new plaything. I determined to speak to Nick, nonetheless. The hall was too public; I would make no plea in plain view, nor would I seek him in his lodgings, for fear that word would reach Tom. One afternoon, I saw him leave the hall alone and followed.

My breath caught when I realized his destination was the tiny chamber where we had met so often. Perhaps he went to retrieve something left behind; it could not be an assignation. Almost convinced of this, it still took time to nerve myself to enter the room.

My eyes were met with a tableau so appalling that I reeled back against the door, my hands coming to cover my mouth.

Nick was half-dressed, his velvet doublet thrown carelessly on the floor. His hose were untied and bagged around his knees. He still wore his fine Holland shirt, but it bore the creases of rough handling. There was a smear of rouge on one shoulder.

The woman on her knees before him was mother-naked, her only covering a mane of shining chestnut hair. Her flesh was rose-gold in the candlelight.

"Bess, for God's sake!" Nick hissed, and pushed the girl away from his loins. She sprawled backward onto the floor and swore. I did not need to see her face to know it was Gwen.

She showed it anyway, her lips swollen with kisses. "You aren't needed here," she said, reaching up beneath his shirt to fondle him. "Darling, did you call for someone to sing for us?"

Her words woke me from my trance. I looked at her, but my words were for Nick, who was shrugging into his clothes as if I'd never seen him naked. "I want to talk to you."

Nick cupped Gwen's breast absently, his eyes never leaving my face. "We've no need of music or discussion. The chamber is, as you recall, quite cramped."

Tears welled in my eyes, but they would not see me cry. "I do wish you both in hell," I said and walked out, leaving the door flung wide.

～～～～～

As in any time of trial, I spent long periods alone with my music. I found a small harp in the storerooms and was trying to get the knack of it on my own; my mood would not bear instruction. I showed no more promise than on the virginals, but its sound fit my ill humor.

"Tom isn't happy," Robin said as if I had not noticed.

"It's that new lutenist. When the novelty wears off, he will be fine." I listened to the gossip in the common rooms and prayed Tom would get over his gloom. Even if the king dropped Gianni, he did not like melancholy minstrels.

Robin brushed an invisible smudge from the sleeve of his well-cut dark coat. "He's been asking about positions in the cardinal's household."

I felt the color drain from my face. It never occurred to me that not everyone had my faith in things coming out aright or the patience to wait out unpleasantness. "He can't leave."

Robin laughed. "Why not? What's to keep him here?"

"I would miss him," I said. Missing him was not the proper term, but I didn't know how to describe the emptiness I felt during our brief partings. Even now, though we did not speak, I drew comfort from his presence.

"What better reason to flee? He's got no life here—his prize spot as king's lutenist gone, no woman of his own. He might as well come to us."

"You convinced him, didn't you?" I was suddenly sure this was Robin's doing, as Gianni had been Nick's. Tom would not think of leaving, not after all his lectures to me about appreciating the value of our lives here. "Someone has pushed him."

Shaking his head, Robin told me, "The idea was his, Bess. I merely found a place for him. If anyone has pushed him, it's you."

Put that way, it was surprising that he hadn't run further and sooner.

I dropped into the nearest chair and buried my face in my hands.

"You're not a queen, Bess; you've no need of a courtier." Robin's voice was harsh, a fair echo of his master's tone. I looked up in surprise. "That's what you've made of him. I believe you've worn out his patience."

"You don't know that! I would know if Tom wanted to leave." I gathered my skirts in preparation for a sweeping exit, but his voice stopped me.

"Think beyond yourself. Think of how he must feel."

Tom would never leave, and yet I was suddenly afraid. I tried to forget the conversation after Robin left, but he imbued me with a cold, dry fear that it was possible, and if Tom did leave, I would be alone. I turned the fear around: where would Tom be, if not alone, starting over after spending most of his life at court.

In that moment, my selfishness fled. I was aghast at how far this had gone without my seeing it. I knew of Tom's unhappiness, but as with Agnes, I pushed it aside, not believing it to be serious. I, who felt his sorrows as clearly as my own—if I wished to—had downplayed the worst blow he'd ever sustained.

Nick's introduction of Gianni was meant to injure me. It was logical: to strike at Tom would hurt me, yet how could I not have realized the depth of Tom's devastation? His lute and his lovely, heartfelt songs were all he had, and Nick, in one blow, took all from him. To lose his position as the king's favorite, to be supplanted by a stranger in a place indisputably his own. I thought it was probably very like how he'd felt when Nick took me.

⁓⌣⌣⌐

The Master of Minstrels' door was closed. My ear to the smooth panel, I ascertained Tom was within and sat on the bench outside to wait. My impatience grew, and at last, unable to keep still, I rose and made my way to the household quarters. It was not in my mind to go to the men's chamber, but when I found myself near, I slipped in. Better to speak privately, I thought, than to make a fool of myself in public by begging him to stay.

Having been with the Music so long, Tom was fortunate in that when we were at Greenwich, he had a tiny cell of his own in a corner of the chamber, closed off by a faded arras. This advantage owed, as well, to his position as the king's favored lutenist. Tom appreciated the privilege, for every surface, save the narrow bed, was strewn with music, and I saw the failed attempts of a new piece crumpled under the small table. His few clothes were hung neatly on pegs. There were no personal items in the room but a worn prayer book and a small, framed sketch. I peered at it: a beautiful fair-haired woman, drawn in chalk on yellowed paper.

There was but one seat, a small stool at the writing table, and I perched upon it. I tried not to look at the table, knowing Tom disliked anyone to see his work before it was finished, but as the minutes drew out, I could not resist. The top sheet bore a few scrawled and crossed-out lines.

It has been many years now
Since I first saw her face,
Just a child full of laughter
With no home and no place.

She dwells in my heart now;
She never will leave.
Yet she loves another,
And I cannot but grieve.

She seems not to know
Love devours my heart—

This song would never be performed; it was too personal to expose to scrutiny. I could not leave him to face such desolation without knowing my feelings.

Had I ever told Tom how much I cared? I thought not. Nay, I knew not, for I always avoided putting my feelings into words. It seemed silly—Nick was full of casual endearments, and Tom called me 'sweetheart' almost since the night we met, yet I never told either of them, especially Tom, what they meant to me. Nick took me to his bed, not knowing I had worshipped him for years; perhaps Tom would be able to leave without realizing he was as necessary to me as air.

I had to do something.

He was a while longer, long enough to make me reconsider talking to him in his room, but the outer chamber began to fill, and I was trapped. Staying was easier than letting the others know I had been lingering in Tom's chamber like a lovelorn girl. He would be back any moment, and I would see this thing through to its finish.

The arras swung aside, and I jumped, sending papers all over the floor. "You're an unexpected visitor." His voice was rough. "To what do I owe the honor?"

"Robin told me you're thinking of leaving," I said, trying to pitch my voice low.

"News spreads quickly." He took the music from my hands and tidied it into a neat stack.

I couldn't bear it any longer, his tone or his evasion. "It's true, then?" I put my hand on his arm. "You're leaving the court?"

"What's the matter, Bess?" he asked. His body tensed at my touch. "Aren't you pleased to be rid of one who does nothing but judge you?"

I did not remove my hand. "You always said you worried because you cared." I let my palm slide around to his back. "I can't imagine life here without you."

Tom stepped away, backing into the hard edge of the table. "You shall learn, I'm sure. You're a good student."

"A better student than friend," I said, sitting on the bed. "Tom, I don't know if it makes any difference, but I'm sorry. I'm so sorry. For everything." I looked up to see the effect of my words. "I know how hard this has been for you—Gianni, all of it. I should have tried to help, but instead, I was afraid, afraid you'd send me away. I should have risked it."

He let me say my piece without interruption, leaning against the wall, out of reach. Finally, he moved, touching flint to a dip on the writing table. As the room grew lighter, my mood swung further to the dark because I saw my words had not swayed him.

"Tom." My voice was a whisper, tears nearly upon me. "Please say something."

"What would you have me say?" He swept a hand across the table and scattered the music again and waved me back when I would have retrieved it. "That I understand and forgive you? That I've wanted to come to you on my knees because I've been so miserable, but I was afraid as well?"

"Yes." I was closer to prayer at that moment than ever I had been in chapel.

"I do forgive you. I always forgive you, but it's too late this time." His eyes met mine, and I saw his will soften as I held his gaze. "I'm joining Wolsey's household on the morrow."

"No." I could not speak the word aloud, but he saw my lips move.

"I have to, Bess. There's nothing left for me here. At least at Hampton, there is anonymity. I'll no longer be the king's ousted favorite nor the minstrel who pens love ballads to another man's mistress. To be no one again, that's all I want."

I picked up the sheet of telltale verse. "I read this. I didn't mean to, but..."

Tom tore the sheet into small bits. "I don't mind that you saw it, but it's for no one else." He touched me for the first time, gently, on the cheek. "And it's not all your fault. Did Gianni come because you asked?"

"Nick brought him, to hurt me." I pleated my skirt between my fingers. "That night, Tom, on the stairs—"

He turned away but not before I saw the memory darken his eyes. "We don't need to speak of it."

"I need you to understand. Nick was angry because I told him I was ashamed. I said it would have been the same no matter who had seen us, but he didn't believe me." I tucked my hands into my sleeves. "And he was right. I was ashamed because it was you." Closing my eyes, I remembered the cold rush of shame. "Gianni is his revenge," I said. "There's no point in saying it again, but I am sorry. Most of all, I'm sorry I can't change your mind."

There was a rustle of paper as he shuffled through the music again. At last, he left it alone and turned toward me. "It means a great deal that you don't want me to leave, but you must understand why I'm going."

He was beside me then, and I turned and pressed my face to his heart, feeling the rough texture of his shirt beneath my cheek. Nick's shirts were cambric or fine Holland cloth, but servants made do with less.

"I understand, but I hate it." Tears ran unchecked down my face. "Tell me how to bear it without you."

His arms went around me, one hand stroking my back. "You are cruel," he said. "How far must I go to be free of you?"

Despite Nick, despite Gianni, I was still the cause of his leaving. "If I left court, would you stay?"

"Don't be an idiot. Your family can ill afford to take you in, if that's what you're thinking. They'd marry you to the first man who offered." He tapped my chin with his fingertip. "I've made my decision. You're happy here, and I need someplace new."

"To escape me."

A loud quarrel erupted on the other side of the curtain.

"A land hasn't been discovered where I could escape you," he said over the sound of Harry and Ned scuffling, "but I need to try. I'm twenty-four, Bess, and I live like a monk. Perhaps, if I'm away from you, I can learn how else to live."

I hated that I understood. It was the curse of our relationship, this sensitivity to each other. He would learn to live without me, and I would have to learn to live without him. "It doesn't have to be like this," I said. "We can find a way."

He shook his head. "I've loved you since I was thirteen. I've been throwing myself against a barred door for ten years, and I'm tired."

I knew how he felt, but he'd never been so blunt before. "Why?"

"It doesn't pay to question such things."

I laughed at his serious tone. "Now you know why I haven't as much faith as you. If this is what God does, I don't think I'll ever hear mass again."

"Bess!"

"Have I've offended you? Well, I'm offended we've been made at such cross purposes." I began to cry again and sat down on the bed. The straw mattress crackled beneath me, and I stiffened, afraid of drawing attention to us. "I want so much for you to stay," I said through my hands.

Tom sat down too, a safe distance from me. "I can't tell you how to feel, sweet, but it's pointless to be angry."

I reached for his hand. "Please don't go," I said, unable to imagine life without him. I could live without Nick, but I could not do without Tom.

"Don't ask me," he said. "I can't bear to see you so distraught. I might give in."

"Good." I smiled hopefully through my tears and saw the pain behind his answering smile.

"I can't, Bess. Being this close to you"—he gestured at the scant inches between us—"is torture. I'd sooner face the rack. At least there would be an end to it."

There would be an end to this, I vowed and reached out to touch his face. I drew my fingertips along his jaw, feeling the light prickle of his beard, the quick intake of breath before he pulled away. I touched his mouth, running my finger along his lower lip. Then I leaned in and kissed him gently, a mere brushing of our lips.

The contact shattered his stillness, and he grasped my shoulders and shook me quite hard. "You'll not change my mind."

I put my hands over his, moved them to my waist. "You said once, you'd never leave me." His hands were warm. I felt the shape of them through my stays.

"I'm not the boy who made that promise."

"I'm still the girl who believed it." I wound my arms around his neck and pressed myself to him. "I won't let you leave."

"You won't let me?" he repeated, and I felt his resistance vanish. He kissed me, tilting my head back and taking my mouth roughly. My lips parted, and he kissed me harder, meeting a response I could not control. The drowning sensation which had scared me before was back, but this time, I flung myself into the torrent, knowing Tom would not let me drown. I closed my eyes and followed him.

His longing surged through me, making me cling to him. I sensed the frantic twisting of his thoughts: it was wrong; he should not—he was drowning as surely as I. And he gave himself as surely to it, despite his fears.

My back arched with pleasure as his lips sought my throat, his breath warm against my flesh. I felt my skin come alive at his touch, burning to feel the same caresses everywhere. He began to unlace my gown, and I helped, pulling it from my shoulders. "My little gypsy," he said and lowered his head to my breast. His mouth was warm through the flimsy linen, then hot and moist as he pushed the cloth aside.

I kept one hand on the back of his head, while the other fumbled with the carved bone buttons of his doublet. I was filled with a sense of urgency: this act, which had been avoided for so long, had to be taken to its completion, or we would never emerge from this thing that held us. Perhaps, on the other side, we would be able to see clearly.

Drawing back, I finished unlacing my gown. Beneath, I wore nothing but stays and my shift, poorly mended from its previous rough handling. Tom helped with my stays, dropping them onto the rushes. I tugged at my shift, and the seam parted, baring me to the waist.

"Sweet girl, come here." He lay back on the bed, pulling me onto him. Loosened, my hair hung around us like a curtain. I dropped my head back as his gentle hands, with their rough musician's fingers, stroked my breasts until I thought I would cry out with the pain and pleasure of it.

I rolled aside so he could shed his clothes. Instead, he followed me, running his hands the length of my legs and dealing with slippers, stockings, and garters.

All my experience counted for nothing as I reached for him, trembling and uncertain. I touched my fingertips to the strong muscles of his thighs, feeling the sharp quiver of flesh beneath the cloth. Because of another, my touch was confident and sure of pleasing, but I put the thought from my mind. This was not an exercise of skill, but a gift given with more love than I had ever known.

The light guttered and went out, drenching the chamber in darkness. He moved away, making me reach for him. "Patience, love," he said. I heard the soft sounds of his clothes falling to the floor. The mattress gave as he sat down again and found me waiting.

As my eyes grew accustomed to the dark, I made out the shape of him against the coverlet, but I used my hands to learn his body, pushing my fingers through the light mat of hair that covered him from chest to groin, stroking his lean muscled arms and legs. My fingers strayed, clasping him, feeling him hot and hard against my palm. He made a sound of surprised pleasure and rolled me over, pinning my arms above my head.

"Trying to escape?" he murmured, his mouth close to my ear. I strained toward him, desperate to feel flesh against mine. He rubbed his face across my breasts, making me whimper with wanting him.

"I'll never leave you." The words were said, and through my passion, I heard and knew I spoke true. It seemed that everything I ever experienced with Nick was a rehearsal for this moment. Every sensation was sharper, all my nerve endings closer to the surface.

It was my turn to be patient as Tom turned my own tricks upon me. His hands and mouth were everywhere, seeking to know me, finding the shape of me and committing it to memory. He found the hollow of my shoulder, the sensitive area beneath my breast, the ridge of my hipbone, and to each spot, he paid tribute with fingers and tongue. Remembering the others in the room outside, I tried to quiet my moans, but I could not keep my hips from bucking beneath him.

At once, his touch became gentle. The bed shifted as he knelt between my legs, and I could not breathe for waiting. I stifled a gasp of surprise against his shoulder, for our joining was a revelation, a feeling unknown with Nick; it was as if something lost had been returned to me. Tom stopped, bearing his weight on his elbows, and though I could not see his face, I knew he looked at me and that his expression was one of wonder. He began to move, slowly at first, then with greater intensity as he felt my response.

It was a continuation of what we had always had together, though I never imagined we could be one with our bodies as we were with our minds. My own pleasure and his mounting passion, in combination, were nearly unbearable, except I could bear it—and more—now that I knew.

When his spasms began at last, I thrust myself into his rhythm, muffling his cry in my hair and opening my eyes, knowing his eyes were open too, the starry black haze clearing from his mind. Breast to breast, our hearts pounded.

Separating was a physical pain, the opening of a half-healed wound, and I thought of tales I'd heard of twins, who often knew what happened to the other, though they might be miles apart. Tom and I were like that, I thought and drifted to sleep with my head pillowed on his chest and his seed sticky on my thighs.

His absence drew me toward consciousness, and I listened to the quiet sounds of his movements, hoping he would return to the warm bed. When he did not, I opened my eyes.

The chamber was stripped of its few personal possessions, and Tom was folding his clothes into a small trunk. I sat up, the covers falling to my waist. "What are you doing?"

He turned to face me. In his hands was the doublet I'd embroidered for him at Christmas. "Leaving, as well you know."

I scrambled from the bed and flung myself at him. "But you can't! I thought—"

"You thought last night changed everything." He draped the bed cover around me and put his hand on my forehead, like a blessing. His touch was tender yet somehow impersonal.

"Why are you still going?"

"Did you sleep well last night?" he asked.

"Yes," I replied, confused at the change of subject. "I slept very well. Did you?"

"No. I felt you fall asleep in my arms, and I was so happy, I was afraid to breathe. It was all I ever prayed for." He bent over the trunk, unwilling to look at me. "Then I realized I was wrong. God answered my prayers, Bess. He said no.

"What you did last night was a grand gesture, the kind you do best. I don't mean it with any malice, love, but it's true. You think only with your heart when you're upset, and the result isn't always as you'd wish."

I didn't understand any of this. I tried to catch his hand, but he avoided me deftly and leaned against the edge of his writing table.

"You came to my bed because you wanted to keep me here. It might have worked if I'd fallen asleep sooner. But it was a long night," he said, "and while I thank you from my heart for what you gave me, I can't stay."

"Don't you love me anymore?"

His blue-gray gaze was simultaneously affectionate and exasperated. "Of course I love you. I doubt I'll ever stop. And I'll always be your friend. I just won't be here."

My eyes burned. "For a long time, you wanted to be more than my friend."

"I did."

"Well, now I want that too. Doesn't it matter?"

He sighed. "You don't, Bess. You're just afraid of losing me. You'll exist without me, and I shall learn to exist without you."

"So nothing has changed," I said, feeling my throat tighten. I pulled the coverlet around me with numb hands.

"No. If you thought you had brought that about, I'm sorry." Tom picked up my scattered clothes and laid them on the bed in an orderly fashion: stockings, shift, stays, gown. He reached under the table for an errant slipper.

"I didn't plan what happened," I said in a small voice. I drew my shift over my head and regarded the shredded cloth with dismay. "I'm not so calculating."

A myriad of expressions crossed his face as he debated what to say. He decided, as only Tom would, on the unadorned truth. "You're not; you're impulsive. I'm sure you acted from the heart, but did you think about this morning?" Watching as I struggled with my stays, he began to pull the laces as he spoke. "What if I'd gone to sleep imagining you loved me? What would you have done today? I would stay, but I would expect you to love me this way all the time." He tied the laces and shoved me lightly away. "What then?"

"What then?" I repeated. "Don't make last night less than it was. It wasn't just to change your mind." I saw the distance in his eyes. Part of him was at Hampton already. "There's no way to convince you, is there?"

"No. 'Tis best if we leave things as they are." Closing the trunk, he stood by the curtain. "I'll take this down now. You can dress in private."

"May I come down to say goodbye?" My voice was muffled by the bedcovers, where I had submerged in shame. Dress in private! That was rich, coming from a man who gloried in my nakedness only hours before.

"I'd rather you didn't." Tom's lips brushed my hair, light as the wings of a moth. There was a draft as the curtain swung closed.

Part III

The Reckoning – 1527

Chapter 17

Could one simply shed a wife when she lost her usefulness? One could, it seemed, if one were a king.

That spring, the court moved from place to place with an air of desperation as the king tried to find the perfect setting for his jewel. Trying also, I believed, to avoid the memories of his wife and child lurking in all the chambers of all the palaces they had occupied as a family.

We were preparing to leave Westminster. Around me, the palace was emptying; it mirrored the desolation I still felt. I was hiding in the attics, but sound carried up the stairs, disturbing my thoughts and shattering any chance of peace.

Since Tom's departure, I had kept up appearances, performing, eating, and talking to the others as if nothing had changed. Inside, I was a different person. It was as if by opening myself to Tom, I'd peeled away a protective covering from my heart. I mourned him as surely as if he'd died on that awful morning.

It took a long time to understand his farewell; it is never easy to face such truths. Tom painted a picture of my character I did not wish to see, but in the weeks following his leaving, unable to think of anything else, I recalled his words.

I had gone to his room with no plan, expecting instinct to guide me. And it had—into his bed and out of his heart, with no one to blame but myself. If I loved him, and I knew now that I always had, throwing myself into his arms at that moment was the worst sort of self-sabotage. Knowing my feelings for Nick, Tom would not believe that my words and actions were anything more than empty gestures to make him stay.

The others, even Edith, trod lightly around me. One by one, they approached, saying how much they missed him, and capped those sentiments by adding that I was sure to miss him more than anyone. I uttered only the most banal responses to my well-wishers. I didn't want their condolences; I wanted to be left alone to wallow in my heartache.

I had not anticipated all the ways I would miss Tom. Cut off from the source of the love which had nourished me for so long, I found myself yearning to brush the hair from his eyes, to listen as he plucked random notes and turned them into music, to find out what I believed by trying my ideas against his.

With the exception of brief separations brought about by the king's travels, we had seen each other every day for more than ten years. Even during periods of strain, I knew that if I needed him, he would be there. What guarantee was there now that I would even see him again?

If I found our separation difficult, what must he feel? Dear, single-hearted Tom, who'd had the strength to leave. Tom had not been brought up to express himself in words; he spoke through music. Now I no longer heard him play or compose some new song, I knew not what he felt about me, if indeed he felt anything at all.

"Why could you not believe?" I asked and listened to my words come back to me from the bare walls. "Why, Tom?"

Tom was gone; I was alone.

He was alone. Alone, and if he felt half the loneliness I felt, alone was too easy a word. The attic door creaked open enough for Joan put her head inside. "The barges are ready, Bess."

I wiped my eyes with my sleeve before turning. If my face showed traces of tears, it would not matter with Joan; she understood. "How did you know I was up here?"

Her freckled face showed compassion. "It's one of the places I come when I need to be alone, to think about Will."

"After all this time?" I asked, wondering how many years of emptiness we were sentenced to serve.

"It does get better," she said, linking her arm through mine. "The pain fades, and there are still memories. You have a lifetime of those." She produced a handkerchief and dabbed under my eyes, showing me the telltale smudges of dust. "You said goodbye, didn't you?"

"In a manner of speaking," I said. "We said a lot of things, but goodbye was among them."

"Don't, Bess." Her mild voice was unusually sharp. "Don't make light of it. It doesn't help you to bear it, and later, you'll feel worse for having tried." She paused, twisting the scrap of cambric in her hands. "The king has changed his mind again. We are going upriver...to Hampton."

"The roses will be lovely." My smile was forced. "We can walk the garden together, Joan, and try not to dwell on our losses." I shivered with a sudden chill. "A cheerful prospect, is it not?"

We were on the last barge but one to arrive at Hampton Court Palace. Our visit lasted two weeks, until the middle of June, and in that time, I did not see Tom once.

Cardinal Wolsey left for France in July, his procession threading its way through the jeering London streets. His entourage, wearing his colors and carrying silver crosses, remained as expressionless as the scarlet-clad prelate, but the taunts were relentless. Robin was there, in his sober garments, following close behind the cardinal. His face was set and stony, but his eyes roamed over the faces on either side.

Joan and I watched them leave, and I followed alone until they reached London Bridge, hoping for a glimpse of Tom. I turned back as the last of the procession, consisting of wagons and pack animals, trundled over the bridge. Tom was gone, off to France for as long as it took to right things with King Francis.

"And good riddance to him!" I heard an old man cackle on my way back to Westminster. "The king's not a king when the cardinal's in England."

"What's he doing in France but finding a new queen?" another voice asked. "Bloody whoremaster, replacing good Queen Katherine with a French princess."

Rumors of Wolsey's policies spread far and wide, and I believed the cardinal had indeed gone to France to promote King Henry to Princess Renée in the hope of procuring a French marriage. Wolsey's plans and the king's plans had been one for so long that when his royal master's eye wandered to Anne Boleyn, the cardinal took no notice because he had not seen her first.

The king was fixed in his affections; through that summer, when he moved from one country house to another, he kept a steady flow of messengers moving between them, carrying letters and gifts.

Through the summer, until we returned to Greenwich in September, it seemed we lived on the verge of a constantly brewing storm. The weather was unseasonably hot, damaging the few crops that survived the spring rains; people spoke against both Wolsey and Anne Boleyn, blaming them for all the disasters; the king hunted and ate and drank himself to distraction and presented to his frequent visitors the picture of a merry monarch.

To return to the rolling hills around Greenwich was heaven: at that moment, I wanted nothing more than to close myself in my memories, to dream of a time when I had Tom, and the king had a queen, and Wolsey was disliked only for his ambition.

The next day, I found myself in a coach bound for London. I had been back but a few hours when a small page tracked me down. He peered around the corner, and I gestured for him to enter.

"I've a letter," he said. He was a skinny child dressed in green livery, with wide, hungry eyes. "For Elizabeth Davydd. My lord steward says that's you, mistress."

Elizabeth Davydd! How long since I'd even thought of myself by that name?

The handwriting was unfamiliar, but the name at the bottom was not. I read the letter slowly, my surprise at hearing from Madlen tempered by the news she imparted.

Bess,

Father is ill. Come before it's too late. You needn't stay.

Madlen and I had not spoken since her marriage. I knew from my father she had two children now, a boy and a girl. On my rare visits, she would bid my parents farewell and hurry home to her family, rather than spend time with me.

I sent word that I must go to London for several days. Putting together a small bundle, I wondered at her message. How ill was he? And for how long? Had no one thought of me before now?

Travel by water would be fastest, but when I reached the water stairs, all the barges and boats which normally jostled for position were gone, out on the river, and not even a small boat remained for hire. I turned back to the courtyard. I was hailed almost immediately, but when I saw the young man wore a hawk badge on his livery, I looked away.

"My master wants you, mistress."

"I've no time for him." I looked around the courtyard again. There must be some conveyance that could get me to London.

"He was insistent. He said if you refused, I should bring you to explain yourself." A smile flitted over his features.

Great God, did the whole court know I'd slept with him? "I've been called to London on an urgent matter."

The fellow stood his ground, arms folded. "I'm expected to bring you, mistress. If I do not—I'm sure you're acquainted with his nature."

"Oh, all right." I had no desire to see Nick, but I did not want his ire to land on this hapless fellow's head, despite his sly grin. I could explain myself to Nick with a minimum of words, preferably rude ones.

The outer chamber of his apartments was empty, but at the sound of my step, the inner door was flung open. "Bess, come in."

I entered, carefully looking past him. "I came because your man is afraid of being beaten. He brought me here, and now, I am leaving."

"Don't be ridiculous." His voice was low, velvety. I shivered in spite of myself. "I wanted to offer my coach to get you to London."

I wondered how he knew. "Thank you, I'll find my own passage."

He folded himself into a chair, crossing his long legs. "Are you refusing my offer?"

"Yes." I cast my eyes down. "I won't ride into London in your coach, looking like your whore."

"I won't have you think that of yourself. Look at me."

I obeyed, and my flickering glance took in the dark curling hair, the broad shoulders under the tawny doublet, the easy smile that had filled my dreams for so many years. I hated him for hurting Tom, for humiliating me with Gwen, and for a myriad of other reasons. It was a blow to look at him and still feel something.

I took a step backward.

"Wait." He leaned forward, caught my wrist in an iron grip. "You'll not turn away my offer for such a reason, Bess. I know your father's ill—one of my servants brought the news."

"It sounds like a deal with the devil," I said.

Nick raised his hands in protest. "I ask nothing but that you take my coach. I will even instruct my man to put you out at the next street so that no one will see."

The door of the house stood open when I arrived. I heard footsteps above, and in a moment, Madlen came down the stairs. She stopped short at the sight of me.

"You've come."

"You sent for me," I countered. "What is wrong with our father?"

"Fever," she said. Now that we were older, I could see the resemblance between us, yet Madlen looked haggard and older than her twenty-four years. Her dark hair was straggling out from beneath its covering, and there were stains on her skirt.

"Not the sweat?" I asked in horror, for we had not been visited by that particular demon in many years.

"No. Just a fever—now high, now low—but draining the life out of him sure enough." Madlen put her hands over her face and sat very still. "I know not what else to do," she said through her fingers.

"Is our mother upstairs with him?"

She nodded and pressed her hands against her knees, heaving herself upright. "Yes."

I put my hand on her shoulder. "Come up with me. I must see him, and you know how it is between us."

Our mother knelt on the rushes at his bedside. Her face changed when I entered the stuffy little chamber, her exhaustion replaced with something harsher.

"Madlen sent for me," I said before she could speak. I walked around her to the other side of the bed.

Da was asleep. His skin was waxy, and there was a bluish tinge along his jaw that worried me. A limp shirt covered shoulders that appeared stick-thin. I knelt across from her, noting with distaste the filthy rushes on the floor.

"She wants to be alone with him," Madlen said.

Mum struck her hand away and remained on her knees. "What right has she? Why has she come?"

"I came because he is my father," I said, my voice low so as not to wake him. "I came because Madlen at least thought to let me know he was ill."

"You're an unnatural child!" she hissed. "Never caring what befalls us, so long as you're warm and fed. What do you care?"

I knew grief caused her harshness, yet I could not help the evil that rose to my lips. "And who sold me like a piece of unwanted goods?" I asked her. "He did it to better me, but you just wanted the money." I looked around the shabby room. "What did you do with it that improved his life at all?" I met her gaze across the bed and saw I had shaken her. "Now leave me with him."

"You have a quick tongue, child, but your heart is good." His weak voice startled me, and I saw his eyes were open. "You'll ask forgiveness."

"Yes," I said, more shocked at his appearance now that he was awake.

His face was pale with red fever patches on his cheeks, and the hand that sought mine was dry and hot. "You heard..."

"All of it," he said, and his brown eyes burned brightly. "She harbors a deep hurt of her own. She's never gotten over losing Cefin."

"She's never gotten over not losing me instead," I said, ancient injuries rising to the surface. I had always blamed myself for my brother's death, but I had come to see God took those He wanted, without thought for those left behind.

I adjusted his covers when he threw them off. "Can I get you something? Has a doctor come?"

"No doctor," he said, speaking with difficulty. "I've not been able to work since the rains."

"They should have sent for me," I said, exasperated. "They may not want me, but I can do something." I pressed a kiss on his hot forehead and went to the head of the stairs. They were below, talking quietly, and I called down to Madlen to fetch a doctor, that I would pay. No response came, but I heard the door bang.

"Tell me of your life," his dry voice insisted.

I held a cup to his cracked lips. "Drink first. You need the water to sweat the fever away."

"The fever won't go away," Da said, but he drank, water running down the creases on his leathery face. "Tell me, Bethan."

"I am happy," I said, wondering if he knew I lied. "My role has not changed much over the years. I play the lute, and the harp now, a little."

Da smiled at that. There was nothing left of him but bone and spirit, wrapped in a tissue-thin layer of burning flesh.

"There was talk, months ago, brought by a merchant who comes to the tavern." He took a harsh breath and paused. "He said one of the king's minstrels, a pretty, dark girl, was taken as mistress to a nobleman. I kept it from your mother. Was it you?"

I ducked my head, my shame discovered in the one place I would have it hidden. "Yes."

"And do you love him?" His voice was stern, even in its weakness.

"I believed I did," I said. "But my heart lies elsewhere, and that is the end of it."

"Ah." Talking wearied him. He relaxed against the flattened pillow and seemed to doze, then opened his eyes. "So I'm not to be graced by any grandchildren from you, child?"

His directness brought a smile to my lips. "Not yet, thanks be to God, and not for some time."

"I'll not see them, then." He slept again before I could reassure him. He did not want reassuring, I suspected. He knew the truth better than anyone in the house.

Footsteps scraped on the stairs, and the doctor entered. He was a tall, thick-set man, with good dark clothes and well-shaped hands. He cast an eye on the shrunken figure on the bed, then turned his glance on me. "What do you expect me to do?"

"Whatever you can. I know it's gone on too long, but please try." I pulled Nick's ring from my finger and handed it to him. "I hope this will pay for your pains, sir. I'll be downstairs if you have need of me."

I sat in a corner on a low stool, while Madlen and Mum wept across the room. The faint glow from the window was enough to show me the groove on my finger where Nick's ring had been. I felt no sorrow at giving it up, only the knowledge it had gone for a better purpose than the last ring I surrendered.

"How have you paid him?" my mother asked, her hands knotted in her apron. "With some of your whore's gold?"

"Mum!" Madlen was shocked.

"I know how you live," she said, and her voice was tinged with venom. "I heard the tale from your sister's own husband, and he from some other merchant, that you've set yourself up as a whore, and you live in great wealth on your earnings."

Madlen turned pale, and I wanted to comfort her for having such a weak, woman-tongued man. She looked at our mother in horror.

"I paid the doctor with something that belonged to me," I replied. "Since I did it to save my father, it should not matter if I earned it on my back or not."

Struck dumb for a moment, she began to cry noisily, putting her head on Madlen's breast. My sister recoiled, then began to stroke her hair. "It's all right, Mum. Mayhap the doctor will be able to help."

When he came down, he spoke to us all and then called me aside. "Your father is resting, but his fever persists. How many days has it been?"

"Seven," I said, having discovered this from Madlen. "Some time before that, he complained of weakness and pains."

"Ah." The doctor rubbed his brow. "You are his daughter?"

"Yes."

"Why did no one call for me sooner, when there might have been hope?"

His words struck me like a dull blade. It was clear my father had not long to live, but I wanted to be wrong. "I was only told today. There was no money before." "The ring more than covers my fee," he said. "Is there anything else?"

"Make him comfortable," I told him. "If he has pain, make it cease. If you can do anything at all to ease his time in that foul room..." I broke off. There was no reason to admit a stranger to my feelings. "Thank you, sir. You have already helped us greatly."

That night, we took turns sitting with him, feeding him an infusion for the fever when he woke, listening to his breathing when he slept. My sister was more relaxed with me, but Mum was worse; she protested at my being left alone with him, and it took Madlen and her husband to carry her off to rest.

Da slept most of the time, such a peace on his face, it was hard to believe he was ill. The heat emanated from him in a steady wave, yet he shook with chills beneath the covers. I put another blanket on him, fingering it and wondering where my purchase price had gone; the bedding was as threadbare as everything else.

I got a broom and swept the filthy rushes into a pile, opened the window and threw them down into the street below. The reeking contents of the chamber pot followed. When I was done, I left the window open a hand's breadth, feeling the stir of the October breeze through the stifling sickroom.

"Gwynnedd," he said, and when I turned, he was awake and lucid. "The air smells of Gwynnedd."

When he spoke of Wales, I knew he was dying; his homeland had been but a name to me, a few tales of village life before joining the young Henry Tudor to unseat King Richard. His voice had never held this quality of yearning.

"Tell me, Da." I sat on the edge of the bed. He took my hand, and I thought his flesh seemed cooler.

"It's a hard place. The land is not so rich as England, but it makes up in its beauty." His soft voice was musical as he described for me the rocks and glens of his home, the cold, blue-green rivers, the temper of the people. "We're a proud, fierce breed, always ready to fight, even when there's no cause. No one loves a quarrel like a Welshman."

"I know that," I said.

His face creased in a smile. "For all their temper, the Welsh are full of music. You know that too. I wish I could give you their songs."

"You've given me so much," I said with a lump high in my throat. "You gave me my own music."

After that, he slept again, and I dozed beside him until Madlen came in the gray dawn to push me off to bed. She eyed the open window and bare floorboards with some skepticism, but even she admitted the chamber no longer reeked like the Fleet River at low tide.

I thought a lot during the hours at his bedside. I thought of Nick, by whose kindness I was here but whose presence in my life disappointed my father. I thought of Tom more frequently than I would have wished.

Perhaps it was being in London. We shared so much in those narrow, dirty streets—the secrets of our pasts and our families, the tragedy of Agnes—it seemed appropriate that his shadow was beside me.

The next afternoon, I left the house and walked to the Southwark church my parents had taken me to as a child. I knew praying for Da's recovery would be futile, so I commended his soul to God as sincerely as I knew how.

At some point, Tom infiltrated my prayers. I heard him say God had answered his prayer by saying no, and tears filled my eyes.

When I left the church, I took a different route back and soon found myself in the street where his mother lived. I wondered if she was still alive. It had been more than six months since his last visit; she could be dead or lingering still, suffering whatever horrors the pox had inflicted upon her.

I paused before the door, then turned away. A respectable woman did not walk into a brothel.

Sleep was rare, between the devils of my mind and my father's fever. I was at his side for most of the night, resting at daybreak when Madlen or my mother took their turn. There were periods when he knew me and would clutch my hand and ask me to sing. I sang until tears stole my voice. When the fever took him, he spoke of my mother as a young woman and talked to my dead brother. Once, he wept. I mentioned these wanderings to the doctor, who came each day. He repeated his earlier prognosis. Even if the fever broke, he would not live, all his strength gone. It was a wonder he had lasted this long. I knew the doctor felt helpless, but the whole situation made me so angry, I was often sharp with him.

"Now you've driven him off," my mother said. "He'll let Peter die because of you."

"Haven't you heard anything he's said? He's going to die. All we can do is pray."

I was accustomed to the ways of the palace: when someone was ill, a physician was called immediately. There was nothing the king's doctors could not cure but sweat or plague. That my father was going to die of a lingering fever outraged me, and I realized my life could have ended thus, had he not sent me away.

There must be something, I thought, walking from the house to lose myself in the city. When I found myself in Southwark again, I knew I was meant to talk to Tom's mother. Some things—most things having to do with Tom—must be taken on instinct.

The door opened at my knock, and the face that peered out at me was young and unpainted. I explained who I sought, and she let me inside, hurrying me along before I could get a proper glimpse of the house. I saw only a flash of a lewd mural through partly closed curtains before I was herded up a flight of narrow stairs to a small alcove at the top of the house. The girl knocked on the wall and left me to stand by the curtain, wondering what there was to say to this woman.

"Come," a voice said at last, hoarsely, not the raucous tone I remembered. I girded myself to deal with another dying parent.

The room was warm as my father's, the one tiny window covered with a heavy cloth, which blocked the sun. In the dim light, I could scarcely make out the wasted figure beneath the bedcovers.

"I'm sorry," I said, backing toward the stairs. This was not Tom's mother. "I must have the wrong place."

"I know you," she said and beckoned me forward.

Standing by the bed, I could see vestiges of the woman I'd met when I was twelve. Her face was sunken, for she had almost no teeth left, and her mouth was stained and blurred by years of carmine.

"My name is Elizabeth."

The grotesque mask cracked as she smiled at me. "You're my Tom's Bess."

Embarrassed, I said, "Yes, I suppose so."

"How is he?" she asked. "I don't see him much now that he's with that pox-ridden churchman. Is he well?"

"Yes," I said, thinking she had chosen an odd insult, considering her condition. "I don't see him often myself, Mistress—"

"Call me Rose," she said and looked at me. I was shocked when I saw

Tom's eyes in her haggard face, clear and blue-gray. She must have been lovely once.

"I'm sorry," I said. "I don't know why I came."

"Sit down; you're no bother. The girls don't come up to see me like they should. You're a breath of air, and you know my boy. You can tell me how he is."

I pulled up a stool and sat next to her. The room smelled of sickness and medicine, but it was a different smell than my father's room. It was not yet the smell of death.

"My father is dying," I told her, "and I've just realized how much I love him."

Rose reached took my hand. "He knows," she said. "Just like I know Tom loves me, though I shame him."

"But he visits you, and I've not seen my parents in years." I blinked back tears and felt a trickle of sweat between my breasts. "I can't even tell him—he's not conscious, and my mother, she blames me."

She patted my hand as though I were a child. I felt a tear slip free and wiped it away. After a few minutes, I sat up straight, and she let me go.

"Tom is lucky," I said. "You care very much for him." I wondered how I'd not seen it before.

"I have nothing left to do but care," she said. "Once, I was too full of life and myself to remember I had a child, and then he was gone. The king plucked him from the street and took him away, did he tell you? Sent me a packet of money, but my Tommy never came back. He's better for it, of course. I wouldn't want to think of him growing up here, but I missed him." She sagged in the bed, looking even older. "He was so like his father."

"He told me you called him Thomas of Southwark."

"Being a bastard does not rest lightly on him. Perhaps I should have told him, but I was afraid if his father saw what a fine boy he had, he would claim him. If that happened, I would lose him completely."

The rumor was true then, that his father was of noble birth. Tom had said it once but with such a mocking tone that I always wondered if he believed it himself.

"You wouldn't know it, but I was a beauty once. The king's young men often came here to sample the pleasures of Southwark." Her hand went to her hair, a young, vain gesture. "Some painter sketched me once, instead of paying."

I did not have to ask what had become of the drawing.

"When I found out about the baby, I didn't want to keep it, but after he was born, I couldn't give him up." She closed her eyes for a moment. "He looked so much like his father, in ways only a woman can see. It isn't clear now, which is a blessing. No man needs to find he has a full-grown son. It makes him feel his death coming on."

I looked at Rose and knew it would not be long before she made the journey to the Single Women's Churchyard. I shivered and turned my thoughts away. "Thank you for talking to me. I must get back before it's too late." The sliver of light that edged the curtain was gone. I did not want to walk back in the dark.

"It's always too late." She smiled, and I no longer saw the fading paint, but a woman who suffered yet still cared for a stranger. "I thank you, Bess. You've made me feel I've had a visit from my boy."

Rose said something as I parted the curtain, and I turned. "I'm sorry?"

She repeated the name very softly and added, "I won't live forever. Someday, he may need to know."

Her words haunted me all the way back to Aldgate, where Madlen met me at the door and told me my father had died in my absence.

Chapter 18

Winter came early. The snows blew all night, and in the morning, the ground was crusted white, hard as iron until the sun found its way through the clouds. I felt much the same, except the sun did not shine on me, and I remained wintry and frozen within.

Before my father was cold, my mother turned me out, and I sheltered at Anne's house until after the burial, which I paid for with my best undersleeves and an ornament from my gown. I fled back to court under my own power and sank like a stone into the bottomless routine of the Music. When alone, I played sad songs on the lute or the harp, but I never put them on paper; they were my mourning.

I grieved as much for Tom as for myself. His gain of a father was perhaps more traumatic than my loss. It was a secret that ought not to have been shared. Seeing what her silence had done to Tom, had Rose ever regretted not telling him? Why had she entrusted the secret to me?

Robin, who returned from the continent triumphant, despite Wolsey's dour mood, was silent on the subject of Tom and pleaded an excess of work each time I saw him. I did not believe his excuses; the cardinal burdened his staff, it was true, but he kept the main of the work for himself, and Robin was never too busy for gossip.

By my arrangement, we sat side-by-side one night at table. He turned to me over the meat, his pale face pinched. "You've trapped me, is that it?"

I took a bite of the joint, wiped the grease from my fingers. "You're hiding something, and I would know what it is."

He busied himself with his plate. "I know not how to dissemble, Bess."

"By all the saints," I said, "if there is one art you have learned in that household, you have just named it." Heads turned, and I lowered my voice. "You will tell me, or I will go to Hampton myself. Is he not well?" That was all I could think, that Tom was ill or unhappy, in need and too proud to ask.

"If you must know," Robin said, "he has a woman." He smiled at the serving wench who deposited more food before us.

"Who is she?"

He regarded me with those calculating pale eyes. "Kitchen girl much like that one, if you must know," he said. "A sweet, simple lass who causes him no pain, if she gives him no great pleasure. Her name is Lucy."

I felt as though the ceiling of smoke-blacked beams had fallen on my head. My fine dinner swam before my eyes.

A hand grasped my arm. "Bess, are you all right?"

Robin's freckles mixed with the spots in my vision. I blinked, and the room righted itself. "Yes," I said. "You've just given me a shock. You tell me that the world is ended and then ask if I'm all right."

"It's your own fault, prying it out of me in a room full of people." He pressed a cup into it my hand. "Take a little of this; it will clear your head."

The cardinal had no need of Robin for several hours, so after the meal, he led me out of the dining chamber, one arm solicitously about my waist. In the main hall, we came face to face with Nick, who focused all the magnetism of his dark gaze on my companion.

"Secretary Lewis," he said, "I have not yet had an opportunity to welcome you back. The cardinal keeps you busy, I fear."

"I would fear if he did not," Robin returned, giving Nick a rare smile. "You are well, sir?"

"Well in all but one respect," he said. "I have a great desire to speak with Mistress Bess, if you would but relinquish her."

I stared at Robin as he said, "It is an honor to surrender her to you, sir." He dropped my arm and bowed low to Nick.

I ignored Nick's proffered arm. "What have we to say?"

"Many things, Bess, some not easy for me." He paused. In the glow of the candles, he was all golden brown, still beautiful. "May we speak?"

"If the words are not easy, then keep them to yourself." I thought of Tom with his Lucy and grew angry; this would never have happened if Nick hadn't driven Tom away.

"Bess!" he said, and there was an unfamiliar note of pleading in his voice. I did not want to be alone with my thoughts, and when he offered his arm again, I took it and felt him tense beneath my hand.

We walked through the hall without words. At last, he stopped before an unfamiliar door, and we entered. The chamber was small and sparsely furnished. A door led to further rooms, all similarly situated. If it were anyone else, I would have wondered at their boldness in entering an empty apartment, but Nick lacked neither nerve nor royal favor and went where he would.

Weak light filtered in through windows overlooking the snowy grounds. I sat down on a carved bench beneath the window and looked at Nick. "You haven't brought me here to comment on the view?"

I startled him, but he laughed and seated himself beside me. "I have missed you," he said. "There it is—there's no other way to say it. I did not think it possible, but my life is darker for the lack of you."

I fixed my eyes on the sluggish, ice-choked river. "It's a very nice view."

"I made a mistake, letting you go." Nick stood up, paced the room, his every movement showing discomfort at this unfamiliar situation. "I would like to remedy that mistake." His words rang true, but I thought of his voice on the night when I'd tried to plead for Tom and did not have to harden my heart.

"Several mistakes."

A cloud passed over, casting the room into shadow. "I've apologized for that, Bess."

"You've hurt too many people," I said, thinking of one who had never hurt anyone, born low but with a keener sense of honor than my highborn lover.

"Let us get beyond mistakes. They are the past, and ahead is a future in which, I hope, we will not be long apart." He sat beside me again, clasped my cold hands. "I ask you to reconsider."

"I'm not the girl who let herself be taken in the tiltyard like a common kitchen wench," I said and felt something inside me shatter at my choice of words. Whatever Tom's kitchen wench might be, she was not common. "I've changed. I thought I loved you, but I know myself better now."

His smile was rueful. "I know your heart lies elsewhere, but have you plans to enter a convent?"

"No. Nor a brothel."

"You must not think that of yourself," he reproved. "Londoners call Anne Boleyn the Great Whore, did you know?"

Queen Katherine was loved by the common people, who did not mask their feelings as courtiers and household servants must. This was but the latest—and worst—of their names for her.

"I won't hear her called that."

"You've always had a fondness for Lady Anne, haven't you?"

"I want nothing but her happiness." Which I doubted would be with King Henry, despite his ardor. I recalled poor Harry Percy and contrasted him with the king. I believe Anne would have been happier with the man sprung from that lovesick, spotty boy.

"She's near enough to achieving it," Nick said. "The queen—the queen dowager, rather—banished, Mary put away, even the cardinal treads lightly. Why, she has all but the wedding ceremony now." He fingered his fur-trimmed robe. "And a prince."

"A prince? Speak you of children before they've even made their vows?"

"It won't matter how he loves her if she doesn't produce a son. She will have served no purpose but to cause upheaval with the Church."

I rose and picked my way across the darkening room. "Thank you for the conversation, Nick. It has been very interesting, but my mind is unchanged."

He followed me, stumbling in his haste. "Bess!" He caught my sleeve and drew me back. "You're a woman of considerable passion. It should not all be given to playing and singing."

"I would not call that a waste," I said, backing toward the door. It was strange to see him in the role of supplicant.

"Think on it," he called after me. "You'll find me here, in my new apartments."

~~~~~

There was something worse than being without Tom: the knowledge that Tom, who belonged with me, had found someone else. Was he happy? I wondered. Did she bring him the same love, the same passion we had shared, which took more than ten years to ripen? Each time I closed my eyes, I saw him with her.

As a result, I was unable to put Nick from my mind. He was right: I did not love him, but I swung back and forth between a vision of Tom and Lucy, which battered my heart, to a picture of myself with Nick.

I hesitated to go to Joan with such a quandary. She would not condemn me if I went with Nick; it was not in her. Neither would she understand my apparent renunciation, faithful as she was to her own lost love.

The cardinal's entourage lingered at the palace for several more days. I sent word to Robin to meet me in the practice rooms. He arrived promptly, his rusty hair and disarming smile preventing him from a wholly clerical appearance, or even from looking properly secretarial. He seemed puzzled at my summons.

"I won't keep you but a moment," I said, gesturing for him to be seated. "I've a few questions, if you'll answer them."

"If I can."

"Is Tom in love with that girl?"

Robin's face crumpled. "I wish I'd never told you. I knew you'd upset yourself."

"Don't fret; just answer me. Is he in love with her?" I hid my hands in my skirts, the pain of my nails digging into my palms keeping me from showing the despair I felt.

"I think so." He shrugged. "He's happy with her; I know that much."

I bit my lip. I would be able to tell, just by looking at him. "And has he taken her into his bed?"

"Bess!"

"Tell me."

"Yes."

I had been holding my breath. Robin's answer told me more than he could know. Tom would not allow himself to bed this girl unless he cared for her, unless he'd driven me from his heart. For a moment, I felt bereft. Then a sharper pain struck me. Not jealousy, as I would have expected, but anger. I pushed it away.

"Thank you," I said, trying to keep my voice from shaking. "That's all I needed to know."

He squeezed my hand. "Life gives us all hard decisions, Bess. If you need to speak again, I'm here."

"I must go, Robin. If I do not see you before you leave, I thank you again."

He walked out with me, and as we parted at a turning of the corridor, he grasped my arm. "I shouldn't tell him so soon," he said. "Make him wait."

"Who?"

"Hawkins."

I pulled him to one side. "What do you know?"

"I hear much," he stammered. "That's all. When he approached us the other evening, I assumed..." His face was still blanched, his freckles standing out like birdseed strewn upon the snow. "You are too good for him."

"I can't spend my life alone," I said.

"You're never alone." Robin waved a hand around us. "You've got everyone in the Music and on, up to the king. You don't have to be any man's mistress unless you want to."

I never reached Nick's apartments that night. As I passed through the hall, Flora called to me. "The Lady Anne has requested you."

To her apartments I went with all haste, forgetting Nick altogether; a summons from Anne Boleyn in those days was of no small importance.

A select group crowded her large chamber, milling about, Anne a dark butterfly in their midst. Her sallow skin and black hair were striking among the fair women of the court, few of whom, I noted, were in evidence here. Anne did not like women; her spell did not work as well on her own sex.

Chief among her guests was her brother. He was a favorite of the king and had risen with his sister, who was scarce parted from him.

George Boleyn had enough of Anne's looks to be striking, but his attractiveness was far more conventional, relying on a warm and pleasant smile and sparkling brown eyes, rather than his sister's indefinable magic. He was more popular than Anne; George posed no threat to anyone, stirred no controversy.

He reminded me of Nick, being slim, dark, and meticulously dressed. But George's face spoke of pleasantry and dalliance, while Nick's was all arrogance and darker passions. My skin prickled. I must make my decision soon, to acknowledge Tom as lost and salvage what happiness I could or to remain on my own.

How odd Robin had been, telling me to make Nick wait. It wasn't his usual light tone, and earlier, they had gotten on so well, Robin being almost obsequious with Nick.

The doors were flung open. Preoccupied, my voice trailed off several notes after the musicians ceased playing. The king strode into the room and bowed before the Lady Anne.

"We would speak to you alone," he said, waving us all toward the door. The courtiers scattered, only George Boleyn remaining at his sister's side.

I heard her say, as we gathered ourselves, "May my brother stay, Your Grace?"

"No," came the decided response. "We do not wish to speak to George."

The door closed behind us. George stood apart, then sighed and walked away. Someone murmured, "A lover's quarrel, I wager! Did you see the king's face?"

Gilbert whispered for him to be quiet, and we dispersed. I could have gone to Nick's chamber, but I chose instead to go to bed. Whatever I had to say would be clearer, I hoped, after a night's sleep.

Morning brought a harsh, blustery day and a corresponding grayness in my soul. I felt stifled indoors, but I ventured but a few steps outside before the icy sleet drove me back.

I ate alone, wrestling to overturn the decision I discovered in my mind upon waking. It remained firmly lodged, and after the midday meal, I went alone through the corridors to Nick's rooms.

His manservant opened the door. When he said Nick was gone, I felt a reprieve, a second chance. "Don't leave," he said, moving in front of me as I turned to go. "My master said, should you arrive, I should make you comfortable and send for him."

What of comfort? I thought, looking at the still-empty room. My eye was caught by the open door to the inner chamber, and I saw that it was now fully furnished. How had he done so much in a day's time?

I took a seat by the fire, and he brought me a cup of sweet wine before retiring to the outer room to wait for Nick. I drank and admired the dark red and gold Turkey carpet. Carpets were quite rare, though Cardinal Wolsey had a considerable collection of them at Hampton Court.

I recognized some of the furniture from my visit to Nick's rooms during the time of my father's illness, but there was an enormous tapestry which was new, and when I gathered my nerve to peek into the final chamber, I was astounded by the richness of its decoration. There was another carpet, grander than the first, in deep shades of red and blue. The bed was elaborately carved with roses and beasts and hung with red velvet curtains. The counterpane was also red, embroidered in gold with his coat of arms. The entire chamber spoke of elegance and wealth and the good favor of his sovereign.

They were close, of course, but I wondered how Nick had ingratiated himself as to deserve this new apartment. My puzzling was cut short by sounds in the outer chamber, and I retreated. I arranged the folds of my best blue gown, trying to look as though I had not been snooping. The door opened, and the servant looked in. "I've sent a page for him, mistress—he's outside somewhere."

The wine and the fire combined to make me drowsy, and I was almost asleep when the door from the corridor banged open, and I heard Nick's clipped tones. "Is she here, Terrence?"

"She is, sir."

Their voices lowered, and I could not make out more of their conversation. A few moments later, the corridor door closed, and Nick entered, throwing his damp cloak aside and coming to stand by the fire. His boots were spattered with mud, and I knew if I had not been there, Terrence would have had him undressed, with fresh clothes at the ready; Nick could not to be untidy.

"Bess!" His tone was oddly eager. When he took my hands, I flinched because his were like ice. "I'm sorry, how thoughtless." He held them toward the fire. "I'm glad you've come."

"I wasn't certain I would," I said, "not until this morning."

"Would you like more wine?" He filled my cup and poured one for himself.

I concentrated on the fire, as uncomfortable as he seemed to be. Was it because we were so long apart, or were there other reasons? Did Tom think of me as he went to his Lucy? If he did, it did not stop his going.

Nick moved another chair to the fire and sat down, his long legs outstretched. He drained his cup and set it on the carpet. "I am glad you came," he said. "But sorry the decision was difficult."

"How could it be anything else?" I asked. "There was much to overcome just to see you again, before giving your offer any serious thought." I thought of his crime against Tom, his many offenses to my sensibilities, and wondered how I could even contemplate accepting his proposal.

He smiled then, and I felt as if I'd drawn too close to the fire. "May I take it your response is yes?" he asked, and there was no hint of mockery in his voice.

I nodded, unable to say the word. My heart told me not to agree, but the rest of me, which had felt nothing but hopelessness since Tom's departure, pushed me toward him. If I could not be wife to the man I loved, I would be mistress to one whom I at least cared for. I would take happiness where I found it, for it was not so abundant as I had once assumed.

Nick held out his hands, and I gave mine into his grasp, let him draw me to my feet and slowly into his embrace. He pressed his face to my hair as if he could not be close enough. I moved my hand tentatively, touched his back, and that woke him from his spell.

"God, but I have missed you," he murmured, bringing his mouth down on mine. It was not Tom, I thought, but it would do.

He lifted me as if I were a child, carrying me through the door and into his private chamber where that glorious bed awaited us. Gently, he lowered me to the velvet counterpane, spreading my hair in a fan beneath me. His mouth traced the square neckline of my gown, and he slid one hand beneath me to work at my laces.

My mind was done with regrets; perhaps on the morrow, I would be ashamed of my desire, but I felt none then. I let him love me on top of his family's coat of arms, in the middle of the afternoon, with the full knowledge of at least one of his servants. Before nightfall, it would be known in the Music, and at breakfast, Robin would know.

Our liaison was perhaps more passionate because I did not care as much as before. We met regularly, but though Nick left my body pleased and frequently exhausted, he never touched my heart. He was generous, carelessly handing me small gifts before or after love, tokens that meant little enough to him but were nonetheless far beyond what I could afford.

He gave me another gift. On that first afternoon, as he held me in his arms, he told me he'd pensioned off Gianni and sent him home to Italy. "The king will be furious!" I said. "Why did you do it?"

"For you," he said. "I can't make up for what I did, but I can do this much. The king will find someone else to amuse him."

I came and went as I pleased, no longer afraid of being seen. I even had my own entrance, a small door on a side passage that led to the inner chamber. I arrived late, when my duties were done, to find him waiting with a tray of food and a jug of wine. Occasionally, he would be with the king, in which case Terrence, with whom I had become easy, would gossip with me until he heard his master's footsteps. It was Terrence who aroused my suspicions.

"My master will be quite late, Mistress Bess," he said, pouring wine for me. "I do believe he is celebrating with the king."

I had performed for a sulky, disgruntled Anne and wondered at King Henry's absence. "What have they to celebrate, Terrence?"

The servant reddened and busied himself arranging tiny cakes on a plate. "I may be mistaken," he said. "Please do not mention of it."

"I won't," I assured him. As the apartments neared completion, I could not keep from wondering at the source of Nick's newfound wealth, and I determined to find out.

Nick arrived much later, flushed with exuberance and drink, and seized me without even a proper greeting. After kissing me until I was breathless, he put me off at arm's length to admire me. "That's a lovely gown, Bess. You look most fetching in green."

The gown was new and had claimed all the spare time I did not spend with him. Joan had helped me with the fittings, but I had not really liked the dress until the end when, in frustration, I had torn off the trimmings and made painstaking inserts of the cream lace Tom had given me. I used the rest of it to add ruffles to the wrists of my lawn undersleeves. The outfit was completed by a green and gold headdress in the latest fashion.

"Quite fetching," he repeated and smiled. "I shall be very careful in removing it." He was true to his word, unlacing me gingerly and draping all the pieces of my costume over a chair.

I tried to help, but he brushed my hands aside, intent on his work in the way only a drunkard can be intent. My shift flew over my head, and I heard him sigh as he dropped to his knees to address himself to the ribbons which held up my stockings. He kissed the back of each knee as he removed them, breaking me out in a flurry of anticipatory gooseflesh. Reaching for him, instead, I found myself deposited on the bed while Nick, still dressed, brought wine to the bedside.

"I think you've had enough of that," I said and attempted to pull him onto the bed with me.

"It's for you." He shed his clothes so quickly, I scarce had a chance to see him before the candles were blown out. Nick strode naked to the window and flung open the shutters, bathing the bed in moonlight. I admired his silhouette against the glass, all clean lines and hard muscle, like a statue.

"I don't need any wine," I said. I wanted him badly by this point.

Nick chuckled. "Oh, but you must, Bess. I insist." He poured a cup and brought it into bed with him, balancing it with care as he came to kneel beside me. "Close your eyes, love." His fingers brushed my lips. I obeyed, waiting to feel his mouth on mine.

What I felt instead made me shriek and Nick laugh, as he dribbled the warm wine between my breasts and down over my belly. Moments later, I felt his hot mouth tracing the trail of the liquid. He continued downward, avoiding my frantic hands, until he came to kneel between my thighs. He reached for the cup again.

"No," I said, catching his wrist. "You can't."

"I can," Nick said and did.

Our skins stuck as we lay together afterward. "Shall I call Terrence?" he asked, one hand still caressing my breast. "Would you like a bath?"

I would have done murder for a bath but not at the expense of Terrence wondering why I needed one. "No, I said. "I don't believe I have the strength."

He laughed heartily and took a gulp of wine. "It was a fine evening," he said reflectively.

"You look to have been celebrating," I said, deeming it a wise time to explore the subject.

"I was indeed," he said. "The king has granted me the manor of Kelton, along with its title. I will be Lord Nicholas of Kelton."

I would be a lord's mistress, I thought. "That's wonderful. Why?"

His face darkened, reminding me momentarily of the old Nick. "I'm in no mood to discuss reasons," he said, feigning lightness. "Not when I've a girl in my bed who does not look to have been properly pleased this night."

"I have," I said in protest. "Truly, I have."

Pinning my hands on the pillow, Nick straddled me and looked down into my face. "Oh, no, I don't think so. It's a long time until morning."

I saw little of Nick as December wore on. He spent much time with his cronies, dicing and drinking, and when he sent for me, he was impatient and rough and never wanted to talk. It kept our attachment from deepening. Neglected, I was able to step back and see our odd partnership for it was.

He slept immediately after love these days, and I was able to slip from his bed unnoticed. Dressing quietly, I lifted the arras and left by the rear door. The corridor was cold, and I pulled my cloak about me as I hurried along. At the corner, I collided with someone far larger than myself, who swore softly as he saved me from falling.

Looking up, I dropped into a curtsy. The king was as tumbled and untidy as I, but he was unmistakable even in the uncertain light of the torches. "Your Majesty," I said, "I am most heartily sorry—I did not see—"

"Hush, child," he replied and raised me up, looking with a glimmer of a smile at my unbound hair and the mantle clutched over my loosened clothes. "We appear to have been on the same errand, though I do think that Master Cupid could have brought us a more temperate night."

I realized we were close to Anne Boleyn's rooms. That explained the king moving about without his gentlemen; the king was never unattended, even while he slept.

He kept pace with me for a few steps. After a few moments, he said, "You have been with us a long time, Bess. How do you like our court?"

I spoke from my heart. "In truth, Your Majesty, I cannot imagine life anywhere but here. This is the only home I've ever known."

"And yet you are no longer our happy songbird," the king chided.

"Only children are truly happy, Your Majesty."

The king made a sound of agreement. "We were told of the death of your father and are sorry. Are you missing him?"

"Yes, but he was ill and in pain." For some reason, I told the truth. "Most of all, I am missing my dear friend who joined the cardinal's household."

"Which friend is that?"

"Tom, the lutenist." I cast my eyes upward to the king's face. "He was the first person here to be kind to me."

The king sighed, sounding for all the world like a lovesick youth. "Life leads us all a merry dance, toward and away from our heart's choices. What seems right one day can be a mistake on the morrow."

I said not a word. I scarcely breathed. Was the king regretting Anne Boleyn as he crept from her chambers, even as I wished for Tom fresh from Nick's bed? The air quivered with the weight of those words.

The silence was broken when the king sighed again and laid a huge hand on my shoulder. "Christmas is hard upon us," he said, and he looked weary. "We shall request the cardinal bring your friend. It will be a joy to hear him again."

Chapter 19

It seemed the whole world came to court for Christmas—all but Wolsey and his household. I played and sang and participated in the masques and plays the king so loved, night after night, wearing my holiday finery. Beneath it all, I was empty, waiting.

The king sat on the dais with Lady Anne at his side. She looked lovelier than ever in the gowns and jewels which were the king's gifts to her. She wore them carelessly, which made them all the more magnificent.

The New Year's Eve masque marked the halfway point of the holiday celebrations. I performed that night, singing and dancing in a gown of silver tissue. My hair was intricately bound and covered with a fashionable silver headdress studded with pearls. A girdle of more pearls encircled my waist.

As we took our bows before the assembled company, there was a commotion at the doors, and I looked to see Cardinal Wolsey enter the chamber, with his usual enormous retinue. I caught a glimpse of Robin, but I did not see Tom.

The music began for dancing, and I retreated. Anne and the king led, moving gracefully down the floor, their eyes locked. She wore a gown of cloth-of-gold with sleeves of rich, figured black velvet, and the metallic fabric caught the light as she moved.

I felt a touch on my arm. Nick stood to my left, resplendent in russet and his own cloth-of-gold, offering me his hand. "May I have this dance, my lady?" he asked, doffing the feathered flat cap that was the king's latest fashion. My hand was in his, but my eyes fastened on a head of wheaten hair across the chamber, hair that could belong only to one person.

"No, thank you," I said. "I've promised this dance already." I made my way across the floor. Looking about, I saw Tom against the wall, not watching the dancers. I approached, my heart thudding in my chest.

"I've just told someone I promised this dance to you. Please don't make me look a liar." I held out my hands. He hesitated. "Please, Tom," I said, and my voice trembled.

He did not look at me as we danced, nor did he speak.

"It's good to see you."

"I was ordered to come," he said. I was shocked to see a tracery of fine lines around his eyes. The dance swept him away before I was able to respond.

The king had remembered! I felt a thrill of pleasure, but it faded at the expression on Tom's face. When he circled back to me, I said, "I hoped you would come. I've missed you."

His eyebrow quirked. "I saw the partner you turned away."

"I wanted to dance with you."

We followed the intricate steps, but there was no heart in either of us. I knew not what Tom felt; for my part, all I wanted was for him to smile at me. The music stopped, and he stepped away.

I caught his sleeve. "How long do you stay?"

"The cardinal journeys back to Hampton after mass on the Epiphany."

"And when do you journey back to Hampton?" I asked.

Tom did smile then, unwillingly. "When my lord cardinal does, Bess. I shall see you before then."

I released him, able to breathe. Let him warm to me, I prayed. Even if he did not give up Lucy, let him at least care. I could not imagine a world without Tom in it.

Joan waved, and I threaded my way through the dancers to join her. She looked worried and a bit cross, an expression most unlike her. "What's wrong?" I asked. Hope sang in my blood like wine.

"Nick Hawkins," she said. "His face was not pretty to look upon when you left him standing there."

"He is always pretty to look upon," I said. "It is his most important quality." I never thought what a snub might mean to such a man. He had never acknowledged me in public, though our relationship was known by all. Asking me to dance before the court was quite a step, and I'd refused.

More eyes than Nick's had seen our dance, and before the night was done, I heard my name called. The king stood on the dais, his face radiant with hippocras and happiness, pointing a plump finger at me. "We have a vast entertainment this evening," he boomed. "A reunion of two of our most talented musicians. Bess, please come forward."

I blanched, not knowing how Tom would react. I sought him out among the crowd. He looked trapped.

"Our finest lutenist," the king went on, "whom we foolishly gave up to our lord cardinal. Thomas, please join us." Behind me, someone scurried to fetch a lute, and by the time Tom joined me, Ned had found one, gilded and beribboned, and presented it with a grin and a flourish. The king beamed. "The airs we leave to your discretion," he said and seated himself beside Lady Anne, taking her hand and caressing it.

Tom's grip on the lute was so tight, I feared he would break it. "I did not ask for this," I said beneath the murmur of the crowd, "but we must do it. Play 'Greensleeves,' if you know it."

It was the newest of the king's compositions, a poignant, lilting air written with Anne in mind. I knew it would please him and hoped he would let us go with one song. Tom plucked the opening notes, and I let him play the first verse through before I joined in.

> *Alas, my love you do me wrong*
> *To cast me off discourteously,*
> *And I have loved you so long,*
> *Delighting in your company.*

To sing again with Tom was unspeakable joy. My voice was never better than it was that night. Through the haze of my happiness, I saw the king's pleased expression. The entire court was smiling and attentive. I glanced at Tom. For a moment, he forgot himself and blazed back the brilliant smile of the time before he left me. I looked away before he could realize and mask himself again.

> *I have been ready at your hand*
> *To grant whatever you would crave;*
> *I have both wagered life and land,*
> *Your love and good will for to have*
>
> *Greensleeves was all my joy.*
> *Greensleeves was my delight.*
> *Greensleeves was my heart of gold*
> *And who but my Lady Greensleeves.*

We came to the last verse. I took a breath, looked at Tom's pale head bent over the lute, and sang:

> *Greensleeves, now farewell! Adieu!*
> *God I pray to prosper thee.*
> *For I am still thy lover true;*
> *Come once again and love me.*[6]

I sang my love to them all, as I could not sing it to Tom. When the song ended, he did not stop playing but turned to other of the king's melodies, light and happy tunes, until we had done them all. When at last we stopped, I was trembling. The applause came at us like thunder from all sides. The king rose himself to applaud, smiling and looking like the golden giant of my childhood. Tom reached for my hand, and we bowed as one, then backed from the room.

"That was wonderful," I said, breathless, as the doors closed behind us.

"The cardinal does not have your equal," Tom said. I could not tell his meaning straight away. "I have missed performing with you."

"Is that all you've missed?" I asked before I could catch myself. I did not want to have this conversation now, while we were both so disturbed from performing. "I'm sorry."

He leaned against the wall, crossing his arms over his chest. "It's only right you should ask. I've missed you, all of you, not just your voice, the way you miss a tooth after it's been pulled. Glad of the respite, yet missing the pain that's been a part of you for so long."

I did not know whether to laugh or cry. "You can be such a poet," I said, "and then you compare me to a sore tooth."

Tom shrugged and brushed the hair from his eyes. "I'm tired, Bess."

His tone drained the exhilaration from me. "May we talk before Epiphany?"

"As you wish."

"Don't you wish?" I was suddenly frightened that Robin's tales were true, and Lucy meant more to him than I could guess.

His smile should have lit the halls. Instead, he murmured his good night and left me at the door.

Torn between going to my room and returning to the festivities, I ducked back inside. The chamber was alive again with music and dancing, and I realized my mistake as soon as I entered. I did not wish to be alone, but I could not be with people.

I took a cup from an overflowing fountain and retreated to a corner. The wine lightened the burden on my heart, and when Nick approached, I was able to face him. "Happy New Year!" I said.

"And to you, Bess." He fussed with the pearls decorating his sleeve. "May I have the honor of your presence tonight, or are you promised elsewhere?"

I ignored the edge to his voice. "I thought I would do something novel and spend the night in my own bed."

"Be in my chamber in one hour, or I'll send Terrence to beat your door down."

He would do it. Nick was not accustomed to being embarrassed. Terrence's horror at the task, and the reactions of Flora, Mary and the others, made me move quickly. I changed out of my costume and back into a plain gown and made it to the side entrance just as the hour struck two.

Nick was waiting on the bed, half-dressed, a cup in his hand. The bottle nestled in the curve of his arm. "Terrence, there's no need to search for her!"

Terrence put his head in the door, looked at me and his intoxicated master. "Thank you, mistress. Good night, sir." He disappeared before either of us could perish from mortification.

"Of course I came," I said. "I couldn't let you send him on a fool's errand."

"You came for his sake." Nick eased himself upright, catching the bottle before it tipped. "You don't want to be here."

"I told you I didn't want to come tonight." I sat down on the other side of the bed. "Can't you be pleasant?"

"Was it pleasant to be left standing like an ass while you fluttered off to dance with your musician? You looked like Venus in that gown, with your hair up and your long neck. The neck of a goddess, a curve to make a man weep." He threw the cup across the room, and it struck the wall, spraying the hangings with dark red liquid. "Don't fuss with it, Bess, come back here."

"You've had too much to drink," I said and smoothed the black curls from his forehead.

"I haven't had enough."

He began to caress me. I sat very still. My heart would not respond, but my body might. I thought of Tom and what I needed to say to him, and desire drained away. Nick's hands were on my body, and I took no more notice than if he were Edith feeling my pulse. So it was possible, I thought, to shut desire away.

Nick pushed me back against the pillows and lowered himself over me, his lips at my throat. "It's the New Year, Bess," he murmured, between kisses. "What would you like as your New Year's gift?"

His Christmas gift had been a fine ring. I was about to protest, when I thought of a gift that would cost him nothing.

"Anything?" I tried to squirm free.

"Anything," he said, reaching under my skirts.

I clamped my knees together. "I want the truth."

Nick looked bewildered beyond drunkenness. "I've never lied to you."

"Mayhap I just haven't asked the right questions," I said. "I'll wager what's left of my virtue that you have a secret."

Nick rolled off me, crossing the room to stare through the mullioned window into the darkness. "I never realized you had such a suspicious nature."

The comment was so obviously formulated to distract me that I laughed. "My nature is too trusting, else I would have asked already. Something is different. You've always been a friend of the king, but all this?" I gestured at the chamber. "New apartments, a title—I'm not so stupid that I don't notice."

He closed the shutters and came to sit beside me on the bed, hands resting on his thighs. "The king's gifts are rarely without a price," he said. "You realize much of the old nobility refuses to support the idea of divorce? Some, he will deal with later, as he sees fit, but others, he would try to retain their loyalty and change their minds." He pressed mouth to my wrist. "That is where I come in."

"How can you help?"

"The lord in whose house I was raised keeps to Queen Katherine. The king, knowing my ties to the family, endeavors to sway his loyalty." He took a deep breath and began to speak rapidly. "It won't make any difference to us; she'll never be at court, but it is the king's wish, and I will abide by it."

In the muddle of his words, I heard only one. "And who," I asked, "is she?"

Nick looked discomfited. "The youngest daughter, Elinor."

"You are to be married, then." I was not surprised.

"At Easter," he said. "The king thinks it a grand idea. She's always been her father's darling."

"Why so downhearted?" I poured a cup of wine for Nick, who looked to need it, despite his earlier excesses, and one for myself. "Does she not want the match?"

He looked astonished. "I don't know if anyone has asked her," he said. "If the king were not so set upon it, I wouldn't want the match. Elinor is a child, younger than you by several years. She knows nothing of court or of men. I doubt she's left the North in her entire life."

"I once knew nothing of court or of men," I said. "There are worse things."

Nick dropped into his chair before the fire. "You sound pleased."

I considered him: the hours we'd spent together, the innocent happiness of my unrequited love, the passionate, turbulent times since I'd grown up. "Everything must end," I said. "Don't begrudge her that."

He shoved the chair back so hard, it toppled over. Crossing the room in long strides, he caught my arms and raised me up. "What end, Bess? I've said she'll not be here at court—good Christ, what would I do with her here?"

"The same that you do with me, my lord, if she may serve no other purpose," I said, feeling sorry for the girl. "She'll be your wife. A married man has no need of a mistress."

"No man needs one more!" he cried. "You can't mean this. You're overwrought. I broke the news too suddenly."

I laughed and saw his start of surprise. "You nearly told me not at all." I peeled his fingers away and straightened my gown. "No, Nick. When you were unattached, I felt no shame at being your mistress, but I won't be the one to hurt her. I'll leave that to you."

My explanation was clumsy but true. No longer loving him, I could not split him in two for selfishness. Having seen Tom again made me all the more adamant. What I had with Nick was pleasant, but it was not real and was better done.

"The girl will never know." He was imposing, even in his disordered state.

"She will know," I said. "I would know if the man I loved slept each night with someone else."

The firelight showed me his scornful face, shadowed with stubble. "You speak as if you know she will love me."

"She was a child as you grew to a man. If she did not fight the marriage, she doesn't hate you. All it will take is kindness. And what if she is innocent? Would you rather marry the spoils of some other man?" My tone turned persuasive. "Think of all the delights you may teach her."

"Christ!" he swore. "You discuss it coldly, as if I meant nothing. Do you love your lutenist so much?"

"We are talking about you and the Lady Elinor," I said. I had no wish to bring Tom into this.

"Well, I wish to discuss you and that bastard musician!" he flared. "You left me standing like a fool to go to him tonight. I should have known then—you came here to end it, without my telling you anything at all. You're using my marriage as an excuse."

I pressed my fingers to my temples. "You said when we began again that you knew my heart was elsewhere. How could you be surprised I would go to him tonight, when I haven't seen him in months?" Turning away, I smoothed rumpled bedcover, running my fingertips over the raised embroidery. "Still, I'm not leaving you for him."

"I've known how you felt about him since that night on the stairs. That was why I brought Gianni—to drive him from your heart. I thought I had until tonight."

"You never did," I said and met Nick's eyes. He reeled back when he saw the truth there. "I would walk through fire for Tom."

"Then why come back to me?" He reached again for the wine bottle.

I shrugged. "I loved you once. I thought..." Unable to finish, I gathered my wrap around my shoulders. He had already made me shout at him; I wanted to leave before he made me cry. My hand was on the door when his next words stopped me.

"Speak to your friend Secretary Lewis," Nick said, his voice slurred. "I did not act alone, Bess. I could not offer a place in the cardinal's household or smooth his way. Ask him why he did it, for I do not see my gold upon his back."

It was early, the revelers yet abed, the household staff clearing away all evidence of merrymaking. I climbed to the attics to ponder Nick's words. At first, I felt sick from the shock, but when that faded, I was left with bone-deep exhaustion. How could Robin console me after being the cause of my loss? How could he call himself my friend?

I remembered the odd camaraderie between them on the day Robin put me into Nick's hands; Nick's jovial tone, when he disliked anyone having to do with the cardinal; Robin's warning not to go to Nick too quickly. It explained everything and nothing.

The call for music was constant. By the end of the week, I was hoarse, but it kept my mind occupied, and I had earned a nice little purse for my work.

I saw Nick frequently, but we did not speak. I heard he was traveling north after the festivities were over. January was an odd time to travel, and I wondered if he was curious about his new property or his bride. I did not credit I might be the reason for his departure.

As for Tom, he neither ignored me nor sought me out. We performed together several times, though never with the magic of that first night, and after each occasion, he made his excuses. I had to ask if he would sit with me at supper the day before Epiphany.

The dining hall was packed with the two households, and the table where we sat was filled with Wolsey's undersecretaries and hangers-on, all chattering about their lord and his business. Robin was not among them.

I turned toward Tom, trying to shut out their din, and spoke quietly. "I hoped we would have more chance to talk than this."

He prodded his meat with the side of his knife. "There's little to talk about. It's a quiet life there."

"I think I'd like that," I said, and he smiled at the rough edge to my voice. "It is busy enough here but lonely."

"You have Joan," Tom pointed out, raising his cup. "And Robin says he sees you often."

So Robin's gossip went both ways! I was pleased to hear it; if Tom did not ask, he nevertheless heard my name, and I knew it took but a mention to keep a memory alive in the heart.

"I heard about your father," Tom said after an uncomfortable silence. "I am sorry. He was the last link to your old life."

I smiled. "That is true enough. My mother cares not what becomes of me, and my sister is occupied with her own family now." I looked at my plate, remembering my father's careworn face. "But I was there to say goodbye, and that is what matters."

The men behind us burst into hearty laughter, and one of them caught me in the ribs with an elbow. "How is your mother?" I asked, pushing my food away.

"I was in London last month. She is dead. They wrote, but the message never reached me at Hampton." I knew, despite his tone, that the loss had shaken him. "I hadn't visited her since April."

"I saw her in October," I said, knowing as I spoke that it was a mistake.

Tom turned unbelieving eyes on me. "Why?"

"I don't know, truthfully. She was your mother," I said. "It seemed a way to be with you when I could not. She seemed more tired than ill. She asked about you, when I had seen you last, if you were happy. We spent an hour together."

He dropped his knife. "It was you! The women said she'd had a visitor the week before she died, and she seemed more at peace after."

Rose's secret rose up in me. I pushed it down. There might be a time when he needed to know, as she said, but this was not it.

"Bess?" Tom touched my shoulder. "What did she say?"

"Only that she was sorry all her days she gave you up," I said. It was a sin of omission, I thought, not a lie. "She said she loved you, though she'd never shown it."

"I knew," Tom said. His eyes glittered. "I knew, but I never told her either."

Beneath the table, I took his hand. "And she knew. She missed seeing you, but she understood." I pressed his unresisting fingers. "I don't know what I expected, Tom, but...I liked her."

He let out a pent-up breath. "You've taken a weight off my heart. I thank you for that."

The noise level rose, and I tugged at his hand. "Can we please go out of here?"

It was cold outside and dark, but we agreed to meet at the western doors in ten minutes' time. I ran to fetch my hood and mantle, my heart giving wings to my feet. Time alone with Tom! He had already warmed to me because of his mother; we just needed time before our old understanding returned. Peering anxiously into the square of polished steel Nick had given me, I fussed with my hair and arranged my hood in its most becoming manner. Before I left, I pulled Nick's ring from my finger and shoved it under my pillow.

As I sped down the stairs and through the great hall, a voice hailed me. I turned to see Robin.

"I haven't time for you," I said. He had been ducking me for days; it was my turn.

"But Bess—"

"Not now." I flashed him a look of disdain and disappointment. "Nick told me about you."

Robin went white beneath his freckles. "I had reason."

"Yes. Nick's gold." I pulled my cloak about me. "How could you pretend to be my friend?"

He followed me. "I am your friend and a faithful one. I acted for my own gain, but also because I worried about you."

"And you thought removing Tom from my life would help?"

Robin sighed. "I just saw you at table with him. I never realized—I would not have interfered if I'd known—but Hawkins wanted you, and I thought it would make you happy not to be torn between them."

"I don't love Nick," I said, impatient to go to Tom. "Your interference did nothing but drive us further apart."

214

He looked chastened. "I am sorry, Bess." He kissed me on the forehead and disappeared into the shadows.

I continued to the western doors, but the joy was gone from my step. Tom was there and ushered me outdoors with a solicitous air. "Did you take the stairs too quickly? You look pale."

"I'm fine." I braced myself against the wind that buffeted around the corner of the building and sent me stumbling into him.

He offered me his arm. "Perhaps we should stay indoors."

I shook my head. It was numbingly cold, but between the clouds, the moon was high, and the grounds were lit with an eerie pinkish light. We turned toward the trees, rather than the ice-clotted Thames, and soon, we were wrapped in silence.

My breath was a white cloud before my face as I spoke. "Robin tells me news of you ofttimes."

"He does the same for me."

We walked for several minutes before I could bring myself to say anything more. "He says you have a woman."

The silence grew until I could hear my own heartbeat. Tom did not seem to breathe at all. At last, he moved, and as my hand still clutched his arm, I moved with him. "Robin says too much," he said. "I would not have you hurt for the world."

His words were a balm. "I'm not hurt if you are happy."

"Dear Bess!" He tipped my chin up, and my hood slipped back. "I am...content."

"Content," I repeated. He would not have used such a tame word about me.

The wind took my cap, and my hair swirled free. Tom gathered it up and secured my hood again. "I went to Hampton to escape you," he said, bending to shelter me from the wind. "I felt cut loose, with nothing to cling to."

"You could have clung to me." I put my hand over his, impatient with the gloves separating our flesh.

He shook his head. "I sought out Lucy as well. I needed to care for someone without involving my whole heart."

"Do you love her?" I could not imagine that he loved her.

Tom's smile was rueful, his dimple nowhere in evidence. "I have tried."

"And?"

"She cannot make me angry."

I blinked. "What?"

"Sweetheart, you can make me insane by lifting your eyebrow. Lucy is not woven deep enough into me to cause me that kind of upset."

I thought of all the times I must have driven him to fury, and winced.

"Do you need to hear it?" he asked. "I'll never love her as I loved you, but now... She bears a child in the spring." He took my hands, held them to his chest beneath his cloak. "When she told me, I asked permission to marry her, but the cardinal refused."

This was what Robin had wanted to tell me. It was hard enough hearing it from Tom; I was glad I had not let Robin speak. "I wish you'd given me a child that night," I said, shocking him.

"You know, Bess, what this means?"

"I know." Whether he loved her or me, whether they were permitted to wed, the child tied him to her.

"I do care," he said, oblivious to the biting wind. "And I will not forsake my child. I know too well what it feels like."

My hood fell back again, and I let my hair blow, hoping it hid the tears that burned my eyes, hot then cold. "Then we are nothing to each other."

He saw the tears on my face. "We can neither of us forget, and we should not. But what else is there?"

I wiped my eyes with the edge of my cloak. "It will be like a knife in my heart, knowing you will have love and happiness and a child, when I will have none of these."

He flinched. "I will never feel for Lucy what I have felt for you," he said, wrapping an arm around me. "And your life is hardly lonely, Bess."

In his self-appointed role as go-between, Robin gave me news of Tom, told me of his affair with Lucy; why had I never thought he would tell Tom of my return to Nick?

"Nick's marrying at Eastertide," I said. "When he told me, I gave him up. I'll not be mistress to a married man."

"Oh, Bess." His arm tightened around me, and I snuggled against him, sharing his warmth.

"It doesn't matter," I murmured. "I love him not."

His body stiffened against mine; I felt the change and turned to him. We swayed in the wind, and when he drew my face to his, I put my arms around his neck and let him kiss me.

The aching chill was at once tempered by his hot mouth, regardless for once of all consequence. His hand sought my hair, bundled it against my neck and tilted my head back. Tom's warmth beneath his cloak was tremendous; I pressed myself against him.

I remembered that night in his chamber and his body, lean and strong, and felt a weakening in my legs. It did not matter how many times Nick loved me, or to what heights he raised my passion; I had never felt such an aching need. I dropped my gloves and ran my hands down Tom's back, feeling the smooth muscle beneath his doublet, and shivered again.

He broke the kiss, his hands seizing my waist and setting me apart from him. "Jesu. We'd best stop, love, or I'll be taking you right here in the snow."

I traced a fingertip round his lower lip. "I shouldn't mind the cold one bit if you did," I said and kissed him again. Differently, this time, for I knew though his hunger was as great as my own, he would not love me there on the ground; his respect for Lucy, and for me, was too great. I drew away slowly and touched his cheek.

"What is it?" he asked, bending over me, nothing but concern in his voice.

How could I tell him that his face just then, well-known as it was, struck me as being so beautiful, it brought me to tears? He would laugh at me for being sentimental, which I was, but there was something in the intensity of his expression that made me wish I could forget my own feelings and just hold him and make everything well for him.

"Nothing," I told him, meeting his gaze. "Nothing but loving you and wanting you with me so badly, it hurts."

"Bess." His hands gripped my shoulders so hard, I would bear the marks of his fingers for days. "If you knew how many years I waited on those words and what it costs to hear them now."

"I never meant for it to hurt so." A gust blew my cloak around us, and we stood together, wrapped in one garment, my head on his chest.

The wind began to subside, and he moved away. "We should not stay so long outdoors." His ragged breathing betrayed his calm tone. "You'll catch a chill."

"I'll be all right," I said and knew that my simple words covered a multitude of ills, not all of them physical. Despite our kiss and the love writ plain on his face, Tom would still leave me in the morning.

Through the palace we walked, arm in arm, our cloaks dusted with snow. Many eyes were upon us, but we saw nothing. Tom escorted me up to my chamber and stopped before the door. I raised his hands to my lips and slipped inside. I did not hear him walk away.

Chapter 20

The cardinal's household departed after morning mass. At table that afternoon, I was surprised to see Robin still among us. He made his way over and sat down, ignoring the fact that I was ignoring him. He said that he had been left behind with a few others to finish some paperwork, and he would remain for several days.

"Are you not over being angry?" he asked. "I saw you with Tom last night. You had eyes for naught but each other, coming in all covered with snow and marching straight up the stairs."

How terrible he made it sound! I put down my knife so I would not be tempted to jab it into his hand. "We went outside to talk. We came back in. He walked me up to my room to say goodbye. Your eyes saw more than what happened."

"You are still angry," he concluded. "I thought I was doing the right thing."

"And you enriched yourself in the process."

"Well, yes, Hawkins did pay me rather well, and it never hurts to have a powerful man in your debt, but that is no excuse. I thought—mistakenly, it seems—that I was doing you a service." He rubbed his chin, newly shadowed by a beard grown in imitation of the king. It did not flatter him. "I am sorry I made you unhappy. Please don't let my stupidity ruin our friendship."

I wanted to scream, to slap him, yet at the same time, I pitied how little insight he had into the hearts of others. If I abandoned him, he would lose what little humanity he had left and become just another one of Wolsey's bloodless, efficient creatures.

"You know I will never trust you again."

"I deserve that," Robin said. "But tell me you still have some affection for me. Don't send me back to Hampton desolate."

I laughed. Only the king and cardinal could matter that much to him; he knew it as well as I. "I hope I send you back chastened."

He sighed. "That you do."

"Then I am satisfied." I returned to my food, glad this at least was settled. I still had my remaining link to Tom. I turned then and spoke with more vehemence than I intended. "You must promise me one thing, Robin."

"Anything within my power." He rubbed at his beard again and smiled when he caught me watching.

"Never speak to me of him," I said. "Not his name nor his health nor his relations with her. We are as if we'd never met, and I wish it to remain that way. He will likely tell you the same."

Robin's eyes widened. I'd shocked the man who witnessed the tantrums of royalty. "You cannot wish that; it's like a death."

"I wish him life," I said, "and the same for myself." His expression was skeptical. "It is all we can do."

❧

The doors of the hall burst open to admit two staggering couriers and a swirl of snow. A chill blew through the room, and I shivered in my seat and drew my cloak further around my shoulders. The wind was loud enough to be heard through the stone walls, and the tapestries and hangings failed to keep out the drafts.

The hall was filled to capacity, everyone trapped by the snow. The king had retired to play cards, taking several of his cronies with him. Those who remained stood or sat, talking quietly, even the musicians at rest or too benumbed to play.

A babble of sound broke out behind me, and I looked around. During the holiday, King Henry received visits from several Welsh lords, whose presence enlivened the festivities. When the dreadful weather set in, making the roads west impassable, they decided to winter with us. They were talking amongst themselves as if the rest of us did not exist.

I watched one man in particular. He was perhaps forty years old, with a weathered golden skin and a smooth cap of dark brown hair with the first wings of gray lighting his temples. He also had but one leg and sometimes moved with a halting gait that in no way impaired his attractiveness to the ladies of the court, who fluttered about, asking him questions about Wales. He answered them politely, but I don't believe he ever looked at them.

My attention fastened on him, not for his appearance or the novelty of his accent, but because of the instrument he cradled with the same devotion Tom showed his lute. As he took the small harp from its protective wrapping, I heard him speaking to it in a mixture of Welsh and English.

"Come, cariad," he said to the harp, caressing the glossy carved wood and running his fingertips lightly over the gut strings.

It was as if, somewhere deep inside, a note had been struck.

Cariad. The Welsh love-word was wrenchingly familiar, though I did not remember ever hearing it. Cariad. I repeated it to myself. It must have been my father's word, said perhaps when I was very small, before Cefin's death and my mother's denial of all that still lived.

It was strange to hear it again from this unknown Welshman. With one soft utterance, he had returned something to me I hadn't known was lost.

I reached out and touched the smooth curve of the harp with one finger. "Would you teach me to play, Master Ewan?"

His keen eyes fastened on me, and for a moment, I feared he would think me like the other women who approached him. Then he said, "The harp cannot be taught." He lowered his head again, his fingers barely touching the strings. The sound that issued mirrored the wind outside yet was a poignant echo of my own sorrows. "I have heard you sing. With such a gift, you need never learn an instrument."

I glanced at the seat beside him, and he nodded. "My father was Welsh, you see, and when he gave me to the court, he said I should learn the harp. He never knew how himself."

"He gave you your voice, a true Welsh voice. I knew it from the first note." Sliding closer, he said, "There's a bit of the hiraeth in your voice."

"Hiraeth?"

He plucked a few notes. "There's no word for it in your tongue. It's a sort of homesickness, perhaps, for the past. It's not mourning, exactly, but more a grief for a life not lived." He closed his eyes. "Does that make sense?"

I thought of my life had Jenny Keith not died; if Agnes and I had grown to womanhood together. I thought of Tom. "It does."

"I thought it might. Your voice has a touch of sadness to it, though you're still young."

I thought I had sufficient hiraeth—and loss, for that matter—for someone far older. "About the harp..."

"Only a Welshman can play the harp as it is meant to be played." He raised a graying eyebrow. "And it does look to be a long winter here."

My heart lightened at what seemed to be assent. "Will your party stay that long?"

"'Tis difficult going where we're bound. Until the snow melts, no one will be traveling anywhere."

There was a brazier within a few feet of us, and I stretched my legs toward the warmth. "Have you family in Wales?" I asked and realized that, once again, my words might be taken as flirtatious.

"A wife," he said and smiled. "I've left her at the Abbey in Shrewsbury. She'll pass a pleasant winter there, and I'll greet her in the springtime."

I still did not understand the workings of the male mind. Tom and Nick were poles apart, and now came this changeling man, who left his wife at a monastery and did not seem upset to be parted for some three months. "May I ask a question of you?" The brow raised again, eloquent as his voice. "Aye."

"Don't you miss her?"

He smiled. I couldn't tell from that simple curving of his lips if he laughed at my question. "Of course," he said, "but I can feel her in my heart, even from Shrewsbury."

This was something I understood. I knew from all the times we'd not needed words, or sensed when to soothe a hurt, that Tom felt the same connection, but I'd never heard another man voice such a sentiment. I knew this man not at all, yet I felt I comfortable asking, "Is it...have you ever found it frightening? Being that close to someone?"

He laughed again but not unkindly. "In the beginning, perhaps, before we realized the beauty of it. I've known Bronwyn since we were children. She's like my leg."

I looked down at his legs, one strongly muscled, clad in black hose, the other withered, ending in a carved peg below the knee. "Which one?"

Raising the stump, he said, "The one that's not there. When first they took it, they said I'd feel it for the rest of my life—not the pain of having it crushed under a horse, but the leg itself. I didn't know what they meant, but I soon found out." He raised his hands, then dropped them to his thighs. "It's hell, trying to scratch an itch on a foot that isn't there." He reached for his harp again. "Bronwyn is like that. I can always feel her, even when she's not there."

"An itch." I laughed. I had not enjoyed myself so much in months.

"Sometimes. And sometimes a pain, but more often, she's just the beating of my heart."

Still struggling, I said, "Do you believe people can be born to know just one person in that way?"

Ewan played a short passage of something lilting and wild. "The Welsh believe many strange and wonderful things. But that sort of knowledge, between a man and a woman, is something special. Yes, I believe it."

The doors banged open again to admit another traveler, and I shivered in the draft. Ewan leaned over and settled my cloak closer around my neck. "You mustn't take a chill in your throat." He nudged the brazier closer with his wooden leg. "If your hands aren't too stiff, I could give you your first lesson."

I explained I knew a little, but he scoffed. "You learned from an Englishman, I'll be bound. Stay with me, and learn to play as a Welshwoman."

~~~

When I was not with Ewan, learning the harp, I spent time with Joan. She had received a blow after Christmas when a friend wrote to say William was married. She said, with determined cheer, that she would not begrudge him happiness, but I think those days were as difficult for her as they were for me.

I assumed she had seen me with Tom and drawn her own conclusions, but she was tactful and never asked what transpired that night. She never mentioned him, as I never mentioned Will after she told me of his marriage.

It was strange and peaceful, rather what I thought being a nun would be like, but with better music. I enjoyed the quiet routine of meals, lessons and stitchery, the soft murmur of female voices over a tapestry frame. Such would have been my life at court if Nick had never set me apart. I tried to become more skillful with a needle, only to find my talents unappreciated.

"Bess, you're dreaming again," came the voice of one of the other women. "Why don't you put that down and sing for us instead? I'll pick your stitches for you."

"I'd rather do this," I objected, looking down at the length of frayed cloth that stretched across our laps. It was not a complex repair, but I had no clue what I was doing.

As one, they looked at me, and I rose and took a seat near the fire with my little harp. "It's not that you can't sew," Margaret said with an apologetic smile, "but this is a difficult task, after all, and none of us can sing."

"It does pass the time," Joan added.

I could not refuse my friend. "All right," I said with good humor, "but you will get a tasting of Wales for this." I inflicted my imperfect playing upon my friends and saw with surprise that they listened intently and asked for more.

Thus the measure of our days: stitching in the morning while I played, my mastery of the harp growing as the days lengthened. In the afternoons, I would have my lessons or a rehearsal for an evening performance.

Rarely did I perform for the king, who rampaged about the palace, bored and cranky as a child. Everyone suffered for it—Wolsey and Lady Anne especially, being the closest to the royal person. Will Somers, his fool, was kept weary with trying new tricks to make his master smile; no one envied him the task.

March came and, with it, St. David's day, a celebration for the Welshmen. Though the weather was still gray and blowing, it was better than the past months, and they made ready to depart. Ewan bade me farewell with an affectionate squeeze and an admonition not to forget my lessons.

"Do not worry," I told him. "I shall never forget nor he who taught me." I would miss my new friend exceedingly. He was a natural storyteller, and in the weeks of our acquaintance, he had imparted to me a sense of my heritage by telling me of Llewelyn Fahr and his grandson and namesake, of Owain Glendower and many other heroes and villains of Welsh history. The drama enthralled me as the songs had taken my heart.

In a way, Ewan ap Meredydd was a gift beyond death from my father, giving me a sense of myself as a Welshwoman he had not been able to do himself.

I embraced him and kissed his cheek. "I do thank you for all you've given me," I said. "We shall all miss you, but you are too great a prize for us to keep."

"Men like me are all too common, Bess. Full of dreams and songs and stories and little else. Find yourself an Englishman who cares not for music, and then you'll have a husband." He clasped my hand once and was gone, and with him went much of the music of our days.

~~~~~

No sooner did the ice give way on the Thames than the river was once again clogged with all manner of boats and barges. One of the first to tie up at the water stairs was a new, brightly painted barge carrying a large and boisterous party. From the window, I watched them disembark. One of the first to be handed down was a small figure in a blue cloak, who turned and raised her hands to a man, dark as she was fair, his mantle a bright russet against the dead shades of winter.

Nick Hawkins had brought his bride to court.

I gathered my skirts and ran down to witness their entrance. The passage ahead of me was full; after the wearying months of cold, any arrival was interesting. But they saw my face and let me pass, so I reached the great hall as the doors opened to admit the party.

The king stood in the center of the hall, his arms flung wide. "Hawkins!" he bellowed. "Did you find your lands to your liking?"

Nick came forward and knelt before the king. "My lands were much to my liking, Your Majesty. And see, I have brought back a bit of treasure." He turned and motioned to the girl, who hung back. "Come forward, Elinor, and greet the king."

A servant took her cloak, and she joined Nick, her step hesitant but her eyes shining as she looked at him. She curtsied prettily and kissed the king's outstretched hand. "Your Majesty."

King Henry raised her up. His small eyes evinced pleasure as he looked upon her, and with a flourish, he turned her about to face the crowd gathered around. "The newest member of our court," he announced. "Hawkins, when do you wed?"

It was the first time I'd ever seen Nick look uncomfortable. Certainly, I'd never heard him stammer as he did when he said, "We were married two weeks ago, Your Majesty." He cast his eyes away and noticed me on the stairs. I met his gaze, letting him break the contact.

There was a long silence, but at last, the king shouted with laughter and clapped Nick on the back, hard enough to make him stagger. "Tonight," he called out, "we celebrate the impatient bridegroom!"

I would be required to sing at the wedding feast. It did not matter that we had been lovers—or still were, for all anyone knew.

Nick and his bride were trying to leave the hall, and I was trying to avoid them, but the tides of the crowd carried us together. I stopped a few feet away as Nick accepted the felicitations of Thomas Cromwell, and when he turned, he stepped on the hem of my gown.

"Congratulations," I said, bending my knee to both of them.

She was young, I thought, perhaps seventeen or eighteen, and she had the translucent skin seen only on young country-bred girls. Dominating her heart-shaped face, however, were her eyes, large and light lavender-blue as an early morning sky. Though she was now married, her hair was loose, falling below her waist, and of course, it was the bright gold of a new-minted coin.

"May I present my wife, Elinor," he said, taking my hand. "Elinor, this is Bess Llewelyn, the most talented musician at court."

224

"I'm happy to meet you," she said, looking at Nick when he did not immediately release me. "What instrument do you play?"

"The harp and the lute, my lady."

"And she sings like an angel," Nick interposed. "I am sure you will have the pleasure of hearing Bess one day soon."

"This very evening," I said. "I will sing in honor of your wedding."

"I shall look forward to it," said the girl, Elinor. She put her arm through his. "My lord?"

"Your wife is tired from her journey," I said. "I wish you every blessing in your union, my lord."

It was cruel, but he was enmeshed in the situation I'd predicted for him some months ago. The girl was besotted, and she was not a stupid creature, not with those eyes in her head. If Nick strayed, she would know in an instant and break her heart over it.

When I performed that evening, he twitched in his seat like a restless boy, and his eyes were all over the room. When Elinor reached for his hand, he jerked away as if burned.

After that, he did not attempt to see me, and I was grateful. I had my nun-like existence with the women and my music. I did not need the complications of Nick Hawkins and his difficult heart.

⁓⁓⁓

Anne Boleyn sent for me regularly to sing while she and her ladies played cards or gossiped, but I never saw Nick's wife in her chambers. I assumed Lady Elinor shared her father's distaste for the Boleyn family.

Nevertheless, we soon had occasion to meet. She appeared one morning at the door of the practice room, looking very young and uncertain, despite her fine gown and fashionable French hood.

I put down my lute and went to her, for she would not leave the doorway. "Yes, my lady?"

"May we speak, mistress?" she asked. "Alone—not here."

"If you wish." I followed her to Nick's apartments and tried to look as if I'd never seen the rooms before. When Terrence appeared with a tray, I averted my eyes for fear he would wink and set me to smiling in front of this poor, solemn girl.

"I do not know how to say this and not offend. It is about my husband." Her fingers twisted together, and I saw she wore three fine rings. They looked odd on her small hands.

"What can I do for you?" I watched with sympathy. Once, I had been young and in love with him, though without the bonds of marriage to add to the strain of those feelings.

"I am planning a party in his honor. I must show myself capable of being his wife. I would not presume to ask you to sing for us again, but..." She twisted a lock of that wondrous gold hair around her finger. "I have known my husband all my life, and yet he is not the same here as in Yorkshire. In the country, he cared not what people said or thought, but here, he worries about it all the time.

"His tastes are different as well. At my father's house, a joint of beef and a mug of ale suited him well enough, but now, he must have the best hippocras, for fear he'll be thought less of if he drinks what he likes." Lady Elinor took courage from her cup. "What I need from you, mistress, is advice. Your knowledge of my husband is something I lack. You see," she finished, putting down the cup and looking me full in the face, "I do not wish to shame him."

I turned my surprised laugh into a cough, trying to make sense of what she'd said. My 'knowledge of her husband' meant she knew about us, but asking my advice said she did not. What wife would go to her husband's mistress to learn his likes and dislikes? I decided she did not suspect, for if she did, Nick had landed himself a far rarer bird than he ever anticipated. "How can I help, my lady?"

"Everyone has taken much pleasure in pointing out my husband's mistresses. All of them." Her tone was momentarily bitter. "You are the only one I dared approach."

"You know?" I was at a loss. I heard a sound and knew that Terrence was behind the door, near expiring at this conversation.

"I suspected that first day. He looked at you so strangely, and you were so quiet and pleased for us. Everyone else seemed to want something, but you actually sounded as if you wished us well."

"I do," I said. "I told Nick—your husband—that I wished him all happiness in his marriage."

"You must think me very naïve," Lady Elinor said, moving from her chair to the fire. "I don't suppose what I've done is normal."

"Not at all," I told her. "But it comes from the heart."

"It does." She knelt on the carpet beside my chair. "I love him, you see, ever since I was a child, I've loved him. And I know I could make him love me if we stayed in the north; I know it. But here"—she clenched her small fists in frustration—"he is so distant that he frightens me. If I don't do the right thing, he'll send me back to my father's house." Her voice caught, and she began to sob.

I had not expected this girl at my feet, so scared of losing her husband, she would humble herself to please him. I put my hand on her shoulder. "Get up, my lady. I will help you."

She wiped her eyes. "I feel such a fool, but I was not raised at court, and I know no other way to find answers. My mother always said I'm too straightforward." Rubbing her eyes again, she asked, "How long were you his mistress?"

"A year, more or less," I said, though in truth, I might have numbered the days if she had asked. "He was away often, and then we parted once."

"Parted?" Lady Elinor asked with interest, distracted from her tears. "Why?"

"Because I loved someone else," I answered, wanting to be honest with her, both for my own sake and to set at least some of her fears at rest. "It angered him that he did not claim all of my heart."

She sighed. "He claims all of mine."

"As he should. At the time, I believed my heart was his; he saw the truth where I could not, and we quarreled over it."

Terrence entered to remove the tray and made faces behind his new mistress's back. I gestured for him to go away.

"What about the man you loved?" she asked. "Is he at court?"

I hesitated before giving too many harsh facts to the active mind that lay beneath the childish façade. No matter how I phrased it, she would know. "He was, but is no longer."

"Nick made him go," she said. "Don't look surprised. I do know him, a little. He can be strong-willed, and his temper is not so pretty to look upon as he is. I am sorry he separated you. Perhaps I ask too much?"

I leaned forward in my seat. "We have made our peace. I should like to help you."

The rest of the morning was spent in searching conversation with Lady Elinor as she probed my memory for endless details about Nick. Some of her questions made me blush, but I answered with enough frankness to redden her cheeks. Reluctantly, I told her I had a rehearsal and was making ready to leave, when we heard Nick's voice in the corridor. Elinor turned pale. "What shall we do? He mustn't see you."

I looked around for a place to conceal myself in the outer chamber until she lured him away. "There's nothing to be done," I said and felt a stab of pity. Nick would not be pleased to see us chatting together so cozily.

Her enormous eyes showed fear, and I sighed. I owed no loyalty to Nick. Another thought surfaced. I did not want Nick using his secret entrance to his wife's disadvantage. "There is a way," I said, leading her into the inner chamber. "Follow me."

"That's the bedchamber," she said, stopping my hand as I reached for the final door. "Nick does not like strangers there."

"I know that well enough, my lady," I told her, my voice unnecessarily sharp. She opened the door herself and gave me entrance, her expression bewildered. The room hadn't changed, I noted, except for the addition of a few feminine things on a carved chest. Pushing back the arras, I exposed the door. "It leads to a back corridor. He won't see me this way."

Lady Elinor's face showed a myriad of emotions she was still too young to conceal. "Seeing you in this room—it never really meant anything until now, what you were to him."

I touched her arm with genuine affection. "I am no longer his mistress. You are his wife, and I will not come between you. I told him that, and I tell you the same."

In a fortnight, Elinor held her first small party at court. Though she spent the day in terror, it was a great success. The king danced with her, and with that royal approval, Elinor's reputation was made. I was there at her insistence, but I would not sing. There must be some limit on my participation, else Nick would suspect too much. I chose the music, supervised the musicians, and stayed well out of his way.

The evening went well, even when Nick's dark eyes challenged me with questions. These instances I ignored until Lady Elinor appeared at my side in the small gallery, her face flushed and happy, looking like a flower in a new rose-colored gown. "Bess, isn't it lovely?"

I moved to shield her from the view of the dancers. "Yes, my lady, but your place is with your husband. You should rejoin the party before he misses you."

"He knows where I am. As he knows you are here at my asking." She moved and sent a stand of music crashing to the floor. "I wish you would come down. Nick would like to dance with you."

"You're mad," I said. "You've done what you wanted tonight—you've pleased your husband and silenced your critics. Now you want me to dance with him?"

"It will make him happy, and my critics will remain silent because they'll not know what to say." Her laugh was like a tinkling of bells. "You see, Bess, I'm learning."

She was. I did not wish to dance with Nick, but neither did I want to disappoint her. I hadn't expected to like Nick's wife; it made everything more difficult.

Nick was standing with Charles Brandon and George Boleyn, laughing at some jest. He smiled when he saw his wife approaching, but his expression changed when he saw me behind her. Mischief took over, and I dropped a deep curtsy to him.

"My best wishes again on your marriage, my lord."

"Many thanks, Bess." He turned back to Boleyn. "I say, have you—"

Lady Elinor's voice cut sweetly through the masculine conversation. "My lord husband, I brought Bess down so we could express our thanks for all the help she has given me. I thought perhaps you would like to dance with her."

Boleyn guffawed, and Brandon choked on his wine. One of them planted a hand in Nick's back, sending him stumbling toward me. He turned the clumsy movement into a bow, and I dipped again as he led me out to dance.

The music had scarce begun when he spoke, his voice taut. "How came you to be a part of this?"

I looked up through my lashes. "How could I refuse her request?"

"Envy is an ugly thing, Bess."

"I feel no envy of the Lady Elinor."

Cajoling, he said, "I've missed you." It was the tone of voice that once turned my knees to water. "I need you in my life."

The dance ended, and I removed my hand from his. "My needs are different, Nick. I need to belong with someone."

Lowering his voice as we approached his wife, he said, "You belonged to me—you still do."

"Then I ask you to release me. I may have belonged to you, but you never belonged to anyone but yourself. It must go both ways with me."

Chapter 21

Lady Elinor's party marked a turning point. I no longer quivered at the sight of Nick, but I was also no longer angry with him. He was not the only reason Tom had left court. A larger portion of that guilt rested with me, and I would have to learn to live with it.

Though I knew better, every time a barge arrived from Hampton, I wondered if he would be on it. If I could resign myself to Nick's marriage, I should've been able to do the same for Tom. I would never stop loving him, but I had to stop hoping. Each time I looked toward the river, the wound bled afresh.

Ewan and our lessons had been a welcome distraction during those first difficult months. As well, his union with Bronwyn comforted me; he did not find my connection with Tom strange or frightening, and I looked at our relationship with new eyes, realizing how much I'd refused to see.

"Born with one soul between you." It was apt, though it surprised me Robin had been the one to say it. For all his books, he was no poet.

I focused on my music, practicing until my fingers ached, and helped Mistress Edith when she would allow. I still had no aptitude for herbs, but being with her was a comfort. I knew she missed Tom, but she never mentioned him during our quiet hours in her workroom.

Lady Elinor sometimes called on me to sing when she entertained in the afternoons, though more often, her requests were for my company alone, as she struggled to make her way at court, which she found unnecessarily baffling.

"It's so different." Her bemused expression showed she knew she was repeating herself. "We were not so formal in my father's house nor so easy. Nick laughs at me, but it is strange."

"It must have once been strange to him," I commented, playing softly so as not to distract her. "Does he not remember? He came from a place not so different."

Elinor shook her head, and strands of golden hair floated free from beneath the pinned-up folds of her French hood. "He says I am an innocent."

How long would she stay that way, I wondered, married to Nick and dropped into a place like the court?

She was not all innocence; she knew something distressed me, and she worried at me like a dog with a bone until I finally asked her to stop. "Whatever it is," she said, "Nick is the cause, isn't he?"

I looked at her from under my eyebrows. "Your pavane, Lady Elinor, lacks skill. You should practice."

Thus distracted, she asked about my life in the Music, fascinated with its difference from hers. "It's not all performing," I told her. "It's a lot of work—always new music to learn, and as you've seen already, masques take no little preparation."

She giggled, recalling her disastrous performance at rehearsal, where she had sent the other dancers over like bowling pins. "I can dance," she said. "This is just—"

"Different," I finished, and we both laughed. She failed to comprehend the gap between us, and it was difficult not to think of her as a friend.

"I can't call you Nell," I said when she persisted. "I should not rightly be calling you Elinor without 'Mistress' or 'Lady' before."

Her face puckered, making her look even younger. "But you call my husband Nick."

I looked at her, not wanting to miss the blush I was about to cause. "I've bedded your husband, my lady. But until then, I called him 'sir.'"

A barge was tying up as I passed the river stairs. By its colors, I knew it was from Hampton, and I turned away. I'd slept badly, dreams of my father tangling with thoughts of Tom, and a solitary walk was what I needed to clear my head.

I found no peace on the hill nor in the gardens, for my thoughts followed me wherever I went. Who was I without Tom? It was an extension of the question that plagued my early life: who was I, without my family? Belonging to no one, I alternately clung too hard or kept my distance, and I learned that neither behavior did any good, nor would it keep the people I loved close by if they chose to leave.

As I started back toward the palace, Flora and Mary, walking arm-in-arm along the river path, called to me. "You've had a message, Bess!"

Since my father's death, I'd heard nothing from my family, and I did not expect to. No one would write, except Tom. I found the courier in the hall, a cup of ale in his hand, and claimed my missive.

"He chased me down to the barge," the man said, wiping his face with the back of his hand. "He said it was important you read it right away."

"Who did?" The paper was tight in my fingers.

"Secretary Lewis."

I let out a breath and broke the seal. The note contained one line in Robin's precise hand, and I stared at it until the letters blurred.

The woman and the child are dead.

Dead! If they were both gone, and so abruptly, it must have been the birth. I'd wished Lucy out of his life many times but never imagined her dying; I'd simply imagined a perfect world, and in that world, there was no woman to whom honor held him fast, no child who would call him father.

I thought of a world without Lucy and felt a brief surge of happiness, then caught myself. How could I be happy at the death of a blameless girl? I wondered if Tom felt any guilt because he hadn't loved her. No, I thought, ashamed of myself. He was too good. I was the one with those feelings. Unnatural, my mother had said. Perhaps she was right.

Breaking free of my thoughts, I looked at the courier. He'd freshened his cup and was deep in conversation. "Does the barge go back today?" I asked.

"Aye," he said. "We should be gone in an hour."

I stood up. "Wait for me."

"He'll see no one," I was told, a scant few hours later. "He's suffered a terrible loss."

Normally, the steward, an enormously tall, thickset man in the cardinal's livery, would have cowed me, but I folded my arms and stared back at him. "He'll see me."

My response flustered him. He softened, and I was reminded how easily people cared for Tom. "He is in mourning, lass. I don't think now is the time for a visit, however well meant."

I edged toward the open door. "I have been his friend these ten years and more. Who knows better how to comfort him?"

He gave way at last and called for a page, who led me to the area allotted for the cardinal's household. Most of the space belonged to the king's servants after he'd been given Hampton some three years earlier, and those who remained lived in cramped quarters. I knocked several times before looking inside. The tiny, low-ceilinged room was as bleak as his old chamber at Greenwich, stacks of music and the drawing of his mother the only clues to the identity of the occupant. It was also empty.

I knew where he would take refuge.

The stables were as immaculate as anything touched by the cardinal's hand, a long and graceful building ornamented with the royal crest above the wide open doors. At the near end were his magnificent mules, a perfect, even gray and of such pleasing temperament, they seemed as noble as horses. Then there were the household beasts and, at the other end, some of the king's own horses. And Tom.

I took a deep breath and entered.

He stood at the door of a stall, stroking the neck of a fine-boned chestnut. Sun streamed through the door at the opposite end, glinting on his fair hair, making all the more startling the effect of his black clothing. He looked older, thinner. Devastated.

What was I doing? I stopped, realizing I had traveled all this way without a plan. Again. On reading Robin's note, my first instinct was to go to Tom, and I'd followed it, never thinking I might be the last person he would wish to see. How could he take any comfort from my presence when his memories of Christmas were sure to be as vivid as my own?

I backed slowly away. Perhaps I could return to court and send a note or, at least, linger in the garden until I marshaled my thoughts and came up with a better idea. Anything but springing myself on him unawares.

Then, of course, I sneezed.

Tom looked up. "Robin wasted no time." His very posture was antagonistic, yet his feelings did not transmit themselves to the horse, which continued to nuzzle his neck, oblivious to the tension in the air.

My eyes began to burn and then to water. I wiped them discreetly with my sleeve. I had cried for Tom and for Lucy, but I did not yet know the path his grief would take and wanted no charge of insincerity. If I touched him, he might give in and shed the anguish which wrapped him like a cloak, or he might turn on me. For once, I would think before I acted. "I came because I thought you might have need—"

"Of you?" His fist struck the wall, and the horse whinnied. "Go back to Greenwich, Bess."

I approached, jittery as the mare, fighting another sneeze. I did not recognize the man before me. "I thought you might need a friend, and I knew not if you had anyone here, save Robin." It was obvious he did not, else he would not be hiding in the stables and comforting himself with horses.

He stared at me, and for a moment, I saw my Tom looking out of those glacial eyes. "Bess, I—"

A stable lad entered at the other end, whistling, and Tom swore at the intrusion. He grabbed my forearm, and we stumbled into the yard. After the dim stables, the sun was almost too bright. I took a deep, grateful breath and wiped my eyes again.

"Why the tears?" he asked, letting go of me and wiping his hand on his sleeve. "You haven't lost anyone."

I bit my lip. His brusqueness hurt, but I remembered my fury at Jenny Keith's desertion, and also my helplessness. As a rule, I could sense the direction of his feelings, but this time, there was no need: I had felt these same things and remembered, in addition to the anger, the horror I'd felt at my selfishness.

Everything Tom had ever valued or loved had been taken from him, by whimsy or malice or simple accident. No wonder he was angry at Lucy's death; he'd thought himself safe from the pain of loss by not loving her completely.

He walked out of the stable yard without looking to see if I followed. I matched my stride to his and waited for him to speak. We passed through the gatehouse and beyond, to the rolling dirt road that led, a mile or so hence, to the village. Tom walked, and I followed.

This was not what I'd expected—for now, I realized I'd had some expectation of this meeting, perhaps that he would look at me, see my love, let me comfort him. Beyond that, I hadn't bothered to think. It should have been enough. It would have been, before.

The day was warm, and as he strode along, sweat gathered along my hairline and made a slow path down my back beneath my stays. He must have been sweltering in his dark clothes, but he showed no sign. The road was rough beneath my slippers, and I began to lag. Were we walking all the way to the village?

"You have the timing of a carrion bird."

"I did not come to pick her bones or yours." My voice shook, despite my best efforts. "I thought you might need me. I shouldn't have bothered. You don't need anyone."

I turned so he would not see the tears welling in my eyes and began to walk back. I'd ruined everything again, and I could not watch him break apart from loving, and losing, someone else.

How could I expect his love to weather what had passed between us? He could never bring himself to love me again, not after losing her. I hated to leave him alone, but there seemed no other choice. He needed someone, but not me. My caution in the stable was meaningless; I had managed nothing more than to make him angry. There were feelings beneath the anger, and those were the emotions he must confront, but I did not know how to talk to this withdrawn, prickly version of Tom.

Risking a glance back, I saw him standing on the rise, his head bowed. Even from a distance, his pain came to me in waves.

Come to me, I thought, digging my nails into my palms. I want to help. Please, Tom. Come to me.

After a few moments, I heard his footsteps, soft on the parched earth. "Bess, wait."

I started breathing again. Looking over my shoulder, I said, "If I had known I would be unwelcome, I wouldn't have come. I'm sorry."

He took my hand. His skin was hot to the touch, but I'd never felt a more welcome sensation. "You are not unwelcome, and it is I who should apologize. My anger is not directed at you." Squeezing my fingers, he said, "You're right—there is no one here for me to talk to, but having you appear took me aback. Once, I could have said anything to you."

"You still can." I dried the last of my tears.

He turned me around so I faced him and tipped my chin up. "I am glad to see you, but I cannot share my grief, Bess. Not with you. Not with anyone."

Hampton Court loomed ahead of us, its red brick lit with the afternoon sun. A shaft of light caught the cluster of turrets and chimneys at the top of the building, and I thought it was not a day for sorrow. We walked for some time, regaining our comfort with each other. It had been months since we'd spoken, and in such circumstances, it was hard to judge boundaries. Tom would have been content, I believe, to put me on a boat with no further talk at all.

I took his hand this time. He did not object, and I led him away from the road and into the palace grounds. With the king not in residence, they were not crowded, while on a pleasant day, the gardens and woods at Greenwich were as busy as the hall. I stopped on a hill overlooking a plot of early roses.

"Was it the birth, Tom?" I thought of Jenny Keith and our long-ago conversation.

"It was," he said after a long silence. "A breech birth, and the baby born dead besides. The cord was wrapped 'round his neck." His mouth tightened, sharp creases appearing on either side. "The midwife let me come in when there was no hope of saving her."

His anguish twisted something deep inside. I was there with him, saw the tumbled, bloody sheets and the white, exhausted face of the rival I had never known. I felt his pain and the emptiness that followed.

"Such agony, and for what?" he asked. "To die and know her baby was dead before her? The priests say it's God's will, but I can't believe that. God couldn't hate Lucy. It's me He hates." Tom sat down on the grass, as if the strength had gone from his legs. "I used her as a substitute for you," he said, misery thick in his voice. "I chose her because she could not hurt me."

But she had hurt him, by dying, by leaving him to remember what he had not been able to give her. I dropped to my knees beside him, looking at the shadows beneath his eyes. How long had it been since he'd slept? "You cared for her."

He sighed. "I am cursed, Bess. Everyone I care for either dies or is driven away."

If he was still the Tom of my childhood, I would have put my arms around him, but this heartsore man was someone new, someone who would mistrust my embrace. "You're not cursed. I cannot believe it was God's will either, but it wasn't your fault. Women die in childbirth; you know that."

He pulled a ragged handful of grass. "My mother cursed me with bastardy, and that has tainted everything I've ever touched. This babe, had he lived, would have been a bastard as well."

It had been a boy, a chance for Tom to right all the wrongs done to him. "He would have known you," I said, removing the tortured stems from his fingers. "It's not the same."

"It is as well he died," he said. "He was spared that, at least." His voice broke, and he turned away and cried for his son.

I was no longer afraid, and I gathered him into my arms as I would any grieving person. He clung to me while I stroked his hair, his whole body shaking with the force of his sobs. "She shouldn't have died," he choked. "She didn't deserve that." Tom buried his face against my shoulder, and I felt his tears on my neck. "I needed her."

"I know," I said and held him tighter. My own face was wet, and I wondered that I could cry for Lucy as well as for him. "You were there. She knew you loved her. She died knowing, and that's something."

It was something. Lucy had given Tom more than I ever had, and would have given him still more if she and the baby had lived. I knew he was grieving for her, but it was the loss of the child that would truly gut him when he allowed himself to think about it.

It was always the babies. Jenny Keith's husband never returned to court, so I had never met my namesake. Agnes was unable to bear life with or without her child. Queen Katherine could not bear a living son and was put away because of it. Anne Boleyn would feel that pressure soon enough.

And now Tom had lost his child.

His grip on me loosened at last, and we sat together on the grass, our bodies so close that an observer would think us lovers. He'd been there for me countless times, and I was glad to be able to comfort him now. "It will be all right," I said and wondered how I could give him that hope. "I'll always be here when you need me."

He turned his head, and his lips grazed my cheek. The air shimmered between us. Barely seeming to breathe, he raised his hands, placing them on either side of my face. Something strange and fierce and ineffably sad shone in his eyes.

I expected a kiss—I wanted him to kiss me—but there was desperation in the way his mouth covered mine and in his clutching hands, one on my breast, the other hard on my thigh. It didn't matter if this was a part of his healing or if something deeper drove him; he would hate himself for betraying her memory so quickly. I let the caress continue just a moment too long before I drew back.

As swiftly as it had come, his hunger drained away. He drew back, looking shaken. "Christ, I'm weak." He passed a hand over his eyes. "She's only been dead for a day."

I put my hand on his shoulder, trying not to think of the flesh beneath the rough, new-dyed linen. "You don't need to kiss me to prove you're still alive." I felt his breathing calm and removed my hand.

Tom's eyes were red rimmed, but they held a clarity that had not been there earlier. "It's the first time I've cried for them." He leaned over and kissed my cheek, and this time, there was nothing in the gesture save gratitude. "I thank you, Bess."

"I didn't cry for my father until long after." I thought to console, but I should have kept quiet, for at the word, his face clouded. "Don't think about it. Why must you know who he was?"

"He was ashamed to admit he sired a child on a whore." Tom lay back on the grass, one arm across his face to block the sun.

I had always known we felt differently about this. It didn't matter to me who my parents were or, once I joined the Music, that I had parents at all. Once I became a minstrel, I became one with my whole heart. For Tom, it was never enough. He was a friend to everyone at court, golden Tom, celebrated for his talents, but no one had touched his heart until I arrived.

I moved away and plucked wildflowers from the hillside, his mother's confession bubbling in me like a spring. When I had a handful of blooms, I began to weave them together. "She never told him of your birth," I said, unable to keep silent. "She told me that much."

He sat up. "You spoke of my father?"

"No more than that." I stretched to pick another daisy, using it as an excuse to look away.

"You're lying."

"No," I said, "I told you her words, those and no other."

In a moment, he rolled over and pinned me to the ground. The flowers scattered as his fingers dug into my arms. His grip hurt, but it was his gaze that seared my soul. "What else did she tell you?" This was Tom. He saw my secrets, and he would have them.

"You're hurting me," I gasped, trying to squirm free. "Tom, please!"

Relaxing his grip, he said, "She told you something, else you would have repeated the whole conversation last year, not in bits and pieces, sorting first to make certain I could bear them." He kept one hand on my shoulder as I tried to sit up. "I will have his name from you, Bess, or—"

"Or what?" I asked from my undignified position. "You'll kill me, so there is no one left to love you, and you can glory in your bastardy and self-pity?" His hands fell away, and I scrambled free, shaking the crushed flowers from my skirts. "She said, one day, you might need to know. This is the day, it seems, else you would not try to break my arms."

I felt his struggle, so close to knowing the truth and yet shrinking from it.

"Tell me," he said, and his voice was calm; he had mastered himself through some unimaginable effort. "Tell me his name."

"She never told him about you," I said again. I wanted Rose to bear no blame.

"I believe you."

I saw his closed eyes, his pale, waiting face, and my resolve broke. "Suffolk."

He flinched as though I had struck him. "Brandon?"

Tom was almost old enough to be the father of Brandon's children. The court had celebrated their births, a son and two daughters, and we'd performed in their honor—his siblings, whom he would never know as equals. I watched him process this extraordinary information.

He got to his feet, brushing the grass from his clothes. "I must be alone now, Bess."

I followed him back to the road, no longer paying any mind to the heat. "She thought it might help you to know." Tom maintained his silence, and I added, "I have permission to stay on for a bit if you need me."

His beautiful eyes were empty again. "We've had need of each other too often, and it's done neither of us any good. You should go."

It was a dismissal. I stood still, waiting. "Do you mean for the moment? Or forever?"

"I have lost a wife and a son and gained a father in two days." He pushed his sleeves down over tanned forearms. "Yet somehow, the hardest thing for me to bear is that you've lied to me."

Tom had spent his youth believing Rose hated him; it never occurred to him she might have done him the same kindness my father had done me. After years of dutiful visits, he now saw a woman starved for him, who'd kept his father's name secret to save him the pain of knowing. Nothing was as it seemed; the earth tilted beneath his feet, and I had taken from him the means to deal with it.

He turned, and I recoiled. For a moment, he looked like an old man. Then, the sun caught his hair in a flash of gold, and the illusion fled.

"What was I to do?" I asked, "Tell you then, when you were just settled at Hampton, trying to start over?"

I held my ground when he stood before me, so close that I could see the gold hairs glinting above the roughly knotted ties of his shirt. His familiar scent filled my nostrils, making me want to lean into him.

"It is not for you to decide." He trailed a fingertip down my cheek. "You can't know how it's haunted me, that it might have been you in her place, lying dead because of me."

"I wish it had been," I said, pulling away from his gentle touch. "I wish I were as dead as Lucy, because then, you could still love me."

I watched as my words struck home and undid all the good our conversation had done. Appalled, I put my hands over my face and cried until I was sick.

And finally, Tom, whose grief was greater than mine, put his arms around me. His embrace was comforting, but I could feel him holding back. At last, I stopped crying, and he set me away from him. The light was gone from his face. "Go back to court, Bess. I cannot see you."

"For how long?" The thought of never seeing him again was impossible. Before, when I had asked Robin to spare me his name, it was not this cold cutting loose; it was for both our sakes. This was far worse.

He shook his head. "I don't know. I can't even look at you now."

"I'm sorry I kept it from you." I reached for out, then dropped my hand before it was rebuffed. "What else can I say?"

"It's not just that," he said. "I can't look at you without thinking of them. If I'd been able to let you go, there might never have been a child, and she would be alive."

It was always his gift to me: the truth. Even in his anger, he was straightforward, and he was no longer angry. No matter that he loved me; Tom could not see me without remembering what he had lost and gained and lost again.

"So that's it, then," I said. "I pay for her sins as she paid for mine."

"What sin did Lucy commit?"

Trying to ignore the way my heart pounded in my chest, I asked, "Is it not obvious? She left you—the greatest sin of all. And if I do not leave, you will drive me away." I pressed a kiss to his cheek. "God bless you," I said, my voice thick with tears. I picked up my skirts and ran toward Hampton before I could say more.

Chapter 22

It was as if Tom were truly dead this time, in fact rather than imagination, and I could not take it in. Often, I would wake trembling, afraid I was going mad because I couldn't remember his voice. Worse were the nights when I woke and felt his presence beside the bed. I pressed my face into the pillow so that my tears didn't wake Flora and the others.

Still, it was impossible to live at court and remain aloof. I forced myself to spend time with others, and slowly, my heart began to thaw. I could not have Tom, but I was yet alive, and I had friends, though they would, I realized, never stay the same.

Joan received a message not long after I returned from Hampton. It was the first she'd heard from her guardian since her arrival at court, and his news must have been a shock.

"So you see," she said, calmly stitching, "I will be leaving at the end of May."

Shifting in her chair near the window, the sun caught her, allowing me a closer look. There were no traces of tears on her pale, freckled skin, nor yet was there any joy in her eyes. "That's just a few weeks away," I said, stunned. "Couldn't they allow you time to adjust?"

"I'm sure it's been discussed for months. My guardian says the details are settled; only the marriage remains to be transacted." For all that she'd been haggled over like a prize cow, Joan's placid face showed no upset, but she had showed little emotion since hearing of Will's marriage. "I regret how quickly I must leave you, Bess. I've been happy here, and you've been a good friend to me."

I put my embroidery aside; it was already marred by my wandering thoughts. "Do they not think to wonder about your life? What if you had a young man here?"

"What is the likelihood of that?" Joan asked, always practical. "With all the pretty girls at court, who would look at me? It's not as if I have a large dowry."

"But you're lovely," I said. "You're the kindest person I know, and everyone in the Music adores you."

Her laugh was genuine. "That's not what I mean, and you know it."

I squeezed my eyes shut, thinking how bleak the court would feel when she was gone. "I don't know what I'll do without you."

"You'll be all right," she said. Her stitches, unlike my own, were flawless. "You belong here in a way I never have. You've a purpose, a talent; all I have is myself, and I can be of more use married to Edward Cope."

I picked at a few stitches before putting the cloth down again. "Don't you mind?" I asked. "You don't even know him."

Joan smiled, and though her face was not pretty, the sweetness of her expression was transfiguring. "I remember him from Christmas many years ago, when his wife was alive. He was kind." She put her hand over mine, light as a butterfly. "I do not fear him, Bess."

"But neither do you love him."

"I don't need to love him," she said with touching simplicity. "I've had my love, which is more than many women are blessed with. I can respect Edward Cope; I will be a good wife, mother his sons, and bear him children, if we are so blessed."

Her acceptance saddened me. To marry a man she had seen but once and of whom she had nothing better to say than that she did not fear him. "I could not do it."

"I don't require love as you do," Joan said. Her eyes were serious. "I can be happy with him. Perhaps I will be happier if I do not pin all my hopes on him—men, after all, are rarely faithful, and this way, I'll never break my heart."

"Oh, Joan." I bridged the space between us, and in my arms, I felt her sob, just once. When we separated, her eyes were dry, and she smiled, but I knew what was inside.

"You are lucky, Bess," she declared as I left to go to practice. "You have what I've always wanted. You've found your place. You belong."

Her words came back to me as I lay in bed that night, trying to keep thoughts of Tom at bay. She had touched the very essence of my own problem.

A sense of belonging was what I had always sought. I was comfortable at court, happy in my position, but I always defined belonging as being with someone, as in belonging to the family which had given me up or belonging with Nick or with Tom. I had come closest to the truth when I told Nick that belonging must go both ways.

Tom's rejection set me adrift, and I might have drowned but for the port provided by the court. I found the idea of belonging to my own life novel but not unpleasant. It seemed that everything I yearned for had been mine, and of my own making, all along. I belonged with the court but to myself first and foremost. I was the only one who could make me feel unwanted or a stranger, as I had done for so many years. I would endeavor to realize what I was and what I meant to those around me. I deserved as much, and I owed it to Joan, who made me see it.

As I drifted off to sleep, I thought that truly religious people must feel this way, knowing God was in them. I wasn't certain about God in me; I had discovered myself in me, and for now, that was enough.

⌒⌒⌒

I spent as much time as possible with Joan before she left, and when the time came for her to depart, I was able to produce a genuine smile.

"I will write, my darling friend," she assured me as the last of her things were stowed on the coach. "And please, do not give up."

This was the closest we came to discussing Tom. I found some meaningless words to cover my feelings and embraced her again. I could not see for tears as she disappeared from view.

"Will you come to my wife this afternoon?" asked a voice at my shoulder.

Wiping my eyes, I turned to see Nick. "I had not planned to."

"Please do. She's not well and craves your company." His expression was wry. "She's quite attached to you."

"I am fond of her."

He laughed harshly. "As am I, but it's a damned uncomfortable situation, you must admit. Wife and mistress, the closest of friends."

"Former mistress," I said.

"I do wonder what you talk about."

It was cheering to know we caused him discomfort. "Harmless things," I assured him. "Most of the time."

"Bess!"

It was my turn to laugh. "We've not discussed you intimately since our first meeting. And then she just wanted confirmation of certain rumors."

"Damn. I was afraid she might have guessed something." His expression told me more than he would have liked about his feelings.

"She guessed nothing," I said. "She was told about me and any number of others. It was an impressive list, I wasn't aware of all of them myself."

Nick gave every indication of being shocked to his core. "I've thrown that poor, defenseless kitten in with a pack of lions," he said. "They'll eat her alive."

"If they haven't eaten her already, she's quite safe," I told him. "And besides, your kitten has grown a few claws, or at least a good set of defenses. I've even seen her talking to Anne Boleyn without going up in flames."

Nick looked up as thunder rumbled overhead. "I'm glad. I've encouraged that, for her father's sake." Taking my arm, he walked me to the door. "Will you see her?"

Relenting, I said, "I should not, but if she doesn't mind my harp, I will come and gladly." I shut the door as rain blew across the floor. "How is she unwell?"

His face suffused with unfamiliar color. "She is with child."

Elinor looked restless, not sick, and their chamber was strewn with attempts to busy her mind and her hands. When Terrence ushered me in, she threw her book aside and patted the place beside her.

"I hoped you would come!" she cried, brightening. "Nick said he would persuade you."

"He did." I sat on the bed, my harp resting in my lap. "I should be at practice, but when he said you were ill—"

"I'm not ill," she declared. "I've never felt better. Women have been bearing children since Eve, and most of us don't require bed rest to do it."

"I'm glad you're well. Nick looks worried."

Elinor threw back the covers. "I'm glad he's suffering, he's left me here to fret and miss all the fun. I hate staying in bed, even when I am sick." She paced, stopping every so often to curl her bare toes in the carpet. "Would you believe he's dismissed my woman and left me with Terrence, so I'm not able to dress?"

"I'll act as maid," I offered.

Elinor's eyes widened. "I couldn't ask that of you. You're my friend, not my servant."

"Let your friend be your servant this once." It was another mark of her naiveté not to remember I was a servant. "What will you wear today, my lady?"

Once Elinor realized I would not heed her objections, she got into the spirit of the game and chose garments with abandon. She had no modesty at all, which surprised me in such a young girl. When I held out her shift, she dropped her bedgown around her feet and stood naked before me, unconcerned as a child.

244

For all her slenderness, Elinor was surprisingly rich in flesh. Her legs were sweetly curved, her breasts full and high. Except for a small bulge in her otherwise flat stomach, she was perfect. What pleasure Nick must take in her!

"When is the babe due?" I asked.

"October, I believe," she said, confirming that she had conceived almost immediately. "I shall be huge, and I shall have the most beautiful babies."

"With such parents, how could they not be beautiful?" I could not keep the edge from my voice. One parent fair and one dark. I thought of the children I would never have with Tom.

Sobering, she took my arm. "I'm sorry, Bess. Have I said something wrong?"

"No," I assured her and meant it. "You are lovely, and all the world knows Nick is handsome."

My gaze landed on a small table near the bed on which were tumbled several trinkets and an expensively bound book. The cover was marked with a familiar monogram. "Lady Anne has been to see you?"

"This very morning," Elinor said. She lifted her mass of hair while I laced her up the back. "She is quite kind, not at all what I expected."

"Your family declares for Queen Katherine." I fussed with her sleeves, which were of pale blue satin.

"My father would beat me bloody for even speaking to her," she admitted. "But that is Nick's job now, and he wants me to like her. I expected some demon in the guise of a female and a king too besotted to notice, but it's not like that, is it? I've never seen the queen dowager."

"I have seen both," I said. I tried to dress her hair and failed, coils sliding loose each time I had them pinned. "I've no talent at this, Elinor; see what I have to work with."

"You have beautiful hair. I'd rather it than mine." Elinor stepped in front of the glass and divided her hair into three parts, laying them neatly over her shoulders. Taking a length of ribbon, she knotted it through her hair and braided it swiftly. The effect, with her brilliant eyes and white and blue dress, was breathtaking. She stabbed pins into the mass and settled a French hood on top, its folds of fabric concealing her handiwork.

"The Lady Anne has few women friends."

"That is true. She prefers male company, especially her brother. And the king, of course." I leaned on the back of her chair, met her eyes in the mirror. "I am glad she has taken a liking to you."

Elinor was pleased by any compliment. "She inquired of my acquaintances here, and I told her of you."

"You've friends at court other than me."

Scampering to the window with no more dignity than the child she sometimes resembled, she pressed her palms to the glass. It still rained, and she made a disgusted face. "Not very many and none such as you, who tell me the truth because you care and not to hurt." She flung herself on the window seat. "The Lady Anne was interested to hear of you. She said you once did her a kindness, and she thinks of you with great affection."

I recalled my punishment for meddling in Anne Boleyn's affairs. While it pleased me to be thought well of, I did not wish to risk my life at court over some new mishap pertaining to her—as if that could happen now, beloved as she was of the king!

"She said one curious thing, that she envied me my baby. The king wants a son, and when he divorces the queen dowager, she must present him with one as soon as possible, to reassure him he's done the right thing." Her forehead wrinkled. "Isn't that strange?"

My heart went out then to Lady Anne, who knew too well that love had a dark side. What a load to put on her proud, narrow shoulders: the succession to the throne of England and the love of its king.

We were yet at Greenwich, drawing out the days until the king's progress was charted and the court broken up for the summer. Spring had arrived with sunshine, flowers, and festivals, all of which helped to drive away the last of the winter gloom. It was almost possible to ignore the news from London.

Since the turning of the season, there had been rumors of deaths in the city, but it was put up to ordinary illness and the weather, though the signs pointed to a visit from England's worst enemy. There had been an outbreak of the sweat during my first year at court but nothing since. I scarcely remembered the epidemic of 1511 that had carried off my brother and spared me, but my father had described it, and his words lodged in my heart.

Londoners were not wont to panic, but at the first sign of the sweat, they gave themselves over to an ecstasy of fear, boarding up shops and houses, fleeing as from an invading army. Merchants from the city arrived at court and were refused entry. I heard some of their conversation at the gate and shivered with dread. The sweat was among us, and it showed no mercy.

Church bells tolled, the sound mingling with the rumbling of the carts, taking hundreds of bodies to unmarked graves. There were corpses on every corner, and fires burned constantly, filling the air with choking, purifying smoke.

The gaiety of May surrendered to the specter of June. It was as if Death himself stepped up and cast a shadow over the palace. Courtiers who, weeks before, had decked themselves in flowers and danced on Shooter's Hill, were huddled in corners, discussing the merits of their distant estates and how long they should remain there. The huge, many-legged beast that was the court struggled to its feet and hurried its preparations.

The king would go to Waltham, much to the dismay of Anne Boleyn, who was to stay behind. It was not said outright, but it was felt that a woman, no matter how skillful a rider, could not keep up with the blistering pace set by the king when trying to escape the perils of London. It was suggested she go to Hever, to her family. Kent was isolated; she would be safe there.

Anne raged at being abandoned. She stalked her chamber and cursed Henry in vivid French. I sat in a corner with my harp, watching as her women, including Elinor Hawkins, tried to calm her.

"My lady, you must rest!" she said. "You'll wear yourself out with all this pacing."

Anne's black eyes regarded her with fondness. "It's you who should rest. Your husband should take you from court. A woman with child is not safe here."

"I am fine," Elinor said. Pregnancy suited her, bringing a bloom to her cheeks and making her extraordinary eyes even more luminous. "It is you we worry about, my lady. The king would be wroth if you became ill."

"Ah, he is so concerned!" Anne cried, striking his miniature from the table. It spun across the floor and came to rest at my feet. "He claims to love me unto death, but he rides to Waltham with his doctor, his fool, his fear, and my brother."

We were silent, knowing she spoke truth. Henry's morbid dread of sickness made him see a death mask on every face.

The chamber echoed with her shrill, sudden laughter. "Do you know what the people say?" she asked, breaking away from Elinor again. "This latest plague is my fault. Because of me, Henry has offended God."

I'd heard the same ugly rumors. One of the names for the sweat was the Lord's Visitation, and it did not take much imagination to tie the king's maneuvering with cardinals, popes, and wives to a plague upon his people.

It was superstitious nonsense, but there were many, even in the palace, who took it seriously.

I did not doubt that God was offended by the king's manipulations, but I could not bring myself to believe in a God who punished the innocent. It was treason to think further, but I did: if King Henry so angered God, then let him be struck, and spare those who had no part in putting away Queen Katherine.

I put the king's portrait back on the table and dodged as Anne's pacing carried her in my direction. She put a light hand on my shoulder. "Play something cheerful; they are leaving now."

Elinor went to the window, but Anne did not. She sang softly along with me, her skirts swaying. She reminded me then of Harry Percy's happy sweetheart, not the king's mistress, approaching thirty and growing short-tempered with waiting.

"I'm glad they're gone," she said. "Someone fetch a drink; my head hurts."

Her first declaration was puzzling in light of her anger at being left behind, but we had learned not to question her capricious statements. The rest of her words frightened me. "Are you well, my lady?"

"'Tis but a headache—do not worry. If it was the sweat, I'd be dead by now, and then where would Harry be?" She was amused by her own flippancy. "Please, Elinor, call for a servant, and have them to bring something for the pain."

Elinor returned a few minutes later, shutting the door and leaning against it as if to protect us all from the news she carried.

"What's wrong?" Anne asked. "Please don't make riddles today."

Elinor smoothed her skirts and folded her hands over her belly. "The servant just told me that two kitchen lads have died since daybreak."

Even Anne had nothing to say to that, and she did not chide me when my harp faltered into silence.

⁓～⌣⁓

The sweat did not take a particularly virulent form at Greenwich, not compared to the tales that came from London. Many were stricken there, and most died. Still more fled the palace for the areas without contagion.

Since I was able to move among the infected without fear, I gave up music and nursed the servants who were taken ill. Several members of the Music were stricken. I worked with Mistress Edith, dispensing herbs and changing soaked linens, wiping sweat from fevered bodies. Mary Wynne took sick and lingered for two days, burning up inside her dry skin, before she died.

"That's the worst of it," Mistress Edith said, wearily closing Mary's eyes. "When it turns inward, it always kills."

"Turns inward?" I repeated, looking down at my childhood tormentor. She was only twenty-four.

"When the sweat stops flowing," she explained, "the poisons turn inward and stop the heart. Pray we don't see more like that."

I did pray, harder and more sincerely than I had prayed in my life, coming into the back of the chapel when mass was being said, leaving before it ended to go back to the sick. Despite my prayers, despite our work, people still died, and I turned from the windows when I heard the carts rumbling away with their bodies.

After an endless week, the worst seemed over. Mistress Edith, afraid for my health, forced me to rest, and my sleep was instant and dreamless.

An insistent hand shook my shoulder. "Mistress Bess, wake up." I opened my eyes to a young page kneeling by my bed.

"What is it?"

"The Lady Elinor sent me," he said, his voice high and frightened. "She has fallen sick."

I scrambled up. "Elinor is ill?"

"No," he said, explaining more slowly, "Lady Elinor sent me. She is sick."

I knew then, by his tone, that "she" was Anne Boleyn; there was no other. "Is the Lady Anne in her chambers?"

"Aye, and the Lady Elinor with her."

"Find Mistress Edith," I directed. My stride was longer than the child's, and I called back over my shoulder. "Tell her the Lady Anne is in sore need."

I invaded Edith's chamber and took some of her fever herbs before I went to the king's mistress. When I entered the room, the air was already reeking. A disheveled Elinor met me at the door, her hands clasped to her breast.

"Bess, she collapsed, just like a poppet. One moment, she was telling me about the French court, and the next—" She looked at the carpet, and I saw the spray of spilled wine.

"How long ago?"

"A quarter hour, at most. Her maid and I got her into a night-robe and put her to bed, and I sent the boy for you."

I put my hand on Anne's forehead. It was like touching a boiling pot. "Is there no physician left at court?"

"No." Elinor looked ready to burst into tears. "Dr. Chambers is with the king, of course, and I heard Dr. Butts was himself ill."

I stayed all that day, mopping her brow, watching as Anne writhed and murmured in her fever. A messenger arrived near midnight, bringing a letter from the king. He was reluctant to give it over to any of us.

"Lady Anne is in yon bed, if you dare approach," I said, my voice sharp with exhaustion and worry. Elinor rose from her chair to join me, as if her slight support might intimidate the king's messenger. "I'll accept it for her," she said. "Please, tell the king the Lady Anne is very ill, and we have no physician here."

Elinor held the letter warily. "What ought we to do with it?"

I was more concerned with the woman in the bed than her royal lover. Mistress Edith was bent over her pillow, pushing back the thick dark hair the king so loved. Fine for him if Anne died while he was in hiding, I thought and was ashamed.

The king could not risk his own health, even for those he loved, for what would happen if he died? There was the Princess Mary, of course, but she was the child of a discarded wife and a girl besides; there was the young Duke of Richmond, Bess Blount's boy, not yet ten and illegitimate for all his titles. Wisdom said King Henry must live to sire an heir the kingdom would accept.

And besides, everyone knew how the king felt about illness; there was no use in hoping his affection for Anne would diminish an abhorrence held since childhood.

"It's so stuffy," Elinor said from behind me. Her face was waxen, and she held tight to the doorjamb. I moved to prop her up and called Mistress Edith, ignoring my friend's protest that it was but lack of air that made her feel faint. I remembered Anne's breezy dismissal of her headache the week before.

I waited alone while the stubborn Elinor was removed. Mistress Edith returned, wiping her hands on her apron. "Is she ill?"

"She was sick just now," the older woman said and smiled. "She's had an easy time of it, but the poor girl has worked like a drudge these past days."

Relief flooded through me. "Then it's just the baby?"

"That's enough," Mistress Edith said. "I think I've frightened her enough to keep her in bed." She rinsed a cloth in cold water, then began to tidy her jars and potions, her hands never still. "I can't imagine why she's still here."

"She won't leave without Nick, and he is with the king." Their quarrel, when she refused to journey to Hawkmoor without him, was fresh in my mind. It was the first time Nick had encountered his wife's will, and he'd wilted before it. When he left, he'd asked me to watch over her. Letting her work herself into a rag, even for Anne Boleyn, did not constitute proper watching over.

"Harry!" Anne said clearly from the bed. Our heads turned, and the village doctor hurried in from the antechamber. "Harry, where are you?"

"She seeks the king," Mistress Edith said.

I heard the yearning note in her voice and thought it was not Harry Tudor she sought, but another Harry, lost to her.

"Lady Anne," I said, kneeling beside the bed, "you have a letter from the king."

Her dark eyes opened and stared through me.

I took her hand and squeezed it very hard, to bring reason to her mind before she betrayed herself before Edith and this bumbling, anonymous physician. "Your letter, lady, would you like me to read it?"

I felt her hand return weak pressure. "Thank you."

Breaking the seal on the heavy paper, I saw in dismay it was written in French, which I spoke but haltingly. "Excuse my clumsiness, my lady."

She closed her eyes for the affectionate greeting and listened until I reached the passage concerning the health of the king and his followers. "'When we were at Waltham, two ushers, two grooms of the chamber, and your brother, the Master Treasurer, fell ill and are receiving every care, and since then, we have been well physicked in our house at Hunsdon, where we are well established and, God be praised, with no sickness.'"

Her eyes fluttered open. "George?"

"The letter says he receives every care, my lady." I read on, struggling with both the language and the king's uneven spelling, and smiled at the closing. "Listen, my lady, to what the king says: 'It may comfort you to know it is true, as they say, that few women or none have this malady, and moreover none of our court, and that few elsewhere have died of it.'"

I folded the letter away, exchanging glances with Mistress Edith. We were both skeptical of the king's medical opinions; he busied himself with charms and remedies, but for him, as well as anyone, the best remedy for the sweat was to simply outrun it and stay safe until it passed.

"So hot." The voice from the bed was faint. Mistress Edith pulled back the blankets and began to wipe her down with a wet cloth. Lady Anne was already slender, but the fever wasted her so that all her ribs were visible through the thin linen bedgown.

Elinor returned the next day, looking shaky but claiming to feel better. She sat with Lady Anne, talking to her whenever the fever allowed her to be lucid. She was in the bedchamber when the outer doors swung open and Nick strode in, several steps ahead of a pale Dr. Butts, still shrugging into his long green physician's coat.

"The king sent a doctor," he said to me. "Where is Lady Elinor?"

I gestured toward the bedchamber. "With the Lady Anne."

"Damn her!" He barged into the room, pushing the doctor aside again, and came out seconds later with a struggling Elinor in his arms. "You are done with nursing. I care not who lies in that bed—you'll soon lie at Hawkmoor and not stray from there until our child is born, if I have to tie you to the bed."

"Nick!" Elinor twisted and pulled, but he towed her down the corridor. I heard them arguing until they turned the corner.

I peered into the inner chamber and watched Dr. Butts. He ignored the other doctor, much as we had, and seemed to approve of our ministrations. "Call for a litter," he said to his assistant. "And bring more blankets. We're moving her to Hever."

"To Hever?" I spoke without thinking.

Dr. Butts looked around. "The king's orders. Her father is also ill, and he wishes them to be together."

I saw the direction the rumors would now take: it was not the king with whom God was angry; it was the Boleyns, and the innocent who suffered were mere victims in a haphazard search for the true sinners.

The doctor thanked Mistress Edith for her hard work, then turned to me. "You have been here as well?" His eyes were red and tired, circled by purple shadows. He was only just out of his own sickbed.

"Yes, doctor." I looked at the woman in the bed. "May I go to Hever with her?"

His brow creased, no doubt trying to place me among her maids. Then, recognizing me, he said, "I cannot allow it. She will be well cared for." He regarded me with curiosity. "Do you not fear the disease?"

"I survived it as a babe," I told him. "I've nothing to fear."

He sighed. "That may be your best protection. Those who worry most are invariably stricken." He watched as they swaddled Anne in blankets and lifted her onto the litter. "If you wish to nurse, there's a boat on the river bound for Hampton. They've been taken badly, and your cool head might be of some help there."

I had taken a few steps toward the door before the name penetrated through the haze of my exhaustion. Sickness at Hampton!

My second realization was more chilling. Tom would not wish to see my face again, not even at his deathbed.

Chapter 23

"The Lady Elinor wishes to see you."

I had only slept for a few hours, but it felt like days. My spine crackled pleasurably when I stretched. "I thought the Lady Elinor journeyed to Hawkmoor today."

"So did her lord husband," the maid said with a stifled smile. "She has agreed to stay away from the sick, but she will not agree to go."

Elinor stamped her foot. "He can't make me leave!"

"Of course he can," I said. "He's your husband."

"And I am his wife. He should love me and honor my wishes," she said, "not order me about like chattel."

Under the law, chattel was precisely what Elinor was. It spoke well of her parents' marriage that Nick's casual mastery angered her; the usual manner in which a husband dealt with a recalcitrant wife was to order her to do his bidding, and give weight to his words with a blow or a beating besides. Nick might not strike her, but he would not let her have her way.

"The change will be good for you," I told her. "You're in no condition to tire yourself."

"But I'm not tired," she protested. "Everyone thinks I'm delicate. I'm stronger than I look."

That much was obvious. "It's your first babe. Can you blame him for worrying?"

Elinor dropped her face into her hands, looking, for a moment, like a terrified child. "I don't want to go back there! I did when we first came, but I've gotten over that—I'm not afraid of losing him to every woman he dances with now."

"It's only until the baby comes. That's not so long."

She was silent for a moment. "I might be able to bear it," she said, her lips twitching into a smile, "if you came with me."

"I can't leave the court." My response was automatic; her suggestion never really reached my brain.

Elinor pulled away. "Of course you can. The king will not return for months. You're just wasting away here. Oh, Bess, please consider it! Having you with me would make such a difference."

Her earnestness made me squirm. Was I was being selfish? Surely, Elinor needed me more than Hampton, where I would only risk breaking

254

my heart again. Cardinal Wolsey had many fine physicians; I would just encounter a repeat of Dr. Butts's dismissal.

I did not want to be dismissed. I wanted to be necessary to someone. Elinor pleaded her case so well, I began to waver. "I cannot stay until the birth," I said.

She crowed with joy. "Bess, you are too kind!"

I did not see Nick's reaction when he was informed both wife and mistress would journey to Hawkmoor, but by evening, our plans were in order. Out of concern for his unborn heir, Nick chose to travel to his new manor in Hertfordshire rather than the longer trip to Yorkshire.

Their constant genial wrangling entertained me for the duration of the journey. She wanted to ride, and he insisted she stay in the coach. The compromise involved Elinor beside me and Nick riding alongside, holding her gloved hand through the window.

Kelton had come to Nick on his marriage. I remembered him grumbling that the hunting was good, but the house was in poor condition and inconveniently situated. For all its supposed neglect, when we crested the hill, it looked to be a charming place.

It may have been small for a manor, but the rooms were nicely arranged and the windows large and well-placed. The furnishings were faded and shabby from use, yet I noticed none of this when Nick presented me to the steward as Mistress Elizabeth Llewelyn, the Lady Elinor's friend. This designation earned me a handsome timbered chamber with a high bed wrapped in blue curtains and a view of the river from the diamond-paned casement window.

It was a lady's room, and I said as much to Elinor that night at table.

Her eyes widened. "But why should you not have a nice chamber?"

"We sleep three to a bed in the Music," I said. "I'm not accustomed to such luxury."

"Would you rather a cramped little space under the roof with no window and the servants thinking you're one of them?"

"I am one of them."

"Take your chamber, and be happy." She took my hand across the table. "Bess, you are doing me a great favor by being here. Allow me to treat you as my guest and give you the comforts you can't have at court."

I felt a sudden unease and looked up to find Nick watching us. "I agree with Elinor," he said. "It pleases her to give you things, as it pleases me."

His words returned in the days that followed, when my new environment threatened to overwhelm me: the strangeness of being served, the feel of a soft feather bed, scented rushes, rich food, good wine. I thought we lived well at court, but this visit proved me wrong. It felt almost unnatural to live in such a manner, but I grew accustomed to it.

Eight weeks passed in morning walks, riding lessons, delicious meals, and pleasant musical evenings. One morning, I woke to see the leaves outside my window tinged with gold.

It was September. The sweat would soon falter as it always did in cooler weather, and the king would return. Life would begin again.

When I ventured down for breakfast, Elinor looked at me and knew at once. "You can't leave yet." She put a hand on her belly, which was enormous as she'd predicted.

"It's time." I had never before lived without work or duty, and while Elinor claimed to need me, her body made clear she could do as well absent the lot of us. She had perhaps the easiest pregnancy I'd ever witnessed and would bear her child with a minimum of fuss.

When she protested, I looked to Nick. He'd been a perfect host, always nearby yet never too close. If he found our household arrangements bizarre, no one knew but himself and his confessor, if he had one. Religion was pleasantly lax at Kelton.

"Don't plague her," he said. I thought he understood. "The coach is at your disposal."

I thought of arriving at Greenwich in his coach, and it tasted too much of my father's dying. "If I might just borrow a horse," I suggested. "Elinor insisted I learn to ride, and I've little enough to carry."

"Horse and escort are yours, then. I wish it were more," he said, "for all you've done to cheer her."

We left the following day as the bells of the nearby monastery tolled prime. Nick provided an admirable horse and, for conversation, my old friend Terrence. A groom lagged behind, carrying my baggage.

"This marriage has done him good," I said, thinking Nick was much gentled.

"Yes, mistress." Terrence watched his horse's ears. His bearing made it plain he was uncomfortable discussing his master. "I didn't favor it myself."

"You had another candidate in mind?"

"I've been his man a long time. I've seen a dozen mistresses if I've seen one, and telling you true, you're the only one of them he loved."

"Terrence!" His candid words brought color to my cheeks.

"He loves Lady Elinor, but you made him shout and stamp and throw pitchers," Terrence said, approval in his tone. "He made himself ridiculous for you."

The homing instinct was on me. From the inn where we rested, all the way to Greenwich, I felt the eagerness of a horse nearing its stable. I wanted to race ahead, find my place again. It had come to me during the night, the grace note to Joan's lesson, illuminating my sleep as though a door had been flung open. This place, and any other that housed the court, was mine. I needed no other to make me whole.

Greenwich's familiar front hove into view at last, and without embarrassment, I found my eyes damp. All was quiet, but it was the peace of tranquility, not death.

Terrence saw me inside, sending the groom off with our mounts. I thanked him, almost loath to see him go. "I enjoyed your company on the journey. You may tell the Lady Elinor I arrived safely."

"And the master?" His smile reminded me of all he had witnessed.

"You may tell him," I said, my expression reproving though my heart was not, "that I thank him again for his hospitality."

Terrence's eyes narrowed. "And that be all?"

"What would you have me say?" I tweaked the sleeve of his brown coat. "Do not take me wrong, I am grateful for his kindness. But that is the past, and I've other things to live for than a man's gaze."

I followed the porter upstairs and found Flora in our chamber, staring at the ceiling. She sat up, looking at my box with interest. "It's good to see you back and ahead of the king. He won't be with us for weeks yet, and it's been right quiet."

"The sweat has gone, then?" I asked. I shook out my new gowns and put them away with care, my hands lingering on the rich cloth. They were gifts from Nick and Elinor, made by her seamstress, one ginger-colored and one a deep blue-green, finer than anything I'd ever worn, even for a masque. "There's no sickness here?"

"Not very much. A few cases in the week just past, but no deaths. The worst is over now. I had a touch of it myself," Flora said, "but it was only a day of fever, and since then, I've just been very tired."

"Have you been outdoors?" I asked, shaking the dust of travel from my skirts. I saw from her pallor, the lilac shadows of exhaustion beneath her eyes, how it must have been and felt a pang for deserting Edith and the others.

She looked shocked. "They said I must rest."

"It's a beautiful day," I coaxed. "Warm, with a fine sun. Must you rest indoors?"

She held my arm as we walked slowly through the gardens and found a quiet spot near the river. The scent of autumn roses hung like a haze over the slope, and Flora smiled in spite of her determination not to enjoy herself. "It scarce feels like September," she said. "The summer was so harsh, it doesn't seem it should be autumn yet."

I stretched out beside her, closing my eyes. "And soon, the king will return, and we'll start preparing for Christmas."

"And who will be queen at Christmas?" Flora asked, a touch of rancor in her voice.

I sat up. "The Lady Anne recovered, did she not?"

"Through no excess of care on the king's part." Flora's lips thinned with disapproval.

"He sent his physician." I was surprised at her tone. She had always favored Queen Katherine.

"Dr. Butts is his second best, as we all know." She heaved herself up to watch a barge drift past. "She might have died, and he wouldn't have known for days!"

I understood then. Flora supported Queen Katherine, but she sympathized with Anne Boleyn, who, for all her airs, was still a woman at the mercy of a man. Perhaps, if more women thought that way, the abominable name, "The Great Whore," would lose its popularity.

We watched the languorous river traffic. I'd never realized how much of the constant parade of boats, large and small, was caused by the king's presence.

"What news from Hampton?" I asked.

Flora brushed grass from her skirt. "I thought Tom's well-being would have been the first question on your lips."

"I did not mean him so particularly," I said. "I have other friends there."

"Hampton had a bad time, but both Tom and Robin were well, last I heard."

I had been back a week. The king was still away, so I spent most of my days near the river, playing the harp and watching the boats. It was not as bad as Kelton, but I still felt at loose ends.

A familiar voice intruded over my music, and I saw Robin waving from the landing. I put my harp aside and called him over. His coat flew about him as he ran, and he carried his hat in one hand.

"It's warm indeed," I said, "if you are going about all unbuttoned."

"Hellish weather," he said, "and the last thing we need with all this sickness. I see you've taken advantage, though—you're positively brown."

"No doubt, Edith will find a way to bleach me," I said, "before I perform again in public."

"You look like a gypsy."

Tom had once called me that. I found the memory no longer hurt. "It's the Welsh in me," I said. "What brings you to Greenwich? Is the cardinal come?"

He shook his head. "My lord cardinal is with the king. He'll be returning any day."

"With the king?"

"He'll come soon. There is some fine hunting near Eltham." He grinned like a boy. "Actually, I journeyed down to see you. There's a Welshman at Hampton who claims to know you," he said. "Fellow named Ewan something-or-other. Older fellow, with a peg leg."

"Ewan?" I smiled, remembering his teaching and his wonderful Welsh songs. "He is at Hampton? I thought he'd returned to Wales."

"He was sent with a dispatch from his lord about a church matter. It seems the man wants to divorce his English wife and thinks my lord cardinal is the man he should appeal to."

Laughing, I said, "As if Cardinal Wolsey did not have enough on his hands with one divorce!"

"Indeed. I thought perhaps you might spend a day or two at Hampton if you'd like to see your friend." He squinted at the river. "I would enjoy the visit, if Ewan is not reason enough."

My first instinct was to go, if only to see Ewan and continue my lessons; playing made me realize how much I still had to learn. But Tom was at Hampton. I hesitated.

"I need to be here should the king return."

Robin looked exasperated. "The king will not come south for a week or more. You can't use him as an excuse."

"I'm not," I said. "It's just better I stay here. Perhaps Ewan—"

"He will not budge until the cardinal returns. He does his lord's bidding to the letter and thus gives himself time to wander in the gardens, playing and singing." He glanced at my small harp. "Isn't that some enticement? I shall keep you separate from Tom if that is what you wish. But do come."

It was foolish to miss seeing Ewan because I wished to avoid Tom. The very thought of him made me warm, and I knew I could not see him without those feelings showing on my tanned face.

A boat waited at the water stairs. Robin went to tell the boatmen we were coming while I went inside to pack. Along with my harp, I brought some new music Ewan would enjoy, and impulsively, I bundled my new gowns into the box.

━◡◡◠

I roamed from side to side in the barge, taking in the perfect day. Thrushes sang along the banks, and I raised my voice to echo theirs, bringing enthusiastic cheers from the oarsmen.

Robin smiled, leaning against the side, his dark coat whipping in the breeze. "Still the show-off."

"There are days when I just can't keep it in."

"You blush like the roses on the bank," he said and colored himself. "You'll have plenty of time to sing with your Welsh friend—he's filled the palace with new songs. All the maids are singing in Welsh these days."

Ewan had had a powerful attraction for the women at Greenwich, and I did not wonder at the maids' sudden interest in music.

The boatmen had scarcely tied up before I was over the side. "Where do you think he will be?"

"I'll have someone take your things, shall I?" Robin asked, smiling at my impatience. "Look for him in the gardens."

"Tell them to be careful with my harp."

"If you do not see him, just listen," he called. "His music can reach dead men's ears."

It was by my ears that I found him, not in the gardens, but further on, in the beginnings of the forest. The liquid sound of his harp led me over the grass, and when I saw him sitting with his back against the bole of a beech tree, it was as if we had never parted.

"Ewan!"

He looked up. The year had put more gray in his hair, but his brown eyes were still merry. "Bess!" He set the harp on the grass and rose awkwardly. "Has the king come?"

"Not yet," I said. "Secretary Lewis told me you were here, and I've come for a visit."

Spreading his jacket on the ground, he bade me sit with him. "I would have journeyed to see you, but I dare not move for fear of missing the cardinal."

I settled myself, touched the harp with a finger. "Robin told me you've been spreading music all over."

His fingers brought a throat-tightening sound from the harp. "I've been teaching one of the cardinal's minstrels," he said.

"Do you mind having two pupils? You must teach me more songs."

"I'm glad you've enjoyed them. You look as if you've had a bit of sadness this year."

"A bit." Was it visible in my face, or had Robin been spreading tales again?

The birds sang for a full minute before he broke the silence. "You were unhappy after Christmas, but this looks different."

"I had hope then."

He frowned. "You cannot live without hope."

"It's just hope of love I've lost, not hope of life."

"Bess, if I did not have a wife waiting for me in Shrewsbury, I would put you on the back of my saddle and take you pillion to Wales." He squeezed my hand in his strong fingers. "Hope of life indeed."

I returned the pressure. "If you did not have a wife in Shrewsbury, I would come, and gladly."

We began to walk, our backs to the palace, until I realized our road was the same one Tom and I had walked before we parted so bitterly. I stopped. "I cannot go this way."

Ewan looked at me. "Is it beyond help, then?"

I nodded.

"You haven't spoken?"

"It's been months. I fear this is past mending. He does not want to see me again." I felt the weight of our estrangement settle on my shoulders.

Ewan made a diplomatic, ungraceful turn. "Shall we go inside then and find your harp? I've a new song that will suit you."

The next few days were spent making music, either in Ewan's small chamber or at the edge of the forest. He was busy with his pupil in the mornings, and I was told those lessons were private. Robin walked with me in the gardens until midday.

"Wolsey is old," he said, "and grows unsure. The pressure of this divorce will be his undoing, even if he procures it."

"I've a riddle for you, Rob—which does Anne Boleyn want more? The divorce or the cardinal's downfall?"

He looked surprised. "You believe she wants that?"

"Once, she did not feel so gentle toward him," I reminded. "He cost her four years at court."

"The Northumberland affair? That was long ago, and she has the king's affection now."

I let him believe what he wished, but I was not so sure. She had the king's love, but would she have traded it for the less risky affections of Harry Percy, Earl of Northumberland since his father's death? I could read her no better than anyone else.

That afternoon, I sat in Ewan's chamber while he tidied up the music strewn on every surface. There were several sheets on the table, and I glanced at them while I waited. The first was "Darkest Beauty," Tom's song about the king's foolish pursuit of Lady Anne. I read the lyric with a wistful smile.

"Where did you—" I broke off when I realized the music was set down in Tom's hand.

"That's his work," Ewan said, "the minstrel who's learning the harp. He's written me out a few of his compositions, but that one is my favorite."

I touched the black-inked notes. "I know it well."

"He wrote it for his ladylove."

Not the king, but Tom. Tom was the foolish lover. "It's an old song," I said, "but I remember it."

He joined me, leaning over my shoulder. "Still fresh to him—he wrote it out this morning, along with several others."

My smile must have dazzled, and when I grabbed Ewan by the shoulders and kissed him, he blinked in surprise. He'd given me back some of the hope of which he himself lamented the loss, for Tom had, this very day, written out a love song to me which he might well have avoided, had he not still cared.

"May I join your lesson tomorrow? Please?"

Ewan looked doubtful. "You've known him long?"

"Aye, we were children together."

He agreed then and further promised he would not warn Tom of my coming. The hours flew by after that, and though the next day dawned stormy, it could have been sunny as springtime for all I noticed.

"The rain has eased," Robin said, appearing at my elbow, "but I'm afraid it's still too wet to walk. I've thought of something else for us."

"Ewan asked me to come up this morning." I tried not to smile.

"But you don't see him until afternoon," he said. "In the mornings, he—"

"He sees Tom," I finished. "He told me."

Still flustered, he said, "I thought you would like to see the cardinal's library."

I shook my head. "I thank you for being so careful with me, but this must be done. Even if it comes to nothing, we will have spoken, and the sword will disappear from above our heads."

Robin surrendered and took me to fetch my harp. I primped hastily in the window. I wore my new popinjay gown, and my hair was loose but for a matching band. My skin was unfashionably tanned, but it was clear and comely enough.

When we entered, Ewan was alone. His eyes met Robin's over my shoulder, and a look passed between them.

"Have you two been playing puppets, and I too dull-witted to feel the strings?" I asked after Robin had gone. "How long have you known?"

His expression was sheepish. "Since the beginning. First from Robin, then from Tom himself. Robin said we had to keep you apart. I thought he knew best, knowing you longer." He began to play, and I recognized one of Tom's melodies. "Your man's had his own pain this year, Bess. Don't expect he will be gentle with you."

"I will know as soon as I see him." I set myself to following Ewan's lead. I had never tried to play Tom's music, and my fingers fumbled on the strings.

When the door opened and Tom's shadow fell across the rushes, my breath stopped. I stayed out of sight, to watch him and judge how I should behave. He placed his lute on the table. "I brought this as a change," he said, and there was a smile in his voice. "Some of my songs cannot be played on anything else."

"Today, I have a singer for your songs," Ewan said, his face full of concern.

My insides were quaking, and I could not feel my legs. I pressed my hands on the table as I rose. "Hello, Tom." The words were said; I had not choked nor lost my voice.

"Bess." In his eyes, I searched for the mirror to myself, but I found nothing. The glass had been broken, and I saw only that he had not sought our meeting. "I didn't know you had a guest, Ewan. I'll come back when it's convenient."

My mouth opened, but this time, no sound came forth.

"No." Ewan said it for me. "Please—I've heard tales of your performances. I would hear for myself before I return, if you'll favor me?"

Tom's hand strayed toward the lute, whether to take it and leave or to give in, I couldn't be sure. As soon as he touched it, I began to sing. After a moment, he picked up the tune, his touch sure and sensitive on the strings.

> *Do 'way, dear heart, not so!*
> *Let no thought you dismay;*
> *Though ye now part me fro,*
> *We shall meet when we may.*

> *I make you fast and sure;*
> *It is to me great pain*
> *Thus long to endure*
> *Till that we meet again.*[7]

It was an old song of the king's but new to Ewan. He was enchanted. He sprawled on the bench and listened, his eyes burning with the joy of a true musician. Short of the angels, he said later, there had never been a sound in heaven or earth to equal us.

Tom played like one possessed. Perhaps I was his demon, infecting him all over again. He took his lead from me on the first song, I from him on the second, and we continued thus until I felt my voice would break and his fingers bleed, and still we went on until he began, unthinking, the notes of a song certainly taboo in his heart but so welcome in my own that when he stopped, I said, "Please," and he began again.

> *I will rise up and meet him*
> *As the evening draws nigh.*
> *I will meet him as the evening,*
> *As the evening draws nigh.*

And if you love another, your mind for to ease.
Oh, why must you love another
When this one yearns to please?[1]

Ewan would not notice the alteration in the words, there being so many versions of this song, but Tom's head snapped up, and his eyes were blue fire. I held his gaze and sang the last verses. When the song ended, I stopped.

Soft applause came from Ewan's corner, and he rose to his feet, smiling like a moonstruck boy. "I would love to take you back with me," he said. "You are flawless, the pair of you!"

I spared a glance at Tom and found him pleased by the praise but wary of my presence.

There was a knock at the door, and a page looked in. Ewan went to speak with him. As soon as he was out of earshot, I said, "Don't blame him. I asked to be here."

"Why?" Tom's face was thinner, and there were creases around his eyes and bracketing his mouth. That same stubborn fall of hair swept his brow, and I ached for the boy who knew only one parent, to whom women were but friends and not a means of sadness. I ached for the days when I would have brushed that lock of hair from his eyes without causing him even to blink.

I gave him the same answer I gave Ewan. "I had to." His hand lay on the table before me. I ran my fingertip lightly along the web of flesh between his thumb and forefinger. There was a sharp intake of breath, and he jerked his hand away.

"What are you doing?"

"I wanted to make sure you knew it was me." He was not unaffected by my presence, no matter what he wanted me to believe.

He turned his back. "I know it well enough."

The rain had passed, and a weak shaft of sunlight streamed in the window opposite, catching on a cracked pane and fracturing into a rainbow. I stared at it, afraid to look at him. "I cannot bear this."

"And yet you must, for I cannot bear it any other way." The sound of paper rustling told me he gathered his music. "We said goodbye in the spring." He took up his lute. "We needn't say it again."

I grabbed his arm and felt the shock that went through us both. "You said goodbye. You said it, not me."

"The cardinal will be back by week's end," Ewan said, tactfully pretending not to notice me clinging to Tom's sleeve. When he made his exit, I followed, leaving Ewan to stare after us.

We went through the hall and into the courtyard, filled at this noon hour with a score or more people, carts, horses, and dogs. He stopped, and I almost trod on his heel. "Come along if you must."

I thought he would lead me back to the spot where we'd last parted, but he turned into the gardens and stopped finally at a small stone bench surrounded by trees. As we approached, a light breeze caused a shower of leaves like gold coins. It was not a place for unhappiness. He gestured for me to sit, but I would not until he did.

The sun warmed my face, but inside, I was still cold and uncertain. I said at last, "I was afraid you wouldn't talk to me."

"I knew not if I could," he admitted. "We've been angry before, but this was something worse than anger. And we've never been apart so long."

My heart pounded as if I'd raced him to the bench. "I've made confession, Tom, but priests can't help me. I must have absolution from you or none at all."

He shook his head. "I've long forgiven you. There was no malice in your withholding nor in your telling. You followed her wishes." He covered his eyes briefly with one hand. "I've almost been able to forgive myself."

Unable to look at him, I focused instead on his worn shoes, but that was no good either, for my eyes strayed to the muscular leg above. I wanted to nestle myself in the curve of his body and forget everything. "You said you never wanted to see me again."

"It was hastily but wisely said." He scuffed his foot in the damp grass. "We cause each other nothing but grief."

I expected the words, but anticipation made them no easier to hear. "You still believe that?"

"I have to." He rose but did not yet pick up his lute.

To put my head on his breast and tell him he was wrong! His stance told me I had exhausted such familiarities. The air between us prickled with tension, and I turned away so that I would not reach for him. It would only make things worse.

"Are you easier now?" I asked. "Knowing about Brandon?"

"At times," Tom said after a moment. His gaze was fixed on the gravel path. "I wish I could ask her why she kept it from me."

"I'm sorry," I said again. I might have been forgiven, but he would never recover from my meddling in a matter so close to his heart.

"The worst of it," he said, "is that knowing makes no difference at all. It doesn't change who I am. It doesn't change anything."

"You once told me, we made our own families here at court. You said it to comfort me, but it's just as true for you."

"All my life, I thought knowing would make me feel better, but instead, I felt cheated."

"How?"

His expression was troubled. "I always imagined he would be someone I would be proud to call father."

Charles Brandon was wealthy and powerful, the king's dearest companion, but he was also harsh, and his checkered personal history would not appeal to someone as honorable as Tom. In addition to his children by the king's sister, there were three more by his second wife as well as bastards scattered throughout England and rumors of a by-blow from his campaign with the emperor. As Brandon's son, Tom gained more than a father; he had acquired, if he cared, a veritable tribe of siblings.

"Should I return to the palace?" I asked, turning from the topic of his parentage to face the inevitable.

Greenwich would still be there, even without Tom. The larks would sing, the roses would bloom, the Thames would flow, all without Tom, and my heart would still beat, but I would be less alive.

"Finish your visit," he said, looking like a man who has lost everything. "The cardinal will return by Saturday, and Ewan will be gone once he has obtained his audience."

"I will absent myself when you come to court," I said, almost eager to please.

Tom's expression softened. "I thank you, Bess, for understanding so well."

His gratitude was hard to bear, but I did understand, as I had understood when he left court. All his pain was wrapped up with me. It hurt to part, but he would bear it as I would, with public smiles and private tears. And music.

Ewan knew all was not well. He sat me down with a cup of wine and played Welsh love-ballads for me, so wrenchingly poignant that I found myself weeping. He played until my tears stopped. "That is what music is for," he said with a smile of pure goodness. "You must be able to move your audience to tears."

I sniffed one last time. "You had an unfair advantage."

He put the harp aside. "We'll be gone soon, me back to Wales and you to Greenwich, but we have our memories. The bad ones will dim over time, and the good will grow stronger."

"Will I ever be so wise?"

"I hope not." Ewan dropped a kiss on the top of my head. "It takes much heartbreak to become wise. Given the choice, I'd rather be a fool and be happy."

Chapter 24

Two days later, I packed my things, including a thick folio of Welsh music, and joined Robin in the courtyard. He tried to hide his concern as we walked to the barge.

"I've enjoyed having you here." For a moment, I saw no more than the solemn, freckled face of my old friend. "I wish it had turned out differently."

"I'm no worse off than when I came. What happened was my own doing—you tried to keep us apart."

He put his hand on my shoulder. "I'll visit you next time, shall I?"

"That would be best."

A piping voice made me turn. One of the cardinal's boys hurtled over the grass, his arms pinwheeling with effort. As he neared, I made out what he shouted. Back out of the boat I came, to the top of the water stairs. The child was bent double, gulping air, his face red as a berry. "The Welshman sent me, mistress. Tom's fallen sick."

I felt the blood drain from my face. Was this how I was to finally lose him? Was the living death of separation not punishment enough for loving him too late? I passed my bundle to Robin and made to follow the boy.

"Bess, it's the sweat!" Robin caught my arm. "Leave him to the physicians; don't risk yourself."

I slipped on the wet marble, wrenching my ankle. "It doesn't matter."

We found Ewan by the stable doors. "Tom's inside," he said, "but the physician's away on the cardinal's business." The darkness blinded me for a moment, but even before my vision cleared, I located Tom by the smell of the sweat rising from his body, stronger already than the hay scent I abhorred. I knelt and laid my wrist on his forehead and found him burning hot.

From behind me, Ewan said, "I suggested we ride, to take his mind off your leaving. He was leading his horse out of the box when he said he felt dizzy."

For the first time, I noticed the Welsh pony at my shoulder. "It strikes like that," I said, letting him help me up. "We must get him inside. Not his room, though, it has no window."

"The last thing he needs is air." Robin's voice came from the doorway. He stood well back, still holding my things. "He needs to be in a room with a fire."

"I assume you'll not volunteer your chamber?" I asked, knowing full well he would not.

"Take mine." Ewan bent down, and together, we balanced Tom's limp form over his shoulder. Concerned for his balance, I held fast all the way to his room, which had both window and fire and plenty of space around the narrow bed.

I threw back the covers, and we manhandled Tom onto the straw mattress. "You needn't stay," I said, folding back my hanging sleeves. "Send a servant, and I'll manage until the physician comes. I've done this before."

"You'll need assistance," Ewan objected, hovering at my shoulder.

"Only in authority," I said, beginning to remove Tom's clothes. I found I was able to function if I didn't think about the body on the bed as his. "If you tell them to obey me, they will. I'm going to need cold water, more blankets, dry bedding, and lots of rags to wipe him down."

Before the door shut behind Ewan, Tom was stripped of shirt and hose. I tossed them on the rushes and covered him to the chin with a light blanket, as I would any other patient. I'd never had anyone strictly in my care. Always, Edith or one of the other women had been there to direct me, to measure out doses of medicine, which had little or no effect. To be responsible.

When he came to take charge of Anne Boleyn, Dr. Butts had treated me, as well as Edith, as ignorant women poaching on his preserve. Perhaps we were; the fact that I'd survived the sweat and knew some possets and remedies made me no better than any other female with pretensions to learning, and possibly more dangerous. But not everyone at Greenwich died; most, in fact, had lived. Without fear of catching the disease, it meant no more than hard work and worry for me until the crisis was past.

For Tom, it meant no less than his life.

For a moment, I panicked. Then, common sense took over. There was no doctor, I told myself, and after the severity of the attacks earlier in the season, where eight of the cardinal's household had died in four hours, few at Hampton would risk infection to help me. "If loving you makes a difference," I said, "you will live."

He moaned, and I dropped to my knees at the bedside, searching his face. Where were the rags? I looked around the room, but short of using Ewan's clothing or the bedding, there was nothing. I reached inside my neckline and undid the ties to my undersleeves, pulling them loose and using them to wipe his forehead. Moisture soaked his hair, and I was glad to see it. That meant there was no immediate threat of the fever turning inwards. If that did not happen, he had as good a chance as any at recovery.

His eyes flickered open, and I saw that he recognized me. "Bess." His voice was cracked, weakened already. "Leave me."

I wiped his face again, my sleeve growing damp. "You're ill, Tom. Do you hurt anywhere?"

He pushed my hand away. "You can't be here. You'll catch it."

Leaning over so my mouth was close to his ear, I said, "I've had it, remember? Let me tend you."

His eyes closed, and pain washed over his face. "Go back to Greenwich, sweetheart," he said, almost inaudible. "Let me die and have peace."

I thought of my dead: sweet Jenny Keith, who had mothered me; poor, lost Agnes, whom none of us could save; my father, who gave me up and gave me life; Master Cornysh, who taught me to use my gifts. Even Tom's mother was among my dead now. My dead were my history, my past.

Tom was my life and any hope I had of future happiness; I would not allow him to join my dead. "No," I said. "I will not let you die."

The door opened, and a servant put her head in. "I've got blankets, mistress, and water." She put two brimming buckets on the floor and reached behind her for an armload of bedding. "What else will you be needing?"

"Cloths to wipe him down, unless you'd have me tear the sheets," I said, fetching one of the buckets. "And I'll need more water than this—and medicine. I know the doctor is away, but is there anyone who works with herbs?"

She nodded. "Old Brother John takes care of the herb garden."

"Ask him for an infusion for fever"—I tried to remember Edith's favorites, regretting every occasion I'd found to avoid learning something that might save Tom's life—"agrimony or feverfew, whichever he prefers, and perhaps some sage to cleanse the air." I was annoyed by her frightened face. "And I need those cloths!"

The rags arrived by way of the same boy who'd found me with Ewan's message. "Nan's afraid," he said, smiling from beneath a crop of chestnut curls. "I sent her to Brother John. Can I help? I like Tom."

I let him soak the towels and hand them to me. Throwing aside the damp blanket, I wiped each fever-baked limb and repeatedly cooled his face and wrists. He shook with chills, despite the scorching heat radiating from his body, and I covered him with more blankets to still the shaking.

He muttered unintelligibly, never quite passing into sleep. I feared how quickly the fever had taken him, though I knew the ways of the disease as well as any: one minute upright and ready to ride, the next, unconscious in a fever of sweat and just as likely to die as see another dawn.

I held his hand under the covers, as if my touch might preserve his dwindling strength. His breathing was labored but steady. Some struggled for breath almost immediately, the fever causing their lungs to seize. Still, its course was harsh enough; it was clear on his face already, his cheekbones like dull blades beneath the skin.

I sent the boy, Jamie, to the chapel and hoped his prayers were more effective than my own, which were a litany of "Please, God, let him live" over and over, while holding fast to his hand.

The day was suddenly gone. Dusk fell, and still his fever mounted. I stood, wincing at the pain in my ankle. Crossing to the window, I saw lights on the river; the cardinal had returned. I opened the casement, and fresh air flooded the chamber, dispelling the foulness of the sweat and bringing hope to last me through the night.

Soon after, there was a tap on the door, and an old monk peered in, his face nearly obscured by a cloud of untidy hair. "You're caring for Tom?" His brown robes had seen better days. Despite his rumpled appearance, the glass flagon in his hand sparkled with cleanliness.

"Are you Brother John?" I asked, already reaching for the bottle. "What have you brought?"

He ducked his head. "It's a special brew I make for fever."

"I've always heard feverfew or agrimony for the sweat." I removed the stopper and drew back as my nostrils were assailed by an odor as rank as it was familiar. I knew it from Edith's herber, but it was more: in the bitter scent, with its underlying trace of mint, was the memory of Agnes. "Is it pennyroyal?"

He was impressed. "Have you worked with herbs yourself?"

"Not a lot." I remembered Edith's bowed head. "Can it...hurt him in any way?" I asked, trying to be delicate. Brother John worked with herbs, but it was obvious he dealt rarely with women.

"No." His glare said I had no business knowing the herb's more questionable uses.

"Why this, rather than feverfew?"

"It keeps the sweat flowing." He approached and felt Tom's forehead, wiping his hand on his robe. "Other herbs—the sage you asked for, for instance—can dry it up."

I nodded, wondering if Edith possessed this knowledge. "I but wanted the sage to freshen the air."

Brother John bowed in my direction, and his perfectly round tonsure gleamed. "I would use hyssop, myself, and sprinkle it on the rushes. I'll send some to you, along with the sage." He reached into a fold of his robe and produced another bottle, smaller. "This is for tomorrow, when he is past the worst."

I was grateful as much for his optimism as his remedies, and I put this last offering on the table without smelling it. In spite of his discomfort, I found Brother John interesting and wished I had time to question him further.

"It's an infusion of willow bark. It will reduce the fever," he explained, "as well as help with the aches and chills, but don't use it with pennyroyal; the herb is too potent."

Most with knowledge of herbal lore were natural healers and would have been loath to leave their medicines with someone untrained in their use, but Brother John seemed to enjoy the art without feeling a need to put it into practice.

Closing the door and leaning against it, I surveyed the scene before me. Ewan was a tidy man, and the space showed little evidence of his occupancy other than his music and some neatly folded clothes. I put his possessions in one corner and readied for the siege ahead.

Before I sponged Tom down again, I poured a little of the pennyroyal brew. Sitting on the edge of the bed, I hauled Tom upright and put the cup to his lips. He tried to drink and choked, some of the liquid running down his chin, but I saw him swallow and knew at least some of Brother John's medicine had made it down his throat. I kissed his damp forehead and tasted bitter sweat on my lips.

He slept in fits and starts. During the sickness at Greenwich, Edith had told me that medical custom held the afflicted should not be permitted to sleep for fear they would fall into a slumber so deep, they would not awaken.

"Why?" I asked. It seemed that sleep would heal the body.

Edith shrugged. "Physicians' silliness, if you ask me. What's worse, dying in your sleep, unawares, or burning alive and knowing it?"

Hours passed as I changed his linens, whispered reassurances, forced him to drink. His skin was so hot, it dried the cloth as I passed it over him.

I heard Ewan's harp outside the door and, later, voices singing with him. I hoped Tom could hear them.

The priest came at daybreak. He'd discovered Jamie sleeping on the marble floor before the altar and hurried to Tom's side, expecting me to welcome him. I had been up for more than twenty-four hours; I was frightened, exhausted, and as sweaty as Tom, my hair bundled into an untidy braid, my sleeves and underskirt turned to rags.

"It is dawn, my child," he said, placing his large palm on Tom's forehead. "I must be alone with him now."

"No." I spoke before I realized his intention, and when I did, I was doubly sure. Tom had made it through the night without help from the Church. I knew if the priest administered the sacraments, I would lose him. "He's not dying."

"Nonsense, look at his face." The priest's expression was stern and grew darker when he saw the small dish of sage smoldering on the table. He poured water on it and wiped his hands fastidiously. "You have done good work here, but you cannot protect him from God's will."

I put myself between the priest and the bed, wondering if this was the same man who'd tried to reassure Tom after Lucy's death. "It is not God's will that he die."

He put out a hand, and I struck at him blindly, catching him on his shoulder. "Wait outside if you must, but you will not touch him!"

"If he dies—" The priest stared down at me. His eyes were black, like Anne Boleyn's, and just as frightening.

"Then the sin is mine," I said. "Leave us."

It was no small sin to disrespect the Church, and I had gone far beyond that: I'd denied Tom salvation and condemned him to hell because of my own superstitions. His faith was stronger than mine, but I wasn't sure how he would feel about being given extreme unction by the priest who'd dismissed Lucy's death as God's will. I thought he would not want it.

Outside, the priest was praying, his words but a murmur through the door. Odd, how clear the sound of Ewan's harp had been, and yet the prayers of a man of God seemed no more than a gnat's buzzing.

"I won't let you die." I knelt beside the bed and took his hot hand in mine. "You must understand how important you are to me. You always have been, ever since the night you first played for me. The night you named me." With my other hand, I stroked the side of his face, wanting more than anything to see the slack muscles curve into a smile. "You have been the one true thing in all my years at court, the one person I could count on. I was foolish not to see it sooner."

The room had cooled. I dragged the brazier close to the bed and stirred up the fire. Tom did not move, and I resumed my vigil. "I know the truth, Tom. Ewan broke faith with you to soothe my heart."

How many times could hope be renewed before it was worn through? Ewan had repeated Tom's words to me as we brought him to bed, and outside my worry, I felt the same surge of joy I always felt when there was a chance to mend what was broken between us. It did not matter how many times I hoped and was disappointed.

As the day grew brighter, I continued my one-sided conversation. Tom was unconscious, but I hoped my voice would reach him through the fever. "You told Ewan you still wrote your songs for me. You said loving me was your life, but it was impossible for us to be together." I stroked his hair, separating the wet strands with my fingers. "You've stopped believing you can be happy. Please don't turn away from me."

Ewan's uneven footsteps made me turn. "It's near to noon. You've been with him over a full day. You should rest."

"Not yet."

He put his arm around me, and I sagged against him. "You'll do him no good if you fall ill yourself."

"I've already had the sweat. I can't get it again."

Ewan raised his brows. "You can still take sick with exhaustion. Just sleep a bit; that's all I ask. I've had a pallet laid outside. I'll sit with him."

The thought of sleep made me weak, but I would not leave Tom, even with Ewan. "Bring it in here, and I'll sleep. I won't go where I can't hear him."

He gave a quiet order, and two men brought in clean bedding and made up a pallet for me in sight of the bed. I took off my shoes and sank down gratefully on the floor. Ewan watched me like an anxious parent.

"If he makes the slightest change, wake me!"

"I'll not hear his breath change without calling."

I let him draw the coverlet up to my shoulders. As I closed my eyes, I said, "Thank you for all your kindness. You needn't risk yourself for us."

He smoothed my braid and said, "I care for you both. I can't stand by while you work yourself to the bone."

"I must save his life," I said, on the edge of sleep, "so I can give it back to him."

When Ewan woke me, the sun was already slanting across the floor. I sat upright and rubbed my face. "You've let me sleep for hours!"

"You needed the rest," he said, offering his hand. "And he hasn't moved or spoken, so there was no reason to disturb you."

I listened to Tom's breathing, felt his forehead. It still burned, but it seemed perhaps a little less hot. "He has not come to himself at all?"

"Once or twice he spoke, but I couldn't make out the words." Seeing I had again taken charge, Ewan seated himself and watched me. "Before you slept, Bess, you said a curious thing. What did you mean, you had to give him back his life?"

Said on the verge of unconsciousness, the words had a truth I found difficult to explain. "I owe him so much," I said, the words coming haltingly. "He's always been my friend and my support, and for all he has done, I've never given him what he deserves. He loved me, and I made myself mistress to another man. When he found a woman of his own and lost her, I gave him more pain." I felt a flush of shame at the thought. "He says he's forgiven me, but I've not forgiven myself."

"Tom told me," Ewan said. "Not the man's name, but the fact of him. He said it was the greatest wound he'd ever received, and at the same time, the healer of all wounds. He was grateful, in the end."

Busying myself with the covers so he would not see the tears in my eyes, I said, "I'm glad to know it. Now, if we never speak again…"

His shadow moved, fell across the bed. "Tom will live to tell you himself."

I looked up into his face, saw his eyes worried yet clear of the murky feelings that bound the rest of us. "The last time we spoke, he said he never wanted to see me again."

"It was said in anger. I've seen the man look at you."

"He was very calm. He said we cause each other nothing but grief."

"Well, that does seem true enough." Ewan stared out at the fading sky as if searching for a solution. "What if, when he recovers, he still feels that way? What of you, Bess?"

That was a topic on which I had spent much thought over the past day. "I shall be all right," I said. "I have my place at court."

"Is that enough?" he asked. "Nothing for the rest of your life but music and a remembered love?"

"It's been enough for him all this time."

In the evening, Ewan left for his audience with the cardinal. I was grateful for the silence, needing to be alone with my thoughts. I did not light the candles immediately.

Earlier, Jamie had brought food, but the plate remained untouched. I drank a cup of warm, sour wine and felt it reach my blood moments later, lending strength to my heavy limbs.

As the darkness grew, Tom's fever rose again. I'd hoped the worst was over, but he became so hot, I could feel it an arm's length from the bed. I wasn't certain he could withstand another such night. As I bathed him, he began to shake. This was the worst chill since he'd been stricken. Before stirring up the fire, I gave him another dose of Brother John's infusion and covered him with more blankets. He still shivered, and I watched him helplessly, thinking, if he had been one of the patients I'd nursed in the summer, I would have already given up.

A thought came to me, and I did not wait to see if it was right. I undid my sleeves and pulled the laces of my gown so I could step out of it. Wearing only shift and stockings, I crawled into the damp bed, wrapping my arms tight around his shaking frame. "It will be well, Tom," I whispered, rocking him like a babe, his burning head on my breast. "It will all be well."

"So cold," he said through chattering teeth. "Bess..."

"I'm here, my love." I stroked his wet hair, the back of his neck. "You must be strong."

He burrowed against me. "Could you sing?" A spasm shook him, and I pulled him closer, racking my tired brain for a song. I chose one of his, written in the days of his mocking love songs, the ones we assumed were about Anne and the king.

> *I sit and sigh and wait forbye*
> *To join her in the dance.*
> *But those who sigh and wait forbye*
> *May never have a chance.*
>
> *Though she is young and bright of eye,*
> *My suit will not advance.*
> *For those who sigh and wait forbye*
> *Shall never find romance.*

It was not the most comforting lyric, I realized, but he slept again, and for a time, I joined him.

When I woke, I was swaddled in sodden, stinking sheets. The sweat poured off him, and I hurried to strip the bed, ignoring the dead fire and my own wet shift. Once he was dry and covered, I stirred the fire and took off my shift, drawing my gown onto my clammy flesh. I laced myself loosely, my hands too stiff to do a decent job of it.

If the priest returned, he would disapprove of more than burning sage, I thought and almost laughed. I was growing hysterical from exhaustion. When Ewan came back, I would rest again.

Before, Tom was thin, and now, with the fever burning at him, he looked almost skeletal. I barely recognized the face on the pillow, so gaunt had it become in a few short days. His hands and wrists, lying on the coverlet, were all bones.

Weariness encroached, but I pushed it back, plunging my arms into cold water to rinse his towels and splashing my face. As I wiped the water from my skin, I heard a subtle change in his breathing and flung myself across the chamber.

His eyes were open, bottomlessly blue. Heat still emanated from him, but his skin was dry.

"No!" Fear clutched at my heart, and I knelt beside the bed, folding my hands and dropping my head on them, unable to look. If the fever turned inward now, he would never survive it.

He took a deep, rattling breath and was silent. When his breathing started again, regular and soft, I was scared to touch him. At last, I did and found the cheek beneath my fingertips moist and only slightly warm. I dropped my forehead to the blanket and sobbed.

As with the turning of a tide, his fever receded, and by the time I heard the bell for compline, he was asleep, with just a light sheen of moisture on his brow. I gave him the willow bark infusion, finding it much more pleasant than pennyroyal.

I called for a pitcher of wine, mixing some with water in case he thirsted, and drank an undiluted cup myself. It made me drowsy, but my heart was too full for sleep.

It was hours before he stirred. I was deep within myself when I heard his voice. "Bess?"

From the window, I turned and dropped to my knees beside the bed. "I'm here."

He took a shaky breath. Ringed as they were with gray, sunk deep in

278

their sockets, his eyes were beautiful because they held recognition; in their depths, I saw my Tom. "You've been here all this time," he said. "I remember..."

I leaned closer. "You remember?"

"You sang for me." I held the cup to his lips, and he sipped greedily at the watered wine. "How long have I been like this?"

"This is the third day." I told him where he lay and how tirelessly Ewan had waited on him while I slept.

Tom smiled faintly. "The brotherhood of musicians."

He was weak, so I fixed his pillows and smoothed the covers. "I'll be here if you have need of me," I said, and he caught my wrist in a grasp weak as a child's. "I have need. Stay with me."

The doctor found Tom sleeping peacefully with me across his chest, our hands still linked. He shook me briskly. "Your friends are outside," he said.

"I'm staying—"

"You will go," the physician said, brooking no argument. He lifted his furred robe away from a pile of wet rags, topped with what might have been the remains of my shift. "He will not die now."

Both Ewan and Robin were outside, and both reached for me as I stumbled and fainted for the second time in my life.

It was suppertime before I was permitted to see Tom, and while I waited, Robin made certain I ate and rested, providing me with hourly reports on his condition.

I paced, barely feeling the throbbing of my ankle. "Where was the doctor when Tom was in need of him?"

"The sweat struck again in the village. He was coming back to Hampton but stopped there. He never got our message," Robin said. "And Tom never had need of him. He had you, and you weren't about to let him die. I heard you chased Father Francis from the room."

"He wanted to give Tom the sacraments," I said. "I couldn't let him, don't you see?"

Robin laughed. "No, I don't see, but I trust your judgment. You did everything possible, and everything right, by the look of it. I doubt even Father Francis is gravely annoyed now—he has seen Tom, and he's satisfied with his recovery."

That stopped my pacing. "The priest has seen him before me?" I made for the door. If the doctor barred my entry, I would climb in through the window.

Robin followed at a more sedate pace as I ran down the hall. He did not have to help me through the window, however; upon my arrival, the doctor waved me in, shutting the door as he left.

Tom lay in the bed, which was made up again with clean clothes. I approached slowly, afraid now his mind was clear, he might not wish to see me, but he held out his hand.

"I've been hearing tales from everyone," he said. "Father Francis's dignity may never recover."

"Well, he wouldn't listen," I said. While still pale, he looked much improved.

"And you have no great love for the priesthood," Tom said. "He said you hit him."

I looked at him through lowered lashes. "If I meant to hit him, I would have hit him harder. It was an accident."

"And Dr. Byrd was met by a half-naked virago who tried to refuse him entrance."

I felt a blush mount to my cheeks. "You make me sound a terrible shrew."

"Rather a lioness protecting her cub, or an eagle, her nest."

It was all that and more. I neither wanted nor needed anyone else; his life rested with me, and the priest and the doctor tried to usurp a place I could not give up. Perhaps it was foolish to think only I could make him well, but he was well, and whether it was because of me or Father Francis's God, I did not care.

"I wasn't certain you'd see me." It was a risk, but I had to know if he was still lost to me. I'd been preparing myself, trying to see my life as anything other than empty without him.

"How could I not? I must thank you." He sounded weak but purposeful. "I know you did it because you feel you owe me."

I looked up, amazed. "I didn't nurse you because I owe you. I did it because I love you. If you died, it would have killed me."

His raised hand cut off my impetuous flow of words. "I can bear no more of this," he said. By his voice, I knew it to be true. "Why did you not let me die and let death wipe you from my heart? I'll never rid myself of you otherwise."

I wanted to take his hand then, as I had when he was ill. "I could never rid myself of you either," I said. "You're a part of me."

He struggled to sit up and reluctantly allowed me to arrange the pillows behind him. "You say it as if you understand. Do you, Bess? We laugh and cry as one, our joy and our pain eternally mingled. I feel your tears on my face as I feel my own. Do you think I didn't feel your anguish when you cared for me?" He touched my cheek, his fingertips rough, the caress gentle as a babe's. "Can you explain that in your easy words?" "I've always feared to try."

"You're not alone inside yourself, is that what you mean?" His tone was of one who had encountered that terrifying feeling and dealt with it.

I nodded, taking his hand. I recalled to him the Christmas when he'd kissed me, alone in the girls' chamber, when I'd fought him with such violence. "It was then I realized the depth of our connection. My own feelings scared me; yours were something I wasn't prepared for."

"And later?" He meant the eve of his departure for Hampton, when I had given myself to him with such abandon. "Did you not feel it then?"

"Aye, stronger than before." The frankness of the conversation made me warm, but I saw Tom was not embarrassed, only interested in hearing how I felt. "I was afraid, remembering, but I loved you and knew you'd never hurt me, so I let go of the fear. And then it was gone."

I felt a tremor go through him.

"You think what happened was a gesture to make you stay, but it was more than that," I said. "I know it was clumsy, but I wanted to show you how much I loved you and for how long. I didn't know how else to say it so you would believe me." My eyes filled with tears. "The memory of that night is precious because, for a little while, you did not doubt my love."

"You've been a threat to my peace of mind for twelve years," Tom said at last. "At first, I prayed you would grow up flawed in some way, ugly or selfish or cruel. Then, I realized it wouldn't matter if you did; I could not break our bond if I tried."

"I tried," I said, "with Nick."

"And I with Lucy."

We were silent for a bit; then he sighed. "The worst was when you went back to him."

I hadn't yet forgiven myself for that weakness. "I did it," I said, "after I heard about her. It hurt less, being with him."

"Poor Lucy. I tried to love her." Tom's hands knotted together. "I did love her, and for the child...I would have stayed by her, no matter what."

I stroked his hand, felt him squeeze my fingers. "Everyone assumed you and I were meant to be together, and I felt smothered by it. When Nick noticed me, I didn't know how to respond." I could not explain my obsession with Nick, which had begun the same night fate had tied me irretrievably to Tom.

"You never knew how lovely you were."

I tried to stifle a grin. "I have never recovered from being called a dirty little gypsy. That memory has clung like a nettle."

"My gypsy," Tom said and kissed me. It was a mingling of fear and desire, of secrets shared and wounds exposed. It was a joining of our souls and the greatest comfort I have ever known.

After a moment, he backed away, my face still in his hands. They were so cold, I feared for his health. Then I saw the heat in his eyes and knew his strength was returning.

"You'll marry me."

Agnes told me true all those years ago: love is never just. It was not all ease and happiness, as I thought then, but pain and separation, followed by a sharper joy for having endured and emerged on the other side. It was all I wanted.

"I'll marry you," I said and leaned into his kiss.

"We could leave," he suggested when at last we drew apart. "The court is changing. Wolsey falls in the king's estimation every day. The queen is all but imprisoned."

I felt their unjust treatment keenly, but I was not ready to criticize the king. He was wrong, and history would prove him so, but he loved Anne Boleyn.

"What would we be without the court?" I asked, knowing I would leave if he wished it. "We're creatures of its making."

I could feel his exhalation through his fever-thinned frame. "The king's creatures we are, and so we shall remain, even if it means—may God forbid—Queen Anne on the throne."

I had my own feelings about that, but I would not share them, even with Tom. "What of the cardinal?" I asked, recalling uneasily his refusal to allow Tom to marry Lucy.

"His days have number now; I think even he realizes it. Robin has been currying favor with Thomas Cromwell. Whatever happens, Robin will survive."

Robin was an opportunist, wise beyond his years, and careful always to preserve himself. To give up Wolsey so easily gave me a glimpse of that other Robin, the stranger who'd taken Nick's money to plead his case with me. That Tom understood this, proved he was not the lighthearted boy I had grown up with; the young Tom would never have taken such a cynical view.

What would he think of my friendship with Elinor? Would he and Nick ever trust each other enough for us to pass a night in the bed with the blue velvet curtains? I knew not to wish for miracles, but I also learned that hope, if renewed often enough, paid for itself in abundance.

"As soon as I am able to make the journey to Greenwich," Tom said, drawing me closer, "I'll ask the king when we may wed and if he'll have me back."

I remembered the king's radiant expression when we'd last performed and knew both requests would be granted. "He will have you," I said. "He will have both of us. And if he is lucky, he will be as happy as we shall be."

Tom's mouth twisted. "I do not know if I am strong enough for happiness," he said, but there was a smile in his voice. "It is not a habit I've had of late."

We were not the Tom and Bess we would have been if we'd come together sooner. Those two had lost their chance, but Tom and I, as we were now, would not be parted and would end where we had begun, together. Leaning back against his shoulder, I closed my eyes and allowed myself to believe.

"Nor have I," I said, "but I think it is a habit we can acquire. We've always worked well together, you and I."

Epilogue
January 14, 1559

As always, the bells were the first sound I heard. With the blankets pulled high, I listened and named them: St. Mary-Le-Bow, hard by; St. Katherine, St. Saviour, St. Margaret, all further away but adding their music to the morning. Beneath their clangor was the hiss of sleet against the shutters. Snow had fallen for a week, and all London worried that the weather would spoil a day that could not be spoiled. Our fears were unfounded; by noon, the clouds parted, and a watery sun brightened the sky.

I stood with my family along the side of our street, bodies pressed tight with those of our neighbors. I welcomed the discomfort because it brought warmth; the afternoon, though clear, was still bitterly cold. The crowd was packed ten deep from the narrow houses to the edge of the passage reserved for the procession, and we were held back from that space by guards and wooden barricades. Those who would not brave the cold hung from upper windows, calling a commentary on what passed below.

Cheapside was where we lived, and the dwellings in our street were mostly those of small merchants and tradesmen, their shop fronts scrubbed clean, wares neatly displayed. It was always tidy and well cared for, but on this day, it was transformed, the roadway packed down that very morning with gravel and the houses hung with flags and tapestries.

For more than two hours, the brilliant display passed before us: sable-trimmed purple and scarlet for the aldermen and other officials; sober black for the clergy; velvets and brocades of every hue for the nobility; horses with trappings of gold and silver for all.

It had been a very long time since we had seen such finery.

Wild cheers alerted us to the queen's approach. At the Eleanor Cross, just beyond, a platform had been built by the local guilds. The musicians onstage struck up a lively air, and their song was taken up by a group of children costumed to represent the virtues of the new queen. Our granddaughter, Jenny, had been chosen to perform; even at a distance, I could separate her clear soprano from the voices of the other children.

The procession halted, and for a moment, my breath caught. I leaned forward, my gloved hands gripping the barrier, straining to get a glimpse of the queen. I had not seen her since she was a child, but when sunlight caught on hair the hue of burnished copper, my heart lurched in my chest. She sat easily in her litter, her posture straight and graceful, her girlish figure magnificently arrayed in a gown of cloth-of-gold studded with pearls.

No one would ever call her pretty, I thought, but Elizabeth Tudor, watching the children with genuine pleasure, was certainly striking. And she was young and fresh of face, which in English girls, for many years does pass for beauty. It was said she had her father's gift for instilling loyalty; doubtless, many friends had guided her through the uncertain period of her brother's reign and the turbulence of Catholic Mary's five years on the throne.

I leaned against Tom's solid shoulder and directed my words toward his ear. "How she favors them!"

"Her father," he said, and put his arm around me to temper his words. "Not her."

Most of those watching Elizabeth's triumph would see only the unmistakable Tudor characteristics—the red-gold hair, the fair skin, the regal bearing. But beneath the surface, I saw the shade of Anne Boleyn and was glad.

"Witch" was the word they'd flung at her mother, but no one would dare say that now, not of the new young queen whose reign promised stability and freedom from persecution. The fires of Smithfield were extinguished, but the ashes of the martyrs were still warm in the common memory.

Elizabeth held for us all a promise of peace. She was her father come again, they said, calling up fond memories of Henry Tudor in his prime, bluff King Hal returned to them in the body of his daughter. The people of England were prepared to love her for that reason alone.

The song ended, and the procession began to move. In a moment, the golden litter would be gone. I prayed for a last glimpse of her face, and as if by my will, she turned to speak to a gentleman riding beside her. Her expression when she addressed him, imperious and fond, was so clearly that of her father, I could not repress a shiver.

"God save Queen Elizabeth! God save the queen!"

From further down the route, a man's voice took up the cry. "God save Elizabeth! God bless old King Harry!"

The crowd roared, and I wondered if the queen's eyes had also filled with sudden tears.

Endnotes

1. "Cuckoo," Traditional English folk song.
2. Thomas Campion, "Change and Fate," *An Hour's Recreation in Music*, ed. Richard Alison, 1606, lines 13-14.
3. John Skelton, *Why Come Ye Not to Court?* ed. R. Kele, 1568, lines 398-406.
4. King Henry VIII of England, "My Heart She Hath."
5. King Henry VIII of England, "Pastime in Good Company," verse 2.
6. "Greensleeves," Traditional English folk song.
7. King Henry VIII of England, "Whereto Should I Express," verses 2 & 5.

Author's Note

I've been fascinated by this period of history since I was about six (thanks to my mom and the BBC/Masterpiece Theater production of *The Six Wives of Henry VIII*).

Improbable as it sounds, this story is based on fact—though the fact would lead to Tom, not Bess. While reading a biography of Henry VIII, I ran across a mention of the king once buying a child to sing in the chapel choir. That lodged itself somewhere in my brain and wouldn't let go. Eventually, like a pearl—or perhaps not—this story was born.

I hope it is the first of many. And I hope readers of this book will come back and give my future work a chance, whether or not it involves Bess, Tom, Henry, or Anne.

I would like to thank several people who have been instrumental in my journey from reader to stealth writer to aspiring-to-be-published to published author.

First, my parents. I learned to read at age four to see what all the fuss was about. My mom always had her nose in a book, and the phrase, "Just let me finish the chapter," resounded through my childhood. My dad left school in sixth grade to help support his family. While he could read, he didn't find it comfortable or pleasant, but as soon as I learned how, he asked me to read to him every evening after work. (He also got me my first typewriter, an ancient, open-topped Olivetti that disappeared in a move probably 30 years ago.)

It doesn't matter. The writing never stopped.

Next, and far from least, is my husband, Mario Giorno. Someone I never expected and strive to deserve. He reads drafts, helps name characters, and his eyes don't glaze over when I start discussing plot points or research rabbit holes. He makes me a better—and certainly a nicer—person.

Then there are the women. Every woman should be lucky enough to have a tribe of women who have her back, and I do. Thanks especially to Wendy Hutchison, Dianne Dichter, Jennifer Summerfield, Elizabeth Larsen, Andrea Peart, Debra Kimelman, Eva Seyler, Karen Patterson, and the lovely women at Authors 4 Authors: Rebecca, Renee, and Brandi.

To all these and so many others, all my thanks for coming along for the ride.

About the Author

Karen Heenan was born and raised in Philadelphia. She fell in love with books and stories before she learned to read and has wanted to write for nearly as long. After far too many years in a cubicle, she set herself free to follow her dreams—which include gardening, sewing, traveling, and of course, lots of writing. She lives in Lansdowne, PA, not far from Philadelphia, with four cats and a very patient husband.

Follow her online:

www.karenheenan.com
Twitter: @karen_heenan
Facebook: @karenheenanwriter